Truth Games

BOBBIE DARBYSHIRE

Cinnamon Press
independent ... national

The right of Bobbie Darbyshire to be identified as the author of this work has been asserted by her in accordance with the Copyright, Designs and Patent Act, 1988. © Bobbie Darbyshiret 2009. ISBN 978-1-905614-72-1

British Library Cataloguing in Publication Data. A CIP record for this book can be obtained from the British Library

All the characters in this book are fictitious and any resemblance to actual persons, living or dead, is purely coincidental.

Designed and typeset in Garamond by Cinnamon Press
Cover design by Mike Fortune-Wood from original artwork 'dreamstime' by 'loveliestdreams'; agency: dreamstime.com.
Le Cheval Rouge by Jacques Prévert translation copyright c 1958 by Lawrence Ferlinghetti. Reprinted by kind permission of City Lights Books.
Printed and bound in Great Britain by the MPG Books Group, Bodmin and King's Lynn.

Acknowledgements

I owe a debt to many kind people who commented on the draft. My thanks go to:

Jan Fortune-Wood and Stella at Cinnamon Press; Jüri Gabriel; Joan Deitch at *Pollinger*; my mother Beryl and sister Pip; Bob, Colin, David, Faye, Joan, Julie, Keith, Marek, Nick, Nina, Peter and Sarah at *West Hampstead Writers*; Brad, David, Kevin, Richard, Rupert, Vicky and Wendy at *Original Writers*; Adam, Angela, Berend, Carla, Joe, Julie, Kathryn, Neil, Paul and Peter at *Writers Together*; Andy, Bruce, David, Nicola, Richard, Robert, Sophie and Tamsin at *National Academy of Writing*; Alison Gray, Barry Weatherstone, Bernadette Mongellaz, Dave Quinton, Debbie Collier, Elizabeth Barton, Graham Perry, Ian Jewesbury, Janet Mitchell, Jonathan Masters, Liz Adams, Luc Richez, Maurice Paley, Peter Huitson, Richard Colombo, Roger Hurrey; Bill, whom I never met, who saw the manuscript and left a letter for me in St Ives;

and most of all to Jan Fortune-Wood at Cinnamon Press for saying yes.

The Author

Bobbie Darbyshire's novel *The Real McCoy* has been serialised in *First Edition* magazine. She won the 2008 fiction prize at the National Academy of Writing and was published in their anthology, *Finding a Voice*. Bobbie has worked as barmaid, mushroom picker, film extra, maths coach, Minister's private secretary and care assistant, as well as in social research and policy. She hosts a writers' group and is a volunteer adult-literacy teacher. She lives in Clapham.

In memory of Richard Colombo

Truth Games

London 1975

After the hippies and before the yuppies,
between the advent of The Pill and the onset of AIDS,
between the 'summer of love' and the 'winter of discontent',
the newest game in town was sex.

In merry-go-rounds of lies
The red horse of your smile
Goes round
And I stand rooted there
With the sad whip of reality
And I have nothing to say
Your smile is as true
As my home truths.

Jacques Prévert
(translated by Lawrence Ferlinghetti)

JUNE

New Rules

Lois sighed, and Hugh drew back hurt into his own warm space in the bed. He would have to say something soon.

He made himself speak, as though it were nothing. 'You don't fancy me much lately, petal.'

'I never really did.' She rolled away and lay still.

It had him catching his breath. Insults were standard, she never pulled her punches, but calling her 'petal' was cue for her to counter by calling him 'prawn', a reference to his sun-shy skin and red hair. 'I never really did, prawn' was what she ought to have said.

He stared at her tangle of dark curls. He was being foolish; she was probably hung over. Saturday night with the Goldings was getting to be a habit, and too often they paid for it on Sunday morning. His own head was clear. At forty, he was feeling the need to go slow with the wine, to put a hand over his glass when Jack lurched by on his life mission to top everyone up.

He snuggled close again, kissed Lois's freckled shoulder, breathed in the lazy, sleepy smell of her. 'Poor petal. Shall I bring you a cuppa?'

She half-turned her head. 'Not even at the start, I didn't. Not properly.' She sounded despairing. 'It wasn't really physical. You know?'

It was happening, what he'd dreaded so long. He tried to see her eyes.

'But we had something back then,' he said, 'We still do.'

'If you say so.' She shook her head, chewed her lip. 'Although sometimes I wonder—was I just showing off?'

She was sliding from his arms, launching herself into the day. She had swung her legs clear of the bed and was reaching to open the curtain. The stream of sunshine dazzled him, bouncing off her naked flesh and revealing the hot dust in the air around her.

Horatio struggled from his basket, wagging and snorting and sneezing. When Hugh leant to fondle his ears, the dog promptly heaved himself onto the bed and covered his face with slobber. 'Ugh! No! Get down, you beast! Now I understand how my poor wife feels.'

He looked up, hoping for a smile, but she showed no sign of having heard. She was contemplating her reflection in the long mirror on the wardrobe door, no light in her eyes. And he knew he'd lost her. Ten years, his time up and she'd be gone. He couldn't bear it. No choice, no more time to consider; he must make his offer at once. Hugging the dog to his chest, he took a steadying breath and made himself speak the words.

'I wouldn't mind.' They snagged in his throat. 'You know, if you wanted adventures.'

She turned from the mirror.

'Seriously, Lois.'

A second went by.

'If I fuck someone else, you mean?'

He closed his eyes. 'Truly, I would the gods had made thee poetical.'

'You won't go all hurt and holier-than-thou?'

Won't, not wouldn't.

'No,' his voice hoarse, 'I won't.'

He was off the bed, taking a step towards her, wanting to rewind the ten years and see the starry-eyed student who'd seduced him. 'My love, I tried to teach you ethics once and failed. I've learned my lesson.'

She pulled a face and turned back to the mirror. 'There you go. Pompous already.'

My god, she was right. In that case, 'Lois, listen.' He took another step. 'I mean it. I promise. No moralising.'

Her dark-blue eyes observed him from the depths of the mirror. He gathered himself to speak plainly.

'I will not, repeat not, go all hurt and holier-than-thou if you sleep with another man. With a dozen other men. I know

12

I'm not all you need. I love you. You're free. Use your freedom. I'll still love you.'

He paused, then added, 'Try not to leave me.'

'Do you mean this?'

At last she was smiling.

'Yes, I do.'

Like a child on Christmas morning.

'You honestly won't mind?'

'Cross my heart.'

He cupped her face in his hands. She had her arms round him now. 'Thank you, prawn.'

He swallowed. The transaction was oddly exciting. Come back to bed, he wanted to say, but she was pulling on jeans.

'Yes... time for breakfast.' He backed away, groping for his dressing-gown and the door handle and nearly tripping over Horatio, who lumbered ahead. As he reached the bathroom, he found he was trembling and sweating. He'd promised too much. And what could it buy him but time? She would despise him; she would still leave him. But even if the gamble was futile, what other way was there? Love wasn't a chain.

He stared into the mirror, forcing his hands to manage toothbrush and paste. Why *did* she marry him? He examined his nondescript, middle-aged features. He'd never understand it. Why did she detach herself from the crowd of wide-eyed eighteen-year-olds and waylay her tutor? And how had he persuaded himself it wasn't lunacy to let himself love her, this impulsive, unsuitable student who put his heartbeat on hold, standing too close, with her eyes on his lips? Who told him she wasn't the lovey-dovey type, but really liked him. Liked the way he explained this ethics nonsense—when did he get pompous?—and knew the best bits from the boring books.

'Shakespeare's not boring.'

'If you say so. Go on then, tell me another.'

'It were all one that I should love a bright particular star and think to wed it, she is so above me.' That was her favourite.

It was impossible, he told her. 'I'm your philosophy tutor...

13

your *moral* tutor.'

She was shameless. 'Okay,' she said, '*let's* get wed, have a party, go public. Sort out all that rubbish.'

'*Marriage?*' He'd fought vainly to hang on to reality. 'You'd regret it in no time. I'd make you unhappy. Then you'd make me unhappy.'

'So what?'

And suddenly that had been his thought as well. So what? His life was too sheltered. The world was full of young people taking no care for tomorrow. He wasn't yet old. Why shouldn't he join in?

'Don't worry,' she'd murmured in his ear as he finally succumbed. 'It doesn't have to be forever.'

There it was, from the start. Joy and uncertainty, it was always the deal: in Fulham 1975 as in Brighton 1965. The stakes were higher, but he still wanted in, which meant keeping this impossible promise. He mustn't hide a moment longer. He must show there was nothing amiss.

He left the bathroom; checked the bedroom, empty; then found them both, Lois and Horatio, guzzling their breakfasts in the kitchen. She was piling Old English marmalade onto a slice of burnt toast.

'So what shall we do today, prawn? Give Jack and Tessa a ring? Tell them, stuff your headaches. See if they fancy that *Cuckoo's Nest* film?'

Her exuberance lifted him. When she was happy, how could he be sad?

'Good idea, petal. And Ann, too.'

He spooned coffee into a mug, poured muesli into a bowl. The nausea was gone. His hand was steady. Yes, he was equal to this. He would keep his word and perhaps, in spite of everything, he wouldn't lose her.

He would try very hard not to be pompous.

Playing Gooseberry

'God, Lois, I miss you,' Ann laughed, 'I thought work could never stop being heaven, but it isn't the same with you gone.'

It was Thursday, and the two of them were sharing a scratch supper in Fulham while Hugh attended some end-of-term do at the university. The day had been another scorcher, and the air in Lois's big, jumbled kitchen was gluey with heat. Lois was throwing red wine down her throat, one bottle already half-empty when Ann arrived. Lois looked radiant, more teenage than twenty-eight in a shocking-pink T-shirt and hipster flares, while Ann felt a wreck in her sweaty work clothes.

Lois came round the table and squashed Ann in her arms. 'How can you be missing me? This makes three times you've seen me this week. And we'll all of us be in Italy soon.'

'All of us. Exactly. I never have you to myself any more. I don't want to whinge, but it's always the Fairchilds and the Goldings these days.'

'Oh help,' Lois said. 'Have we gone all married-coupley?'

'Yes, you have.'

'It's Tessa's fault,' Lois protested. 'She's the one who issued gold-embossed invites and keeps saying "my husband". Anyway,' she paused to swallow more wine, 'no way am I coming back to work, because, darling,' she drawled, 'I'm a photographer now.'

'And a kept woman,' said Ann.

'But, of course. Cheers, Hugh.' Lois toasted the ceiling.

She was half-pissed. Ann wished that she could be too, but the drink was going nowhere.

'So. Did you develop the picture from Tuesday yet? The one you took of Tessa?'

Lois nodded. 'It wasn't of Tess exactly. Wait, I'll show you.' She ran to fetch it, past Horatio, who'd padded in looking for Hugh.

'Hi, doggo,' Ann said. He wagged his tail, but then padded

out again, back to his favourite leather armchair in the living-room.

Ann moaned softly. Rod Stewart's abrasively seductive voice wasn't helping her mood. Lois had played nothing else all evening. 'Rod's edible,' she'd announced as she flung open the front door and lifted Ann half off her feet. 'I always put him on when I'm randy.' Which had Ann feeling randy herself and acutely frustrated. Was it really two years since Ed left?

Here came Lois with the photo. 'It's good, don't you think, Ann? Tell me it's good.'

The picture wasn't of Tessa, although she was in it, frowning in the foreground, hunched over her ravioli. Stripped of the clatter of cutlery and the smell of smoke, wine and pasta, the wide-angle view showed a sea of mouthing faces. Across the crowded trattoria, so many people were animated, arguing or gesturing, furious or exultant. Had the hot weather made them excitable?

'Gosh, Lois, it's fabulous.'

'Forget "fabulous". Do you think it's professional? Do you think I could sell it?'

'I'm sure so.'

'No, be serious. Hugh thinks I will.'

'This photo?'

'Lots of them. He really believes in me. He...'

Ann looked at her. 'What?'

Lois grinned, shook her head, took a swig of wine.

'What?'

'You won't tell?'

Ann shook her head. She never told anyone anything.

'It's amazing,' said Lois. 'Whatever I want, he finds it out and says go ahead, do it. First photography and now... wait for it,' she paused naughtily, 'sex. Other men.'

Ann sat back.

'But, Ann, he could see I was dying of boredom. He says I'm free. He won't mind. And he means it.'

She leant forward again anxiously, her eyes on Ann's face. Ann tore the cellophane off a new pack of Bensons, lit one and started to flatten the gold paper with a finger.

Lois was crouched at her feet now. 'He promises he won't. And with Hugh a promise is like putting his soul on the line.'

Ann shook her head.

'It's only sex, Ann. It won't hurt us.'

Only sex? She tried to imagine it. Maybe Lois was right, but how must Hugh be feeling?

'Won't it?'

'Quite the opposite,' Lois said eagerly. 'I really *was* fed up— I was getting niggly with him for no reason. Whereas now I keep looking at him and thinking how lucky I am.'

When Ann snorted, 'Yes, you jammy sod, you are,' Lois let out a whoop, leapt up from the floor and hugged her again. Ann nuzzled into the hug, trying to feel better. 'Okay, my lover, you're persuading me.' She used the West-Country endearment for all of her friends, but for Lois it wasn't too strong. She couldn't always agree with her, but she loved her nonetheless. Hugh too. Like family. Better than her annoying brothers and sisters.

She leant out of the hug to take a drag on the ciggie. 'So did you come clean about the rugger-bugger?'

Lois fell back on a chair. 'Oh... shit... maybe I should. Do you think?'

'Have him round to tea and a discussion of ethics with Hugh?'

That was snide.

Lois contemplated her wine. 'Problem is,' she said at last, 'it would be like rubbing Hugh's nose in it.'

Ann sucked hard on the ciggie, wishing she didn't feel so horribly priggish.

'Look, whatever he asks me I'll tell him, okay? And whatever he doesn't I won't. Then, no lies, it'll be up to him.'

There was no point in arguing. Lois was irrepressible.

'But thank you, because now I've decided, clean slate. I'm going to kick Rug-bug into touch. Or is that football?'

'Lois, I didn't mean—'

'It's fine,' she was insisting. 'I'm seeing him tomorrow night

17

while you lot play bridge. I'll tell him thanks and goodbye.'

She raised her glass, 'Bye bye, Rug-bug,' and drained it. 'Plus I'll be discretion incarnate, nobody knowing. You'll be my only exception.' She reached for the bottle. 'Isn't Hugh wonderful?'

Ann nodded. 'He's a lovely man.'

Lois was up, dancing around the kitchen to Rod Stewart. Ann watched her and smoked and thought of poor Hugh. Not much to look at: she could understand why Lois, having all, kept wanting more; but special nonetheless. A bit like Fred Astaire, she often thought, with his sandy, straight hair and his wide-mouthed grin, and that touch of the old-fashioned about him, as though he might spin you off on his arm into the moonlight. So kind, so gentle and clever, and so much in love with Lois.

Lois paused to refill her glass. 'To Hugh!'

'To Hugh,' echoed Ann. She stubbed the cigarette.

'Who is so brilliant,' Lois said earnestly. 'Cos what a palaver, when you come to think about it. What incredible nonsense this monogamy stuff is.' She waved the glass, splashing wine on the floor. 'Take Jack and Tess. Good for each other, happy together in their argumentative way. So it shouldn't make a blind bit of difference that he's fucking that silly cow.'

'*Lois!*' Ann struggled to keep her face straight. 'Pamela's my *friend.*'

'Come off it. As I was saying, no difference at all. But Tess'd blow a gasket if she knew.'

She was off again, swaying dreamily in the space between fridge, cooker and sink, observed by Horatio, who stood in the doorway wagging his tail. Ann lit another cigarette and watched the glowing tip start to eat its way down. Tomorrow night the Drunken Bridge Club would meet in her flat, as it did every alternate Friday: Jack and Pamela, herself and Hugh, while Tessa worked overtime and Rug-bug scored his last try. She rolled the scrap of gold paper, then unrolled it again.

Jack and Pamela had been at her place this afternoon. She

18

hadn't been home yet; she had that to face. Soon, she would have to leave Lois's hugs and this warm, untidy kitchen and take the tube to Camden Town, where there'd be no option but to drag her feet along the High Street and through into her road, to kick the day's crop of chip papers into the gutter, tiptoe down the area steps to the shadowed front door and reluctantly turn the key. And there she would be again, prowling like an interloper in her own home, catching the drift of Jack's classy cigarettes in the hallway, fingering the glasses gleaming on the draining board, staring at the neatly remade bed with its tight hospital corners.

Pamela, the staff nurse: how Ann detested her pedantic tidiness. And how had it come to this? It was high time she saw action herself.

The music had stopped and Lois was enveloping her in another hug. She looked anxious all of a sudden. 'We mustn't tell Tess about me and Hugh.'

She hiccupped.

'I won't tell a soul.'

She hadn't even told Lois about Jack and Pamela; it was Hugh who'd done that.

Lois hiccupped again. 'It's tempting. I keep wanting to say, "Hey Tess, why don't you give meaningless sex a whirl, same as your Jack does."' She took another swig of wine. 'How *are* Jack and Pam, by the way? Has he managed to ditch her yet?'

'Not yet.'

'Hugh says, can't be long.'

Ann nodded. 'He's right. You can see Jack's pissed off. He'll soon be telling her in words of one syllable.'

She watched gratification, jolted by hiccups, spread across Lois's face. The penny dropped, and her stomach. 'Oh Lois, you *don't*? You and *Jack*? Oh my *God*, Lois!'

Lois grinned, hand to mouth. 'I fancy him something chronic. Oh help, aren't I awful?'

'Yes, you *are!*'

'It's only sex, Ann, I promise. He's safer with me than with Pamela. And Tessa won't know.' She grinned, showing her

19

little white teeth. 'New bottle. New toast. Turn Rod over.' She stumbled out of the kitchen.

Ann sprang from her chair, almost ran after her. She wanted to smack her, to shake her and tell her to wake up. Lois and Jack? Too much, God, how horrible! How could she even think of it? Hugh pretending not to mind; Tessa unable to see. As if that made it okay. God!

But already the shock was subsiding. It began to seem possible. More than that, unavoidable. A done deed, the stain already spreading.

Why not me? The thought sprang like rage in her head. And why not poor Hugh?

Horatio, sensing excitement, was snorting and nudging her hand with his nose. The image of Hugh's face was floating before her. Fred Astaire's smile. She closed her eyes and dropped back on her chair. A sigh spread through her, starting in her shoulders and settling through her limbs. Her muscles relaxing. Hugh, of course, Hugh.

Lois was back with the new bottle, filling their glasses. 'So here's the toast. To Italy.'

Ann patted Horatio's head under the table. 'To Italy,' she agreed, shouting above Rod Stewart. 'Let's face the music and dance.'

Advertising

The next day, when Ann lunched with Tessa in a pub on the Strand, Tessa launched immediately into a rant about Alan, her boss. Ann could barely concentrate; her head was too full of secrets.

'You wouldn't believe what a sadist he is, Ann. He knows just how to wind me up.'

Ann nodded and murmured sympathy. Tessa was looking older than her years, she was thinking. Broad shoulders, square jaw: there'd always been something a touch masculine, but lately she seemed deliberately androgynous with her tailored suits and close-cropped hair.

'He's a pig, my lover. But you can't win, so ignore him. Don't rise to it.'

Might as well tell her to stand on her head.

'It's him that won't stop. He picks his times, waits until there's someone else there so I can't defend myself. This morning he gatecrashed my budget review meeting, and...'

Ann's attention drifted. She shaded her eyes against the glare of sun from the high leaded windows and scanned the bar. It was like Lois's photograph again: everyone shouting and animated, packed tightly around the oak-barrel tables, or standing, crushed together, in the spaces between. Three feet from Ann's eyes, a man's hand slid confidently over the curve of a woman's buttock. Ann shifted on her seat, pushed her food aside, lit a cigarette and took a gulp of wine. She needed to calm down. She sat back, willing the alcohol into her system, adding her exhalation to the smoke, hearing the tetchy stop-go of the traffic beyond the window. She tuned in to Tessa again.

'When I'm alone with him, you'd think butter wouldn't melt, he's so smarmy. "My dear young lady, what a marvellous job you're doing" blah, blah.'

Ann tried smiling, but Tessa didn't smile back. The frown that Lois had caught with her camera was getting to be semi-permanent. She'd been just as belligerent three years ago when she marched into ATP, the little market research company where Ann still worked. Tessa had been a whizz kid at twenty-four: nipping uneconomic projects in the bud, scrutinising the contracts, terrifying the partners but impressing the clients. Then, this year, she'd been head hunted by Rex Advertising for the top job in their administrative department, where her unwritten main duty was to keep the vile MD off everyone's backs.

'... and I know, if I tackle him, he'll deny all knowledge, make me look paranoid.'

Ann thought of Lois. 'So why don't you quit?'

'Quit?' Tessa's nostrils were flaring.

'Jack makes enough money. Think what you really want to do, and go for it, Tess. Like Lois is doing.'

'Thank you, but I'm no one's dependent.'

'Don't bite my head off.'

'You think Lois is a model? She seduces her tutor, flunks out of a degree, spends ten years sponging off him—'

Ann couldn't bear this. 'Lois loves Hugh.'

Did she though? Was Tessa right?

'Italy.' She changed the subject. 'Two weeks with your husband in Italy and you'll forget your horrid boss.'

Tessa's scowl deepened. 'I'm right off the word "husband."'

Ann nearly choked on a lungful of smoke. For an awful moment Tessa seemed unable to say more, and Ann thought: she must know.

'It's my lousy father. He's packed a bag and moved in with some floozy. It's been going on for two years apparently.'

'Tess, I'm so sorry.'

'It's a shock.'

'I should think so. How old is he?'

'Fifty-one.'

'And this woman?'

'I don't know. Some bint from his office. Much younger. What an idiot. But the worst thing is Mum. She's drinking. I mean drinking.'

'Ah, Tess...'

'It's like she's making herself ill to make him feel bad. But he doesn't feel bad—he's not even *there*. She rings him up, pissed as an Irish wake, and he says, "Get some sleep."'

Ann nodded dumbly, stubbing out one cigarette, reaching for another.

Tessa touched her hand. 'Are *you* all right, Ann? You seem edgy.'

'Me. Sorry. No. Tell me more about your mum.'

'That's it, really. I'm done. So, come on. Your turn. What's the matter?'

'Really, nothing. Just feeling my age.'

'Don't be daft.'

'Thirty in October.'

'That's not old.'

'Okay, I'm sex-starved. Will that do you?'

'No, because you could shag Charlie's brains out tomorrow, so why don't you?'

'Be serious.'

'So it isn't just sex, then.'

'Okay. You've got me. I want the real deal.' She pulled a face. 'Hearts and flowers. My youngest sister got decked out in orange blossom last month. That's all of them hitched, and half of them sprogging.'

Tessa was rearranging her big shoulders in a businesslike fashion. 'So let's be systematic. Is there someone you've missed? Not Charlie, I'll grant you, but you really should think about Sebastian.'

Ann laughed. 'Tess, give it a rest.'

'But he's nice—'

'*Nice?*'

'And good-looking once you get past the beard and the glasses.'

'And the belly. And the DIY haircut.'

'But Ann, he's sensible. Okay, wrong word, what I mean is mature and grown up. He's got a fabulous smile, and—'

'So why didn't *you* snap him up, eh Tessa, answer me that? All those months you shared an office with him. No, you're all right, *Jack*, and you don't care what rubbish I get.'

Tessa looked pained. 'Of course I care. And I might have thought of Sebastian, only Jack came along.'

'Pull the other one. Always with his nose in some book on statistics. Or regurgitating *The Times'* leader for want of an opinion of his own.'

'Ann, be fair—'

'I am being. *The Times* this, *The Times* that. Friday, in the pub, he was still droning on about the referendum, for heaven's sake. Do we really need to know the count in the

23

Outer Hebrides?'

'Sorry I spoke.'

'Oh Tess, don't be huffy. You're right,' Ann conceded, 'he is "nice", as you so enticingly put it, but he never shows any interest in women.'

Tessa didn't reply. She was fiddling with her glass and glancing distractedly around the bar, as if she half expected to see someone she knew.

'Nor men either,' Ann teased, 'or Charlie wouldn't have moved in with him.'

Tessa sat up straight and leant forward. 'Okay. How about this?' Her cheeks had flushed pink. 'Have you thought... what I mean is... why not have a go at *Time Out*?'

'*Time Out*?'

'Yes, you know. Don't rush to dismiss it. Lonely hearts.'

How dare she! 'Ugh! Come off it, I'm not that desperate. And the man I'm looking for isn't that desperate either!'

Tessa looked as if she'd been slapped. For a moment Ann couldn't think why. Then, 'Oh my God, was *that* how you met Jack?'

Tessa was bright crimson now, the flush spreading to her ears, exposed by the savage haircut. 'For your information, we weren't desperate, either of us. It's an efficient way to meet, that's all. Lots of people do it these days.'

'Yes, of course. I wasn't thinking. I didn't mean—'

'Yes, you did.'

'No, really. This is far more glamorous than your French evening class. And brave. Tell me what happened. Did you advertise, or did he?'

Tessa was grinning in spite of herself. 'He did. "Builder with a brain. Short, dark and handsome." I wrote a letter. He rang. I warmed to his voice. And we met.' She paused. 'Here.'

She gazed round happily.

'Here?'

'Yes. I came in out of the wind, and he was over there, at the bar. And he hadn't seen me yet, and we hadn't exchanged photos, but I knew it was him.'

24

Tessa looked quite unlike herself. Ann couldn't help smiling. 'Love at first sight.'

'No, of course not. I'm not stupid. And please, Ann, don't say anything. Jack would be ever so cross.'

'I won't breathe a word.'

It *had* been love at first sight, she was realising. And who could blame Tess, because Jack might be short, but he was a real looker. Broad shoulders, dark eyes, dark, wavy hair, and a way of looking right into you. She tried to imagine their meeting, to picture Jack as a stranger in a blue haze of pub smoke, scanning the crowd for the woman he would marry.

It made her jealous as hell, so she thought about Hugh again, to calm herself down.

House of Cards

That evening, Hugh fidgeted by Ann's open French window in Camden Town, impatient to distract his thoughts into the discipline of dealing cards and counting points. It wasn't fear or jealousy he was battling right now, it was acute longing. He was falling in love all over again. Lois was so vivid, so extraordinary; he ached to look at her. He'd hardly been able to tear himself away from her to come here tonight.

Outside, on the flaking concrete among the weedy, unwatered tubs, Jack and Pamela hovered, their dark and blonde heads bent close, cooking up some private angst. 'Let's to billiards,' he called hopefully.

'Hold your water, Hamlet. We're coming.'

They showed no sign of it. He sucked in his breath. Oh Lois, Lois.

Ann arrived at his side and leant into him, head against shoulder. He swallowed the lump in his throat. 'Hello, little Annie. I like your new haircut.'

She lifted her face, exhaling smoke and smiles. 'Vidal Sassoon. It cost me a fortune, and you're the only person to notice. You are a lovely man, Hugh.'

'Am I, though?'

'Definitely.'

'Thank you, Annie.' He stepped back to deliver a bow, a hand on the hilt of his sword as he doffed a velvet cap. 'Evermore thanks, the exchequer of the poor.' He'd lost his own voice tonight.

'Hey, where did that man go?' She swayed on one leg for a moment, mock-pouting, before toppling sideways. Then sighed. 'I'd better get the table set up.'

Dear Annie, always acting the clown. He moved away from the window and kept his mind busy by watching her. She wasn't beautiful, but her style made her seem so. Faded jeans and white shirt, silver jewellery, and her chestnut-brown hair, expertly bobbed, bouncing and swinging as she charged around the dank, stuffy room, dislodging dead leaves from the fossilised grape-ivy. She was humming as she bent to fold out the legs of the card-table, practically dancing as she shook the cards from their boxes and arranged coasters and ashtrays, all the while giving him quick sideways grins.

She was on strange form tonight, jubilant in a forced way. But so pale. She should take better care of herself. And of this nice little flat. Jack kept nagging her to 'get a foot on the property ladder', but Hugh understood why she hung on here, renting. It might be pokey and dark, but it had character. It just needed a good hoovering. A bit of leaf shine, and a break from being kippered in nicotine. And a scrub-down with bleach in the bathroom, where the avocado suite looked grubby and the wallpaper was sooty with mould.

There was noise from the patio; they were coming at last. Jack knuckle-gripped the door-frame, while Pamela whispered and tugged at his sleeve.

Ann heckled them, 'Come along, you star-crossed lovers,' and was off again, laughing and spinning on her heel. 'Hey, everyone's so uptight tonight. We need to get happy. I'll fetch more wine.' She bounded off into the kitchen, calling, 'It'll help us to a slam, Hugh my lover,' in habitual self-parody of her Devonshire roots.

'An unmakeable slam,' he confided to Horatio.

The dog was sprawled untidily on Ann's brown-cord sofa, a large portion of his black-and-pink stomach drooping over the front. He cocked an ear, half-wagged his tail, then grunted and returned to his dreams.

Jack and Pamela were still whispering by the window. Hugh took a seat at the table and channelled his nerves into cutting and mixing the decks. The activity brought more thoughts of Lois, but safe ones. It was Lois who'd taught him to shuffle like a hustler, interleaving the cards in this satisfying blur of crisp noise. It took her a term to master the technique and two to teach it to him. She said it was the most important thing she learned at university, nicely ironic given that she'd refused to play cards ever since. 'Yawn,' she'd pronounced when Ann first suggested bridge.

The memory calmed him, making the present seem bearably transient. He was humming, he realised. He'd picked up the tune Ann had left hanging in the air: *Let's face the music and dance*. He lifted his eyes from the cards to contemplate the fractured pair who approached the table at last. Jack scowling, drawing heavily on one of his slim, brown cigarettes, his saturnine face, which others thought so handsome, full of ill will. Pamela, her eyes fixed mournfully on the back of her lover's head.

'Ja-ack.'

It couldn't be long. She would see straight, or Jack would put her straight. He was clearly done with her.

Jack produced his winning smile for Hugh, gripping his shoulder. 'Sorry to keep you, mate. Good to see you. Did you spot my new Rover outside?'

'Can't say I did, but then, you know me—car-blind. Are you pleased with it?'

'Oh boy, am I ever! Automatic. Huge engine. Three-and-a-half litre V8. Three-and-a-half grand.'

'It's gorgeous,' said Pamela. 'All shiny and green.'

'Cameron green,' Jack clarified, detaching himself from her

27

grasp.

'The inside is cream leather,' she sighed. 'It smells heavenly.'

Jack nodded. 'She'll do a hundred and eighteen, Hugh. Nought to sixty in ten and a half seconds!'

'Amazing. What power, eh?'

He didn't know what else to say. His Vauxhall Viva had been resprayed bronze by the previous owner. Lois hated the colour, but it hid the rust. The inside smelled mostly of Horatio.

'Be nice to me.' Pamela clutched at Jack's elbow.

She's like a doll, Hugh thought suddenly. Her face was too round, the nose too precisely upturned, the cheeks too prettily pink. Her hair, harsh as spun nylon, was cut in a blonde bubble across her brow and the lobes of her ears. She even spoke in a mechanical whine, "Mama, Mama", a voice like water torture; no wonder Jack had had enough. Her eyes, swimming with tears, were baby blue, fringed with thick, pale lashes. Did they roll when you tipped her horizontal?

Lois had asked after them as he ate his lamb chop tonight. 'How is it with Jack Sprat and Sugarpam?'

'Uncomfortable to watch,' he'd replied. 'She hangs on like grim death.' Which had Lois objecting, 'Why doesn't he just tell her? What on earth is he playing at?'

Her annoyance seemed curious in retrospect; usually she giggled and pumped him for details. He'd been too busy noticing that she was wearing no bra, while she grumbled on about Jack and Pamela.

'Lord knows how he got sucked in in the first place. He needs a lesson in taste. How long do you give them?'

'What, petal?'

Her breasts had been free beneath a blouse he hadn't seen before: silky-soft, peach-coloured, with small covered buttons.

'Sprat and Sugar. How long do you give them?'

Her timing was odd. Normally she asked when he got back from bridge.

'Well, Jack could scarcely be plainer. She'll have to take the hint soon.'

At which Lois had smiled enigmatically and fetched strawberries and cream.

'No!'

The shock of incest.

Jack was speaking. 'What's up, mate?'

He could barely answer. 'I... it... it's nothing.'

He stared at the man. Found himself looking at the dark hair on his forearm. Please, no. It hadn't happened, not yet. Perhaps he was wrong. Would Lois do that?

'Ja-ack.' Pamela could give lessons in pleading. 'Jack, don't be cross with me.'

The bastard ignored her. Grinned. Sucked on his expensive cigarette. Said, 'Hey, let's draw for partners for a change.'

'No *way!*' Ann erupted into the room. 'Hugh's *mine! We*'re going to win tonight, aren't we, my lover?'

He didn't feel like a winner. He tore his eyes from Jack; stretched a hand out to Pamela. 'Come on, Pam. Come and play bridge.' Pray God, she had more miles in her. She'd been fun at the start, before she got plaintive. At the start, he'd almost understood what Jack saw in her. He struggled to imagine fancying her, as if this would rekindle Jack's passion, but he couldn't manage it. 'Show us what you're made of. You know you can beat hell out of Annie and me.'

She blinked gratitude through meekly lowered lashes, slid into her seat opposite the still-vertical Jack, and produced one of her mawkish banalities. 'Lucky at cards, unlucky in love.' Her forlorn gaze visited her plump white fingers spread upon the stained green baize. Then she fixed Jack with another abject stare. 'At least let's be happy when we *are* together.'

'For fuck's sake, *be* happy then, for once in your life!'

This shocked them into silence. They were all seated at last. Cutting for dealer, Hugh drew an ace. He dealt rapidly, battling to calm his thoughts, to blot out the idea of this man with—

'The new recruits are arriving on Monday.' He concentrated on listening to Ann. 'Two of them are our age. ATP's been lonely with Lois and Tessa gone. I can't wait to be

29

in Italy with you all.'

Hugh sorted his cards, biting his lip so hard that it hurt. Did Lois plan to seduce Jack in Italy while he, Ann and Tessa looked on?

'Tell you what,' Jack was saying. 'These recruits, Ann, why don't you ask if they play bridge? Let's expand to two tables.'

'I will. That's a brilliant idea.'

'And we'll have another go at persuading Tess and Lo, eh Hugh?' Jack winked at him. 'I'll have a good go at Tessa, I promise.'

Hugh sensed Pamela shrink and felt her pain as his own. For, of course, Lois would come now to the Drunken Bridge Club. She would come for Jack and would take him easily, while he watched in silence, as impotent as poor Pamela, as irrelevant as the unknowing Tess.

'Yes, Jack. I'm not doubting you will,' he snapped. 'But now, let's play, can we?'

Playing House

Zoë Smith slammed the door of her new, glass-fronted oven and saw gravy splash from the plate inside.

'Curse and sod it!'

A second plateful steamed on the round white table at the far end of the kitchen. She stepped over dusty bags of plaster, plonked herself on the rush-bottomed seat of a new pine chair, looped her long hair out of the way and began. Chicken casserole, mash and peas. Surprisingly delicious. For once she'd cooked something edible, and still Tony didn't come home.

She finished and pushed the plate away. 'Sod Tony.'

She felt a bit better now; hunger had made her irritable. And there was no mystery to why he lingered in the pub with the other teachers. If she had some half-decent place to go after work, wouldn't she stay out too? She was as weary as he was of this vile house.

She shook her head, refusing the tears. As she carried the empty plate to the sink, her gaze swam out through the pink primer of the new window-frame into the builder's tip they called the back garden, a cheerless view in the low evening sun. When they first moved in, she'd been eager to dig and plant, her hair tied up in an Indian-silk scarf, imagining shrubs and flowers and buzzing insects. Tony had come out to watch, and she'd smiled up at him, wanting him to share the vision. But what he said was, 'Sorry, lovely, I hate to be a killjoy, but shouldn't we concentrate on the house first?' And he was right, of course. So now the garden was bricks and junk, and heaps of sand around the black crater of ash and fired nails. Not a growing thing to be seen.

It was she who'd found what was growing. 'It's soft here,' she'd pestered six months ago, poking away at the skirting. 'Can't we take up a board, just to be sure?'

'Oh all right, if you must. But do try not to break it. We've far too much to do as it is.'

They'd both been afraid. The floor felt weird; something dreadful was lurking beneath it. The difference was that she needed to look and Tony needed not to, as though by not looking it wouldn't be so. And then, when they looked, he made her feel it was her fault. For looking, for wanting the house.

'A coat of paint and a sunny day, they had you in raptures.'

That was unkind. They'd chosen it together, hadn't they? Wasn't it as much his fault, too mean to pay for a survey?

It was true though, the house had been full of light that first day she'd run down the road with the estate agent's key in her hand. Sunshine bouncing off white walls, a beautiful little house in Balham, south of the river. 'Come and see!' she'd enthused, grinning through the dusty panes of the phone-box at the leafy entrance to the Common and the shop around the corner that would soon be *her* shop around the corner. 'Quick, before it goes!' Houses seemed to fly off the estate agents' lists; there was no time to lose.

'Ye-es.' He'd paced slowly from room to room as she jiggled with impatience, willing him to love it as much as she did. 'Okay, it's got potential. We'll need to replumb and rewire. And replace all the gutters. But look, Zo, we can knock this wall down, and junk all this pastry round the ceiling. Take out the fireplaces, put in a decent kitchen, install a shower.'

Which meant he was saying yes! And she was so full of excitement that she didn't think to wonder or argue. And so they arrived, after the honeymoon, wielding club-hammers and blowtorches and electric drills, and in no time at all they'd transformed the little house with its small, white Victorian rooms into a grey, dusty forest of Acro props and jagged holes and fallen plaster.

Still, things hadn't seemed so bad. Not until that December evening when she threw her weight onto the chisel, splintering the wood. She'd stolen a look at Tony, but he was busy fitting a U-bend, head under the sink, bony knees waving in the air. She tried again, easing the chisel beneath each nail as he'd taught her. With tortured creaks, the nails let go. She yanked the board up and off the joists and shone the torch into the void.

There was a sudden, powerful smell of mushrooms.

Beneath the dusty floor, glistening in the torch beam, lay great luscious pools and beads of honey brown liquid on pallid, grey-yellow plates of fungus.

'What is it, Tony?' Her voice was a whisper.

'Dry rot,' he muttered. 'Just a massive, bloody outbreak of lethal, deadly dry rot.'

She had heard of it, had seen some comedy film when she was a child, which had the bad guys tumbling squealing through a disintegrating staircase before the whole house fell on top of them. Now Tony's DIY books spelt out the reality. They read them avidly, huddled in bed together. *Merulius Lacrymans*: the weeping fungus. Once it takes hold it creates its own conditions, sucking humidity from the air, seeking sound wood with long, rubbery tendrils that can penetrate even brick. You must find it and destroy it, every bit, cut the good wood back at least six feet and souse everything in poisonous spray. Even then you must provide plenty of ventilation, or it will start all over again.

Terrifyingly accurate: they uncovered grey tendrils snaking up inside the lath-and-plaster walls, heading for the bedrooms. Even now Zoë shuddered, imagining it burrowing through the newly-laid concrete.

'We can't do this, Tony,' she'd pleaded. 'We'll have to get builders in.'

But he wouldn't hear of it. 'They cost the earth. And anyway, would you trust them to get it all?'

'I don't know. Will *we* get it all? Can anyone get it all?' And again she'd crept down the uncarpeted stairs in the dark, to peer into the glutinous depths beneath her kitchen floor.

The slower horror began. Each evening when they got in from work, they ate hurriedly, hardly speaking, changed into their oldest clothes and set to. The kitchen became a quarantine zone into which they stepped with disgust and from which they retreated in dread of the spores clinging to their shoes. They burned the rotten wood in the garden, conscious of their neighbours' disapproval, feeling tainted like plague-carriers in old London. It was Zoë's job to tend the bonfire, and often she lingered beside it, stoking the blaze as high as she dared until the flames, beyond her control, roared up into the night, consuming the infection and drying her tears.

If Tony noticed the tracks on her cheeks, he didn't say. His expression was grim. He hacked at the beams with robotic intensity, pausing only to light cigarettes or to stub them out savagely on the pale fronds of *Merulius Lacrymans,* leaving its evil white trails on the beams and the bricks.

Life was primitive without a kitchen, an interminable extension of their wet camping honeymoon in Wales, where she'd learned to carry water from a standpipe and to use the Calor gas ring. In the bedroom she used it again to prepare endless stews in a pressure cooker. Staring about her, waiting for the steam to hiss from the valve, or the kettle to come to

33

the boil for the washing-up, she saw how dust and grime had sullied the wedding presents: the white rug from her grandma, the chintz-covered armchair from Tony's mum and dad, the cotton-lace bedspread from her aunt. Everything hopeless and grey. And Tony, when she looked at him, was grey and hopeless too, all his eagerness and certainty withered. He'd gone on at her for months to marry him, insisted it would be all right, didn't she see, if only she would trust to fate a little.

Her parents said the same thing. 'He's steady,' pronounced her father, shaking his *Telegraph* out wearily. 'Reliable. A bit older than you, I'll grant, but eight years is nothing, enough to show his potential. Head of science already, you can see what you're getting. You'd be daft not to take him. You'll be stuck on the shelf soon—men like Tony don't grow on trees.'

She saw distaste in her father's eyes. He was weary of her impulsive love affairs with fickle men.

'What's wrong with Tony?' her mother whispered in the kitchen. 'He seems very nice and sincere, and you like him, don't you?'

'Yes, but Mum, I don't love him.'

Yet she too was weary of getting her heart broken. So one day she stopped fighting, drew a line under the quest and said, 'Okay, yes, I will marry you.'

'Good God, Zo.' Tony's mouth had dropped open. 'Do you mean it?'

'Yes, I do.'

And amazingly she found it was true. The world brightened. She felt safe and happy. And they *were* happy, making their vows, holding hands under the tablecloth at the reception. She was trying to smile now, but it was no use, this memory. It was true in a way, but not in so many others. She still hadn't loved Tony when she married him, and she knew now that she never would, not as she wanted to love a husband. It was her fault, not his, but knowing that was no help.

She turned back from the window. The kitchen smelled of congealing stew, not of horrible, toxic chemicals. The rot was ripped out, burned, all traces buried under four inches of concrete, yet still she sniffed and prodded, and woke terrified from dreams in which it burst through the new tongue-and-groove panelling.

She bent to touch concrete, as though it might offer an answer. Something had shifted in her head. Not Tony's fault: was that it?

Her job hadn't helped. Musty corridors, chalk-dusty professors, her desk in a broom-cupboard with a barred view of moss and slime and pigeon shit. The university deserved dry rot but was too posh to catch it. And at last she was gone from there! Heading for ATP on Monday, which wasn't at all posh: yellow brick, steel and glass, five floors up with an outlook of sky and chimneypots. With smells of coffee and cigarettes and Xerox ink. And the people mostly young, wearing jeans and short skirts. Yes—

But here was Tony back. The unsteady scratch of his key, the clunk as the door shut, the sound of him in the hall. Her spirits deflated. It wasn't his fault, no, it wasn't at all, but that didn't mend it.

He stumbled into the kitchen wearing a sheepish grin. 'I'm sorry, Zo. I only meant to have one.'

And she was hushing him, smiling, trying to make him smile too, though he wouldn't. 'It's okay, don't be sorry. I've been wrong to be cross. It's fine to get out. You're right to get out. I should get out more myself.'

False Move

As she turned off the Aldwych on Monday morning, Ann concentrated on feeling positive. She always enjoyed this walk up Drury Lane. Narrow and meandering, it still was a "lane" despite the modern frontage of the theatre. The little specialist shops with their dusty display windows spoke of the past. When she'd first sashayed up here seven years ago, the only one of her family to get a degree and leave Exeter, she'd felt shivers of joy, fancying herself to be walking in Nell Gwynn's footsteps, destined to rise in the world and to win some great man's heart.

She was passing the coffee merchant's now, the smell of fresh grinding was delicious, and ATP was in sight against the morning blue of the sky. In the next-to-top storey of the small office block, its windows were lit gold by the sun. The Attwood Thorn Partnership: Ron Attwood, Doug Thorn, where before long she too would be partner, they both hinted as much.

'You've been with us from the beginning, Ann,' marvelled Ron. 'We'd barely begun.'

'Yes, and dear me,' echoed Doug, 'who knows if we'd have made it without you?'

They knew that they wouldn't and didn't mind saying so. 'You're a lifesaver, Ann Wilton. Who else could have landed the contract with Rex?'

It was true; they'd have gone under last year without that five-year, price-indexed deal. Times were hard, inflation scary, rampaging above twenty-five percent now, and market research budgets were always among the first to be cut. But ATP was still comfortably afloat, with no shortage of work for its three-dozen staff and four more arriving today.

Ann quickened her step. Ron and Doug were a bit old-school, a touch "fifties", but not stuffy, no obsession with status or titles. They mightn't pay the best salaries, but they respected their staff, seeking consensus, letting the best ideas win and the odd ideas run. Like when they heard it was Charlie Evans who'd started calling the place "Ask The Punters", they weren't offended. They chuckled and passed the joke on, until before long "Ask The Punters" was what everyone was calling them, even their clients. And then, a month or so back, lift-off! "Ask The Punters" was mentioned in some TV piece about opinion polls on the Common Market, and suddenly it was the in-name in market research.

Whereupon Ron and Doug, bless them, had come to ask

Ann what to do, and agreed 'Good idea', and trooped round to the scruffy office that Charlie now shared with Sebastian Santini, to hand him a posh vellum envelope addressed 'Charles Evans, Esq', containing a grateful letter and a cheque for fifty pounds.

And she'd only suggested twenty.

She was through the street-door now and into the lift with a couple of accountants from floor two. They were hefting the gigantic briefcases like sewing machines that were the badge of their trade. 'Nice weekend?' she teased, and they groaned in unison. She pressed 5. "Attwood Thorn" read the little brass plate. Soon to be Attwood, Thorn and—bother! Because she was the loser from Charlie's *bon mot*. It would look churlish, wouldn't it, not to say commercially dumb, to expect them to add her name? Attwood, Thorn & Wilton? "Ask The World"? "Ask The Wankers"? No, damn it, partner or not, "Ask The Punters" they would have to remain.

The lift cables rattled and jerked into motion, making her think of guillotines. And then of Charlie losing his head over her. For months now he'd been stubbornly besotted, gazing at her across the pub table like an inebriated angel, his face framed by yellow curls, telling her she was his Ingrid Bergman and pleading, 'I love you. I want to go to bed with you.' Which would be flattering if it wasn't such nonsense. In truth, Charlie knew nothing about her and didn't want to know. She wasn't a snob, really not. It wasn't that Charlie was a lazy, charming, beautiful, over-qualified clerk going nowhere, whom they really ought to sack. No, it was because she wanted a real man, not a star-struck fan.

When would her man turn up? Her sisters and sisters-in-law were making sympathetic noises, and her mum kept fishing for news of her love life. How old was Nell Gwynn when she landed the king? Younger than thirty, no doubt. Maybe Charlie would know. His subject was supposed to be history, though he always looked shifty and said 'Not my period' when you asked him anything.

Ding. The lift doors opened at the second floor, the

accountants got out, and the doors shut again. Ann met her own eyes in the lift mirror. God, she looked tired. Her cotton shirt was shapeless and crumpled, her skin sallow, the Sassoon cut lacked bounce. She stuck on a grin.

Ding. The fourth floor. The doors opened, but no one was there. She punched 5 so hard that she broke a nail. Hell! What was she to do to ease this ache? Hugh might take the edge off it, but then again, would he? Because Hugh was lovely, but it was Lois he loved.

Ding. Floor five. And along the corridor, bang on cue, came Sebastian Santini, ATP's resident statistician, as recommended by Tessa. Uninspiring to look at despite the lyrical name, and no zip to him somehow. But he was pleasant enough, and yes, though she'd known him two years, she could never quite make up her mind to rule him out.

'Hi there.'

'Oh, erm, hi...?'

He looked startled. She smiled warmly. 'So how's life with Charlie?'

He'd been intent on transporting a brimming mug of coffee over the much spattered corridor carpet. Now he was considering her question as carefully as he would an enquiry about stratified samples. The coffee was hot, which was causing him a problem. He shifted the mug to his left hand while he fished in his pocket for a handkerchief, blue madras cotton, crumpled but clean, to insulate the handle.

'Fine,' he said finally. 'Yes, definitely fine.'

She smiled, amused, wanting more.

'I'm getting used to his mess. It's good to have company.'

She made an effort to fancy him, though, dear me, even in this heat he was wearing his tired old Marks and Sparks woolly over his comfortable stomach.

He ploughed on. 'Er... We've found a pub that has live jazz on Sundays. The Hackney Stompers.'

She hated jazz.

'Not your thing? Well, it was good fun yesterday, um, and nice weather. There was an interesting article in the paper actually, about the way the weather is going.'

'The weather, Sebastian?'

'Um, yes, the climate.'

She stepped a little closer. There was an awkward pause. She fidgeted with her broken nail.

'Erm—sorry,' he said, 'How rude of me. Was *your* weekend okay?'

'Well, you know how it is,' she said gaily, 'the usual thrills. Shopping, washing, ironing.'

He grinned, sharing the joke. She had to admit he wasn't bad-looking. White teeth and full, curved lips hidden in that beard he was stroking.

'Do you happen to play bridge?' she said.

'Bridge?' His eyes were nice too.

'We've got four, but we're thinking of expanding.'

He looked uncertain. She touched his hand. He looked down at her hand touching his.

'It's not serious. We're "The Drunken Bridge Club."'

'Sounds good.'

The teeth were really something. Good lord, she wasn't persuading herself, was she? How on earth would she live this down with Tessa?

'So we just need three more.' She grinned. 'I suppose we could ask Charlie.'

He nodded, amused. 'Charlie would tell us where to get off.'

'Too right. He'd give us a mouthful about how bourgeois we are.'

They both laughed.

'Anyway, great... I'll organise it when I'm back from Italy.'

'Thanks.'

'Will you be at the welcoming do later?' she asked him.

'Er... yes.'

Her spirits had lifted. She held his eyes a moment longer, then touched him lightly on the arm before speeding away, along to the secretaries' room to see if they needed help with the wine and cheese.

*

At the do, she kept an eye out for the new recruits as the staff drifted in. She was sounding out the fieldwork supervisor about the new survey for Rex when she spotted one of them, David Pratt, hovering in the doorway. 'Duty calls,' she said, and dived to greet him.

'Hello again. Welcome aboard.'

She put a drink in his hand, then steered him through the crowd. 'You'll be working mostly with Sebastian Santini. I'll introduce you.'

So there she was, quite naturally, offering Sebastian more smiles.

David Pratt set about ingratiating himself, asking longwinded questions and hanging obsequiously on Sebastian's replies. What an enormous chin the man had. She hadn't taken to him at the interview, but he was well qualified, so she'd let Ron and Doug over-rule her. Charlie arrived and began pulling faces behind Pratt's back, trying to make her laugh. She frowned at him to stop, though Pratt seemed oblivious.

'I gather that quota sampling is in vogue,' he smarmed.

'Yes,' Ann said. 'You stand on the street with a clipboard and pick so many men, so many women—'

Pratt ignored her. 'But it's too hit and miss, surely, Sebastian?'

'Er, yes,' Sebastian met Ann's eyes, 'you're right, the purists do sneer. They say it's slapdash and cheap. You miss out on the people who drive or stay at home.' He paused. 'And they're right of course—it *is* cheap.'

Pratt brayed sycophantically.

'But actually...'

Sebastian broke off, his attention caught by something across the room. Ann turned to look.

'Mmm,' said Pratt. 'And who's she?'

'I don't know,' said Sebastian.

'Nor me, neither,' Charlie said fervently.

A young woman, tallish with a cloud of soft auburn hair,

hovered near the door, smiling shyly. 'She's new,' Ann told them. 'She'll be helping me. Her name's Zoë Smith.'

'Well, I'm all in favour, eh, boss?'

Ann looked at Pratt startled, but then realised he was addressing Sebastian, still gazing at Zoë, who answered absently, 'Er, well, yes.'

Bloody hell, Ann didn't believe this. How rude! Sebastian was tedious, actually. Scruffy and fat. Good for nothing but news bulletins and bridge.

The partners had spotted Zoë and were doing the honours: shaking her hand, giving her wine, beginning to make introductions.

'Not a patch on my Annie,' murmured Charlie, at Ann's elbow. 'Looks a bit posh to me, like the queen on a visit.'

'Maybe,' Ann said. 'She's been in university research. We did wonder if...'

She stopped. It was indiscreet to reveal the board's doubts.

Pratt grinned at Sebastian. 'Well, I wouldn't say no.'

'Such a pity she's *married*,' Ann said tartly, and marched off towards Zoë Smith.

Friendly Game

'Today's crossword was impossible,' Charlie remarked. 'I had to give it up and do some filing.' He flung back his head, upended the bottle of light ale and waited for the last, slow drop to fall.

Sebastian said nothing. The day had been unsettling, and he was in no mood for banter. He continued to scan the contents page of his new Indian cookbook.

Charlie tossed the empty over the shredded arm of the grey-brown sofa, to crash amongst its fellows in a cardboard box. 'Bulls-eye!' For a few satisfied seconds, he contemplated the ceiling. 'I think we've got a new, keen spider. Some ambitious spinning going on up here.'

Sebastian maintained a poker face and struggled to concentrate. *Pork Vindaloo? Dhall fritters? Bengali Bhaji?*

There was a sound of effortful scrabbling from the sofa, and of Charlie muttering, 'Where the fuck?' The tobacco packet was squashed beneath him. He gingerly extracted a prepared roll-up and lit it with the table lighter that Sebastian kept in fuel. An ashtray toppled to the floor, but he ignored it. 'All mod cons,' he said.

Brinjal Chutney? Kabuli Channa? Prawn Pilau? It had been too quiet before Charlie came, Sebastian reminded himself.

'Hey! Mussolini!'

Damn. He'd frowned, and Charlie was in. Sebastian lowered the book and looked up, squinting against the sun that had made it through the grimy first-floor window of the Hackney flat.

'Wanna know what I heard on the radio this morning? I might've got it wrong —I was only half-awake.'

Sebastian sighed, 'Go on then,' and reached for a pale ale for himself. 'What?'

Charlie grinned. 'It was one of them religious geezers. Telling us how to get through the day all happy 'n holy. I was just reaching over to shut him up and grab another half hour's kip, when I fell out of bed laughing. "Lake all vicars," says 'e, "lake all vicars, after the sairveece I stend at the chairch door and shag hens."'

Charlie got tangled in a paroxysm of half-inhaled smoke.

Sebastian smiled. 'Nice one.' He picked up the bottle opener. 'You know, I have asked you not to call me Mussolini.'

'Why not? You're a bleedin' Eyetie, aren't you?'

The banter was under way and as ever was bringing a sense of wellbeing. The unnamed troubles of the day began to recede.

'I'm British.'

'You've got an Eyetie name and you speaka de lingo.'

'I also speak French and write Fortran. It doesn't make me a frog or a computer.'

'Geddaway!'

'Okay, call me Galileo. I'll answer to that.' He eased the cap off the bottle.

'Bloody immigrants. Come over here. Take our jobs.'

Sebastian decided to play to win. He cleared his throat. 'It's a bizarre tale actually.' He prepared to lob the bottle cap into the cardboard box.

'Oh yeah?'

Bulls-eye. 'How I came to be here.' He stroked his beard and waited.

Charlie slid deep into the sofa and closed his eyes. 'Okay,' he conceded. 'Let's be having it.'

Sebastian took a warm, slow swallow of beer. 'Right, because here's the curious thing. All four of my grandparents are Italian, but neither of my parents is.' He paused, but Charlie said nothing, just blew a smoke ring. 'My grandparents all started off in the same village, up in the Dolomites. They had nothing, no possessions or land of their own. They were peasants—'

'Stands to reason,' said Charlie.

'And times were hard. Everyone who could was getting out, going where there were jobs and money.'

'Didn't I say?'

'So, my father's parents came to England, and he was born here, which makes him British. And my mother's parents went to Lille, in France, where my mother was born. So she's French.'

Charlie yawned ostentatiously, then dropped the stub of the roll-up into a coffee mug. Sebastian waited until he was still.

'I don't know if the two families knew each other in Italy, but they didn't after they left. There wasn't an expat network.'

He took another swallow of beer. It was doing the job; he was feeling benign. The sun had sunk low, backlighting Charlie's corkscrew blond curls. He set course for the punch line.

'And then came the war, and my father enlisted. Nothing

43

special, just a squaddy. So there he was, caught up in the retreat to Dunkirk, asking a French barman if there was somewhere he could doss down for the night. But the barman didn't understand English—'

'Ignorant frog,' chipped in Charlie.

'And my father couldn't speak French. Still can't actually. But he thought, what's to lose, give it a go, he'd try Italian, which, no surprise, the barman didn't understand either. Meanwhile, there in the bar was my French grandfather, in the corner with his cronies, enjoying his constitutional evening grappa.'

Sebastian paused to top up his own constitution. Charlie frowned at the ceiling. 'What's "grappa" when it's at home?'

'Italian grape brandy, and very nice too. Anyway, how amazed do you think my grandfather was to hear some *ignorant* Englishman speaking Italian? And not just any Italian either, his own village dialect!'

Not bad. Another mouthful of beer.

'So, up he jumps and shakes my father by the hand and buys him a drink. And offers him a bed for the night. And takes him home to meet his wife, and his beautiful daughter. My mother.'

Images of his parents floated in Sebastian's mind. His mother still beautiful and charmingly other with her indelible French accent; his father still embarrassingly ignorant. Anti-immigrant, among other failings.

'Actually, my grandparents weren't too keen on her marrying him. But she would insist. Which was just as well for me, I suppose. Anyhow, they all lived reasonably happily ever after.'

Charlie valiantly concealed the extent to which he was impressed. 'What did I say, eh? Closely related to Hitler.'

'So are you probably,' Sebastian countered. 'Who knows where any of us would be if it wasn't for the war.'

'Shagging hens!' cried Charlie. 'No, seriously, mate,' he allowed, raising his bottle to acknowledge defeat, 'your pedigree and conception are not altogether lacking in interest.

It's not a bad tale.'

They supped ale in silence for a few minutes. Then, 'I reckon I was got in the normal way,' Charlie mused sadly. 'Behind the bike sheds.'

He scratched his scalp absently with a bent fork through the dirty yellow curls. Sebastian remembered Zoë Smith's luminous cascade of hair. Like copper, he'd thought at first, but then, no, more like brass. Golden-red, reflective, shiny in the middle, blurred at the edges.

'Did you see any more of the new people?' he asked Charlie.

'Oh yeah.' Scornful. 'Old Attwood got all of us lower orders lined up to say,' sing-song voice, '"your name, who you work for and what you do." And he goes first, to show how, in case we're too thick to catch on. "I'm Ron Attwood," he says. "I'm one of the partners, and I do a little bit of everything." So off we go, creeping death, trying to out-creep each other and make out how important our crappy jobs are. And I'm on the end of the line, right? So when they get to me, everyone's half-asleep, and I say...' He stood up to demonstrate, smiling like a cherub. 'I say, "I'm Charlie Evans, and I work for Sebastian Santini, and I do what I'm told."'

Sebastian grinned. 'Wonderful! What did poor old Attwood make of that?'

'He pretended to be amused—"Huh huh huh." Said, "Of course, we're really very democratic." Then he bundled them off to meet someone grander. He'll probably ask you to have a word with me about all pulling together.'

Charlie examined the end of the fork. 'Are you going to move that Pratt twerp into our office?'

Instead of me, he meant. 'No,' said Sebastian.

'Talking of pulling,' said Charlie, more cheerfully, 'it's time I did. Have you had any lately?'

'You know that I haven't.'

There was a silence while they both thought about sex. Today's encounter in the corridor came into Sebastian's mind. 'Why don't you try Ann again?' he said. 'She might surprise

45

you and say yes.'

Charlie sighed. 'She never will.' His voice had the reverence it always caught around Ann Wilton. 'My Ingrid, my Ilsa, forever unattainable.'

Sebastian stroked his beard. 'Well, I don't see any Victor Laszlo on the scene. And at least Bogart always had Paris.'

'Yeah, well, he was Bogart. I'm just li'l ol' Charlie Evans.'

'And Ann is just Ann.' Sebastian picked up his book. 'Do you know, I think I might have a go at samosas.'

'Fine by me,' said Charlie. 'And anyway, she's going to Italy.'

JULY

Away Game

Ann lit another cigarette and watched uneasily as Lois sized Mario up through her viewfinder. Absorbed in his deft supply of bread and olives from a silver-coloured tray to each sun-dappled table on the evening terrace, pausing to swap pidgin Italian with some fluttering middle-aged housewife, Mario hadn't spotted the lens pointed at him. Lois was readjusting the zoom as he approached, slinking his bum between the tightly packed chairs, bending and straightening over the pink tablecloths, lighting the candle on each from the candle on the one before, closer and closer, until, four tables away, he lifted his head and grinned. The shutter clicked, and Lois winked at him over the camera.

No one else saw. Hugh, on Ann's left, had his back to Mario, while, on her right, Jack and Tessa were oblivious, cuddled together, humming along to the dance band that had just struck up. Lois was behaving like a kitten on heat, but a fortnight of idleness and Chianti had gone to the Goldings' heads, and they only had eyes for each other.

Ann could barely return the smile that Lois shot her across the table. How unsettled she felt, horribly restless, plagued with longings that Italy had inflamed, not assuaged. The mirror in the hotel bedroom showed a scarcely recognisable face, suntanned and glowing with health, but inside she was desolate. Tessa, Jack, Lois, all high on sex, seemed almost to have forgotten she was here, while Hugh was unshakeably brotherly. An American had bought her a drink in the bar one evening, and she fancied him, quite. They'd flirted a bit, and he'd offered, 'What d'you say, honey? Shall we go upstairs?' But he was leaving the next day, which made it seem tacky, so she shook her head, 'Thanks, but I don't think I will.' So he went upstairs on his own, and she thought, did I make a mistake? If Lois can do meaningless sex, why can't I?

'Boy, am I hungry,' said Jack, rubbing his stomach.

'Me too,' said Tessa.

He was tanned like a film star, while she was more freckled than brown. Their eyes were fixed eagerly on the approaching food. Ann pulled a quick face at Lois. They hadn't noticed in London, but here the side dishes had a way of disappearing down Jack and Tessa's throats before you had your share. 'You could photograph us eating,' she said.

'Please don't,' objected Tessa. 'It's a real pain when we're trying to relax.' She rearranged the green silk scarf she had fussily tied round her neck.

Hugh played the diplomat. 'Don't worry, Tess, Lois is superstitious. She thinks it's bad luck to follow other people's suggestions.'

'Dear me.' Tessa frowned. 'That must mean you do practically nothing.'

Lois laughed. 'Not at all, I do practically everything. And you've got it wrong, Hugh. Not every suggestion is bad luck. Only the "shoulds" and "oughts" and "if I were yous". I may very well snap you with your snouts in the trough.' She started changing the lens.

'Well, I'd rather you didn't snap me.'

There was a pause. Ann failed to catch Hugh's eye. Lois was still smiling to herself as she fiddled with the camera.

'Pity we have to go back tomorrow,' said Jack.

'Too right,' Tessa sighed. 'I wish we could stay forever. The time has flown by.'

'No it hasn't,' said Lois. 'We've still got the whole of this evening. Can't you just feel it, stretching ahead of us like a warm cat?'

She leant back in her chair, languidly extending her arms and colliding with Mario, who was leaning to light their candle.

'Whoops, sorry!'

'Prego.'

And Lois was beaming at Hugh as Mario moved smoothly along.

Jack and Tessa fell like gannets on the oily bread and shining purple olives. Lois lifted the camera. Click.

'Lois, don't!' Tessa spat stones into her hand. 'It isn't fair.'

'Foul is fair,' murmured Hugh, picking out an olive.

Did he mean the Goldings or Lois? Ann laughed, but Hugh gazed impassively out across the valley. For the umpteenth time today, she struggled not to feel snubbed. He must know she was flirting with him. Italy didn't suit him: his nose was bright red and his scalp beneath the ginger hair was as pink as the tablecloth. But now he was meeting her gaze, blinking affectionately, and her heart softened again. What if she were just to reach over and touch his—

'Oh wow, these are sublime!' Jack ripped bread to dunk in the garlicky juice. 'I can't get over how wonderful they are. You don't find olives this good in London outside Soho.'

Lois hooted. 'How would you know, Jack? You never shop outside Soho.'

He raised his glass to her and stuck out a messy tongue.

Click.

'See if I care,' he said.

The olives were gone, and the first bottle of Chianti was empty. A heady smell of herbs and tomatoes wafted through the swing-doors to the kitchen as Mario passed back and forth.

'Have you found the tickets yet, Jack?' Tessa wiped oil from her mouth with a pink napkin. 'I'm sure I gave them to you to look after.'

'Maybe he's lost them on purpose so you can stay.' Hugh twiddled a fork on the tablecloth. 'Chewing the food of sweet and bitter fancy.'

And out of Pamela's reach, thought Ann.

'I'm sure you've got them, dearest heart,' said Jack. 'You said I couldn't be trusted.'

Ann was fed up with their banter. 'I've no one but myself to blame when *my* ticket goes missing.'

Tessa smiled. 'There's a lot to be said for self-reliance.'

'Maybe,' Ann countered, 'but I was reading this article the other day. It said more single people get depressed, even when

49

the married people aren't happy with each other. They call it having "a significant other". Apparently, it really helps to have one, even if you hate their guts.'

'Jack doesn't hate my guts. Do you, Jack?'

'No, sweetheart.'

Ann bit her lip. 'I wasn't talking about you.'

'Darling Annie!' Lois leant forward, displaying her cleavage. 'You can hate *me* if it makes you happy.'

'We all love you, Annie,' said Hugh.

'Yeah, yeah. Like brothers and sisters. I've got plenty of those.'

She lit another cigarette and tapped at it fretfully. Had they forgotten how it felt to have no one special? No one to fear losing or to spar with or to bloody well touch in this provocatively sensual place? What a mistake to bring *Couples* as holiday reading. Time and again, lying by the hotel pool amidst the tangle of her friends' untouchable limbs, she'd turned a page and found herself gasping with undirected desire. What gave words such power? Sex seemed so near, so palpable. Just now, John Updike was her "significant other"; she almost expected him to walk onto the terrace.

The last evening of the holiday was sliding by. She needed anything more than this. 'Tell you what,' she said, seizing Hugh's hand, 'after dinner shall we play that truth game I was telling you about?'

His eyebrows shot up. 'Those things are risky, Ann. People get hurt.'

'Aw, come on, we're all friends. It's only a bit of fun.'

'I'm game.'

'Thank you, Jack!'

'You always are.' Tessa.

'Me too.' Lois smiling at Hugh. 'Don't worry, prawn, you'll be safe with me.'

'But how about you, Tess?'

Tessa bridled at Hugh's concern. 'I can handle it, don't worry.'

Ann grinned. 'Motion carried!'

'So how does it go again?'

It was Jack who was asking, acknowledging her gratitude with his stunning white smile. 'It's easy,' she told him. 'We think of a characteristic, like... like greediness for example. Then we each give scores—five for the greediest, one for the least greedy, including ourselves. Then we add up for the group verdict.'

Tessa was frowning. 'Shouldn't it be anonymous?'

'We write the scores down.'

'But we'll recognise the writing.'

'Not a problem,' said Jack. 'List the names first so there's only numbers to add, and all use the same pen. I'll fetch some paper after dinner and meet you back by the pool. Oh wow, look at this.'

The first course was arriving, *zuppa di fagioli*, and a second basket of bread.

'More Chianti, Mario, per favore!' cried Jack.

'Si, signore!'

'I'm not inhibited! I'm not! How can you say so, Jack?'

'Who knows what I said?' He laughed at her. 'It's anonymous.'

'I know what you said. What every one of you said.'

Hugh did his best to calm things. 'It's only relative, Tess love. None of us is all that inhibited.'

Would to God we were, he caught himself thinking.

'And it's only a word,' said Ann. 'What does it *mean* after all?'

He watched as Ann lit yet another cigarette; she was getting to be a chain-smoker. She was looking at him as if wanting an answer. 'We could have a Socratic debate,' he teased her. 'That might be more fun.'

'Silly prawn.' Lois was all mischievous smiles, basking in the pleasure of being voted the least inhibited.

'Well I'm pretty sure I know what it means,' Jack persisted. 'And you're definitely the most inhibited, Tess. By a mile. You're proving it right now.'

51

Tessa took a swipe at him, but he ducked. 'And you're the biggest rat!'

'Hey, that's a good one,' said Lois, sotto voce. 'Shall we do the biggest rat next?'

'No, petal. Let's not.'

Lois dazzled him with a grin. Ann reached to touch Tessa. 'How about we do sincerity?'

'Don't patronise me!'

'You've had too much to drink, my darling wife.'

'Look who's talking! Let's do the most alcoholic.'

Things were getting out of hand. Hugh raised his voice. 'Children. Children.'

'Okay. Fuck it, we'll do sincerity. Give me a piece of paper.'

For a minute or two they were silent, passing the pen. Hugh went first, then leant back, letting his gaze drift into the dark beyond the candlelight and the blue shimmer of the pool. No good would come of this one either, but what the hell if they wanted to make themselves miserable?

He sipped his wine and hummed along with the distant dance band. They were playing *Perfidia* again, making him smile. Was he some kind of masochist? Somehow he was learning to live with the anguish, managing not to reveal it by a flicker, in public or private. Keeping his word.

It had been torture at first, seeing her eyes connect to another man's smile, noticing Mario's careless Latin beauty, the muscles beneath his shirt. And then, that first time she went for a walk, the twist in his gut when it dawned on him that it wasn't "a walk" when she'd returned asking anxiously, 'Are you all right, prawn?' The revulsion at knowing where she'd been, why she was flushed, what it was that she smelled of, why she was ducking from his arms and into the shower. It had happened. Lois with Mario. Their mouths and their fingers, their—

Christ. Hell. Unbearable. Even now his skin crawled and his head was exploding. Then, he'd wanted to drag her from the shower and have her tell him it wasn't so. Or no, to tell him, in every last detail, that it was so, to describe it and more:

52

her sensations, her thoughts, her exact, complete self.

But he hadn't. He'd kept his word, at least on the surface. He had stared through the window at the landscape of umber hills crowned with cypress trees and managed to keep his lunch down. And yes, with repetition it became easier. The trick was to steer his mind away from the beast with two backs, to concentrate on her smile, her concern, the thoughtfulness of her sluicing her body each time before letting him touch her.

How infinitely worse and more testing it could have been. She'd been so discreet. Ann knew about Mario, he could see that, but Jack and Tessa hadn't noticed a thing. He felt stupidly grateful. Because, yes, more than discreet, more even than kind, Lois, washed and scrubbed and smelling of nothing but soap, had been, dare he claim the word, loving? Well, tender at least, in a way he'd never expected to see.

And thank God it wasn't Jack's cuckolding eyes he had to meet at each meal. Not Jack. The greed and cruelty of the man had been much on show these fourteen, slow days, and he'd seen Lois noticing. 'What a carnivore you are!' she snapped at Jack last night, causing him to laugh and growl and bare his teeth at her. Had Mario saved him from Jack?

The band wound up *Perfidia*, cha cha cha, amid a sudden outburst from the cicadas. It put his troubles in perspective to picture poor Marlowe in anonymous exile, here in these Tuscan hills perhaps, pouring his grief into lovesick sonnets, written in another man's name.

'There!' Ann threw down the pen.

Tessa seized the pile. 'I'll score these.'

No one spoke while she added numbers.

'Okay. Sincerity.' She looked happier. 'You're right, Ann. I've come second, with eighteen. But way out in front, as if we didn't know, comes the fabulously sincere Hugh with twenty-three.'

He raised his glass. 'Gosh. Thank you. I must make a good job of pretending.'

'So who's the least sincere?' Ann wanted to know. She was

looking at Lois, he noticed.

'You, Ann, I'm sorry. You got eight. Just behind my admirable husband, who clocks in at eleven. Leaving Lois bang in the middle with fifteen.'

'Good heavens!' Lois looked startled, making him wonder if she deserved the five he'd given her. But yes, she did. She was nothing if not sincere.

Jack snorted. 'It's all right. I know who's gunning for me tonight.'

'Ha!' Tessa brandished the score sheet at him. 'You hide the fact you used to be an estate agent, and you expect to rate high on sincerity.'

'You cow,' Jack hissed.

There was a silence. My, that touched a nerve. No surprise. Lois had passed on the gossip. Apparently Jack was so mortified at failing his eleven-plus, he quit school at fifteen.

The cicadas grew insistent. Jack scowled and stubbed out his cigarette. 'It was a sensible way into property. Hornsey Road was practically a ruin. I got it for a song before it went on the market.'

In jumped Tessa again. 'But darling, you'd still be smarming in a blue suit to pay for it if your dad hadn't died.'

'What's with you, *darling?* Jack hissed. When Tessa didn't move, he pulled her roughly to her feet, where they teetered together, eyeball to eyeball.

She planted a kiss on his mouth. 'Now who's the most inhibited?'

They glared some more, until Jack burst out laughing. 'Come on, enough public brawling. Let's finish this elsewhere.'

He scooped up her bag, took her wrist and yanked her towards the hotel. 'Goodnight, people.'

Hugh watched them depart for what he supposed would be some rather violent sexual intercourse. Then, 'I'm off too, prawn.' Her voice came soft in his ear, making him jump. 'See you in a bit.' Before he could turn or think or speak, she was sliding her camera into his lap, squeezing his shoulder and slipping away into the darkness. Ah, no, please. Not again.

Had he groaned aloud? He cleared his throat and struggled to his feet. 'So much for truth games. I'm for bed.' His voice was wobbling. 'Goodnight, Ann.' He set off fast, stumbling against a tangle of chairs in his way, clutching Lois's camera tightly to his chest.

It was only as he reached the bedroom that it registered that Ann had been crying. But, of course: the game. Should he go back, try to comfort her? Not in this state; he might begin blurting about Lois. And anyway, what could he say? Less sincere than Jack Golding? Well yes, in her likeable way she was, and it could be quite tiresome. False enthusiasm, exaggeration, superlatives, pretended jollity, fake accord, scarcely hidden resentments. More anxious to be liked than to be known, like a puppy without a master. She probably wouldn't thank him for noticing her tears.

One More Player

Zoë saw the gigantic, ugly man as soon as she entered the hotel lounge in Oxford that evening. He towered head and shoulders above a knot of people who were laughing at something he'd said. Why had she noticed him? Something about his eyes: amusement, a suggestion of blue? From behind his glasses, his gaze swooped over the crowd, lingering on one face, returning to another.

She shrank back into the doorway, scanning faces herself, hoping to see someone she knew. Her ATP colleagues must still be safe in their rooms, nibbling the complimentary biscuits and gazing out at the artificial lake and the roses and elegant statuary. Why was she always so punctual?

She took a breath. What a mouse she was being. She held her head high and made her way purposefully towards the bar. The cheap skirt felt stylish with the high heels; its silky lining made her feel sexy. She dared to meet the man's stare. For a brief instant, his odd, lumpy face focused, through the smoke, across the plush carpet. *You are the one.*

She didn't smile, although maybe her eyes did; she moved smoothly on. Her heart was thumping, but she felt light, as if a weight was beginning to lift.

The bar was tricked out with fake wood and wrought iron. She ordered a gin and tonic—beer didn't fit these surroundings—and pretended to watch as the barman speared lemon and clunked ice.

Tony, she thought. She must think of her husband, must picture his face with its large, solemn eyes. But his image eluded her. It hovered just out of range, blocked by the sense of a stranger's gaze on her back. She tried to be offended; she tried to shrug off the gaze. But she wasn't, she couldn't.

The voice at her shoulder was no surprise. 'So, what did you say your name was?'

His eyes weren't at all ugly; they were the colour of blue ink.

'I didn't. It's Zoë Smith. And who are you?'

Already they were smiling in complicity.

'Mick Galway.'

He didn't sit next to her at dinner. The handwritten name-cards along the table were sacrosanct, he said, placed strategically by Rex Advertising's media department to ensure that each weekend guest received due ear-bending. Mick was a senior account director, whatever that meant, and was required to charm two important clients towards the head of the table. Zoë took her seat at the lower end a little nervously, unsure what ear-bending to expect or attempt.

The woman on her left said she was a planning assistant and began to grill her about ATP. Zoë answered as best she could, glancing across the table in the hope that Sebastian Santini would come to her aid. He was deep into explaining something to his own neighbour. To Zoë's relief, the man on her right cut in.

'Now myself, I'm in finance,' he announced. 'I'm a chartered accountant.'

'Oh yes?'

'And you,' he indicated her name card, leering, 'you'd have us believe that you're "Mrs Smith".' He wiggled the tip of his tongue.

His breath smelled bad. Zoë leaned back a little. He moved closer.

'Yet another gorgeous girl from Ask The Punters.'

She pulled a face.

'My lady boss came from there. *Mzz* Tessa Golding. Failed their gorgeousness standards, I'm guessing. A bit of a bra burner. I expect you know her.'

'I'm sorry. I only joined a few weeks ago. Is she here?'

'No. Naughty Tess. She's on holiday.' He chuckled and bracketed his halitosis with a hand. 'Between you and I, the Big Chief was a trifle miffed, expected her to put this shindig first, but you know *Mzz* Golding.'

'Well. No. I don't.'

'She's sunning herself in Tuscany with one of your mob. The fabulous Miss Ann Wilton.'

A couple, Zoë wondered. Was that what he meant?

'I know Ann. I share an office with her. She's sort of my boss. I'm going to help her with this new survey for you, the one on gender stereotypes? We didn't have much time before she went, but she seemed very nice.'

'She's *nice* all right.' The accountant's lower lip glistened. 'Very tasty indeed, your Miss Wilton.'

'So what is it you do exactly?' The planning assistant glared at her colleague across Zoë's smoked salmon.

There was a short silence before Zoë realised the question was for her. 'Well, as I say, not much yet. I'm going to be working with Ann. That's why I'm here, because she's on holiday.'

The accountant, thank goodness, had turned away to torment his other neighbour, and the planning assistant promptly lost interest and did the same. Oh dear, was she supposed to be selling ATP to these people? Zoë glanced along at Mick Galway. He was laughing again, and so were the two important clients. He's good at his job, she thought. He's confident. I want to feel that way.

So think about the job, she scolded herself. Not how to charm these two, but about the survey questions Ann asked her to draft while she was away. Rex wanted to know what stereotypes the punters believed in, so they could decide how to use them in adverts. Who talked more, for example, women or men, and about what kinds of things? And should they talk less, and who listened the best, and was it the same for young and old? The more thought she'd given it, the more Zoë had come to realise that she lacked answers of her own.

She peered down the table to see who was talking most here. The conversational decibels were rising as smoked salmon and white wine gave way to roast lamb and red, and a small army of waitresses spooned vegetables onto each plate. She was surprised at how few women were speaking. Some sat disregarded like her, but mostly they were smiling and nodding, listening to men. The woman opposite, with Sebastian Santini, had a slightly glazed expression.

She spotted an exception. Halfway along, two women, one young, one middle-aged, were deep in conversation, interweaving their words so fast that it wasn't clear who was speaker, who listener. Occasionally they broke into laughter, or paused to swallow food or drink wine, before starting up again. Zoë wished she could eavesdrop, but they were too far away.

Beyond them sat Mick Galway between his two clients. The three weren't looking at each other much. Their voices, if not the words, were audible above the clamour. It was as if they were taking turns to address the table, each waiting for his go.

Tony believed in 'go's. His face sprang clear in her mind now, puckered in a frown just like her father's, because she'd interrupted him again. She tried not to, but she was forever doing it. It felt unnatural to listen for so long without speaking. When he said something interesting it brought ideas bubbling into her mouth. When he told her something she already knew, it was hard not to say so.

These days, even if she managed to stay quiet, she annoyed him. She'd listen attentively, concentrate on letting him finish. And he would stop abruptly, of his own accord, muttering, 'I'm sorry. I'm boring you.' And she would say, 'No, no you're not,' realising that, yes, well, actually, he had been.

Because interrupting wasn't so bad, was it? Those two women were interrupting each other, down along the table, and it made her want to be with them, to listen and join in. They were enjoying themselves.

So was Mick Galway. The boom of his laughter rolled along the table. The laugh of a confident man.

Tony was a man. Older. A teacher. Her respite from heartbreak. Her ticket to approval from her father. But he wasn't all that confident. He was... well, he was Tony. Her husband. Forsaking all other.

She hadn't spoken those words at the registry office, but it meant the same thing. She'd repeated some modern, unpoetic version of the ancient vow and smiled into his disbelieving eyes. She'd squeezed his hand beneath the tablecloth at the reception, and bumped shoulders with him, sharing the joke as her mother got tipsy and his mother frowningly didn't.

She should keep her promise. She didn't want to hurt or betray him. But forsaking all others? Forever and ever?

Mick Galway came back into focus. One of the clients was speaking, and Mick's attention was roaming the table. There was something a bit sleazy about him. What a dreadful, loud jacket. Why on earth did she fancy him?

She struggled to turn herself round. Her marriage shouldn't unravel at the first come-hither. Hold tight, and by tomorrow this cocky stranger would be forgotten. Give in, and she would be sinking again, in confusion and remorse.

His eyes found hers and flashed their signal. Not cocky, almost supplicant: I'm yours if you want me. She smiled, she couldn't help it, and the feeling of lightness coursed through her once more, like bubbles in champagne.

*

'That's it. Duty done, bigwigs safe off to bed, so we can quit toadying. May I buy you a drink?'

'Yes. Thank you.' Impossible to stop smiling. 'White wine. Just a small one.'

No harm in a drink. No harm in talking. He would say something crass, and that would be that.

He sat himself opposite, not beside her as she'd expected. His hands were enormous, she noticed as he set down the drinks, and his face absurdly misshapen.

'Thank you.' She lifted the wine to her lips. She would drink it, then make her excuses.

He didn't speak, just kept smiling. He pulled the top inch off his beer.

'Nice wine,' she said.

Those inky-blue eyes, he must know their power. That was probably why he'd sat opposite.

'So. Zoë Smith. What shall we talk about? Did you run into that crowd on the Strand last night? ATP's near the Strand, isn't it?'

'Yes, it is. No I didn't. What crowd?'

'A swarm of Jamaicans trying to gatecrash a concert. Blokes with hair out to here.' He held his hands a foot from his ears. 'Reggae. Do you dig it?'

She shook her head. 'I'm useless at music. I like it all really.'

'Me too.' He grinned. 'Do you have the same trouble with men?'

She sat back.

He sat back too, and looked her straight in the eye. 'You haven't asked, but I'll tell you. I'm happily married with two kids. And to judge by the ring, so are you?'

'Yes.' She was startled; but she liked the directness, the candour, his physical distance as he stated his terms. 'Thirteen months now. No children.'

'Ah, a novice. It's the proverbial seven years in my case. But the itch set in long ago.' He raised an eyebrow. 'And luckily, my wife doesn't seem to mind.'

Zoë put down her wine. 'You mean, she knows?'

He turned away, his gaze wandering over the other drinkers, the other women in the bar. The question had wrong-footed him. In the pause, it was becoming a comment, not expecting an answer. Because his wife didn't know, did she? Didn't know, didn't ask. Zoë felt weird: half-anxious, half-defiant. He looked back at her. She said nothing.

Finally he smiled, leant forward and touched her finger. 'I like you.'

That did it. She made up her mind.

He flashed his blue eyes. 'What would you say to a walk in the moonlight? It's romantic out there.'

She pulled a face. She couldn't help it. What a line.

'It's up to you.' His gaze was off again, roaming the room.

She found her voice. 'Sorry, it's just... but okay, you're on. Let's walk in the moonlight.'

There was no moon, but the garden was romantic on cue, fresh and tranquil after the bar and scented with honeysuckle. Once out of view of the hotel windows, he offered his hand, and she took it, and her mind filled at once with the sensation of handholding, their fingers and thumbs mismatched in size but fitting easily, their two palms cupped together, disconcertingly intimate.

He said little and seemed in no hurry, strolling her, apparently aimlessly, around the ornamental lake and across the grass towards the topiary screen beyond. She had to admire his competence. But through the hedge she had trouble not laughing: just a fence and some dustbins. What would he do now?

He halted, reached to take her other hand and turned her to face him.

'You're a very lovely lady. May I kiss you?'

Yuck, how ridiculous. Seduction by numbers.

'Why else are we here?' Still time to back out.

Like his hand his mouth fitted, and he knew how to kiss, his tongue welcome not invasive. He tasted of beer, which was fine.

61

'Mmmm,' he breathed, sliding his palms from her shoulders and slowly down to her bum. She stiffened. This felt false and manipulative. She was back in two minds.

He broke for a moment to look at her, then took off his glasses. Why did he do that? Just to flash his blue eyes again?

He slipped light fingers under the curve of her breast. 'May I?'

Sod this. She grabbed the fingers tightly. 'Look. Do we have to play this game? We're going to bed, aren't we?'

Home Runs

Buoyant after two weeks in Italy, Jack Golding was up on Monday with the dawn, leaving Tessa mumbling goodbye in her sleep. He showered and shaved, downed some black coffee, grabbed an apple and was out into the sunshine.

The air was wavy with heat already; this summer was fabulous. And here on the gravel was his beautiful Rover, oh boy, just look at her, waiting to glide him along dappled-green Hornsey Lane and down towards Kentish Town, full of rich pickings in today's fickle property market. His heart swelled with pride at the thought, because he knew how to pick. He'd more than trebled Dad's legacy already, and however much his wife and his friends with their fancy degrees and professional jobs might want to sneer at an estate-agent turned builder, it was he who was getting rich quick while they plodded towards their forty-year pensions. Okay, they had style; but style he could learn, he could buy! He tossed the apple core out of the window.

Ten minutes later, he was steering the Rover snug into the new garage at Bartholomew Road. Off-street parking was definitely worth more than an extra reception room in a family house like this, plus it saved on decoration. And here was the boiler, installed in his absence, with neat pipework all properly lagged. The plaster on the garage walls had dried nicely. He ran his hand over the surface. An excellent job, though he said it himself, a useful skill to have learned. Doing up Hornsey Lane single-handedly, evenings and weekends, had been tough, but it had given him what many developers lacked, a feel for the skills of the trade. Without that he might have squandered Dad's cash, hoarded over a lifetime of selling nails by the dozen in brown paper bags from behind a hinged counter.

Instead, order from chaos, money from thin air. The boys were hammering away upstairs already. It was worth paying the rate for good, keen workers and trusting them to do the job.

He went in through the kitchen, inspecting the tiling and the overhead cupboards. Everything fine, which left just the floor to lay in here and the walls to paint.

Across the hall was his office for now, and, hey, the room looked palatial. The boys had painted it the colour of bleached straw and stripped the old paint from the fireplace. Get an eyeful of those Victorian tiles. Up went the asking price again. Four weeks, six at most, would see this back on the market. And the last two contracts were exchanged now on Brecknock Road. His bank balance would soon be too healthy; there was no point in sitting on cash with inflation like this. It was time to be buying again, making fresh plans, finding a new site for his nomadic HQ. The big, pillared mansion for sale in Lady Margaret Road was tempting: real class. A huge whack of money, but that was for the sheer size of the place. Done up, it would bring in a fortune, and meanwhile he'd keep the ship well afloat with a few roofing jobs. It helped to have contacts and a suave bedside manner.

He was whistling some tune the Italian dance-band had dinned into his head. He perched on a corner of his paint-spattered desk, leafing through the backlog of invoices and estate agents' come-ons.

Oh hell. The whistle dried in his mouth. Pamela's big, loopy handwriting. *Personal. Jack Golding. To await return.*

He fingered the envelope gingerly, willing it to be good news. Please God, she was letting him go. The bloody thing was pink, for fuck's sake, and rustled as though lined with tissue paper.

He tore it open. *Jack darling, how I miss you.* Oh fuck.

'Good break, guv?'

He jumped to his feet. Gary, his foreman, leant in the doorway, grinning. He crumpled the letter into the back pocket of his jeans.

'Yes, grand, thanks. Smashing. Hot.' He was regaining his balance. 'So. Gary. It's looking pretty damn good here. How've things been?'

Zoë surfaced from a dream about dry rot in a life-raft. For a short while she hovered between the anxiety of the dream and the anxiety of opening her eyes. No place, no identity, no difficult questions.

It was useless. The hum and rattle of the milk-float in the street told her where she was. She unglued her eyelids; saw across the pillow the thinning patch on the back of Tony's head, remembered Mick, and her mind was in pieces again. Guilt that she'd done it, disbelief that she'd done it, a sudden, sharp thrill of delight that she'd done it. Hard kisses, hot, slippery bodies, and laughter, yes, both of them laughing, open-eyed, face-to-face, unburdened by guilt, power, apology, shame, insecurity, shedding all that with their clothes. Just sex for its own sake, for the first time in her life.

But at breakfast in the hotel dining-room, the bad feelings had started. Watching this massive stranger at the next table stuff his big, hungry mouth with kippers, she was embarrassed by the physical excitement she felt. Surely it was visible? Surely they could see it, or smell it, these smaller, paler, un-humorous people who flapped the creases from their *Telegraphs* like her father did and passed the milk and the marmalade? She was unable to meet their eyes, or his.

She had already packed. She said yes to the first lift to the station. She saw Mick's head turn. And he was following her out onto the hotel steps, pretending to wave off a client, offering her his hand.

'Safe journey. Good to have met you. I'll be in touch.'

His eyes seeking hers. His hand squeezing hers. If she saw him again, all that stuff would begin: one stronger, one weaker; one wanting more, one less. And there was Tony to think about. Here, now, trusting her, sharing her pillow. Yesterday, lugging her suitcase along the street towards home, she'd dreaded seeing him. And there he was, on the pavement out front, chatting to Mr and Mrs Nosy from next door. Turning his head, brightening at the sight of her, hurrying to meet her, taking her suitcase, asking did she have a good time. Making her want to blurt out there and then what she'd done. He rolled over now and opened his eyes. 'Morning, lovely.'

Even to smile was to lie.

But already it was easier. A one-night stand with a stranger. Gradually the memory would blur, would recede, until it hardly seemed worth confessing.

Safe journey. Good to have met you. I'll be in touch.

Just words. Just politeness. Thank you for having me.

Because an affair, how could that possibly work? How did Mick Galway square what he did with 'I'm happily married'? Lust, sex, mutual pleasure, carrying no baggage, inflicting no harm? Could it possibly be so?

Tony yawned and stretched, scratched his chest. 'Trouble is it's *Monday* bloody morning,' he grumbled. 'No peace for the wicked.'

Ann gasped as the familiar knot tightened. More than a lump in the throat or a sting at the back of the eyes. A massive weight pressing up under her ribs, trying to burst out. There was no point in crying again. It didn't change anything or make her feel better. She'd learned that in the year after Ed.

On Saturday evening, she'd given in to it. After she'd waved Jack and Tessa goodbye and run down the steps from the street. After she turned the key in the lock, and recognised the musty smell of home. After she stumbled around the flat for a while, unpacking and picking up post. After she put on the radio, and then turned it off again because there wasn't room for any more noise in her head. After she'd rung home, and lied about what a great holiday. After she'd poured gin, and stood in the kitchen, staring through the window at the neighbour's dead geraniums. She'd given way, let the tears come, heard the wracking sobs echo around the empty room until, gradually, the pressure migrated from her chest to her head, and the sobs dwindled to hiccups.

And then she'd blown her nose, swallowed an aspirin with the gin, poured another, and begun in a rather blurred way to rummage for food.

Feeling no better. Worse in fact, because nobody came, nobody knew, and she would hate it, and them, and herself if they did. Because what would they see? Only stupid self-pity. And what would they say? There, there, Ann, don't cry?

Why not? Why shouldn't I cry? Too much sincerity for you?

Fuck them. Fuck them all.

And here it was, Monday morning, and she wouldn't give in, no she bloody well wouldn't. She pushed herself up out of bed and stood for a moment, staring at her hateful reflection. What an attractive young woman, eh? Healthy and tanned, in crumpled white-cotton pyjamas. The lovely Ann Wilton. Nothing wrong. Everything hunky-bloody-dory. Choose clothes to set off the golden-brown. Swallow some coffee, some cornflakes. Stick on a smile.

And go.

Before it happened, the room seemed normally colourful to Zoë. The smart, grey desks with their red trim that matched the doorframes. The hot sun slanting through the Venetian blinds, falling in golden wedges across the carpet. The people: Mr Thorn, Sebastian Santini, that Charlie Evans with his cheeky grin and shock of blond curls, and the others, they too seemed interesting and colourful. They were noisily discussing the survey on gender stereotypes, with everyone excitably full of opinions. And Mr Thorn had just interrupted to remind them that it wasn't their views but the punters' that Rex

Advertising was paying for, in that bemused tone of his that made Zoë laugh. And, of course, there was still Mick to think about. With part of her mind she was still remembering, and smiling, and wondering if he would ring, and knowing that he would, and asking herself what would she do when he did, and feeling awful about Tony.

And then it happened.

Ann Wilton came in. The red handle on the grey door turned, and Ann Wilton came in.

Suddenly, beside Ann, the others were monochrome. Striding into the midst of their laughter, bronzed by the Italian sun, dressed in glorious sky-blue, sweeping the air with eloquent brown fingers wreathed in silver rings, dispensing greetings and smiles, Ann was amazing.

Zoë had met her twice and not taken much notice, but now she saw differently. All faces turned to Ann, all welcomed her, all waited for her to speak. And she was so genuinely pleased to see them, so kind and friendly and warm, bestowing herself on all and sundry. A lesbian, that accountant had implied. Was it true? Zoë had never met one before.

Ann's smile rested on Zoë for no more than a moment. Her eyes scarcely took Zoë in, and yet it was done. Willingly enchanted, Zoë succumbed to her spell. This was the person whose office she shared, the person she'd be working with every day from now on. And more, there was going to be more.

Ducks and Drakes

Three days later at noon, Zoë stood on the bridge over the lake in St James's Park, fighting the agitation in her stomach, and waited for Mick Galway.

She was early. She took several deep breaths and tried to empty her mind, closing her eyes and lifting her face to the sky. A light breeze eased the midday heat, and brought the smell of sausages and onions from a vendor's stall nearby. The sounds were of footsteps and quacking ducks and snatches of conversation. She opened her eyes again. The bridge teemed with people, hastening or lingering, some eating, some offering bread to sparrows that perched on their fingers and pecked crumbs from their palms. Out towards the centre of the bridge, a couple leaned on the rail and gazed into each other's eyes. She wouldn't do that with Mick. They would behave as if they barely knew each other, had met by accident and were chatting before moving on.

That was fine. Though his eyes were his asset, she didn't much want to gaze into them. She wanted more hours in a bedroom, his great hairy hands, his earthy smell. Anxiety gripped her again. Why was she doing this? How could she excuse it, to Tony or her parents? Who might she become?

She'd experienced a kind of clairvoyance about Mick's phone call this morning. She'd known he wouldn't ring on Monday or Tuesday—that would look far too keen. Wednesday, well maybe, but no: Mick was a seasoned player, he knew better. So today, yes, though not at nine sharp, and not bang on ten either, but wait, very soon.

At seven minutes past ten, she'd stopped pondering gender stereotypes. She'd put down her biro, sat back from her grey desk with its red trim, checked that Ann wasn't watching, and looked at the telephone.

And it rang. In the way that told you it was an outside call. And Ann's face came up from her work, smiling, in case she needed help with the call. But she didn't need help, because she'd known as she carried the receiver to her ear who it was.

'ATP. Zoë Smith speaking.'

'Well hello, Zoë Smith.'

'Well, hello.'

She'd felt good. Calm and powerful. Because this wasn't love, it was sex. This man only wanted her body, and it was for her to decide, yes or no.

She seized the warm bridge-rail, tilted her body forward and grinned down at the water and the bank of the lake, trampled to mud by the ducks. Directly below, a mallard drake sat in the shallows, ignoring the scatter of bread crusts. For a moment it was a painted ornament, of wood or stone. Then it twitched a wing and blinked an eye, and its feathers became real, plush and oiled. And suddenly, the smug little bird seemed astonishingly beautiful, its dark-green head and navy-blue wing-feathers glistening with sunlight, the two chocolate kiss-curls of its tail framed by molten gold. Standing quite still, her thighs pressed against the bridge, Zoë forgot everything but the duck. She jumped at the sudden voice in her ear.

'Hello, gorgeous.'

Butterflies rose in a cloud through the top of her head. The thrill hadn't lessened. The world kept revealing itself in visions: like Ann Wilton on Monday, like the duck, like the sheer bulk and maleness of this man.

She pointed to cover her grin. 'What do you think of my duck? I think he's special.'

Mick glanced over the rail. The duck was stretching and rearranging its wings, thrusting its beak in little rhythmic jabs among the feathers.

'I think *you're* rather special.'

'Which is what you say to all the girls.'

But his voice had her melting and aware of her nakedness beneath the white cheesecloth top and the blue-denim skirt. And she could only feel glad, glad to be feeling again, wanting and lusting again, seeing the world as though she'd been blind.

'Maybe,' he said. 'But I mean it every time. You're all special. Wonderful creatures.'

'Like my duck.'

As he laughed, she saw his tongue, his teeth. She wanted to kiss him.

'Quack, quack,' he said.

Girl Talk

Tonight Ann didn't have to go home to the empty flat. Tonight was yoga. Pointless really, she didn't know why she still went. It had seemed a good idea to begin with: all that blurb about self-realisation and psychic power; but in reality it was just a clutch of overweight women and two wimpish men in leotards making fools of themselves on rubber mats. And the ban on eating beforehand was a pain. By eight o'clock she was always famished, ready to blow whatever good it had done her in the chippy.

Zoë Smith was coming along; perhaps that would make it fun. Although, truth be told, she wasn't sure she altogether liked Zoë. She didn't know why: there was nothing she could put her finger on. Something about the way she asked questions perhaps, like Alice in Wonderland, though it seemed she really did want to know and wasn't being ironic or judgemental. On the contrary, it felt sometimes as if Zoë believed that she, Ann, held all the answers to life, and was hungry to learn them. Which felt creepy, as though Zoë might steal her soul.

She must stop being paranoid. She was getting everything out of proportion these days.

The muscles in Zoë's left hip screamed. She could ease the tension by letting her right hip move forward, but that wasn't allowed. You had to hold your torso in one plane, lean down over your left thigh, and stretch your arms beyond your head in a perfect triangle, until the instructor said you could stop.

The woman in front wasn't really trying; her arms were curved and her bottom stuck out. There was pain if you did it properly. It wasn't difficult; it just hurt. But actually, the longer you held the position, the more you stretched and pushed and willed yourself, the less it hurt. There was a kind of warmth in her hip now. She grinned to stop herself groaning.

The instructor paused beside her. Checked her over.

'Good. Now don't let go. And don't forget your breathing.' He moved on.

She struggled to hold firm. Pulled in her bum. Straightened her spine. Stretched her arms. Extended her neck. Counted her breaths in and out: one, two, three, four, five. Agony. Surely he must soon say—

'Okay. Gently now. Relax, and straighten up. Then sit yourselves down and rest a minute.'

The rubber mat was a luxurious magic carpet. She was warm all over. Her muscles flooded relief into her bloodstream. She turned to smile at Ann, and Ann smiled back.

They sat on the low wall outside the chippy, gobbling down battered cod and chips, and giggling about their maverick idea for the survey questionnaire. They would end it with an open question: something like, *what do you think is the biggest difference in the way men and women behave?* The punters could say whatever came into their heads. The interviewers would enjoy being let off the leash, and she and Ann would read every scribbled word, and code it for the computer themselves if the coding supervisor said it was too much work for 'her girls'.

'Women giggle—there's one for the list,' said Ann. 'And it's true, isn't it? We'll have to concede it. But I don't give a damn!' She threw a fist at the sky.

They giggled some more. Zoë was flying; the warm wind was lifting her towards the stars.

'It's like we're high on something,' said Ann.

'Yes!' They were flying together. 'I'm high on everything lately.'

'You must be in love.'

Zoë jumped. In love with *her*, did she mean? She held tight to the wall, shaking her head in confusion.

Ann whooped gleefully. 'I should've known! That was him on the phone this morning.'

The wind dropped. Zoë avoided Ann's eyes. 'My husband,' she said.

'Your husband? Sorry. Okay.'

Zoë dared to look up. Ann was munching on chips and watching the traffic. Not smiling suddenly.

'Is something the matter?' said Zoë. 'Sorry, ignore me—' Perhaps Ann had had a row with her girlfriend.

'Thanks,' Ann said. 'It's nice that you notice. I've just been on holiday with four people who wouldn't ask me what the matter was if I was crying my eyes out right in front of them.'

She sounded bitter.

'Four people?'

'Yes. Two married couples. Talk about a spare part.'

'Tessa Golding and her husband?'

'How did you know that?'

'Someone mentioned it last weekend.' Ann still looked glum, and Zoë dared to add, 'So... what *is* the matter?'

'That's it really. I've said it. My friends are married, and I'm not, and sometimes it hurts. I was living with a bloke a couple of years ago, but he left me. Which knocked me sideways. And now the whole world is happily married.'

'I'm not. Not happily.' Zoë felt released to confide. 'I was lying just now. That wasn't my husband this morning.'

Ann brightened. 'Really?'

'It was a man called Mick. Someone else's husband.'

Ann pulled a face. 'Aren't they always?'

She scrunched the chip paper, binned it and lit a cigarette. She pulled hard on it so the end glowed brightly. Did she disapprove? Zoë rushed to placate her.

'I'm sorry. I know it's wrong. When I'm not getting carried away, I feel awful about it.'

'It's okay. You don't have to justify anything to me.'

'But I do to myself.'

Ann didn't reply. Shaming her. She struggled to explain.

'It's only been once. I've known him less than a week. I'm not in love. Or into home breaking. He's married, I'm married, so... I should stop it, right now. Call a halt, shouldn't I?'

'I can't tell you that.'

'No. Of course. But it's hard, working this out on my own.'

'Can't you talk to your mother?'

'Are you kidding?'

Ann took a last pull, dropped the cigarette and ground it under her heel. 'I can't talk to mine either.'

Zoë wasn't sure what to say. Then Ann touched her arm, so lightly that her skin tingled, and she smiled her phenomenal smile. 'I can listen. I don't mind listening. I just don't have the answers.'

'Of course. Thank you. The thing is... the thing is that you know Mick.'

Ann frowned. 'I don't think so.'

'He works at Rex.'

'Good heavens! Mick *Galway?*'

'Yes. Why?'

'No reason. It's a surprise. He's so... how shall I put it?'

Zoë couldn't help laughing: the image of Mick had her flying again. 'How about huge, loud and grotesque? With dreadful, flashy clothes and no table manners?'

Ann smiled. 'Come to think of it, gender stereotypes, it makes perfect sense. Beauty and the Beast!'

The compliment made Zoë shy. She wanted to say, you are beautiful too.

'So. This happened last weekend?'

'Yes. But, Ann, please,' she was scared suddenly, 'no one knows. It's a secret. You mustn't tell anyone.'

'I won't.'

'Promise?'

'Yes. No one. Not ever. Cross my heart.' Ann reached into her bag again. 'Ciggy?'

'I shouldn't. But while I'm sinning, I may as well go the whole hog. Thanks.' She bent to Ann's match. 'But what about you? Is there anyone you like?'

'Not really. Perhaps you should introduce me to your hus—oh, God, that sounds awful!'

Zoë considered. 'No, strangely, it doesn't. I'm not going to break up Mick's marriage, but I think mine may be a lost cause.'

The strong taste of the cigarette was making her head swim.

'Why's that?'

'I shouldn't be saying. Please don't get me wrong. Tony's a good person, and he can be hilarious in a miserable sort of a way. He answers to "Hancock".'

She pulled an illustrative face, and Ann nodded.

'But actually, that can be a downer. Like he never really enjoys himself. And something else... how can I explain it? Do you like sitting quietly with a smile on your face being told things?'

'Nuh-uh.' Ann blew smoke. 'So how come you married him?'

'I was a bit lost, needed my hand holding. It isn't Tony's fault. He's decent, and kind, and—'

'Okay. I get the picture.'

They watched traffic together. Zoë tried to blow a smoke ring. Mick wasn't decent. Or kind probably. Next Wednesday she would be naked with him again. She sucked on the ciggie and smiled. Then looked at Ann, wondering.

'Would you like to be in love?'

'Again,' Ann said sadly. 'Yes. Wouldn't everyone?'

'I don't know. It feels mad, and dangerous. And it'll only mean I'm rolling around in strange beds with a smile on my face being told things.'

'Sounds okay to me.'

'I suppose. But why can't we ever tell them anything?'

She grinned and swayed, light-headed from the cigarette. Ann exhaled smoke with an odd expression.

'What?'

'Nothing. It's just there keeps being more to you than meets the eye.'

'Down with stereotypes!' said Zoë.

She was letting herself fly with the stars again, and Ann was laughing, 'Hear, hear. Tell you what. Do you happen to play bridge?'

AUGUST

Snake and Ladder

Back from Italy a whole week, but who would know it? Jack couldn't remember a hotter summer. White light was transforming London, turning it into somewhere else. Not Italy, nowhere he knew, but itself as it would be if every summer was like this. The dust rose in eddies behind the red buses. Plane leaves and bark crunched under his feet. Sales of ice cream soared, street theatre was happening, cafés ventured tables onto pavements, beautiful women thronged the streets bare-limbed and bra-less, in loose cotton dresses, sporting tans acquired in suburban back-gardens and smelling of fresh sweat.

He wanted to revel in it, but how could he with Pamela nagging at him? He unlocked the desk drawer at Bartholomew Road and pulled out her letter.

I'm never alone. Hundreds of miles away, in a hotel I can't imagine, is the man I know by heart. I have him clear in my mind, every detail, and for the hundredth time since we parted eleven days ago, I find myself smiling secretly over the shape and sound and smell of him. So soon we'll be together, my love. My wonderful Jack, I can hardly wait—but, believe me and trust me, I shall be good and patient. I understand how difficult this is for you. I shall not besiege you on your return, but will wait happily for your call...

Et-bloody-cetera. How could anyone seriously write crap like this? And 'wait happily'? Bollocks! Two calls already, the latest this morning. Gary had relayed her message with sadistic precision.

'A Miss Harrison, guv, same as Friday. In all day, said you've got her number. Bit of a whiner. She knows how you're busy and all, but could you get back to her? Rather you than me, eh?'

'Thanks, Gary. I'll deal with it.'

Fuck! He could see her lying in wait, playing the Paul Simon record he'd given her, wearing her staff-nurse uniform that he once made the god-awful mistake of saying he found sexy. Watching the phone with rabid eyes, bloody relentless.

He couldn't keep putting it off. She was impervious to hints, and who knew what she'd do next? Ring him at home perhaps, and Tessa might answer.

He stared at the phone. How had it got this complicated? At the start it was only an affair, a bit of fun. She'd seemed cheeky, this old school-friend of Ann's from Exeter, playing her games of hard-to-get across the bridge table, all buxom vivacity. And then, when they got going, she'd been so sexy and passionate; he'd been swept along by the adoration she heaped on him. Tessa was forever trying to amend and improve him, while Pamela could see no wrong, none at all. For a while he was thinking maybe he'd been a fool to go sniffing after class and cleverness through that ad in *Time Out*. He should have stuck with his own sort; and he was telling Pam that she was just what he needed, and getting off on her pleasure and excitement. And it wasn't just class either, or being allowed to be himself. She was so pretty and feminine, while Tessa? Well, yes, Tess was attractive in her way, but you would never in a million years say pretty, and he was noticing how even her friends found her difficult. Anyway she was definitely hard work, and Pamela wasn't. And Tessa was a stickler for sexual equality in the bedroom, while Pamela was up for all sorts of erotic games, in the thick of which it had been easy to say that he loved her.

He squirmed, trying to undo it. Because now she had him cornered. Desire came and went, but women hung on to words, and it seemed this woman had saccharine ears, turning everything she heard into fanciful plans.

He crashed his fist on the desk. The telephone jumped and jingled. He must ring her now. Had to. Had somehow to tell her the truth, or some version of it that would release him.

No escape. Get it done. Back of the drawer, the emergency scotch. Single malt. He unscrewed the cap and took a swallow:

silk and smoke. He listened to the boys whistling upstairs. Gary was out; they weren't about to come down. Now. Do it, now. He made himself lift the receiver and dial. Recoiled as it was immediately answered. Heard her voice, full of false lightness.

'Hello?'

'Hi there, Pam.'

'Jack! Oh darling! How are you?'

'Fine. And you?'

'All the better for hearing your voice.'

His mouth dried. Why couldn't she just see?

'Is something the matter?' she said. 'What's happened?' Sudden hope. 'Have you told her?'

'No! Nothing's happened.'

'Oh, Jack.' Her voice thick with disappointment. 'Is it so very difficult?'

'Yes, it is. Look, Pam. We need to talk.'

'What about?' There was that note of frozen pain that said: you can't hurt me, you must not.

'Nothing... I mean... Now look, Pam—'

'I'm sorry.' Heading him off. 'I really am sorry, Jack. I knew I shouldn't have rung you. I don't mean to press you. You know that, don't you?'

An agonising pause.

'But time's been so slow, Jack. It's nearly four weeks. I want you so much. My darling, say I can see you soon. Please.'

He didn't want to see her. He wanted to tell her now, on the phone.

'Jack?'

But he couldn't.

'I'm sorry, Pam. Things are incredibly busy here. The work's piled up, a whole load of stuff to sort out after Italy. Look, there's bridge on Friday. I'll see you th—'

'But Jack, that's four days. And we can't talk at bridge. I need...'

She stopped. Waited again. Oh fuck.

'I need to hold you.'

77

Here came the tears. This was madness, it couldn't be happening. 'Come on, Pam. Four days isn't the end of the world. I'll see you on Friday, okay?'

Silence.

'Okay?'

'Tell me we can have an afternoon soon?'

'I'll try and sort something out.'

'I love you, Jack.'

Oh hell. 'Yes, okay. Friday then.'

He killed the line and reached for the whisky.

'Boy, am I glad the week's over,' said Tessa. 'I'm not sure I can take much more of that awful man.'

'Who?'

'Who do you think, Jack? Alan, my boss, that's who.'

They were sharing spaghetti and salad at their long, scrubbed-pine kitchen table. Jack had finished his meal. Now he dawdled, listlessly turning pages of *The Times* that Tessa had brought home, humming along to tunes on the radio, enjoying the hot breeze from the open door to the terrace. Soon he would set off for bridge. The prospect of seeing Pamela wasn't too daunting, because Ann had invited more people. He could side-step Pam, display his indifference. So, best not to arrive early, allow time for the crowd to gather.

Tessa was angry about work, as she often seemed to be these days. But suddenly he didn't mind, not at all. He looked up from the paper and grinned with new appreciation at his big-boned wife with her cropped hair and clear, hazel eyes. 'So what's the evil toe-rag done now?'

'You wouldn't believe it. He's still not let up about my being in Italy that weekend.'

'Is that all?'

'No, it's not all.'

'What then?'

'It's a male put-down. Like women aren't serious about their careers or something.'

She was hot on male put-downs, a real minefield some

days.

'You're joking. I've never known a woman more serious.'

She stabbed a tomato. 'Maybe he feels threatened.'

'By what?'

'I don't know. He pretends to treat men and women the same, but he doesn't. He's a dreadful hypocrite. I try to tell him.'

'Ah.'

Tessa flung down her cutlery and sprang from her chair. 'Don't say "ah" like that. You're supposed to be on my side. Women will never have equality if they won't stand up and be counted.'

'Okay, I'm counting. One... erm, one?'

It was fun to tease her. She lunged at him across the table. He raised his hands in surrender and saw her smile in spite of herself.

She began to clear the dishes—it was her turn to do them today—swaying her hips in time with Chris Barber. It was rare to hear jazz on the radio.

'But seriously, you've no idea. He browbeats me, outmanoeuvres me somehow.'

'You take too much notice.' He turned another page of the paper, looked idly at the weather forecast. 'Don't let him wind you up. Let him get on with it.'

She swung back from the sink, red rubber gloves flapping in her hand. 'I'll give you an example. I was telling the board today who's on the shortlist for Client Services Director: five men and one woman. And when I get to the woman, Alan jumps in, all oily, and says, "She's a remarkably high-powered lady. Only thirty-five."'

'Is that so young?'

'Exactly! So, when he's finished pontificating, I say, "Actually, she's not the youngest candidate. She and Mick Galway are the *oldest*." And Alan just stares at me, as if I'm making no sense. "So presumably," I say, "it's not her age that amazes you, Alan, it's her gender?"'

'Blimey. And how did he react?'

'He tried to laugh it off. I said he was missing my point.'

'Wow. In front of the board? You don't give up, do you?'

'Why the hell should I, Jack?' She was shouting.

'Okay, so he admitted it, did he? Said yes, you've got me bang to rights, dear Ms Golding. I'm an incorrigible male chauvinist pig. I tender my resignation.'

'No, of course not.' She slumped. 'He just changed the subject. And everyone laughed.'

'Well, it is funny.'

'Jack, whose side are you on?'

'Pass.'

She looked hurt and fragile, the fight leaking out of her.

'Anyway. They all laughed. And it was me as usual who ended up feeling bad. Like I'd been making a silly fuss.'

'Which of course you hadn't,' he said softly, reaching for her hand.

She snatched it away. 'No! I bloody well hadn't!'

'I'm sorry, sweetheart.'

'Thanks a million, sweetheart!' She turned her back and began slamming dishes about in the sink.

'Hey, don't break the crockery!'

She rounded on him, jabbing the air with a red rubber finger, shouting above the jazz. 'Want to know my litmus test for sexism?'

'I've a feeling you're going to tell me.'

'Next time someone makes a remark about a woman, just try saying the same thing about a black man. Or yes, how about this, Jack, a Jewish man.'

Oh fuck. She came close, oozed words in his ear. 'Jack Golding's a remarkable Jew. Hardly out of his twenties, and no education to speak of, but so rich already.'

He jerked his head away. 'Okay. You made your point.'

'Racism not as funny as sexism, eh?'

'You know I don't think sexism is funny.'

'Don't you, though? God, I'm amazed how it keeps on going, the cosy male club.' She rained mock blows on his head.

'Hey, stop. *Stop!*' He fought her off, then drew her towards him and slid an arm around her comfortable hips. She wasn't the easiest woman, but she didn't half have spirit. He'd not made a mistake.

Now that she'd equalised she softened, draping herself heavily across his shoulders and nuzzling his ear. He looked at the paper again. 'Hey, it says here the police are being allowed to take off their ties and undo the top two buttons of their shirts while this weather lasts.'

'Dear me,' she said. 'The end of civilisation as we know it.' She bit his earlobe.

'Ow!' He rough-handled her onto his lap and licked her nose. 'D'you know what, my fine, feminist wife? Yesterday was the hottest August day in London since records began.'

She started upright, new light in her eyes. 'I've a brilliant idea, Jack. Shall we throw a Sunday lunch-party? What d'you think? In the garden, all lazy and French? Invite all the nice people we know?'

'With lots of nice bottles?'

'Yes. We can get squiffy in the sun. I'll cook a salmon in the fish-kettle and make chicken tarragon in aspic.'

He nodded. 'I'll do my salade Niçoise.'

'Yes, and summer pudding and tarte aux pommes. Can you bring the trestle tables? We'll set them up along the terrace, under the vine, with white tablecloths and pots of daisies.'

She leapt up, found a pad of paper and was busy scribbling notes. 'We can seat twenty easily. Or let's make it a buffet.'

The wonderful energy of this woman. And the style. How could he even have considered trading her in for Pamela? She'd unlocked the door to a world that, before he met her, he'd thought inaccessible. A world glimpsed in the elegant houses he used to visit with an estate agent's key. Now he had his own key. Now he too had style. He'd become someone whose life others envied and aspired to enter. One of 'the beautiful people'.

'Who shall we invite?' She tapped her crooked teeth with the biro. Okay, it was stretching a point to describe her as beautiful. But what a strong face. He'd warmed to it the moment they met. The disgruntled crease between her eyebrows. The determined nose and chin. The unblinking gaze. A face to be reckoned with.

'You can start tonight,' she said. 'Float a date with the Drunken Bridge Club. Shall we try for the twenty-fourth?'

'The bridge club's expanding,' he told her. 'Some character from ATP. Sebastian something.'

'Sebastian Santini? He's lovely. Tell him to bring Charlie, his flatmate.'

'Some of their new recruits will be there tonight, too.'

'Fine. Wonderful. Invite everyone.'

The radio burst forth with *Sweet Georgia Brown*, a jolly riot of trumpet and clarinet. Tessa flung down her pen, turned up the volume and danced round the kitchen. 'It's time we met some more people.'

Jack sprang up to dance with her, as happy as he knew how to be. 'And time some more people met us.'

Party Game

Zoë couldn't believe the wondrous things that were happening to her. Sometimes she pinched herself, literally, from fear her luck would run out, and to punish herself for her badness. She gave herself a sharp nip now through her blue Indian-cotton dress.

'Will I like these people?' asked Tony.

He was at the wheel of the stationary car, watching for the next gap in the traffic. He had on the green-cord jacket that he wore each day to school, but no tie, thank goodness. No, she thought, he probably won't like these people. He won't see the point of them.

'*I* like them,' she said carefully.

The car made it into the traffic stream and acquired speed in a series of jerks. 'Well I hope it's not a complete waste of time,' he said. 'We should be stripping wallpaper. There'll be plenty more Sundays for socialising when we've a decent place to invite anyone back to.'

Zoë gazed out rapturously at shops and houses. She was going to a garden party in Highgate with Ann Wilton's friends. She was one of them, one of Ann Wilton's friends.

Tony squeezed her knee. 'But we're on the home stretch, lovely, and you've been a good little builder's mate. Couldn't have managed without you.'

He let go of her knee to change up from third. The ancient Volkswagen coughed and lost power. 'Come on, Gertie,' he coaxed. 'You can do it.'

'It was incredible!'

Ann sloshed wine into Sebastian's glass just as Hugh Fairchild's dog pushed its wet nose against his hand.

'Erm... well... yes, it was actually,' he agreed. He bent to rumple the dog's ears while considering what to say next. His shirt had come free from his trousers, he noticed; he tucked it in quickly. 'Er, so, did you know,' he ventured, 'that in barely an hour, three million tons of water fell on an area of eight square miles? They measured seven inches on Hampstead Heath—four months' worth of normal rain. The odds were one in a thousand years.'

He stopped. Ann was waving a hand in his face. Ash from the cigarette wedged between her fingers fell on the parched grass. The hand was brown with silver rings, the arm bare all the way to her collarbone and cleavage; below that was a cherry-red dress.

'But that's just statistics, Sebastian. I was there. I *saw* it. And it was amazing. Absolutely incredible. Hailstones as big as... as this.' She demonstrated.

She wasn't exaggerating. *The Times* said they were the size of marbles.

'They were thundering on the pavements. Thundering. I had to hide in a shop doorway or I'd have been shot full of holes. I'm not kidding!'

He laughed. Although he wasn't sure he was supposed to.

'You should have seen the subway on the Finchley Road. It filled up like a fishpond, in no time at all.'

He'd read about that too. 'The water had nowhere to go,' he explained. 'The ground's baked hard, and the drains are blocked with leaves. They're falling early because of the drou—'

'Yes, but the point is how spectacular it was. Absolutely amazing. I've never seen anything like it. All those poor people watching their basements fill up. Like Noah's flood. Like the end of the world.'

'Truer than you know.' He smiled. 'There's a new ice age coming.'

'Really?'

She was paying attention. 'Erm, yes.' He cleared his throat. 'Apparently, the climate's been changing without our noticing. The Northern Hemisphere's been cooling for fifty years. The experts met in London this week. They think the inter-glacial period may be over. The aerosols people use may be partly to bl—'

'Aerosols?'

'Um, yes, you know.'

'*Aerosols*, Sebastian?'

'Yes.'

'You've got to be joking.'

'No. It was in *The Time*—'

'Oh, Sebastian, for goodness' sake!'

And Ann was gone.

The small, walled garden was full of roses and honeysuckle and beautiful people. That was how it appeared to Jack, exactly as he and Tessa had planned it. He stood beside the long, white-clothed table under the vine on the terrace, with a glass of good Burgundy in his hand. Ripening grapes dangled above his head; the scent of blossom filled his nostrils. 'How marvellous,' everyone enthused. 'Like paradise,' said that new sidekick of Ann's with the smile in her eyes and daisies in her long auburn hair.

Jack tipped his head back, closed his eyes against the sun filtering through the vine-leaves, and concentrated on the sounds. Louis Armstrong crooning *Ain't Misbehavin'* in that caressing, ironical voice of his, the clink of glasses, the drone of an aeroplane in the high, blue sky, the clamour of tipsy conversation in the sunshine. Heaven.

'Jack.'

Oh fuck. Her hand on his wrist.

'Pamela! You startled me. How are you doing? Can I fill your glass?'

She was wearing some long, frilly number.

'Darling, I've got to talk to you.'

'Not here, Pam, for crying out loud.'

'Please don't be angry.'

'But, Pam, this isn't—'

'When *is?*'

Her fingers clawed at his wrist. Her eyes implored him.

'Soon,' he managed.

'You keep saying that.'

'Pamela. Please.' She mustn't make a scene.

'Because when, Jack, when? No, I'm sorry, don't look at me like that. I know how difficult it is. I do understand.'

Her cheese-grater voice.

'Look, Pam, I've told you, not now.' He scanned the garden nervously for Tessa's floppy-brimmed sunhat. She had her back to him, thank Christ, in conversation with Ann.

'I've been thinking.' Pamela's voice dropped to a whisper, and he had to bend his head to hear. 'It's hard for you, of course it is, so... well... I wondered... would you like me to do it?'

'Do what?'

'Tell Tessa. I could ask her to meet me.'

'Bloody hell, no!' A scalding wave of panic. 'Look, I'll come to Acton this week.'

'Oh, Jack.' Her grip tightened.

'So, which is your day off?'

'Tuesday.'

'That's settled then. I'll be there. Usual time. Now Pam, please. Go and talk to someone else.'

At last she let go of his wrist and was moving away, her shoulders round with reproach.

It was all still to do. He gripped the table-edge as the heat and the noise closed in. The tipsy voices had grown louder, there was a crash and a shriek as a glass broke, Horatio began to bark, and now someone turned up the volume on Louis Armstrong. *Like Jack Horner. In his corner.* Fuck, what a mess!

He took a giant swig of wine, struggling to steady himself. He stared wildly out into the garden.

And met Lois's eyes. She was bending down, shushing the dog, showing her fine cleavage, and looking straight at him. Grinning and shaking her head.

He grimaced, and she raised her eyebrows. She'd seen the whole thing.

He eased his grip on the table, feeling better. Much better. He would sort Pamela. He would tell her on Tuesday, and that would be that. The pressure was easing and, yes, everything was blissful, just as before. The small, walled garden was still full of roses and honeysuckle and beautiful people. He topped up his wine and set off towards Lois.

'There's a piece near your foot.'

With Tessa's help, Ann was hunting for fragments of glass, easy to spot on the drought-shrivelled lawn.

'I think we've got it all.' Tessa straightened up, adjusting the wide brim of her Biba hat against the sun. 'So, where was I?'

'Alan has to get his own back.' Slight dizziness hit Ann as she regained the vertical. 'Hang on a mo.' She had the shards in a paper napkin. 'I'll put this somewhere safe.'

The dizziness receded as she nipped to the terrace. She dumped the napkin, found a new glass and filled it, took a swallow, and did a quick inspection of the party. Her hopes of there being someone here to fancy, or, what the hell, to have meaningless sex with, were evaporating. She went back to

Tessa. 'Sorry about that. So, carry on. What did the nasty bugger do next?' She fished a cigarette from her shoulder-bag, lit it one-handed and took another slug of wine, while trying to pay attention.

'Oh, Ann, it's getting beyond a joke. He can't leave it alone. He's forever finding new ways to goad me.'

'And this time?'

'It's a week later. We're in his car with Mick Galway, the three of us heading off to a meeting, all fine and friendly, and he asks how do we think the new Art Director's settling in.'

Ann smiled. 'Mick Galway, eh?'

'No, Ann, Mick's an *account* director. The Art Director's called Ken.'

'Loach?' Ann giggled. 'Russell?' The wine was freeing her. She swallowed some more and flexed her naked shoulders.

'Ha ha. And I tell him Ken's beginning to relax, and the staff seem to like him. So then the smarmy git says he's so glad I think so, because "Ken has some difficulty dealing with your half of the world, Tessa."'

'Yuck!'

'So I say, "With women, you mean?" And he doesn't answer, of course.'

'Oh Tess, he's ghastly!'

'Isn't he though? I'm not imagining it, am I?'

Ann ducked her head under the brim of Tessa's hat and kissed her cheek. 'No, of course not, my lover.'

'Oh Ann, you don't know what it means to have someone say that.'

Ann suddenly remembered. 'Tess, how terrible of me. I never asked, how's your mum? Did your dad come home yet?'

Tessa shook her head. 'No, and she's frantic, can't accept it, keeps insisting he'll miss his old life.'

'But he doesn't?'

'No, he's adamant. But, Ann, let me finish the Alan story, because that isn't the end. I should have dropped it, but damn fool me, I told him Ken's actually impressed by the women at Rex. He's been saying how effective we are, like it's some big discovery. So then Alan lays it on double-thick. "Of course, Tessa my dear," he says. "It *is* the ladies who keep the place going. We men appreciate that."'

'Hmm.'

'And that riles me, don't you see? It's the kind of oily putdown he specialises in. And he's looking so pleased with himself, so I tell him my sexism test. You have to ask yourself, would you say the same thing of a black man or a Jew? It's the blacks who keep the place going. We whites appreciate that?'

'Good *stuff*, Tess! I like it!'

'But no, Ann, he's won. I'm using these indecent words — "woman", "black", "Jew". So he goes all pretend shocked and wants to know what Mick thinks.'

'Now that *is* interesting.'

'Hardly. Mick just smirks all over his big, ugly mush and says, "Count me out. I'm not saying a thing."'

'The toad!'

'And Alan changes the subject, all smooth and smiling, as if... as if my knickers had fallen down. Asks Mick what questions will come up at the meeting. And that's it. Humiliating.'

Ann laughed. 'But at least now we know. Mick Galway's a meaningless sexist!' She glanced at Zoë, who was standing nearby with her husband, chatting to Charlie.

'Maybe, maybe not,' Tessa said. 'I've had lunch with him since. He said he understood what happened in the car, how male chauvinism works at Rex, and he wanted to apologise.'

'Did he now? Well, that's something.'

'He seemed to mean it, too. He didn't want to let on what Alan said afterwards, but I got it out of him. Apparently the bastard commented how "tetchy" I am.'

'Which Mick agreed with, no doubt.'

'He said not. He said the male togetherness stuff was too easy, a sell-out.'

'Oh yeah? And you believe him?'

'No, of course not. He's hardly going to put his career on the line for some woman from admin.'

'Bloody men, eh?'

'I suppose. But at least Mick sees the game and feels the shame, which is half the battle.'

Ann raised her glass. 'You should have asked Mick to the party.'

'I did, but it was one of his kid's birthdays.'

'Right.' Ann emptied the glass.

'It crossed my mind to say, bring the kids. But what fun would they've had? There are no children here.'

Her head on Tessa's shoulder, tipsy beneath the shade of the Biba brim, Ann scanned the garden at knee-height.

'D'you know, Ann,' Tessa whispered, 'I'm getting worn out with the battle. It's endless, and soul-destroying—it won't be won in our lifetime. Actually,' she nodded across to where Jack was kneeling with Lois and the dog, 'and this is just between you and me, so please don't breathe a word, not even to Lois, because it's only a thought. The thing is, I think I might stop.'

'Stop?'

'Yes.' Tessa's eyes were closed. She was smiling dreamily. 'Stop work, just for a while, you know. Have a baby.'

'...a freak cumulonimbus over the Heath.'

Hugh was half-listening to Sebastian Santini explain the science of the Hampstead cloudburst. The subject was fascinating, and he had no wish to be rude to Sebastian, who seemed a modest, thoughtful sort of chap, but he was distracted by two things. One was Pamela, clutching at the sleeve of his denim jacket, sniffing and occasionally moaning. The other, of course, was Lois. Lois with Jack. They'd been petting Horatio, down on their knees on the ground. But Horatio had gone now, and they were still there, whispering and smiling, their heads close together.

'The hot air rose too fast,' Sebastian said. 'Water started condensing on particles of dust, then swirled around, higher and higher.'

Hugh gave Pamela's shoulder a squeeze, and she burrowed her head against him, sighing with great pathos. Sebastian faltered. 'Do go on,' Hugh said.

'Er, yes, well, so high and so fast that it froze into really massive hailstones and plummeted, slap bang on the evening rush hour.'

Lois had vanished! Where was she? Oh yes, over there, still with Jack. They'd removed themselves into the shade of a wall, which was smothered in some exotic, tangled creeper laden with fleshy blue flowers and heavy yellow fruit. How elegant they were, his lovely Lois and Jack Golding, side by side, their backs to this extravagant greenery. Quite still now, saying nothing, watching the party. Jack in a cream linen suit, Lois in her honey-brown sundress, the skirt spread in a circle on the baked straw of the lawn.

'A couple were struck by lightning on the Heath,' said Sebastian.

Ann had appeared, and was waving her arms at the sky. 'It was absolutely *amazing*,' she slurred. 'Just *incredible*.' She was well on the way.

Sebastian persisted. 'There were flash floods. The water at Farringdon Station was eighteen feet deep.'

Hugh stole another look at Lois. Something was odd in the way she and Jack weren't speaking. Jack had a strange smile on his face, and Hugh saw Lois give a small wriggle, as if something was tickling her. There was a glass in Jack's right hand; his left was hidden from view.

And suddenly Hugh understood what was happening, and his knees nearly gave way. Lois's eyes were closed, her mouth slightly open. The hand was under her skirt.

'It got serious,' said Sebastian. 'The fire brigade had to rescue people from basements. One man was drowned trying to save his furniture.'

Hugh's head was in chaos; he could barely breathe or stand. Denied his support, Pamela threw herself bodily on Ann.

'Oh Ann, tell me what to do. Nothing is right. Everything I say makes him angry.'

Ann ducked the embrace, fishing in her bag for cigarettes.

'So maybe it's over, Pam. Let him go.'

'*No!*'

'Pam.' Hugh stretched out a hand. To offer help or to seek it, he scarcely knew which.

She didn't notice. She stood swaying, staring into Sebastian's bewildered face.

Ann lit up and blew smoke. 'You've got to look on the bright side, Pam. It was good while it lasted.'

It was taking all Hugh's strength to be silent. He could see only Lois, her half-closed eyes, her bosom rising and falling, Jack murmuring now in her ear. He wanted to run at them, howling, smash a fist in Jack's face. But he couldn't. He'd promised.

He'd promised. He'd promised. It was good while it lasted.

Ann blocked his view. And Pamela was hissing at her, 'Don't give me that every-cloud-has-a-silver-lining rubbish. It's not true.'

'Patch grief with proverbs,' he quoted mechanically, praying to Marlowe for aid.

'And it's not funny either, Hugh!'

'Shush, Pam.' Ann brandished her cigarette. 'Besides, it *is* true, ish-ish-ish.' She giggled. 'Most things have a good side.'

'Oh yes?' Pamela raged at her. 'How about drowning in a basement? Oh great, that's the mortgage paid off.'

'But you're not drowning, Pam.'

'How the hell would you know?'

She was in tears now. People nearby fell silent. Sebastian was offering a handkerchief. Ann was glancing across the garden, checking Tessa hadn't seen.

Pamela appealed to Sebastian, who was staring, nonplussed. 'What do *you* think? Haven't I a right to be unhappy?'

At least ten listeners waited on Sebastian's answer, and for a moment Hugh, too, believed it would show the way through.

'Oh help!' said Sebastian. Then, 'Don't ask me. I don't know clouds at all.'

Ann shrieked with glee. Even Pamela grinned. And Hugh found he had no choice but to join in with the general laughter, though it tore at his chest like a sob.

Paris

'Are you okay, Charlie?'

To Zoë this party was wonderful. The garden, the people, the music, the lavish buffet, the tastefully modernised mock-Tudor house, the wafts of scented roses, cigarette smoke and alcohol adrift in the air. But Tony insisted on muttering resentfully about 'how the other half live', and now Charlie Evans, too, was being impenetrably morose. Though she'd never spoken much to Charlie, she'd formed the impression that he was an amusing character, and he was definitely from the same 'half' as Tony, so she'd rushed to introduce them in the hope they would hit it off. Instead, they'd grunted monosyllables at each other, until Tony muttered in her ear, 'Fascinating, I'm sure,' announced, 'Time to demonstrate I'm not tied to the apron-strings,' and stomped off.

Would Charlie now brighten? No, he ignored her 'are you okay?' and hunched his shoulders in a 'don't mess with me' way while he distributed a few, measly strands of tobacco along a Rizla paper. He rolled it with expertise into a slim, tight cylinder, then struck a match, inhaled deeply, dropped the match, still flaming, and ground it out with the weathered toe of his plimsoll. He aimed a jet of smoke at the sky.

'Let's say I'm in love,' he offered finally in an American drawl. 'And I've probably got cancer.'

'Oh my God! I'd no idea. I mean—'

He shook his head gravely. 'These.' He indicated the roll-up. '"Symptomless" it says in the book down the library. Just a dry cough that won't go away. Well, I've got that all right, had it for years. But lately it's, I don't know, sort of drier and more persistent. No proof, you'll say. Maybe I'll never get cancer, I'll fall under a bus, still puffing away, aged a hundred and three. Fat chance, because probably *this* drag,' he drew on the roll up, 'will be the one I never knew killed me.'

Zoë was laughing now. 'You should have said that when Tony was here. It's the kind of humour he likes.'

Charlie scowled. 'Why would I want him to like me?'

She should be offended, but she wasn't, and she didn't pause to feel guilty about it. 'Do you want *me* to like you?'

'Suit yourself.'

'And are you really in love, or was that a joke too?'

Charlie's demeanour became even more peculiar. He drew up his shoulders, pressed his chin to his chest, and tugged at his blond forelock. She'd seen him do the same at work.

'Nuh-uh. No joke.' He spoke from the corner of his mouth.

'Why do you pull your hair? Are you trying to straighten it?'

An exasperated snort. 'I'm Bogart.'

'Pulling his hair?'

'Adjusting the brim of his fedora. God, women are ignorant.'

Zoë's curiosity was growing. 'Is the one you love ignorant?'

He stared across the garden, looking genuinely sad. Zoë followed his gaze and saw Ann, in her cherry-red sundress, laughing with Sebastian Santini and that nice, older man from bridge and some others. Then ceasing to laugh, detaching herself from the group, and heading towards the terrace. Zoë glanced back at Charlie. He was still watching Ann.

Of course.

'I agree with you. She's amazing.'

'My Ingrid Bergman,' said Charlie. 'When she stops laughing, you can see the same trouble in her face.'

They watched as Ann stumbled against the table on the terrace and knocked over some bottles. When she'd righted them, she began scratching in her bag for cigarettes. She fumbled one out, clicked her lighter, missed and clicked again.

'She's drunk,' Zoë said.

'Mussolini says I should ask her again.'

'Mussolini?'

'Santini.'

93

'Oh. So why don't you?'

Charlie stood straighter, rolling his shoulders as if to loosen them. 'I'm out of tobacco. I could cadge one of hers.'

He took a last pull on the roll-up, flicked it away, adjusted the brim of the fedora, and began to mosey towards the terrace.

'Good luck,' Zoë called after him.

Ann slumped against the terrace wall, trying to smoke yet another Benson and Hedges. Her body wasn't co-operating. It kept colliding with people and threatening to fold at the knees, and now her hand was having trouble finding her mouth. Her mind though was clear. She couldn't take any more of these women—Zoë, Tessa, Pamela—each one as bad as the next, badgering her with their problems and secrets, assuming she had none of her own. Except that she hadn't, had she? Good old Ann, no problems, no secrets; everybody's sister. That was why she'd run away from the others. She'd suddenly heard the sound of herself laughing, and she'd wanted to yell, fuck you all!

Where were the friends she'd had back before Ed, and the supply of eager lovers? Nothing felt real anymore; all the hugs and the laughter were phoney. Nobody knew her, or saw her, or cared. She was sozzled out of her mind in this beautiful garden, where Tessa and Jack paraded their marriage and Zoë daydreamed of Mick Galway, and, fuck it, *she* wanted to parade and to daydream.

She shook her head, furious. The ground lurched up at her, she grabbed at the terrace wall, knocking a bottle onto the grass. And she was down on her bottom on the ground, trying to pick up the bottle, thinking, sharp as a razor, ha bloody ha, because, whatever any of them thought, none of them was safe either. They only pretended they were, waving their marriage certificates and love affairs, planning babies, a few self-serving lies away from where she was.

She groped her way back up the wall, clutching the bottle to her chest, trying to feel superior. But who was she kidding?

She scrubbed the stupid cigarette out and flung it into a flowerbed. Because it *wasn't* all sham, what the others had. Look at Lois and Hugh: they had the real thing.

Of course. Hugh and Lois. They cared. Hugh might ignore her passes, but he was still kind and gentle and clever. And Lois might be too lucky by half, and tacky with that Italian waiter, but she was still provocative and funny and cuddly. She'd been jealous of Lois lately, not treating her right. Where was Lois now? She must tell her, apologise. Lois would listen and understand and make her feel better. Lois loved her. Lois's hugs would be real. Ann held tight to the terrace and craned out into the garden.

There she was, by the wall, sitting with Jack, leaning on him, rubbing her head against his chin, a Cheshire-cat smile on her face.

And abruptly Ann was sober. She knew at once. Oh Lois, how could you? She found Hugh's face in the crowd, saw him watching them too, felt his pain. She took a step forward and fell hard on her knees.

'Hello, Annie.'

It was Charlie, helping her up, the sun burnishing his golden curls like a halo. He said nothing; his eyes said it all.

And she said, 'Oh, fuck it, all right then. Why not?'

The room accelerated its whirling, dragging her down, sucking her brain from her skull. She had to open her eyes, but here was Charlie, whom she vaguely recalled snogging violently in the back of a taxi. She shut them again tightly and rode out the spin. And it was okay; she kept hold of her brain, the rotation slowed, she rose blindly into a bubble of lucidity. I'm fucking Charlie. Fine. Don't look. Don't speak. That's the trick. Because touch, smell, taste: these are what sex is about.

She'd been barely alive. How long had this hunger been growing? Food failing to satisfy, bottled scents awakening longings, the touch of her own body tantalising and frustrating her. While now, oh yes, please, here in the spinning dark, came the confusion of sensation that was someone else. Anyone else. The smell of lavender on the sheets, the taste of smoke and beer in his mouth and of sweet salt on his penis, the long, slow-fast, hard-soft exploration of his body, the urgent pressure of his hands, the sound of his breathing, his voice uttering half words, lost in itself.

To look was too much. To speak was too much. The dream would crash, she might throw up. There was nothing real to be done but to close her eyes, to open them safely beneath the curve of a thigh or in a hot, damp armpit. And next, after sex, they would sleep. Tomorrow she would face him and answer him. Now it was enough to stroke and sigh, to touch, smell and taste his anonymous flesh, to let the room spin, and to wish this was all of life.

'Oh boy, Annie. Here I am. Looking at you.'

She said nothing. Had he seen she was awake? Her head throbbed and her mouth tasted foul. Mercifully the room was dark, although through a gap in the curtains she could see the sun already scorching the street. The air was heavy, and the tangled bedclothes reeked of stale smoke.

'Annie?'

She turned her head. 'Charlie. I'm sorry... but I can't...'

'Don't say that. Was I no good? I was pissed. I can do better.'

'It was great. Really.' She hugged him. He tried for a kiss, but she pulled away. 'We've nothing in common.'

He took hold of her shoulders, made her look at him. 'You mean I'm not good enough.'

'No.' She tried to think. 'I mean jazz, for instance. I don't like jazz.'

'That doesn't matter.'

'Or bridge. You don't like bridge.'

'That's balls, Annie.'

Pain stabbed the back of her eyes.

'We're single,' he said, 'and we fancy each other.'

Shaking her head set off waves of nausea.

'You fancied me last night.'

96

'Yes. And I do, Charlie. But it isn't that simple.'

He sat up. 'For fuck's sake, what could be simpler?'

'Please don't shout. My head hurts.'

'I'm just a bit of rough.'

'You're twisting what I'm saying.'

'Because you're not saying anything.'

'Stop *shouting*.'

'I'm sorry.'

'The thing is, Charlie, you only *think* that you love me. You don't really. You don't know me.'

'Don't I, though?'

'You're always painting me as Bergman or Bacall. No, Charlie, please, stop.'

He was trying to kiss her again, but she flung back the sheet and staggered to her feet. Standing there naked, she managed a laugh. 'Come on. I must have a shower, and coffee. I've got to get to work. Is Tessa mad, throwing a party on a Sunday?'

Stumbling over the tangle of her sundress and his jeans on the floor, she was out of the bedroom, across the hall and into the bathroom. The clothes-airer draped with washing straddled the bath. She hefted it off onto the floor, and turned on the taps. Charlie followed her in, was colliding with her in front of the washbasin, his erection prodding at her.

'Oh Charlie, please.'

'There's someone else,' he said. 'Tell me, who is it?' He was sliding incorrigibly into Bogart.

Which couldn't be less funny. 'What utter *junk*, Charlie!'

He opened his mouth.

'No, you listen to me. It was okay, *okay?* It was really nice. But I can't do this *Casablanca* thing.'

'And there's no one else?'

She subsided. She felt horribly miserable, staring past his shoulder into the hall. 'If you must know, that's what I've realised, that there's no one at all. The only person I really love and who really loves me is Lois.'

'Lois?'

'And even she... no, I can't tell you. God, it's getting so I can't tell anyone anything. But now out, Charlie, please.'

She was pushing him back into the hall. Beyond the frosted glass of the front door, the milkman was coming down the steps, whistling and clinking bottles. Behind her, she heard the crash of the clothes-airer collapsing, and the insistent drumming of the shower. Standing there starkers, his erection deflated, Charlie reassembled his Hollywood dignity. Hunching his shoulders, adjusting the brim of his imaginary hat, he sank his chin into the upturned collar of a trench-coat and gave profile to camera.

'See what you've made of me, Annie?' he drawled. 'I'm Rick. At Gare de Lyon. In the rain.'

She smiled. She almost relented. But no, she couldn't spend her life replaying some sweet idiot's favourite movie.

She shut the door, kicked aside the collapsed heap of washing, and stepped into the shower.

Home Truth

Whew, thought Jack, he had done it. Now he just had to ride out the storm.

Pamela's face was whiter than her shag-pile carpet; he couldn't look at it. 'But Jack,' she was saying. 'You don't understand. I'll be different. I promise I will.'

'I'm sorry, Pam, no.'

Stick to that now. Sorry, Pam, no. Keep his eyes on the record player. Paul Simon winding down. Three quiet guitar chords—*sorry*—*Pam*—*no*—before silence. The arm clicked and lifted. He was nauseated by the stench of her air-freshener. He lurched up from the sofa. He needed a pee.

She grabbed his sleeve, pulling him back down. 'But you said you loved me, Jack. And you do. You still do. You know it's true.'

Nothing. Say nothing. Avoid her eyes. Think of Lois,

wearing no knickers under the brown linen sundress. Her suppressed squeaks as she came. Watch the arm of the record-player swing over and smoothly descend, needle to vinyl—oh fuck, no, prevent it, because here, bang on cue, came the lingering, nostalgic intro of *Still crazy after all these years*.

'Their' song.

Pamela clutched his hands, forced him to look at her. 'What we have is so special, Jack. We're meant to be together. I've been a pain, I know it, I'm sorry. But I'll be better now, I promise. We'll get through this and be happy again.'

Hold tight, tune out, listen to the music.

'Give me a chance, Jack.'

'Sorry, Pam, no.' Fixing his gaze on the street door, imagining himself beyond it. A quick visit first to the floral peach bathroom.

A sob in her voice. 'But why not?'

Oh hell.

'Tell me, why not?'

'Pam. Just accept it. It's over. Okay?'

Her eyes wide with fright. Her painful grip on his hands. Her voice frantic. 'No, Jack, it isn't. I know that you love me. I can see what you're going through. That you think you mean this.'

Crazy. Still crazy.

Fucking lunatic, more like. Out of the darkness and into the light with Tessa, yet risking everything. For what? A different body? A different set of tricks? Christ, he needed a piss.

'Answer me, Jack.' She was stroking his hair now and smiling up close. 'Darling Jack.' Her voice lapsing into that cloying, self-satisfied tone.

'No, Pamela!' Managing to free his hands. 'Look, I'll say it again, I'm very sorry, and I don't want to hurt you, but it's no good, we must stop. You've got to understand, it's been better with Tess. I'm going to give my marriage a proper go.'

He made it to his feet. He just needed the lav. He glanced about him, checking he had everything.

Then she screamed.

He couldn't believe it. That piercing noise. He tried to laugh.

She screamed again. He clapped his hands to his ears. 'Stop it, for fuck's sake.'

He'd had enough. He made for the street door, but she was on him, dead weight, her arms clamped round his hips, a fist pummelling his bladder, screeching out words. 'You're murdering our dreams. Murdering our children.'

Children? His body shook. He sniggered with a kind of awful embarrassment.

She shrieked again. 'Murderer!'

'Don't be ridiculous,' he yelled. 'Let me go.'

He struggled towards the door. Her cries were waves trying to drown him, her weight the undertow. He dragged himself against the armlock that had slipped to his thighs.

He'd nearly made it. The handle to sanity was within reach. He paused to peel her from him, gripping her wrists in one hand as he reached for safety with the other. And still she was screaming.

'Stop it! Shut up!' He dug his nails fiercely into her flesh. 'Whatever will the neighbours think?'

He sniggered again. And this time it wasn't only with embarrassment. She was ludicrous; she deserved to be laughed at. What was it Lois had called her? Oh yes.

He grabbed Pamela's head in his hands and pulled it close. She lunged as if to kiss him, then squealed 'No!' as he twisted her face sideways and yanked up her hair. He thrust clenched teeth against her ear and hissed, 'Shut the fuck up, you silly, pudgy, cow!'

She stopped. Her body went limp. She stared at him. He let her go. She slumped to the floor, panting, staring, her eyes glassy. He opened the door. He stepped over the threshold into a world drenched with light. Two women stood in the next front garden, pretending not to look.

'Good afternoon,' he said and marched himself and his near-desperate need to urinate smartly to the car.

SEPTEMBER

Truth Will Out

Mick Galway's body had become an object of wonder and beauty to Zoë, evoking in her a resonance without words as though he were some mysterious sculpture. The curve of his calf muscle, the hollow at the base of his spine, his nipple erect beneath her fingertip, his earlobe between her teeth, his ever unfolding landscape was familiar and strange, repeated and never the same. And as she unfolded him, he unfolded her in return, translating her too into a work of art: *Reclining Nude* by Henry Moore, *The Kiss* by Rodin.

It freed her to be brazen and shameless. They slipped and dripped; their fingers searched deep; his tongue tempted and teased a flood of wanting from her. They touched and retreated, cock and cunt, longing to enter and enfold, to coalesce, to fuck. Making themselves wait.

Then they gave themselves up to it. And there was the never failing sense of coming home. 'Of course,' her body told her. 'This is where you should be, where you belong.' For a few moments, the art, the lust, the rush and muddle in her head, were stilled. She smiled at her beloved and kissed him with her whole body. She and he, turning together, one flesh, babes in the womb, protected and safe.

When she opened her eyes, he was looking at her, his face flushed, his mouth open as if to speak. She smiled and, when he said nothing, turned her face to the window, watching the curtain billow out. From the street beyond the hotel, sounds floated up from the traffic, which slowed and accelerated at the lights and indulged in an occasional bad-tempered horn blast.

'I nearly said something dangerous,' he murmured.

She turned and looked into his eyes. Did she want to hear

this? She spoke carefully. 'Say what you feel. There's no danger.'

'You'll get the wrong idea.' He was shaking his head.

'Trust me, I won't. I'll understand that it doesn't...'

She didn't want to finish the sentence.

'Are you sure?'

'Yes. Definitely. I promise. You can depend on it.'

It was like daring him to jump from an aeroplane.

'Okay.'

He repeated this, 'Okay,' then took a breath, preparing himself for the leap. She watched, anxious suddenly.

He shook his head again. 'I need to say it, but...'

'But what?'

He grinned. Then he said it.

'I love you.'

The words sounded strange. Mick buried his face in the pillow. She held him tight, unsure how to reply.

I love you, too? A trite echo. And what did it mean for Beauty to love the Beast? What did it imply?

'Watch this space,' she said at last. 'I understand exactly.'

It was enough apparently; she felt him relax. He lifted his head and looked at her, close up with his myopic blue eyes. 'No smashed marriages. No ownership. Okay?'

'Absolutely.' She nodded. 'Couldn't agree more.'

He grinned. Then he wound his hand in her hair and tugged till her scalp tingled. 'Love,' he announced loudly. 'Love.' And kissed her hard.

'Love,' she repeated, returning the word to his mouth. Because yes, love, why not? Nothing wrong with a word. Or with this feeling. Nothing easier or more right. And the certainty built, and the relief spread through her, as his body found hers again.

Gone ten the next Saturday morning, she lay in a different bed in a different mood with a different man, procrastinating.

It was an unwritten custom between her and Tony to make love on Saturday morning. But somehow lately they never got round to it. After they made love, or instead if they weren't going to, they were supposed to get up and get on with the house. But today they couldn't face that either.

So okay, they could do with a rest, but at least they should be talking, shouldn't they? Relating work anecdotes, enjoying comfortable, cosy, married chat. Instead they were snoozing and fidgeting, cuddling half-heartedly, and barely exchanging monosyllables. Still at odds after last night.

It should have been fun. Waiting for Tony in the bar of the National Film Theatre, Zoë couldn't have been happier. She'd had a great day giggling with Ann over the answers to the pilot question about the biggest difference between men and women—'Men are into all that physical palaver' was her favourite so far; plus this place always gave her a lift. It reminded her of the bars where she used to hang out as a student: dimly lit and crowded with trendies who spilled off the hard, low benches and tables onto the floor, flirting and chain smoking and discussing art movies at the top of their voices. Eager to be part of it, she'd been imagining Ann there, blowing ribbons of smoke into the fug and waving her hands about. She'd leapt up and run to kiss Tony. 'Hi there, Hancock. Can I cadge a ciggy? How was your day?'

But then, what was this? A long account of some disastrous fourth-year physics practical. Faulty apparatus, no budget for replacements.

'The cretins,' he'd fumed, tugging to loosen his tie, 'forever whining on about underfunding and inflation. Bollocks— they've blown it on crap. Raided the science budget for sport and art and "ologies", wine and cheese parties, handouts spouting waffle about equal opportunities and the creative power of the child. When half of the little dears can't even read properly. And what chance does a child have to create when his blessed Bunsen won't work, I ask you?'

Except he wasn't asking her or looking at her, he was just mouthing off. More acid than angry, muttering and hissing, and she'd heard this rant three dozen times before. Was there going to be a new point or punch line? Was he telling her this because he really needed to, or to hear himself talk? But that was unfair. This stuff mattered, didn't it? More than art movies. She'd nodded and made herself listen.

'...headless chicken of a secretary in a flap at the sight of me, while that useless headmistress smiles like Nurse Rached and recites, 'Yes, I hear you' and all her other meaningless mantras.'

'Why not put it in writing? Say you'll go to the governors?'

'...cycle of deprivation. Pay peanuts, get monkeys. Monkeys can't see that a school's about teaching, not some airy-fairy self-realisation nonsense. Result—kids don't get taught, more monkeys next time round. Sod room 101, we'll be back in the caves by 1984. The trouble with—'

'Why don't you answer me?' she'd exploded. 'You're just spouting as usual.'

He glared, open-mouthed. Marched stonily ahead of her into the film.

Oh Lord, how did that happen? She'd caught up with him, slipped her arm through his, delivered the ritual grovel. 'I'm sorry. I was horrid. We're not communicating again.'

And he'd smiled, but coldly. And after the film, he was the same, or so she imagined. Anyway there'd been no touching, and no question of sex when they got home. And now, Saturday morning, with the question of sex deafeningly loud, they were only pretending to grope.

Zoë made a new effort to concentrate. If she could summon the enthusiasm, he would too, and afterwards they'd feel better, and the weekend would go well. Easy. Just do it. Come on.

She snuggled, and he snuggled back. She slid a hand inside his pyjamas. And yes, he was twitching and rising. He rolled closer and kissed her. She shut her eyes, kissed him back, tried not to mind the stale taste of his saliva—she must taste the same—managed to avert her head as he clambered on top of her. Why didn't she enjoy kissing him? She never had. No, stop worrying about that, think about sex; see how easy it was. He was inside her now, and he was heavy, and the fuzz on his chest was making her nose prickle.

She opened her eyes, saw the pink folds of his ear, and her hand on the back of his head, and beyond that the ceiling, dancing with sunlight. Here I am, she thought, having sex with my husband under this friendly ceiling. And it feels fine. Fine enough. There was something gentle about this back bedroom, sunny and white. Tony was right though: the Victorian cornice was in a bad way. It needed the hundred layers of paint digging out of its cavities. He wanted to replace it with polystyrene coving, which looked good, didn't she agree, in the knocked-through lounge? Only he hadn't mentioned it in a while, and it wasn't on The List. Sometimes she came in here by herself, and lay on the bed, and listened to the blackbirds in next door's garden, and watched the sharp edge of sunshine creep across the paint-blunted flowers and grapes and leaves, and felt blissful for no reason; the same bliss she'd felt when she first saw the house.

'Here it comes. Bloody hell!'

She hugged him tight, meaning it, joining in, enjoying it, kissing his stubble as he roared in her ear. 'Oh f-f-fuck!'

He rolled onto his back. 'Boy, I didn't half need that.' He turned his face to hers. 'We should do it more often.'

She nodded. Of course, nothing easier. And not just on Saturdays, she made up her mind.

'Up 'n at it.' He mock-punched the air.

It was great when he was happy. They didn't argue, they got along fine, they were friends. And for the sexier kind of love, there was Mick. Though she mustn't think of Mick now.

Tony heaved a long Hancock sigh. 'Strewth, I'd forgotten this ceiling.'

She sat up. 'Good. Let's forget it completely, leave this room alone. A shrine to the house as it was.'

'But look at it, Zo. It's only held up by the paper. We've got to keep an eye on the resale value. In a couple of weeks, we'll be done in the main bedroom. We can move back in there and have this one sorted in a—'

'No, Tony.'

'Come again?'

'I like this room as it is.'

'Don't be silly.'

'Why not? Why can't I be silly? You sound like my father.'

'Because how can I argue if you're going to be silly?'

'You could try not arguing.'

He sat up. 'Are you saying my view doesn't count?'

'You've told me it, Tony. I've heard it. It's counted.'

'So you're saying we have to do it your way?'

'Why not, just for once?'

He was silent, his face was quite still, and for a moment she thought he'd conceded. But then she noticed how tightly he was clenching his fist, all but one finger.

'That's rich!' he hissed. 'Who wanted this god-awful house in the first place?' Jabbing the finger. 'Who gets every, single, last thing she wants, when she wants it, and still isn't content, like the fucking princess and the fucking pea?'

She stared at him, struggling to make sense of the argument and her feelings. It was true. He was right. But she was right too, and suddenly she couldn't give a damn about the ceiling.

'It's no good, Tony. You and me. Is it? Tell me, do you really think it is?'

The Meaning of Words

A squall rattled the window behind Sebastian's head and spattered raindrops against the glass. The long, hot summer had ended. Gales were beating the coasts, waterspouts three hundred feet high had been sighted in the Irish Sea, a whirlwind had waltzed across Swansea harbour lifting boats and cars and alarming the natives. The London police had rolled down their sleeves and rebuttoned their shirts, while Viking One headed for Mars.

The room was warmly glowing and comfortable and full of pleasingly unfamiliar objects. On the table at Sebastian's elbow, a petite metal lady, wearing distressed-gilt knickers, stood on tiptoe atop a pyramid of three brown-marble slabs. She leant back, displaying small, uplifted breasts. She supported a delicate sphere of white light on outstretched, slender arms.

It would be entertaining, he thought, to explore second-hand markets and begin to kit out his own place with a few tasteful things. Trouble was, he didn't have much spare cash these days. Sharing with Charlie was supposed to produce some, and Charlie did cough up half the rent now and then. But he 'borrowed' it all back, and more, in the pub, and Sebastian was reconciling himself to looking upon Charlie's company as a luxury he paid for quite dearly. But okay, he could afford it and didn't much begrudge it. Tasteful objects would doubtless accrue in time, and who needed them, really?

He sipped the wine that Hugh Fairchild had thrust into his hand in exchange for his bottle from the off-licence. He felt pleased to be here, gratified to be part of this lively gathering in these agreeable surroundings. His gaze left the metal lady and travelled along the arm of the leather wingback into which he'd retreated. It was scratched and torn, by age or Horatio's attentions or both, into holes with protruding tufts of yellow horsehair. Sebastian's feet in their scuffed Nature-Treks rested on a knotted rug, brown and beige with large blue swirls, over which Horatio, ecstatic at the arrival of so many human friends, was scurrying back and forth, begging pats and compliments from each one.

Sebastian shifted his attention to the people. Jack, Tessa, Hugh, Lois and Ann rushed about, greeting one another with all the noise and exuberance of five more mongrel dogs, while, across the room, Sebastian's new assistant, David Pratt, had taken refuge beside Zoë Smith upon a vast, square, cream-coloured sofa. Pratt's ingratiating smile and big chin loomed above an inappropriate collar and tie. He had the look of a man way out of his depth but determined not to go under. That woman, Pamela somebody, who'd been so upset about something at the garden party, had dropped out of bridge, so

Ann had enlisted Pratt as a last-minute eighth. 'You must come,' she'd hectored him with bizarre logic. 'We've even had to dragoon Tessa.'

Sebastian smiled. He was out of his depth too, but enjoying the feeling. He decided that he liked Hugh and Lois's home. He liked its self-confidence. That huge Victorian oil-painting, for instance, on the wall above Zoë's head: a half-naked woman with a naked child lying on a bed of pink and white roses in an ornately carved, gilded frame. Many people might think it was excessive, kitsch even. But it hung there with confidence, and it was just fine. Sebastian wished that he could show the same confidence in his life. Could it be a matter of practice, of learning to face it out?

So far he was holding his own okay with this alarming group of people. The secret, he was finding, was to say not much at all, and then, when he did speak, to contribute something mildly helpful, not pushy, or else some anecdote: short rather than long, amusing rather than informative. He'd prepared one for this evening. He'd practised it on Pratt as they travelled here on the bus, and Pratt had laughed a good deal. That was no test of course, because Pratt laughed at all his jokes, but the correct sycophantic response was a little tricky to judge given that this joke was at Sebastian's expense. And Pratt's laughter had seemed less insincere than usual.

From the depths of the cushions into which she'd sunk, Zoë marvelled at the sumptuous furnishings. The lamps particularly. Where did people find such lamps? That amazing little dancer beside Sebastian Santini, and then, nearer to her, elaborate metal stems curving up from a claw foot to erupt in two snowdrops of milky glass petals.

Such beauty made her feel sad. Hugh and Lois's taste seemed so effortless, so all of a piece. Thirties, she guessed, in keeping with the jazzy railings outside and the long, horizontal windowpanes. While she and Tony, at enormous effort and cost, had managed to wreck their little Victorian house, to turn it into a soulless travesty of itself, all hessian wallpaper and twist-pile and Habitat light-fittings, in colours that matched Tony's tan-leather sofa. Yes, now she saw that the house was wrecked. And it was too late. Too late in every sense. It was over with Tony.

'No,' he'd said, when she asked did he think it was working. 'No, it isn't.'

No argument. No scowl. Waiting blank-faced for her next question, which formed itself easily, as if it was nothing important.

'And it's no good trying to make it work, is it?'

And again he'd said, 'No,' just like that.

His silence was awful. She'd broken it by saying, 'It's a terrible waste, but there it is.' Which seemed honest. But then she'd stopped being able to speak, or to look at him, and the tears had started, and the tears seemed like lies. So she'd got up from the bed and begun to pull on her clothes, feeling caged and closed in. 'I need air. Do you want to come with me?'

'Okay. Yes.'

And they'd abandoned the house, locking it in on itself, and walked to the common together. And, although there was a chill wind and she wasn't wearing a sweater, she hadn't taken his arm, and he hadn't taken hers. She'd hugged herself and shivered in silence. And he'd lit up a cigarette and circled it in his palm. And still he'd said nothing, walking beside her, staring into the distance. And gradually she'd understood that he never would say anything, because there wasn't anything to say.

The room had calmed, the greetings were done, small gaps were opening in the chatter, and a couple of people had successfully fished for general laughter. Jack Golding was singing the praises of a crate of claret he'd got dirt-cheap from Oddbins. Tessa was grumbling about having to miss *Fawlty Towers*. Sebastian sat forward, gathering his nerve, deciding to risk his anecdote. He cleared his throat and waited for Hugh Fairchild's pale, sandy eyes to meet his. Hugh was older. If he got Hugh's attention, maybe that of the others would follow.

'Something funny happened to me yesterday.'

'Oh yes?' Hugh smiled encouragement, pushing a loose strand of red hair from his forehead.

'I was ringing an old university pal of mine—'

'Which university?' interrupted Jack Golding in a rather belligerent tone.

'Cambridge.'

All eyes were on him. No way back now. 'So, erm, yes. So I rang this pal of mine, to invite him over for a curry, um, because I'm teaching myself Indian cooking.'

'Are you really?' said Ann. 'I'd love to have a go at that.'

'But Ann, French is the queen of cuisines,' said Tessa. 'Only the French know how to combine and bring out flavours.'

'So what happened?' Hugh's eyes held Sebastian's. 'When you rang your friend?'

Sebastian resolved to hold faster to the storyline. 'I was a bit taken aback, because I didn't get straight through to him. He's doing rather well, he's got a secretary, and she was, er, you know, all secretary-like and efficient. "I'll see if he's available" and "Who shall I say is calling?" Which threw me, and for a split second I forgot my own name. You know how you can do that sometimes?'

Zoë laughed. 'Yes, I know.'

'So I stumbled a bit and said, "It's, er, Sebastian Santini." And then she put me on hold, and when I got through my pal was laughing like a drain, because that's how she'd announced me—"Sir Sebastian Santini."'

Jack hooted.

'That's wonderful,' said Zoë.

'Brilliant!' cried Ann.

They were all laughing, and Horatio barked, and there was a flash as Lois took a photograph, for heaven's sake! Sebastian pulled in his stomach too late. He hated having his picture taken.

*

110

'Come on. Let's play,' said Ann. 'Let's cut for partners.'

Zoë drew a queen and found herself paired with David Pratt. 'Are you any good?' he immediately wanted to know.

'No, not at all.' She nearly laughed at his crestfallen expression. 'But hopefully I won't disgrace you.'

Tessa Golding tutted. 'I think it's dreadful how everyone has started to say "hopefully" when they mean "I hope". Another American import.'

Lois's camera flashed again as Zoë felt her face grow hot. More with anger than shame, but she could find no comeback.

'I dare say it'll be in the dictionaries soon,' Hugh Fairchild was saying. 'Language is always evolving. I don't hear the wrongness any more, though I did at first. I'm even beginning to say it myself, though—hopefully—I'll never write it.'

Zoë dared to look at Tessa, who was frowning and shaking her head.

'Actually, I'm indebted to it for one of my few original jokes.' Hugh stood on the knotted hearthrug, beaming and gesturing with his wineglass. Zoë could imagine him entertaining his students. 'I was browsing in the library, and I happened to dip into a thesis by an ever-so-slightly pompous colleague of mine. More pompous even than me. Sorry, than I.'

He met Zoë's eyes, and she tried not to giggle.

'And what should I see, shock, horror, amidst my colleague's erudite, silken prose, but the gruesome phrase, "to arrive hopefully at". And so, at once, tarrah! I uncapped my biro and wrote in the margin, "It is better to *travel* hopefully than to arrive."'

Everyone laughed, even Tessa, whose hand Hugh promptly picked up and kissed. 'But you'll note, Tess my love, I wasn't absolutist. It's not in my nature.'

He's genuinely kind-hearted, thought Zoë. Taking care of me, guiding me in; and looking after Tessa too, who was much less intimidating when she smiled: awkward yet stylish, like a giraffe or an elk.

'Dictionaries change a lot,' Ann was saying. 'I've had a

pocket Oxford since 1960. The other day I looked up "magus", but it wasn't there, and I found "masturbation" instead, as you do. And you'll never believe what it said.'

'What?' Jack Golding stole the question from Zoë's mouth.

'"Bodily self pollution!" Just that. Nothing else at all.'

Ann laughed and ran her fingers through her hair so it swung and shone in the lamplight.

Hugh shook his head. 'That wouldn't get a curious child very far.'

Zoë was fascinated. 'Did you look up any other rude words?'

She thought she'd spoken clearly, but Ann didn't seem to hear. Ann had decamped to the far end of the room and was sitting at the dining table there, looking disgruntled, shuffling and cutting cards onto the maroon-velvet cloth. Above her head hung yet another marvellous lamp: an octagonal glass bowl, glowing with soft light, divided by leaded veins into a patchwork of cream, gold and brown. Lois's camera flashed once again.

Zoë followed Jack and David down the room, leaving the others to play on the low table in front of the fireplace. 'So what other titillating words did you find in your dictionary?' asked Jack.

'Masses!' Ann leant forward eagerly. 'Back then all "virgins" were women, of course. And a "vagina" had something to do with botany!'

Zoë tried not to feel snubbed. It was understandable that Ann paid more attention to Jack. He was good-looking; she remembered thinking so at the party. Short but stocky, with solid, square shoulders, though there was a mean twist to his mouth.

'How about "sex"?' Jack grinned along the room as he gathered up his cards.

'Yup,' Ann giggled. 'Sex meant gender. Male or female. Not even a hint of hanky-panky.'

'Did you try "stork" or "gooseberry bush"?' called Hugh.

Ann shrieked with laughter. 'You've got the idea, Hugh my

112

lover! Growing up with that dictionary, no wonder I'm a late developer!'

Ann picked up her cards. They were lousy, damn it. And life was lousy too. She was bored to tears with how lousy it was. Her thirtieth birthday was only two weeks away, and her mother assumed she'd be having a big party, but everyone in London, even Lois, seemed to have forgotten. Pamela sobbed at her down the phone every blessed day. Lois was hard at it with Jack, neglecting her entirely. And Hugh remained immune to her overtures. Even a cuddle would be nice; couldn't he see how much she needed one? And then, in the hall, when she arrived, came Lois's unsettling news.

She'd sensed immediately that Lois was off with her. No hug, grin or kiss. Just, 'Did you know Charlie rang me today?'

'My Charlie?'

'*Your* Charlie, yes.'

'No. Should I have known?'

'He suggested dinner.'

'Dinner! With Charlie? How very grand. What brought that on?'

'I've no idea.' Lois's voice was cool and her face mistrustful above an uncharacteristically unsexy polo-neck. 'That's exactly what I said. "What brought this on?" He said you would know.'

'*I* would know?'

'Yes.' Icier still.

'Why on earth would he say that?'

'Because you've told him, Ann, haven't you?'

'Told him what?'

'About Hugh. About Jack. About me.'

How could she even think that? 'No Lois, I never, I haven't told anyone.'

'So what did he mean?'

'I don't know, Lois. I'm not his keeper. But I do bloody keep secrets.'

At last Lois smiled and held out her arms. 'Oh Ann, I'm

sorry. I thought you must have put him up to it.'

She'd accepted the hug, but through the affront a weird understanding was dawning. What exactly *had* she told Charlie?

'Did he say what dinner was in aid of?'

'Yes actually, he did.' The mischief was back in Lois's eyes, and sauciness in the swing of her blue-denim hip as she led the way down the hall. 'Which is why I can't think what he meant about you. He says he wants to go to bed with me.'

OCTOBER

Detective Stories

'You're the one person I can say this to, Ann. You have to promise not to tell anyone.'

Hell, not again. Ann forced a smile. 'Of course, Tess.'

Battling her way to the pub through an arid midday wind that stirred up black filth from the Strand and hurled it into her eyes, she'd been hoping that Tessa's summons was to discuss how to celebrate her thirtieth, but obviously not. She almost felt like draining her glass and leaving. She tapped at her cigarette, kicked at the barrel-table and let her attention wander. She couldn't stop thinking about Lois and Charlie.

'The thing is...' Tessa was unlike herself: all stop-start. 'This is bad. I shouldn't be sharing it. Maybe I'm wrong, Ann, and it will be awful, worse than awful if I'm wrong and I've told you. But I can't get the thought out of my head.' She hesitated, then spoke quickly. 'The thing is, I've begun to wonder about Jack.'

Ann focused. 'How do you mean?'

'I think he may be cheating on me.'

Ann concentrated on controlling her face muscles: widening her eyes, raising her eyebrows, aiming for surprise, disbelief, something like that. Tessa was watching her closely. 'What on earth makes you think that?' she managed.

Tessa frowned. 'I've no proof.' Ann held her breath. 'It's more the way he is with me lately. He keeps explaining to me, ever so carefully, where he's been, what he's done. Which you might think was a good thing, except he never used to do that, and why *is* he doing it?' She wasn't taking her eyes from Ann's for a moment. 'I'm not the jealous type, who needs every minute accounted for. And then, yesterday, he really upset me.'

Ann cranked her face into sympathy.

'As I say, maybe it's nothing, but... well... you remember I mentioned about a baby?'

'Of course.'

'So, okay, Jack may not be ready. It's a huge step, and probably the idea came as a shock to him. And he's entitled not to want a child yet. But that wasn't it—it was *how* he reacted. He seemed angry. He snapped at me not to be bloody daft. And that was it. No discussion—he changed the subject.' She was still observing Ann minutely. 'So what do you think?'

'Is that all?'

'I suppose so, but I'm only summarising. It feels like a weird change has come over him. Look, Ann, I'm no fool, no romantic. I know a marriage goes through phases, and these are still early days. I knew from the off that Jack would have feet of clay, and I've been gradually finding them, accepting them. That's what marriage is about—working together to deal with the differences. But that's it—he's not working *with* me anymore. His attention's away somewhere else.'

Just keep listening, Ann told herself. That's all she wants, someone to listen.

'And what's worse, Ann, is that when I let myself suspect him, I have moments of not caring, almost of being glad.'

'Really?'

'Yes, really. Because I'm *not* my poor, shackled mother, pathetic with self-pity. I'm thinking how it would be not to love Jack. Because, if he's cheating on me, I owe him zilch.'

She looked almost triumphant, but then her face fell. 'It's probably dreadful that I'm thinking like this, talking myself out of loving him. He's my husband. Maybe he's worried about something—he's doing some big buying and selling at the moment. Or maybe I've been trampling him with *my* feet of clay. I've asked him, and he says everything's fine, but... still.'

Ann was stuck. She should tell the truth, now, immediately. Brace herself for Tessa's fury. But she couldn't betray Lois.

Tessa was still talking. 'And it's not that you know about marriage, but I thought—'

'Pardon? What did you say?'

'Well, you know what I mean, Ann. You haven't been married, so—'

116

'So nothing!' She was livid. 'I was with Ed for years. And I've got eyes in my head, and *feelings*, God damn it.'

'Exactly. Which is why I thought maybe you'd know why he's acting like this.'

Sod her. Sod her to hell.

'You've really no need to worry.' She let the acid leak into her voice. 'He's perfectly happy with you. Plus he'd be an idiot to leave you, and he knows it.'

Tessa said nothing for a few seconds. Then, 'You're making me wonder if it's you.'

'Me what?'

'You that's having an affair with my husband.'

'Fucking hell!' Ann grabbed her bag and jumped up. 'I don't believe it. How dare you? I'm your friend, I wouldn't do that. Your friend, Zoë's friend, everybody's best mate.' She was spitting, she was so angry. 'But no one is *my* friend. It's my birthday next week and no one's even bothered to remember it, let alone stooping to have an affair with me.'

'Ann. You're right. I'm sorry. Please sit down. Let me get you another drink.'

When she came back from the bar, she took Ann's hand and said, quietly, 'Pamela?'

Oh shit. Ann added the tonic and took a quick swallow, before venturing, 'What about her?'

'Me. Zoë. You didn't say Pamela.'

'I was angry. Names come to mind.'

Tessa was shaking her head. 'It's okay, Ann. I understand.'

She was quiet for a moment. Ann froze, bracing herself to deflect more questions, but they didn't come.

'I knew it. I don't need you to confirm it.' Tessa's voice was alarmingly icy. 'I'm not stupid—I was hoping I was wrong. The way the silly bitch gawps at him, what more proof do I need? The whole thing makes sense, lots of little things. Your shiftiness about her. The sugary way Lois asks after her. The way Jack snaps whenever she's mentioned. And there they were, at our party, right under my nose—my husband and Pamela Harrison, whispering on the terrace. And all I could think was—poor Jack, waylaid by that ridiculous creature in her sprigged Laura Ashley, all ruffles and bows. Thinking nothing of it, the party so perfect.' Tessa's 'p's were explosive. 'Such paradise. Me and Jack so *fucking* happy.'

'Tessa—'

'Shut up. Don't betray any confidences on my account. You've all been whispering, haven't you? And laughing.'

'No, Tess—'

'Shut up, I said. You, sour with envy. Lois, smirking insufferably. Hugh, so unctuously kind.'

Sour with envy? Ann drained her gin, trembling with hurt, but Tessa didn't notice; she was too busy thinking aloud.

'Okay, now I know—so what's my next move? That's what I've been pondering. Kick him out, you might think, but I'm not so sure. What bullshitters men are—how naïve to think my husband was different. He's behaving the way men behave. And that's the point—that's what I have to figure out. It's women who are reinventing the world, Ann. I'm not my wretched, bleating mother. The difference has to be in me. Chucking him out is a cliché. Freeing him, victimising myself. When really Pamela is small fry. He'll be bored to death of her in no time and maybe, who knows, of the whole puerile game.'

'So what will you tell him?'

'Nothing.'

'Nothing?'

Tessa sat back and closed her eyes. Opening them again, she spoke slowly. 'He would lie, and I couldn't stand that. We would end up divorced. No, I'm going to watch and see what happens.' She glanced over at the bar, biting her lip, then muttered, 'I love him, Ann. And from a sea of bullshit, maybe he's still not a bad catch.'

This was where they met, Ann remembered.

'You're going to let him get away with it?'

Tessa shook her head. 'I'm going to even the score. I don't know who with yet, but I'll find someone. And then I'll get away with it too. Come on, drink to my success.'

Startled into obedience, Ann clinked her raised glass.

'He won't notice a thing actually,' Tessa said grimly. 'He's got something way more serious than bloody Pamela to distract him just now.'

'Oh yes?'

'I rang him at work this morning. Working at my marriage, God help me. Apparently there are squatters at Brecknock Road. He's worried shitless—so was I when he told me, but now... Ann, tell me honestly, why should I care about his problems? I've got a lover to find.'

Jack parked the Rover thirty yards from the house, then approached with fast-beating heart and a cold sweat breaking in his armpits. Fuck it, he shouldn't be nervous, he should be angry—no, calmly in charge, and the law on his side, though he'd have to check that out with the solicitor.

This shouldn't be happening. Squatters didn't bother with this kind of place, all freshly done up, the two top flats sold and occupied, the board for the third saying 'UNDER OFFER'. Squatters went for council slums, or for places standing empty, sliding into dereliction after some old biddy snuffed it. Not for his house, not for Brecknock Road.

It was Gary who told him. 'You'd better get round there, guv. Looks like they got in through the bog window. I guess Clive left it open.'

Clive, the central-heating man. A good worker, held out for his price, but fast and sure with no mess, and worth that bit extra to keep everything bowling along. Garden-flat plus freehold. Contracts exchanged. Completion date to be agreed, subject only to finishing off in Clive's wake. And to vacant possession, Jack supposed. Was that a condition? It was bound to be. It was certainly there, in the contract. Those words.

He didn't normally part with the freehold. He liked to watch his little empire of ninety-nine year leases grow, his ground rents begin to add up to an income, and to imagine, way down the line, his descendants come into a fortune. But the buyers had offered over the odds to have the freehold thrown in; it would have been stupid to say no. The estate

119

agent had rung him in Italy, 'You need to make your mind up quick,' and he'd made it.

He eased the key into the lock, let himself into the hall and waited, testing the silence. Despite his agitation, he had to pause to admire the quality of his work. The gracious, high-ceilinged vestibule with its gold and white décor. The oak staircase, painstakingly restored, leading the eye up to the flats above. He didn't deserve squatters. He wasn't some callous, money-grubbing, bodge-it-and-run developer. He'd earned his profit. He was doing London a favour.

Flat A was along beside the stairs, the original door stripped and waxed, embellished tastefully with brass. He paused to find the Yale key, then headed towards it.

He heard something and stalled. What was that? A soft gurgle or chuckle. Had they seen him come in? Fuck them, did they think this was funny?

He lifted the key to the lock. His property. His right to enter. Foolishly, he was unsure. Squatting was complicated; he should have rung the solicitor first. He mustn't use force, it might mess up his case; that much he knew from somewhere.

Listen, there was that chuckle again. As if whoever it was could smell his anxiety through two solid inches of wood. Which they couldn't. Nevertheless he drew back, lifted a hand, tapped with a knuckle, and waited.

Silence. The bastards.

'Hello?' He cleared his throat. 'I know you're there, I can hear you. Open up.'

Still nothing. Then the same mocking sound.

'Watch it, mate,' he said loudly. On impulse, he crouched and peered through the old keyhole, daring his tormentor to meet him eyeball to eyeball.

Beyond the door, on the floor, on a home-made rag rug, sat a baby waving a teething ring, hitting its fists together, then itself on the head, bouncing as if its nappy had springs, and grinning a gummy smile.

Jack straightened up, feeling foolish. He glanced behind him, but no one had witnessed his idiocy. So now, what to do?

He returned to the front doorstep, rang the bell for flat A for twenty or thirty seconds straight, then raced back. The baby was crying, he heard footsteps approaching and the door was opening and he had a toe in the gap.

'What the fuck?' said the young woman.

Down-market blonde, not bad-looking. Jack took a breath, preparing to charm her, but—

'No. Wait. Listen.'

Too late. While he was drawing the breath and widening his smile, she'd kicked his foot away and slammed the door shut in his face.

'Come on now. Be reasonable. I only want to talk.'

'Bugger off!'

Silence. Then scuffling. He put his ear flat to the door. She was lifting and cooing the baby, 'Come on, sweetheart.' And now her footsteps were retreating, along with the sound of its wailing and her grumbling voice. 'Filthy capitalist.'

Bullshit. He wasn't the bad guy here. This was his property. His livelihood. His key. Into the lock and turning.

Except, no, surely, please, it wasn't turning.

Pull it out, take a look, only one way up for it to be. Try again. Turn again. Fuck it, no go.

Straight Talking

'What do you think of it?'

Zoë raced into the bare, white, high-ceilinged room, taking in the explosion of autumn leaves framed in the massive bay of south-facing sash windows, breathing in the clean, dry smell of the place, feeling beneath her feet the springy boards, which told her with the certainty of an expert surveyor that there was no dry rot. It was every bit as wonderful as the first time with the agent.

'Isn't it beautiful. Isn't it huge?'

Only today the building society had said, yes, yes, yes. She ran into the bedroom, also empty. She would have to buy carpets, but she could afford them from the money that Tony had painstakingly agreed was her share of Balham and was increasing the mortgage to pay her. Not much left for curtains; she'd have to make them herself; but that would be fun. She'd sit here, on her own, or perhaps with a cat, sewing the curtains and listening to Desert Island Discs.

The sun came out and flooded the flat with light.

'Speak, Mick, speak.'

She grabbed his big hand, holding his thumb and small finger in her two fists, and pulled him from the entranceway into the bedroom. She nodded towards the bare boards. 'Hey, let's christen it.'

'I don't like it,' he said.

She reeled backwards, collided with a wall, slid down until her bottom hit the floor and sat open-mouthed. She laughed at him. 'Why ever not? What is there not to like?'

'This is it? Two rooms. I thought you wanted a garden.'

'Yes, but the garden flats are so gloomy. I can have boxes on the sills here, come and look.' She scrambled to her feet and ran to the window.

He remained stubbornly where he was, a big, ugly man scowling at a big, beautiful flat. 'It's not you. I can't imagine you here.'

'Of course you can. There'll be carpets and curtains. And a bed, Mick!'

'Yes. I know that.' He spoke slowly.

'So what kind of place do you think I should have?'

He stepped back into the hallway and pushed open the door to the bathroom. He hit the light switch, and the extractor fan began to hum. 'Where you are now,' he said finally.

'In Balham? With Tony?'

'Yes.'

'So it's not this flat. It's any flat?'

'I don't know. I suppose so. Yes.'

What was he saying? 'You don't want me to leave Tony?'

122

He came over to the window at last, stared out into the sea of red and yellow leaves, and grunted, 'No. I don't.'

'But why?'

He shook his head.

'You mustn't worry. I don't want you to leave Elaine. I won't start pressur—'

'Yes, yes. I know that too.'

He sounded angry. Didn't he believe her? She made him look at her.

'I'm not angling for more, Mick, truly. I don't want to live with anyone for a while. That's what's great about you and me.' She stood in the centre of the room and stretched her arms high and wide. 'I've never lived by myself. Don't you see?'

She stopped. He looked like a depressed gorilla. She'd never seen him miserable before. 'Mick. Tell me. What's the matter?'

'I love you, Zoë.'

'Yes, and I love you too, but—'

'And I thought we'd be lovers for years. But now, it'll change. You'll meet someone else, someone available, and it'll be over.'

She listened, watching his inky-blue eyes. There was no one else, she wanted no one else, and yet it was time to leave Tony. She would be here alone; her heart raced with excitement. She didn't want to feel sad or to fear for the future. She pulled off her tank top, unbuttoned her blouse, lifted Mick's hand and offered her breast to his fingers.

'Maybe so. Maybe you're right. But please, Mick, don't do this. Right now, I'm yours with no rivals.'

Slowly she unzipped her skirt, coaxing a smile from him.

'Come on. Show me what dreadful underpants you've got on today.'

'He's upset that I'm leaving Tony,' she told Ann in the office. 'He says I'll meet someone else now and finish with him.'

She was afraid of sounding boastful, but she wanted to

share everything with Ann; she couldn't stop herself, and Mick had unsettled her.

'What a nerve!' Ann blew smoke. She was perched on the edge of Zoë's desk, swinging a foot. 'What does he expect, a faithful little mistress sitting in a loveless marriage in south London waiting for him to drop by?'

'No, it isn't like that. He doesn't expect that. He's just...' Zoë tried to find words. 'Just saying what he feels.'

And, she might have added, her marriage hadn't been altogether loveless, and what was wrong with south London? But she saw, in a way, that Ann was right. She backed off the subject. 'Anyway, the flat is amazing. And mine!' She jumped up and seized Ann's hands. 'And it's wonderfully empty. I'll be in before Christmas. It's in Greencroft Gardens. You know, Finchley Road, behind John Barnes. You'll love it.'

'Can't wait.' Ann lifted an arm for Zoë to spin beneath, as if they were jiving. 'It's great that you've found somewhere. You'll have to have the gang round.'

Zoë stopped spinning. 'Really? For bridge? Do you think they'll come?'

'Of course. Why ever not?'

Incredible to think it was possible, to play host to Ann's friends! How fast her life was changing because of Ann: tossing her razor-cut hair, lighting her Benson and Hedges one after the other, filling the air with throaty laughter, pronouncing on things. Ann's blessing on the flat restored Zoë's happiness. She went back to her work with a sensation of joy.

She was transcribing the questions about gender stereotypes to a fair copy for the typists to work from. There was a huge amount to do, but she was enjoying every bit. By next week the final questionnaires would be printed and she and Ann would be briefing the interviewers. Ann said they'd do some interviews themselves, so they knew the hiccups at first hand. Zoë could hardly wait to be standing on the Aldwych, flagging down strangers and asking them, what did they think?

She completely adored this job. She couldn't get enough of ATP's coffee-smelling corridors and busy atmosphere, or of the neighbourhood around: the Strand, Drury Lane, the eclectic, arty streets and shops of Covent Garden. But most of all, she loved working with Ann. No, most of all she loved *Ann*. Because what was wrong with a word, or with this feeling? It was only a feeling. It didn't have to imply anything.

She wiped her biro; she didn't want blobs. The stereotypes kept making her smile. She had more opinions about them now.

Men are less faithful than women. Agree strongly, tend to agree, neither agree nor disagree...

Well, on her own recent performance, she'd have to disagree.

Women find it easier than men to speak their feelings.

Well, no, not really. Look at Mick, holding her eyes, telling her, 'I love you, Zoë. I don't want to lose you.'

She snuck a look across the room. Ann had pushed her shiny dark hair back behind her ears and was writing fast: a progress report for Rex Advertising. Pausing to puff on her cigarette, immediately writing again. Absorbed in her work, conversation done with for now, completely and mysteriously herself.

I love you, Ann. The feeling was there, and the words, but Zoë didn't dare speak them.

That's the difference, she thought. It isn't that women find it easier, it's that for women it's more expected, more okay. Except when it isn't. Then we're as tongue-tied as men.

Strongly disagree.

Ann lifted her head and smiled. 'How's it going?'

'Okay. These questions don't half make you think.'

'Fancy a cuppa?'

'Please.'

'My turn to fill the kettle.'

Zoë watched her rise, cross the room, pick up the kettle and leave. Why did people say 'I love you', she wondered. What was the point of saying it? To stake a claim? To be loved

125

in return? She and Mick denied such motives, but were both of them lying?

What could it possibly mean to love Ann? There was no reason to expect her to reciprocate. It might be unnerving if she did. With Mick, love merged into sex. Did she desire Ann physically? She tried to imagine it and found herself trembling with a weird mix of feelings: curiosity, fear, hilarity... Ann's return sent a thrill through her veins and the blood to her cheeks. She grinned in confusion.

'Tea or coffee?' said Ann.

'Coffee, please.'

Ann stood gazing out of the window, waiting for the kettle to boil. Zoë tried to imagine her naked. It was easily done. She could see the shape of a breast under the sweater and could guess where the nipple was. She could imagine the bare legs beneath the flared corduroy trousers, the breadth of the back between the hipbones, the descending cleft. She felt dangerous, and intrusive, like a burglar might feel. But not sexy exactly.

So, Mick, think of Mick instead, yesterday. Think of sitting astride him on the dusty boards, in the echoing flat. Think of his face and his body, his urgent erection.

A different sensation shot through her, contracting her stomach, pulling her knees together beneath the desk, and making her draw in her breath. It was different, quite different.

Ann turned from the window and smiled, and all at once Zoë remembered the duck in St James's Park. Miraculously other, making everything around it seem brighter.

I love you, Ann, she thought. Whatever on earth it means. I don't need to say so, or touch.

Spectator Sports

Tessa topped up Ann's glass. 'Thanks ever so much for coming, Ann. I know it's remiss of me, but I usually duck out of these parties. Alan starts playing his power games, I get riled, and before I know it I've sounded off to one of his spies. With you here, I'm safe. And now he's buggered off home, we can relax, let our hair down.'

'Yes. Let's do that.'

Ann was mellow and ready to flirt. She looked across the vast open-plan office to where Mick Galway was carousing with a crowd of giggling typists. Beyond them, slumped in a corner, was the excuse for the festivities: Rex's Client Services Director, whose last day this was. After the speeches he'd fast been forgotten, and now he was badmouthing Alan to anyone who would listen, while his face turned rapidly puce.

'Poor sod,' said Tessa, tracking Ann's gaze. 'People stopped caring weeks ago if he jumped or was pushed. They're more interested in who'll get his job. I know of course—I've had to send out the letters and sort out the salary and so on. But Alan's holding off telling anyone else. No one knows how to behave—should they wish Mick Galway luck, or will that piss Alan off?'

Ann detached a stray length of party streamer from Tessa's pinstriped shoulder and kept on looking at Mick. The typists were having no trouble knowing how to behave towards him.

'So will Mick get the job? You can tell me.'

Tessa had her mouth open to answer, but then pulled a face. 'Oh lord, here comes my obnoxious accountant. He might as well have 'spy' tattooed on his forehead. Say nothing about anything, Ann. Smile frostily.'

'Well, I never! Blow me, if it isn't *Mzzz* Golding. Are you real? May I touch?' He pawed Tessa's arm. 'Cinderella has come to the ball.' He turned to Ann, leering alcohol in her face. 'With fairy godmother in tow. The luscious Ann Wilton, if I'm not very much mistaken.'

'Brian, really, back off,' growled Tessa.

He swung back to her. 'Seriously, Tessa-baby, what brings you here? Is there a party-girl you've been hiding? Or, no, I get it. You don't want to go home to your hubby?'

He was stabbing in the dark, but Ann saw immediately why

127

Tessa, for all her toughness, was so easy to bully. Her face showed he'd got it in one.

'Hey up,' he said. 'Trouble in paradise?'

And Tessa was immediately out of her corner. 'Why, Brian, is that why *you're* here? Or no, sorry, forgive me, I'd forgotten. You've no one to go home *to*, have you? No one but Alan wants *you* to kiss their arse.'

Ann cringed. The man looked seriously offended. 'Fuck you, sweetheart.' He went off, shaking his head.

Tessa groaned. 'Oh dear, not safe after all. Brian is hardly going to parrot that to Alan, but he'll find other ways to discredit me.' She dumped her glass on a windowsill. 'Look, I'm sorry, Ann, but this is a mistake. It was stupid to think of finding a lover amongst this lot. Let's leave before I do any more damage.'

She set off for the lifts, weaving her way between the desks and room-dividers, rabbiting as she went, 'Where on earth *will* I find one? I can't advertise again. No shame in it, it's efficient, but it'd be wrong to pretend to be single. I'll come to the next ATP do.'

Ann stumbled after her, furious. It hadn't crossed Tessa's mind that *she* might want to stay. It was her birthday tomorrow, goddamit.

'Because the ATP men are worth thinking about, not like this lot. Sebastian, especially. Although, come to think of it, Sebastian doesn't seem the adultery type—his family are practising Catholics. And Charlie, of course, though he's far too fixated on you, Ann.'

'What? You're thinking of Charlie?'

'Yes. Prime candidate. But it would be so incestuous.'

Too damn right. First Lois, now Tessa.

'So, an ex-boyfriend, perhaps. There has to be someone.'

They'd arrived at the lifts. Mick Galway was there with the typists, who were clutching bottles to their chests. The sleeves of his shiny purple shirt were rolled up; there were dark patches of sweat under his armpits. He held a tray loaded with glasses of wine and bowls of nuts; his tie trailed from the back

128

pocket of his trousers. He grinned a big, crooked grin and flashed his blue eyes.

'Hi, you two. Fancy coming with us? Private party about to begin on floor seven.'

Ann opened her mouth to say, 'Great,' but Tessa was pushing the 'down' button. 'Sorry, Mick. We've had enough.'

The lift going up arrived. The typists began to crowd in. Ann was pissed off with Tessa; she stepped forward to join them; but Tessa grabbed her arm, pulled her back and cupped a hand to her ear. 'Of course, Mick would be fanciable in a gross kind of way, if he wasn't spoken for. Stunning wife—I've seen the photo. He said it wouldn't have been fair on his kids to marry someone as pig-ugly as himself.'

The lift doors were closing on the typists. 'Hey. Wait for me!' bellowed Mick. Someone inside pressed the button, the doors opened again, and he was backing in holding the tray at arm's length, shouting, 'Make room. Make room.'

'Oh my God,' Ann shrieked. Tessa threw herself at the lift, but too late. While Mick stood there grinning, the doors closed on his big, hairy wrists, so the tray twisted and the glasses crashed to the floor, and Tessa was left standing in a puddle of red wine and nuts, holding his hands.

The doors opened again. Mick didn't let go of Tessa's hands.

He smiled at her. She smiled back.

'Easy come, easy go,' he said, and pulled Tessa into the lift.

The doors closed. Ann watched the floor-numbers light up: five, six, seven. The lift going down arrived and stood waiting.

Hugh surfaced from a difficult dream. He tried to catch hold, but it sank unremembered, leaving him restless and vulnerable, beached in a new dawn. Opening his eyes, he saw Lois, asleep with her mouth open, her palm on his chest, and felt the familiar mix of luck and longing.

He turned himself carefully, so as not to wake her, and worked at memorising her features: the precise curve of her eyebrow, the position of each freckle. How fast a memory could fade. He could conjure his parents only from photographs now, and perhaps in dreams, though who knew what faces one saw in dreams? Lois's eyes trembled beneath their lids, and her lips moved. Was she dreaming of Jack Golding? His heart contracted with jealousy. He must steel himself to ask for a bulletin.

She told him nothing unless he enquired and everything if he did. Scylla and Charybdis. He would let tormented weeks pass, not wanting to hear. Then his imaginings would turn septic, would threaten to leak from him in bitter quips, and he would reluctantly stretch his mouth in a lying, light-hearted smile and say, 'How's your sex life?'

'Are you sure you want to know?' she'd answered the first time. And 'Yes,' he'd replied. Sure that he didn't, but surer still that he had to, for if he swaddled himself in ignorance, he would have nothing left of her at all. There was revenge in it, too. Jack took him for a fool, that much was obvious, but in a way Jack was the fool, unaware that Hugh even suspected, let alone that Lois regaled him with accounts of her lover's pretensions. The robbed that smiles steals something from the thief.

She opened her eyes. He kissed her nose, 'Good morning, petal.' Then he made himself say it. 'How's your sex life these days?'

She smiled and stretched, arching her spine on the mattress, so that her breasts flattened and offered themselves to his lips, giving purpose to his morning erection.

'I'm really glad you asked,' she said. 'I'm a bit out of my depth.'

He kept his voice light. 'Though still swimming strongly, I hope.'

'Oh yes. Across the Channel and back, covered in goose fat.' She smiled to herself. 'But you don't wish to know that.'

'No, indeed.' He shut his mind to the image. 'So what's the problem?'

She wound her arms around him and sighed. 'Well, I was going to say Charlie, but really it's Ann.'

'I'm listening.'

'Charlie's been ringing me for weeks. "Lois, meet me," he says. "Have dinner with me." And the first time, I laughed. I said, "*Dinner*, Charlie?" And he said dinner, a pub, whatever turned me on, because he wanted to go to bed with me.'

She was watching him carefully, but Hugh's first reaction was almost relief. Would she ditch Jack for Charlie? Please, yes. He could cope with Charlie.

'So I said, "What brought this on?" And I was trying him out in my head, you know, because he's really quite sexy. But he went quiet, so I said, "Don't be coy, Charlie, what brought this on?" Whereupon, all gloom and doom, he said, "Ask Ann."'

'Ann?'

'Which had me totally pissed off, thinking she'd told him about you and me. So I said, "Sod off, Charlie," and hung up, and got shirty with Ann, and then, oh shit, had to grovel, because she hadn't breathed a word. Apparently all, absolutely, she'd said to Charlie was, "Stop pestering me, you don't really love me, not like my best friend Lois and I love each other."'

'So why did he say—'

'Exactly. And that's what I mean about being out of my depth. Because why does Charlie suddenly get the hots for Ann's friend? I mean, it's typical of Ann to gush about love, and of course, we *are* best friends—at least we were until she got taken over by that little creep, Zoë. But it seems Charlie's imagination went into overdrive. Apparently he's convinced we're lesbians or something, and if he can't have Ann, he wants me instead. Which takes a whole lot of thinking about.'

Hugh was sceptical. 'Are you sure he thinks that?'

'Well, maybe not literally, but that way inclined. Anyway, whatever's going on in his tiny male brain, I'm still in a quandary, because he kind of belongs to Ann, and is it going to upset her if I sleep with him? Not everyone's as civilised as you, prawn.'

'Have you asked Ann?'

'Yes. The other day, we had lunch, and I put it to her

131

straight. "Suppose I give in to Charlie," I said. "Just for the hell of it, one more notch on my bedpost, would you mind, would you be cross with me?" And she said, "Of course not. Don't be silly."'

'So that's all right then,' Hugh heard himself say. Was he mad, cheering on one lover to drive out another?

'She was lying,' said Lois.

'Maybe not.'

'Hugh, take it from me, she was lying. And meanwhile, he keeps ringing me. "Lois. Meet me. A walk by the river." And I say, "Charlie, how many times?" "But I must go to bed with you," he says. And I say, "Be told, Charlie. Give it a rest." Because I don't need this complication. I'm getting sex by the bucket-load.'

Ouch.

'And then yesterday afternoon, he turns up on the doorstep.'

'Here?'

'Yes, here, and I'm saying, "Charlie, my darling, what's all this about Ann?"'

Suddenly Hugh wasn't cheering. Because he could tell from her face that it had happened, and the idea of 'here' was too awful.

'And he's not answering me. He's standing on the step, with that look on his innocent little face. You know,' she laughed, 'the get-your-knickers-off look. And I'm thinking, if Ann won't have him, she can't seriously object. And he's pleading, "Come on, Lo. Let me in." And he's shaved properly for once, I'm noticing, and put fresh whitener on his plimsolls.' She hooted. 'He's holding out a bottle of plonk, hopefully, like a ticket!'

Had Jack been 'here' too? Had Jack Golding been in his bed?

'And I'm fancying him like crazy, but there I am, barring the door, with my knickers still on, cross-examining him about his motives. And then, bang, I understand it, what's stopping me. Like it's actually insulting, don't you think, to be some kind of body stand-in for Ann?'

She seemed far from insulted, her eyes bright with excitement.

'But I was intrigued, and I could feel myself weakening, and, whoops, it must have shown, because he was through the door, and then there was no stopping him.'

'He forced you?'

'No, rubbish, I caved in. He was kicking the door shut, dumping the wine, propelling me along the hall. All I had to do was navigate! In less than a minute we were at it, with nothing but my knickers off!'

Hugh managed to hold his voice steady. 'In here?'

'No, in the front room.'

The image sprang in his mind. He couldn't help seeing it. The big, square, white sofa, beneath the gold-framed, Victorian painting. The two of them copulating like a randy sailor and his moll.

He recollected himself. 'Okay. Charlie. So... does Jack get his cards?'

She stopped laughing and looked at him. 'Are you okay, prawn?'

'Of course I am, petal.' He hoped he was a better liar than Ann was.

'Are you sure, because...' She flashed him a smile full of mischief. 'Well, when you said a dozen other men would be okay, you didn't say one at a time.'

NOVEMBER

Playing Away

'This has got to be the perfect relationship.' Zoë grinned at Mick across her pie and chips. 'I get to see you just enough to look forward to it, and I don't have to wash your socks.'

They often met in this pub near Paddington Station before Mick boarded the train home to Reading. His mouth was full of pie, so he smiled and nodded and raised his glass. His face floated before her in the warm light: radiant, benign, no longer in the least bit ugly to her, each feature endearingly his own.

She took a swig from her Guinness. 'And you get to seduce any woman you want and to tell me about it.'

He'd just told her about Tessa Golding, which was a surprise. Tessa seemed so strait-laced and judgemental; it was weird to hear that she could kneel provocatively on a hotel bed, sliding the strap of a black-silk petticoat down over her muscular white shoulder. Mildly aroused, Zoë felt the thrill of a voyeur, which made her ask suddenly, 'You don't tell them about me, do you?'

He shook his head, grinning. 'No way.'

They were back to being easy together; his dread of losing her to a host of single suitors seemed to have receded. And today he was cock-a-hoop about landing the promotion to Client Services Director.

'You really don't mind about other women, do you?' he said.

'Not in the slightest—they're fascinating. Each one is so different—from me, from each other.'

His smile broadened. 'It's why I'm addicted. It's not the sex—it's the women. How can I stop sampling?'

He reached across and took her hand. 'Although sometimes, I mind that you don't mind.' He paused, as if wanting her to say something. 'And then I tell myself, come on, Mick, you can't have it both ways.'

'Exactly,' she nodded. 'This is the way love should be, not spoiled by jealousy and lies and suspicion. As I say, perfect. And once I'm into the flat, we can do all the domestic stuff. You can even sample my cooking, though that really is risky!' She raised her fork. 'Safer to stick to pub meals.'

'I'll stay often,' he said. 'New job, new duties, I'll tell Elaine. Out-of-town client meetings, crack-of-dawn starts, late-night kowtowing to Alan, that kind of thing. She won't mind—it'll soon be routine.'

Zoë laughed. 'What more can I want? Oh yes,' she remembered, 'there is one thing, but don't worry, I'll manage without.'

'What's that?'

'Nothing you can help with.'

'Try me.'

She wasn't sure she should say this. 'A holiday. I've been nowhere since my washed-out honeymoon in Wales.'

He put down his Guinness and looked at her. 'So let's go on holiday.'

Was she hearing him right? 'Are you mad?'

'Maybe.'

'But how could you swing it?'

'A management course. A conference abroad.' He gathered her ankles between his under the table. 'When shall we go, foxy lady?'

'You're serious?'

He was nodding, but it didn't seem real.

'In the spring, I suppose,' she said, 'though right now would be nice. Life with Tony's no fun, waiting for the flat to come through. We don't row, but it's like living in a morgue.'

Mick reached beneath the table and slid his hand up her thigh. 'Cornwall in winter,' he said. 'Have you been?'

'Are you kidding me?'

'We'll take the train. Watch out for me salivating on the platform at Reading.' They were both laughing. 'I'll fix it with Elaine tonight. A client visit should cover it. We'll have to go

Monday to Friday—I can't swing a weekend at this notice. Next Monday suit you?'

'Mick, you're wonderful!'

He took a swig of his pint and sat back. 'Cornwall's great at this time of year. No tourists and it can be sunny. But bring your mac.'

'The weather's no problem.' She chased brown sauce with her last chip. 'We'll find plenty to do if it rains.'

In Cornwall a north-easterly gale blew relentlessly, battering against their window at night and making them regret the fine view of St Ives Bay for which they'd paid extra. Massive waves smashed in white-green smithereens against the little granite-block cottages. The lighthouse in the bay failed, and the pubs were full of knowing locals yarning of old shipwrecks and lives lost at sea. They bought cheap cagoules and tried to explore, but after a while they felt stupid hanging onto the harbour rail and slipping on the wet cobbles. So they retreated back to the pubs or, in the afternoons when the pubs were shut, to the coffee shops.

Not to the hotel bedroom. Because, without explanation, Mick seemed altered. He didn't show much interest in sex. Or in talking, or flirting, or laughing. With no warning, he'd become a stranger, his eyes focusing elsewhere each time she smiled into them, reticent, terse, almost as though he were angry. By Wednesday morning he hung broodingly over his breakfast, scarcely responding to the things she said.

He'd been animated on the telephone to his children the evening before. She'd watched across the crowded, steaming bar as he stooped in the narrow alcove, his mammoth shoulders quaking with laughter at the jokes he shared with Ben and Florence, and perhaps with Elaine too. Now, watching him rearrange the sugar for the twentieth time, she said, 'What's the matter?'

'Nothing.'

It wouldn't do. 'You don't want to be here,' she told him. 'You want to go home.'

'Yes.' His face relaxed. 'I'm racked with guilt. I don't know why. It makes no sense.'

It was good he was talking again; that was what mattered. She took his hand.

'It's okay. You must do what you want, what you think is best.'

She spoke the words because they were true, not because she wanted them to be. She had no hold over him. She'd thought she did, but now she saw that she didn't.

They climbed glumly back up the stairs to a room that briefly and irritatingly blazed with sunshine. They packed, and checked out, and took a taxi to Penzance.

'Now I'll be racked with guilt about you.'

'No. Don't. Please.'

She stared through the cab window at the silhouettes of St Michael's Mount and Penzance, black between the malevolent Atlantic swell and the gloomy charcoal sky, and struggled to make sense of her feelings. They'd been so certain they knew what they were doing, so sure they were safe from hurt and confusion.

They couldn't speak about it in the train because a mother and toddler shared their compartment. Zoë welcomed the respite. Across long, wild, Cornish miles, she did nothing, thought nothing, only pretended to read; or watched the mother help the little boy to colour his picture-book: a blue sun, an orange-and-green-striped pig; or tried to guess at Mick's thoughts behind his paper. Was he really immersed in the Queen pushing buttons to start North Sea oil or the new Viking Mars probe?

As they crossed the Tamar, the little boy began asking, 'Are we nearly there?' and his mother pacified him with promises of seeing Daddy. The thought that Mick was 'Daddy' to Ben and Florence made Zoë wistful; but why should that be? Was she envious of people with children? She blanked her mind, inviting a maternal itch to surface, but it didn't. It made no sense. If she wanted a child, she could finish stripping the wallpaper in Balham and stop taking the pill. One day perhaps, but not now. She was feeling envy, or something very like it, but it wasn't envy of motherhood.

Despite all protestations to the contrary, had she been hoping Mick would leave Elaine? From behind her book she watched his dejected gaze slide over the huddled grey roofs of Plymouth and dared herself to suffer the pangs of unrequited love. But no, she hadn't been kidding herself. She loved Mick, a lot, but the pleasure really *was* in loving him without needing more.

So why did she feel so wretched? The train sped on through the November rain. She gazed out across the vast, open sea at Dawlish. It was a fretful, muddy green, and bounced up and down angrily as if pulled by myriad strings.

Mother and child left the train at Exeter. Zoë watched Daddy greet them on the platform, sweeping his son off his feet and whirling him round before setting him down, kissing his wife and picking up their suitcases.

She and Mick were alone now.

'Nothing's changed, Zoë,' Mick said. 'I still love you. I didn't realise how this would affect me. I feel such an idiot.'

He looked tired. He needed a shave. She found words. 'It's okay. No bones broken. I just need to think a bit.'

'Nothing's changed, Zoë,' he repeated.

This time there was a hint of a question in his voice, the flicker of a pleading look in his eye. Of course, she realised, this was what she'd lost in Cornwall: her power over him. Now that she felt it returning, she had a strange aversion to it; she hardly wanted to pick it up again.

'It's okay. Don't worry.'

She understood that one of her emotions was humiliation. How stupid she would feel when she saw Tony this evening— 'Lover boy let you down, did he?'—and Ann tomorrow—'Oh, poor Zoë. What happened?' Was image part of what she wanted from Mick? Look at me, taming this powerful man? She looked at him now, grey-faced and frayed around the edges, and felt ashamed of herself.

They were free to talk, but neither of them did. The

darkness closed in as they sped through Somerset and Wiltshire, the window becoming a shadowy mirror in which they exchanged wan smiles. At last the train halted, waiting for the signals to change to let them into Reading. Mick rose to get his luggage from the rack. Meeting Zoë's eyes, he attempted a wink and a grin. Funny, she thought, the nearer he comes to his family, the warmer the looks he gives me. She understood something new about him. He was like that child, happy as long as his mother was in sight, but bereft when she disappeared for five minutes to nip to the loo.

At last Zoë understood the distress that had been clamouring all day to be named. And yes, it was envy, but not of Elaine. It was Mick she was envious of, of his bond with Elaine and his children, which his actions belied and he never mentioned. She wished she felt that way about someone.

She remembered now, he did mention it. Almost his first words to her back in July, smiling seductively across the Oxford bar table, were, 'I'm happily married.' And Mick didn't tell lies; the word 'happily' wasn't there by thoughtless accident.

What nonsense, to say he didn't tell lies, because he did, all the time, to Elaine. But not to her, she was sure of it. That was her privilege, to know the truth about him: what he did, what women he slept with and lusted after, how he felt about them, how he felt about her and her break-up with Tony, and now how he felt about Elaine. Elaine knew next to nothing, could barely imagine the reality of the man she lived with. Yet it was Elaine who had his commitment.

The train jerked and began to move into the station. He towered above her, his face a crumple of anxiety.

'It's okay,' she repeated, finding a smile. 'I'm fine. I'll see you next week. Shall we have lunch on Monday?'

He bent and whispered in her ear, 'You're a very special lady.'

Zoë smiled. It was his favourite seduction line. She sat stiffly, staring ahead, waiting for him to go.

'And I do love you.' His lips brushing her ear.

She turned, grazing her cheek on his stubble, and kissed his big mouth. 'Yes. Bye then. I hope everything's all right at home.'

He was gone. The train pulled silently out of Reading. The dark winter afternoon slid by the window. Black puddles, pocked with rain, reflected strip-lights. Overhead telephone wires, gathered to wooden poles, dripped in the gloom. Backs of terraced houses. A discarded washing machine. A posh conservatory. Climbing frames. Pollarded trees. Jigsaw puzzle lawns.

The day's unshed tears pressed at her sinuses. No one could see. They began to loosen, to well into her eyes.

But then, no, she decided to fight them. She made herself open her book. It was borrowed from Ann, who said it was wonderful, she absolutely must read it. *The French Lieutenant's Woman*. She focused on the print through the blur of tears, and blinked until the words stopped swimming. She forced herself to pay attention. She read the first sentence several times before she took it in, and the second too. But gradually, as the motion of the train rocked her, she was hooked. The lump in her throat dispersed. It was a story of shame, and when, occasionally, she surfaced from it, she remembered her own shame with amusement and almost looked forward to brazening it out, to laughing about it with Ann.

She felt proud of her self-control. Her mouth, reflected in the rain-streaked window, was widening into a true smile, because she'd had a startling thought. It was possible to decide to be happy. Through all her old heartbreaks and her marriage to Tony, she'd never discovered this. She vowed not to forget it.

Playing Dirty

Jack couldn't get enough of Lois. In Hugh's bed, in Tessa's bed, on the back seat of the Rover with the blood dinning in his ears and the rain drumming on the roof. There was nothing she wouldn't do, or try, or show him, no risk that she refused. She dared him further each time, and he was drunk on her licentiousness, craving more danger, a more exquisite thrill.

The images sang in his brain and rendered him semi-permanently erect. He saw her propped, splay-kneed, on the edge of his worktable in Bartholomew Road, her head thrown back laughing, while the boys hammered upstairs. Or in a dark shop-doorway in Kensington as rowdy pub-leavers ambled past, hooting with comprehension of what they were witnessing. 'You should have worn braces,' she murmured. 'It's such a waste of a hand, holding your trousers up.' Or in that telephone box, for fuck's sake, across the street from the flickering window where Hugh watched some highbrow crap on TV. And, God help them, last week in Ann's tiny, mildewed, avocado bathroom, a drunken, hilarious quickie when they both happened to be dummy and six other people played out three-no-trumps and six-clubs-redoubled in the living-room. He had let out an orgasmic yodel as the others erupted into cheers and howls over the last trick. He'd left Lois sticky and giggling, burst triumphantly in, brazenly met Hugh's eyes and asked, 'Did we make it, partner?' 'Yes,' came Hugh's answer, 'Yes,' and he'd whooped with glee.

Because wow, what excitement! He hadn't felt this physically ablaze since he was fourteen. He woke in the night wanting more, nuzzling up to Tessa, persuading her to move her heavy, protesting limbs and let him in, slumping back afterwards into unconsciousness punctuated by sensual dreams.

Waking or sleeping, he could think of nothing but screwing. Even Brecknock Road wasn't bothering him like it should be. The solicitor had asked him to find out the squatters' names. It would get him to court faster, and make the outcome more certain. So he'd been back four times now, lying in wait for the postman, hoping for letters addressed to flat A, asking the other occupants what they knew, which was damn all, sliding notes under the door and ringing the bell with no answer. So he ought to be frantic, because time was passing, and the sale was on hold, and the buyer's solicitors were getting nasty, and Gary and the boys were running out of work, and he'd need the cash soon to exchange on Lady Margaret Road, which he couldn't let go, he just couldn't. But the solicitor said, not to worry, his rights weren't in question; and rather than fret it was easier to pour a dram or three of the emergency scotch, grab his dick and push the boundaries of his imagination. Because Lois, oh Lois. Witch, trollop, hussy. She didn't half want it, and boy was he giving it to her. At last a woman to match him in appetite and daring, and no asinine talk of love to clutter up the fantastic sex.

But today was a touch disconcerting. He wasn't quite sure he liked it.

They were in Fulham—Hugh was at the university—and the surprise turn-on seemed to be silence. Lois opened the door to him unsmiling, finger to lips, wearing only a bathrobe, her face naked without makeup, and motioned him to follow her, past the closed kitchen where the dog snuffled and half-barked, straight to the bedroom. Which wasn't exactly inviting. The bed was stripped to the white undersheet and the ceiling light was on. But Lois dropped her robe and lay on her back, legs apart, naked, expressionless, not saying a word.

He faltered, hit by the need for a drink. 'Wait. Let me open the wine.'

He escaped to the kitchen to fetch corkscrew and glasses, patting the dog's head and shutting him in again. Back in the bedroom, he pulled the cork, poured two glassfuls and downed a swallow of the rather nice claret he'd brought. She didn't touch hers. She motioned to him to put it on the bedside table. Then she lay there and watched him, almost coldly it seemed. He took another swig and reached for the wall switch. 'Can we have this off?'

But she shook her head sternly and mimed zipping her lips. Then she tossed her curls, flipped onto her hands and knees and waggled her bare arse at him.

And suddenly, whatever she was doing, it worked. He was

142

seized by more lust than he could imagine relieving. He was shedding his clothes and positioning the wardrobe-door so he could watch himself in the mirror, and his face was into her fanny and his hands were clutching her swinging breasts, and they were away. The quiet was exciting now, and the harsh light made it seem dirty. He imagined he was acting in a porn movie, the camera running behind the mirror requiring him to show muscle and inventiveness and staying power. Which he did, but her silence still challenged him, so he flipped her onto her back and set about teasing her, bringing her near, then leaving her dangling, trying to make her beg.

She didn't utter a sound, but when finally he brought her off he could tell it was massive by her arching and her facial contortions. And then he came too, flat out on top of her, heart racing a hundred and sixty a minute.

'Oh boy, wow, fuck, that was good!'

She heaved him off and reached for the kitchen roll. 'If you say so.' She threw him a piece and began mopping herself with another. 'But now, pay attention, Jack. That was the last time.'

'What?' And why was she scowling? 'Come again?'

'You heard me.'

Then immediately she was pulling on clothes, dark curls popping through the polo neck of a red sweater, legs sliding into blue jeans. He waited for the smile, the 'got you' chuckle. It didn't come.

'I don't follow. What do you mean?'

'What I say, Jack. That's it.'

'Just like that?'

'Just like that.'

'But it was you who set this up. Didn't you like it?'

She shook her head. 'That's not the reason.'

Stubbornly unreadable. He could feel his teeth gritting.

'So... tell me, you've met someone else?'

She laughed. 'What if I have? Anyway, that's not it either. I'm going to stick to Hugh for a while.'

'To Hugh?' She couldn't be serious.

'Yes, to Hugh. My husband. Any objections?'

He reached for the wine and took a gulp straight from the bottle. 'What about us, Lois? What about what we've got?'

'And what's that exactly?' She sat on the end of the bed, brushing her hair.

'Sex.' Hadn't he just proved it? 'You love it. You lap it up. And Hugh's a great bloke, but don't try to kid me he's sexy.'

She glared at him. 'What would you know?'

'Come off it. You're telling me Hugh's good in bed?'

'I'm not telling you a thing about Hugh. Or about me for that matter. And you're wrong about me.'

She was staring at her knees, pulling at the bristles of the brush. In the nape of her neck, her hair was fine and short, damp with sweat. Jack moved up close and breathed in her ear. 'I know you inside out.' He lifted the back of the red sweater, began to lick the nobbles on her spine, tasting the salt.

'Lay off!' She leapt apart from him, landing between the wardrobe and dressing-table mirrors, so that he could see dozens of her receding reflections. 'You don't know me. Not at all. You only know what I show you. And I'm finding sex a bit tedious, if you want the truth. A bit of a waste of time. There are things I'd rather be doing.'

'Oh yeah? Like what?'

'Like trying to sell my photographs. Or reading a good book. Or being nice to Hugh. Or shopping for dog food.'

He laughed. She was joking. 'Look, okay, so you're in a bad mood. Your period's due or something.'

'Piss off, you creep!'

She wasn't joking. He started to reach for his clothes. 'Okay, be a bitch.' How dare she do this? 'I think you'll find the thrill of sedate shagging to snippets of second-hand Shakespeare won't last. When you need me, you know where I am.'

She stepped closer, spoke quietly. 'You're nowhere, Jack.' Then she turned and went out, leaving the door open behind her.

Fuck her.

'I'm in your husband's bed, that's where I am,' he shouted,

stuffing his shirt down into his jeans. 'At your most urgent invitation, sweetie.'

He upended the bottle again.

She came back. Stood in the doorway.

'And you've had a good time crowing in my husband's face. So now you can fuck off.'

DECEMBER

Playgroup

Zoë took an afternoon off to go Christmas shopping in the West End. Armed with a list, she was determined to be businesslike, then get home early to cook Tony his favourite dinner: a mixed grill with mushrooms and peas. The solicitor had rung, she had her completion date; she'd be gone in two weeks. She would try to break the news gently to Tony, who'd been so understanding, letting her stay in Balham, letting her feel already free, keeping his pain to himself. Too understanding, really: sometimes she wished he would curse and complain so that she could comfort him. Except she couldn't, of course. Someone else would eventually do that, get him growling and grumbling like before, wheeling out his old Hancock act.

She'd been nearly an hour in John Lewis and bought nothing. She was doubting the list and getting into a state. Christmas was impossible: perfect gifts didn't exist, and imperfect ones wouldn't do. Scent for her mother: how could that make up for the shame of having a daughter headed for divorce for no sensible reason? No ideas at all for her father, who was barely speaking to her; he handed the phone abruptly to her mother whenever she rang. A set of chisels for Tony: for what, so that he could spend months doing up Balham on his own? Even the John Denver for Mick. *Annie's song* was their song. He would take it home, play it, enjoy it. And yet. And yet what?

After Cornwall they'd continued much as before, but something was gone. The word 'love' had a different quality now. From his mouth it sounded more like a plea than a pleasure, and in her own it felt like reassurance.

John Lewis was too matter-of-fact, a great place to shop with a list in your hand, but her list was dead. She abandoned the store, wove her way through the festive crowds that clogged Oxford Circus, and dived into Liberty, where people wandered more slowly, lulled by the sumptuous displays, breathing in the scents of musk and rose and leather. Dozens of lovely, inessential objects began begging her to buy them, for themselves, for the pleasure of taking them home. She found herself torn between miserliness and extravagance, one minute counting her pennies, remembering all the John-Lewisey things she would need for the flat, the next driven to assuage her guilt with generous purchases.

On impulse, she bought a small glass cat made in Russia. It fitted, heavy and smooth, in her palm and glowed with refracted light. It cost far too much. It was a precious thing that she'd love for herself. Her mother would appreciate it, might even cherish it. She might think in years to come, my daughter gave me this treasure.

Buying it reminded her to be happy. She paused in Liberty's doorway, watching the shoppers muddle by, their breath steaming white in the dark. Ann said they used to put up fabulous Christmas lights in Regent Street, but they'd stopped because of the cost. With new resolve, she set off and quickly tracked down the John Denver, the chisels, some socks and a tie for her father—he could stuff his disapproval—plus a chunky red ashtray for Ann to match the grey and red office. Emerging from the last shop, she saw an 88, caught by the traffic-lights. She leapt aboard as it took off and bounded up the stairs, flushed with achievement.

Rain was suddenly bucketing down; the bus was a submarine. Small boys, eight or nine years old, raced about the top deck laughing and shouting. And all at once she was grinning with anticipation. Tomorrow was yoga night, extra special because they were meeting Mick afterwards. She was bringing them together, Ann and Mick, and what she saw in each, the other would see too, without fail. Drink would loosen their tongues, and happiness would be as easy as breathing. Mick and Ann might even fancy each other. It was quite likely; she ought to think about that. And yes—was she

147

mad?—she almost hoped that they would.

She grinned. Would these gifts be perfect: Ann shared with Mick, Mick shared with Ann? The rain was still pelting, the little boys still racing and shouting. Be happy, she told herself. Be generous. Be brave.

Ann watched blearily as Mick came back across the bar with yet another round of drinks clutched to his chest. Two glasses of red wine, three bags of crisps—they hadn't made it to the chippy—and a half of something for himself. He'd been sitting across the table before, next to Zoë, but now he slid in on her side, up close though there was plenty of room on the seat, and gave her what seemed to be a private smile. She grinned back. There was no doubt about it: the pressure of his thigh was intentional.

'That looks like gnat's piss.' She scooped a finger into his drink and licked it. 'Eugh, shandy!'

'You never drink shandy,' said Zoë.

He had his hand on Ann's leg now. 'Well, I thought, maybe someone should stay sober.' He moved the hand to the hem of her skirt. 'To find the way home.'

His fingers separated her knees. Good decision not to wear jeans. She slumped against him, feeling his heat. 'So when *is* the last train to Reading?'

He grinned. 'I'll stay in town. Often do. I warned Elaine not to expect me.'

Zoë was smiling blissfully, her eyes half-closed. Either she hadn't twigged what was happening, or she was too drunk to care.

'Will you book into a hotel?' Ann asked him.

'It has been known.'

'Yes, it has,' echoed Zoë.

His fingers had found her knicker-elastic. Good decision not to wear tights. She leant forward to conceal what was happening from Zoë, and that was it, a finger slid into her body. She gulped wine to cover her gasp.

He was reaching for Zoë's hand across the table. 'Great

idea, meeting up,' he said. 'One of your best.' The finger slid out again, in search of her clitoris. She remembered Lois and Jack on the grass. 'You're a very special lady, Ann Wilton,' Mick whispered, kissing her ear.

Zoë was grinning and wriggling on her seat. 'You're indefatigable, Mick. You'd never believe the game we play sometimes, Ann. We sit in a pub, watching people, and I say which women I think he would fancy, and guess at his points out of ten. Are we depraved, or what?'

'Not at all,' he said, employing more fingers. 'What's depraved about appreciating the finer points of women?'

Ann was laughing, and squeezing his fingers. Zoë gave a little shriek, 'Hey, Mick, you'll get us arrested.' His thigh tensed against Ann's, she discovered his empty shoe by her foot, and she suddenly realised where his toe was.

The rat. But how funny. Inside both their knickers.

He raised his glass. 'To women!'

'To sexy men!' said Zoë, raising hers.

'To sex!' said Ann. And then, 'Look, bugger a hotel. Do you want to come back to mine?'

She hadn't planned it much further, and then, when they got there, it went out of control. After a few grinning minutes in the living-room, they were pulling her into the bedroom, and stripping off her clothes. And there she was under the blankets, reaching for Mick. But Zoë was naked too, and in the tangle of activity, some of the hands were Zoë's, cupping and stroking her breasts. Mick was snogging her, his erection was nudging her thigh, his thumb was working her clitoris and his fingers were deep inside her. But Zoë was wrapped around them both, her breasts against Ann's arm, and was kissing her face. Mick was trying for a three-way French kiss. Ann rolled away to escape it, pulling Mick with her, angling her hips at him, grabbing his penis, trying to guide it towards her. But Zoë clung leech-like, her arms tight round Ann's shoulders, clutching Ann's breasts. And Mick wouldn't start fucking; he was still playing finger games, sitting back, watching and rubbing her clit. Which would be fine, because he knew what he was doing, and his fingers were massive, there were two in there now. But the catch in Zoë's breath showed he was doing similar to her, and even that didn't stop Zoë from pawing Ann, her hands on her buttocks now, her mouth exploring her spine.

She wriggled free of Zoë's attentions, pulled Mick into her and locked her legs tight around him. And yes, at last he was fucking her, though he kept trying to stop, damn him, trying to pause, to include Zoë, or to transfer his fucking to her. But now Zoë was murmuring, 'Yes,' and adding her weight and her rhythm. And Ann's orgasm was building, and so was his, too, she could tell. He'd stopped thinking and stage-managing, he was just fucking and fucking, and her feet were bouncing the bedclothes to the floor, and here she went, flying up on sensation on a long, indrawn breath. And then she was yelping, and she didn't care, and, 'Oh brother,' he grunted, 'here it comes, yes, yes, yes, *yes!*'

She barely slept. Three in a bed was hot and uncomfortable, especially for the one in the middle—they took it in turns—and always someone was twitching or shifting position or beginning to snore, or getting up to fetch more water or to go for a pee. The alcohol had dumped her, and the headache was starting. And the mortification. Why on earth had she done this? What the hell was she thinking? It seemed an adventure, dangerous, outlandish; but it was sordid. And what was Zoë playing at? Was she a lesbian, or turning fancy tricks for Mick, or what? And what was Mick's game? Christ, she felt manipulated and cheap, and furious with herself. Was she so sex-starved she was supposed to be happy with Zoë's leavings? She was on the verge of screaming and kicking them out of her bed. But how could she explain it? They were still so attentive, half-wakefully stroking and nuzzling her. And she was damned if she was going to let them know how she felt.

At last Zoë was asking could she have a shower and slipping naked from the bed, her body a glimmer and her red hair a greyish tangle in the dawn light. And the sense of being with Mick alone had barely time to register before he was stirring himself to smile and to kiss her, whispering compliments, looking into her eyes, going to a great deal of trouble. And despite noticing the bald patch on his head and the hair on his shoulders, and despite knowing she must look a wreck, she was letting it happen again, giving herself up to his stale, sexy smell, parting her knees, feeling her body take over and fly, wanting him and the sex, but all the while knowing that Zoë went for her shower so this could happen, some form of blasted politeness; and even as the orgasm massed and exploded, she sensed misery and shame waiting to swallow her.

The towels were damp and the silvering on the mirror corroded. Behind the mirror, the cabinet was a jumble of grimy bottles and potions: Mogadon, Anadin, Milk of Magnesia, a rusty tin of Andrew's Liver Salts.

Zoë consulted her troubled reflection and wished she'd brought a toothbrush. She wasn't a lesbian, she knew that now, but still she felt rejected by Ann, who'd scarcely even tried when it could at least have been friendly and fun.

She was shivering from lack of sleep. She wrapped one of the towels round her, more cold than damp perhaps, and tiptoed across the hall. A freezing draft from under the front door gripped her ankles.

She wouldn't get back into bed. She'd find her clothes and take them into the living-room. She'd get dressed and have something to eat. She peered round the door.

The room reeked of sweat. There was a moving hump in the bedclothes. She sprang back into the hall, feeling violently confused, then stood there, her jaw rigid with cold, at a loss to know what to do next. What she'd glimpsed seemed a strange, almost alien, activity.

They were going to have to eat breakfast together, she, Mick and Ann. They were going to have to travel to work together, find things to say, meet one another's eyes. Yesterday that would have been a pleasure.

She went into the living-room and lit the gas fire, then huddled on the brown-cord sofa and stared through the French window at the grey morning. She wished she could undo what she'd done.

Confession

The shame gathered weight, darkening Ann's vision and ringing in her ears. She couldn't bear to look at it or touch it. Somehow she'd negotiated Weetabix and the Northern Line and parted awkwardly from Mick on the Strand. But she was still trapped with Zoë, to whom she couldn't trust herself to be civil. Thankfully there was no bridge this evening, but there was a day of work to be endured before she could go to ground for the weekend. A day of avoiding Zoë's eyes across the office, of sidestepping her anxious attempts to reconnect, of skirting the subtext in their discussions of the Rex survey results, all the while dimly aware that her moral queasiness couldn't be blamed on Zoë, or Mick Galway: it was herself she couldn't stomach.

The afternoon crawled by. It became one of those lousy days when nothing could possibly be accomplished. Sapped of energy to make the paper on her desk move or mean anything, she was reduced to watching the clock. At six minutes past three, Charlie trailed in, carrying a wodge of computer printout and looking as morose as she felt. 'There's dozens of errors in this batch,' he said gloomily. 'Want any help sorting them?'

The sight of him cheered her. 'Volunteering, Charlie? Isn't that against your principles?'

'Oh, I don't mind this stuff—it's like the crossword. And... well,' he gave her a mournful look, 'you know.'

Yes, she knew. He wanted to be with her. He'd had Lois, yet he still wanted her. It warmed her; she felt grateful and fond. 'A prime candidate,' Tessa had called him; maybe she should take him more seriously.

He spread the printouts on the table, and she pulled up two chairs. Error hunting was Zoë's job, but Zoë was busy churning out a rough draft of the report, and anyway, sod Zoë, let her be the odd one out for a change.

Charlie leant close, explaining the errors he'd ringed. His knee bumped against hers, his curls brushed her ear. He didn't seem predatory, just in need of comfort the same way she was. She spotted more inconsistencies. They got the stacks of questionnaires from the cupboard, tracked the mistakes down and corrected the codes. Mostly punching errors or respondents giving contradictory replies, nothing wrong with the questionnaire logic.

Charlie made a list. 'I'll drop it round to Computing now, if you like. They'll whinge about "time-slots on the mainframe" and all that bullshit, but if I act impressed I reckon they'll do it by Tuesday.'

'Thanks, Charlie.'

She smiled at him. He smiled back. He made no move to leave.

'Tea, anyone?' When Zoë got up to switch on the kettle, Ann experienced an uprush of pure bile.

'No thanks,' said Charlie, still looking at Ann, and Ann shook her head, 'Not for me,' still looking at Charlie. Zoë went out, to the loo presumably, good riddance, as the kettle began to roar.

Charlie leant confidingly close. 'D'you know what I heard this morning?'

'No. Tell me.'

'I'm going to be an uncle.'

'Hey, wonderful! Your sister?'

'Yeah. Feels kind of weird though. Uncle Charlie.'

'You'll enjoy it.'

'Do you think so?'

'Absolutely. I adore my nephews and nieces.'

They made her feel old. Charlie was looking out at the chimneypots. He was getting crow's feet, she noticed. She remembered Mick's bald patch. Everyone got old.

She glanced at her watch: ten to five. 'Charlie?'

'Yeah?' The crow's feet were nice.

'Do you fancy a drink when the pub opens?'

He looked startled, but pleased. 'I shouldn't. I only made it in at eleven. But you're the boss, eh?'

In the pub, she drank doubles, and Charlie became amorous.

'Can I come back to yours, then?'

'What? Oh no, Charlie. I've had quite enough of that for now.'

He looked stung. 'Enough of me,' he corrected her.

'Enough of falling into bed with just anyone when I'm pissed. The hangover's chronic—it's doing my head in. Even more drink doesn't cure it.'

He shrugged her hand from his shoulder and scowled. 'So that's how you think of me.'

'What? Hey, that rollup's a disaster. Have one of these.'

She gave him a ciggie, then leant to share his match.

'Just anyone. That's how you think of me.'

'Not you, Charlie. I didn't mean you.' Remorse made her soppy; she wound her arms round his neck. 'I'm rotten to you, aren't I?'

'Yes, you are.' He looked suspicious. 'Who else have you been falling into bed with?'

She wanted to blurt everything out; but the whole thing was so shitty. 'Oh Charlie, it's so... it's... oh God, no, I can't.'

'Can't what?'

'Don't shout.'

'So tell me.'

She leant in close again. 'If I do, you've got to promise to understand. Not to laugh or pull faces.'

'Okay.'

'And say nothing to anyone.'

'Fine. I promise.'

She stared at her cigarette.

'Hugh, is it?' he said.

154

'What makes you say that?'

'I've seen you pawing him.'

Her eyes sprang with tears. 'Hugh wouldn't make me feel like this.'

'So who then?'

'I shouldn't say—it's a secret.'

Though why the hell should she keep Zoë's secrets?

'I won't tell,' he repeated.

He detached the cigarette from her fingers and put it in the ashtray, where she saw there was already one burning. He put his own in the ashtray beside her two. He leant near. He took hold of her hands.

'Zoë,' she said. 'Bloody Zoë and Mick Galway from Rex. They're having an affair, that's what I'm not supposed to tell. We got plastered last night and ended up back at mine.'

Charlie's eyes narrowed. 'You went to bed with this Mick bloke?'

'With both of them—and God, it was horrible.'

She picked up the shorter of her cigarettes and dragged on it hard. 'It felt exciting to start with. Daring. I was pissed—we were laughing. And then, eugh, all night and this morning and, oh Charlie, it's freaking me out—they were *using* me.' She scrubbed out the cigarette and picked up the other one. 'Just like everyone does.'

'Zoë?'

'Yes.'

'You and Zoë had sex?'

'Not exactly, just both with Mick Galway.'

'Fucking hell.' Charlie sat back, grinning, then leant forward again. 'So, what did you do?'

'What?'

'With Zoë. You know, to each other?'

For a moment, she didn't understand. Then, 'For Christ's sake, Charlie!' She was up on her feet. 'You just want to lech! No. Stop it. Leave me alone.' She squashed the second cigarette. 'I'm going.'

She steered an uncertain course across the bar to the

155

Ladies.

When she got back, Charlie was counting his change. 'Can you lend us a quid?'

'Oh bloody hell.' She rummaged for her wallet and extracted a fiver. 'Here. A gift. And take these rotten things too.' She pushed the Benson's packet across the table. 'And a kiss, why not. They're cheap enough.'

She landed it unsteadily, somewhere near his nose, then headed for the exit.

Knocked out by the booze and a Mogadon, she dreamt she was terribly afraid. She was in some futuristic flat, nowhere she knew, double-locking the door against the threat. The door was flimsy and had clear glass panels. No key could protect her. There was a light on the landing outside, but down the stairwell the darkness seethed. She ran to the window and found she was hundreds of feet up. Beneath an angry indigo sky stretched a vast cityscape of other flats, like a colony of seabirds on a cliff, precarious in a wasteland. The wind sucked at the glass. She swung back into the room. He'd be here any minute. She sobbed in panic. The phone, of course. Reach it. Dial it. Nine, nine, nine. And yes, she was through. 'Police. Police.' But what could she tell them? He was coming, but who? And what did he want? To steal, murder, rape her? She didn't know. She screamed and dropped the receiver. A man stood in the open doorway. But it wasn't him.

She woke up, inhaled the sour smell of Mick Galway on her pillow, remembered everything and let out a yelp.

Hidden Truth

'I hope it hasn't been a complete waste of time, Zo.'

'Not at all. You mustn't think that. My life was a mess, and you helped. It's your time that's been wasted.'

Tony shook his head. He was wearing his baggy painting

trousers and an old Viyella shirt that she liked. 'Come on then,' he said, 'we'd better get loading. Big things first.'

Her junk-shop wardrobe dismantled into two pieces: a mirror-fronted hanging-cupboard and a base with a large drawer. Tony eased the cupboard free and slid it forward. Together they lowered it to the carpet.

Zoë loves Tony XXX

Oh God, she was there: in her old flatshare, a mug of coffee on paint-splashed newspaper, singing along to Capital Radio as she worked white gloss into the wood grain of the wardrobe, dreaming of happy-ever-after. And then, when she finished, squeezing the dregs from the bristles onto the unpainted back. *Zoë loves Tony XXX*

Tony said nothing, just hefted his end of the base. She picked up the other and followed, along the landing and down the uncarpeted stairs. Bent awkwardly, struggling to keep up, she had to say something. 'It'll always be true. I'll never paint over it.'

He met her eyes and looked grateful. They were passing through the front door. This shouldn't be happening; he shouldn't be helping her move; she would have managed somehow. He should be cantankerous, not kind.

Glancing at next-door's bay window as they manoeuvred the base into the van, she saw Mr Nosy duck back out of sight. Tony would have the Nosies to deal with tomorrow, sidling up to him on his way in or out. 'Getting shot of some furniture, were you?' Heartless, insistent, requiring him to mutter through his teeth, 'We're separating.'

Back upstairs again. 'Wait,' she said. 'It's best this way round.' Rotating the cupboard so the Nosies would see their reflection and not her graffiti. And Tony didn't ask why or argue.

The next bulky item was the bed, the old double her parents donated. Zoë grabbed her end of the mattress, avoiding Tony's eyes.

'The symbolism is deafening,' he said, and they both laughed.

The rest was easy. The van was loaded in no time, and they were away, cruising towards the river, then over it, leaving south London behind. Perched high in the cab beside Tony, watching Belgravia go by and then Hyde Park Corner, it hit Zoë that he would leave. They would get to Greencroft Gardens and unload the van, and when it was empty he would close its back doors and climb into the cab and drive away.

Unloading the van took a while. It was tricky, hauling the mattress, the bed base and then the wardrobe up round the awkward bend and hard left into the flat. The two, high-ceilinged, bare rooms seemed barn-like and unwelcoming, and chilly until Tony got the boiler going. They dragged their feet with the smaller stuff, but in time it was done and he was carrying up the last box. And there was little point in going up with him, because she would only have to come down again to say goodbye. She hovered uselessly at the foot of the stairs, clutching the newel post with tears in her eyes.

Here he came. Tears wouldn't do. 'Thank you for this, Tony.'

'I wanted to make sure you were all right.'

She blinked hard, then grinned and pushed her fist against his chest. 'You're a good person.'

'So are you.'

He put his arms round her. She leant, head on hands, feeling his ribcage beneath the Viyella, and the beat of his heart.

She broke loose, held the banisters instead. 'I'm sorry. This isn't easy. You'd better go.'

A rev of the engine, a wave, a hired van turning the corner. The end of a marriage, and on into the next minute. She climbed the stairs, stepped through the door and let it click shut behind her. She exhaled a breath she couldn't remember taking, and listened.

Nothing. Only the hum of the boiler. The emptiness began to drum in her ears. The solitude she'd dreamed of was palpably here. There would be no sound unless she made it; no object would move unless she touched it; there was no

158

significance unless she gave it.

The transistor radio was on the floor by her feet. She crouched down, switched Capital on. 'GALILEO!' Too much noise; turn it off. The boiler hum was enough.

She sat back against the door for a while, watching and listening, then made a decision to move, through the silent air, to the wardrobe, to look in the mirror. A young woman looked back at her, marriage just ended.

What was this feeling? Not sadness, exactly. But the power to choose happiness seemed pointless, the summer visions used up. She'd lost something with Mick, ruined something with Ann; but even these discomforts were muted. Because she wasn't in love: not with Tony or Mick, or with Ann or this flat.

'We won't always be dropping in on each other,' Ann said on Friday night.

They'd been strap-hanging on the Northern Line again, travelling to Highgate to play bridge one last time before Christmas, and whatever Zoë tried, Ann wouldn't or couldn't chatter or laugh like she used to, and Zoë had been trying to cut through the unease with talk of her move and how near to each other they'd be.

'No, Ann, of course not.'

Wounded, but accepting the snub. Understanding it. Resolving in that moment never to call uninvited.

Because she was changing too. She pressed nose against mirror. Now, when she saw Ann suck on her ciggies and wave her arms in the air, she remembered the sound of her wheezing lungs in the night and the smoker's stink of her breath. And Mick too, he was trying so hard to please her, and he meant it, but all his moves were practised: that was what she was noticing.

It wasn't their fault. Everyone was at it; she was at it herself. Learning tricks: *Zoë loves Tony*, fist against chest, *You're a good person*. Using tricks to charm others, to con herself that she was okay. When there was no way to be true than to stand in an empty room.

159

JANUARY 1976

Guessing Game

Hugh watched Lois sleeping; it was getting to be a habit. He would like to stay here all day, snuggled beneath the eiderdown, the way they used to in Brighton the first winter they were married, reading and talking and making love, getting up to fetch food or to have a bath together, the taps bruising his spine, her body shiny with soap, her face pink with sex and steam. But soon he would have to brave the cold, ride a jam-packed, misted-up bus to Gower Street and have another go at persuading young people to ponder the meaning of moral statements, when, quite rightly, they'd rather be having baths with each other. What a daft way to earn a living.

The tip of his nose was an icicle. Outside it might have snowed, but he thought not. The curtains weren't luminous; there wasn't that cathedral silence. And here came the wind, rattling the windows, stirring the dead leaves in the yard. Oh God.

He must ask soon about Jack, about Charlie, about whomever else. He must brace himself to bear her replies and renew his stoicism. For he began to have bloody thoughts. How could he help it when that bastard swaggered back from Ann's bathroom with the sexual triumph dripping off him, pretending comradeship, insouciantly asking, 'Did we make it, partner?' Thinking to outplay him in irony! The bitterness had found its way out of his mouth as he drove Lois home that night. The macho racetrack down Park Lane had seemed like the final insult.

'Quite the roaring boy, Jack. Don't you find him a bit of a bore?'

'I don't talk to my lovers, you know. I just have sex with them.'

He'd glanced across at her nervously as he played dodgems

round Hyde Park Corner. She sounded angry, and quite rightly. It was a breach of his promise to show his hurt like that. Swinging into Knightsbridge, he'd forced a chuckle and come up with some wisecrack about how, to her, sex was a pleasure as trivial as a boiled egg with Marmite soldiers. But she didn't soften.

'I barely say a word to them. It worked in Italy, so I thought I'd try it in London too.'

He chuckled again. 'Don't they mind?'

'Mind what?'

'Not being talked to.'

'They don't notice. Most men don't notice if you don't talk to them. Just keep smiling and nodding and pretending to listen. It'll never occur to them.'

Her tone was acid, and then she fell silent, withholding speech from him too. *He* noticed; it occurred to *him*. Not a word all the rest of the way. Punishing him for breaking his promise. The game was up, this was it: she would leave him. Locking the car, he broke cover. 'Oh, Lois, please.'

She was climbing the steps ahead of him to the front door. She turned and looked into his face with startled eyes, as though suddenly comprehending his hidden pain. 'Hugh?'

He had nothing to tell her.

She looked at him. She didn't smile. She spoke deliberately. 'Listen. Believe me. I never, ever, discuss you. If they start to ask, I shut them up. If they dare breathe a word against you, they're out.'

Maybe it was Jack she was angry with? Find something to say. 'Do they know that I know?'

She shook her head. 'It's none of their business.' Stared abstractedly at the wood of the front door. 'It's you that I love.' Turned the key and went in.

Freeze the moment forever. He'd wanted to live in it.

She was half-awake now, her eyes open, dark blue like the unseeing eyes of a newborn. He formed the words in his mind: 'How's your sex life?' and realised he could make them a proposition. Nice idea; he tried to will his body into action.

She came fully awake, biting her lip and staring at the ceiling. She was withdrawn from him lately.

He smiled and said softly. 'So, how's it going, petal? Who's the man of the moment?'

'No one.' She frowned at the ceiling. 'There's no one just now. I'm having a rest.'

'Not Jack?'

'No.'

'Or Charlie?'

'I've finished with both of them.'

He should feel pleased, but he didn't. She wasn't happy; she wasn't meeting his eyes.

'Why? Why did you finish with them?'

She looked at him. 'Well, Jack, you know—nasty bastard. It was that evening at Ann's. I came back from the bathroom and saw him practically doing a victory dance, leaping around, fists in the air. So clever, getting away with it. Everyone, even Tessa, thinking it was the slam he was gloating about. And you, smiling, pretending to be congratulated. Looking straight at me.'

Oh, Christ. He cleared his throat. 'It's okay, Lois. My promise stands. In Ann's bathroom, in this bed, with whomever you choose. I won't mind. I don't mind.'

'Hush,' she was telling him, 'it wasn't you, Hugh, it was me. Jack's a wanker, and I thought, what the hell am I fucking him for!'

He breathed more easily, trying to take it in. It was over with Jack. It was over with Jack. And he had survived it.

He put his arms around Lois, struggling to conceal the euphoria; but she didn't hug back.

'Hey,' she said, 'you know those squatters of his? Tessa told me last week, the buyers are threatening to sue. Turns out they're a property company with stroppy lawyers, while Jack's guy's a lazy sod, went off ski-ing for Christmas. So he's no nearer getting them out, doesn't even have a court date, and he's gone and exchanged contracts on something new and doesn't have the money. He's in a complete stew about it,

162

apparently. Serves him right.'

Interesting. Gratifying even, but was she changing the subject, steering him away from something more dangerous? He spoke carefully. 'Maybe... yes... though I wouldn't like to see him ruined.' He paused. 'So, tell me, what about Charlie?'

She was examining the ceiling again, sighing. 'I don't know. He was good fun. Amusing. And sexy in a male-chauvinist-piglet sort of a way. Endearingly off-hand—wham, bam, thank you ma'am. And he likes you, says you're "an okay geezer". But as I said, it's Ann he wants and, I don't know, I started thinking.'

She broke off. He waited. But she didn't go on.

'Thinking what?'

'Well. That it's you that I want. You know.'

That moment again: he was rising on a cloud of bliss. He hugged her more tightly, hoping at last to carry her with him.

She didn't come.

He spoke the reality. 'But I'm not enough for you, petal.'

'No, you're not.' She sighed softly. She was looking straight at him; he tried not to flinch. 'But for now, prawn, you are. I'm hibernating.'

Yes. Good. But she looked miserable.

'You seem unhappy without your lovers,' he said bravely.

'Oh, I expect it's the weather.'

Her tone was abrupt. And then she was gone, rolling from the bed, onto her feet and out of the room in one smooth movement, grabbing her dressing-gown. Averting her gaze, ducking his questions. He wasn't enough for her. He never would be. Horatio lumbered onto the bed and licked his face. 'What's happening?' Hugh whispered. 'Is it over? Will she leave us?'

The dog snuffled and thumped his stubby tail on the eiderdown.

Ann might know.

That evening when her doorbell rang, Ann was on her second gin and tonic, dousing the January blues. Christmas back home

163

had been okay, she supposed. Hard labour, because it was she who'd done most of the cooking while her mother faffed about with holly and silver paint, her sisters and sisters-in-law ran after the kids, and her father and brothers sat about with pink faces. There'd been some carping and niggles, but no actual bloody rows, at least not among the adults. It had been comforting and frightening in the way that Exeter always was, provoking a blend of yearning to go back and start her life again and dreadful certainty that she could never be different because this was where she started. She'd told Hugh about it in the kitchen at bridge on Friday, and he'd listened, then sighed and said, 'Those are the two things we learn from our family—how not to be and who we are. It's the paradox we never escape.'

The bell made her jump, and then cringe. She didn't want to answer it. She considered lying low, pretending not to be in. It was probably Pamela wanting to whine on about Jack; she couldn't take much more of that. It got her speaking of Ed, and then the old grief started up again, which was so futile; but Pam enjoyed nothing better than a good mutual wallow. She peered from the living-room to see the shape behind the glass.

A man.

She went down the hall. Opened the door. And there he stood, with his lovely smile and his straggly red hair. On his own. 'Hugh!'

What on earth did she look like, still in her work clothes and probably stinking of gin?

'Annie, I'm so glad you're in. Do you mind? Is it inconvenient? There's something rather private and personal I need to ask you.'

When he was explaining himself and Ann started to make faces, at first Hugh panicked. 'What is it? Has Lois met someone?' But then, as Ann's desperate brightness gave way to tears, he grasped how insensitive he'd been.

'Annie love, I'm so sorry. I shouldn't have come like this. I've made you think—'

'Yes.' She pulled a grubby, disintegrating tissue from the side pocket of her trousers and blew her nose. 'I've thought it for months. You know I have. And you never do a thing about it.'

He'd been more than insensitive; he'd been unkind.

She paused in wiping her nose and looked at him, her eyes softening with hope. His instinct was to put his arms round her, but he'd done quite enough damage as it was. He stepped back.

'Annie, let me speak plainly. It's nothing personal. You're wonderful, and lovely, and I love you, of course I do.' Was this true? What did it mean anyway? 'And I take no moral stand on this kind of thing, far from it. I've just decided somehow, I don't know when or why, that I'm not in the game. I'm Lois's for as long as she'll have me. Boring, I know, but there it is.'

'Even though she—'

'Yes, even though. It's the deal we've struck. She's enough for me, but I'm not enough for her. She hurts me, but she doesn't deceive me, Ann. And look at me now—deceiving *her*, asking questions behind her back. And hurting you as well. I'm so sorry. I'm just frightened, she seems horribly down, and I'm terrified to ask why, afraid she may leave me. And it was a long shot, but I thought you might know what's on her mind.'

He hated himself for asking again.

Ann flung the soggy tissue at an overflowing wastepaper basket. 'I can't begin to imagine. If I were Lois, I'd be counting my blessings. She doesn't fucking know that she's born.'

'Maybe she does, Ann. Don't be too hard.'

'She's got a lovely, loyal man who worships her.'

'No, look at me, I'm useless.'

'Well, *I* wouldn't complain!'

Ann's anger and misery filled the small room: nicotine emotions, soaking into the walls and furniture. He spoke tentatively.

'I don't think Lois does complain exactly, Ann.'

She was immediately contrite. 'No, I'm sorry. She's never

said a word against you. She loves you very much. I'm being a complete bitch, that's all.'

'No, Annie—'

'Yes, I am. I'm turning all cynical and bitter. No one ever seems to love me like you and Lois love each other. I thought Ed did. But then he went, without saying why. And now he's married, and they have a baby. And all my sisters and brothers are married and having babies.' Her face contorted. 'Tell me what's wrong with me, Hugh? It's like I'm cursed. There's some dreadful thing I can't see that everyone else can.'

'Ah don't, Annie. Please don't cry.' Hugh felt helpless in the face of her grief. He found a Kleenex box on the sofa, pulled a couple of tissues from it and brought them to her. 'Don't lose heart. There's nothing wrong with you. You just haven't met the right person.'

She shook her head violently. 'Don't give me that. I'm done with the fairytale. I've waited for my prince to ride up, and he hasn't, Hugh, and I'm thirty years old. There must be something I'm doing wrong.'

Thirty when he met Lois, forty-one this year. 'You seem fine to me, Annie. As fine as anyone. I guess we each carry a glass slipper and I got lucky, finding the foot that fits.'

'Well, someone needs to give my sodding prince a map.'

Now that she was giggling, it was possible to hug her. Hugh realised for the first time how much he liked to have Ann's face pushed against his chest and the smoky smell of her glossy brown hair invade his nose. How selfish he'd been, accepting her hugs, allowing her to think they meant more.

She was speaking his thoughts. 'Oh Hugh, this is nice. Please don't stop. I don't want this to change.'

'I do love you, Annie.'

It was easy to say it, now that she understood. And yes, no question, whatever it meant, it was true.

Solitaire

Sometimes, when she got home from work, Zoë found a small cat, mottled charcoal and ginger, sitting on the front garden wall. 'Do you want to come in?' she would ask it politely, and the little cat followed her up. She never gave it food or kept it for long, because someone would miss it. But after investigating its gender, she gave it a name—Prunella—and pretended for five or ten minutes that this was her own pet on her knee, purring and stretching and licking her hand with its rough pink tongue.

The carpet was fitted now. She'd spent most of Tony's cheque on it, mindful of her father's advice that it paid to invest in quality. She'd chosen heavy-duty twist-pile, eighty-percent wool, in a khaki colour that wouldn't show stains and that would set off the acres of white wall. The day it was laid, she closed the door on the fitter and ran from one newly sumptuous room to the other and back again, finally flinging herself headlong and rolling about, flexing the pile with her fingers and feeling euphoric.

Comfort and quality seemed the most important things now, worth stretching her budget for. She'd blown a scary amount of money on a duck-down duvet from Heal's, leaving barely enough for curtain material from John Lewis, reduced in the January sale. Everything else must wait. She had the necessities: the double bed, the round white table and four pine chairs that fell to her in the division of the spoils, a cooker and chuntering fridge that came with the flat, her sewing-machine and a black-and-white telly. There was a laundrette nearby. She worked out a tight budget, saving a little each month towards the next luxury: a hi-fi system. There was just one more thing, she decided, that couldn't wait, that had to be classed as a necessity.

In the silence that fell after the children raced shouting into the street, an immense feline sat upright, perfectly and unnaturally still, regarding her. Its pupils, dilated in the dim room, rendered its eyes as full of prophecy as crystal balls. Daunted, almost embarrassed, Zoë lowered her gaze to consider the pincushions of fur below the pink and black spotted nose. From the pinpricks emerged an impressive fan of whiskers of elegantly varied length. Eye contact broken, the cat lifted a paw and began to lick it.

'Thank you,' she breathed. 'I would like to have him.'

'He's called Tommy,' the woman said.

'Oh.' The pretentious names—Maurice, Pirbright, Bootle—she'd been considering flew out of her head. 'Hello, Tommy.'

She scratched behind his ears, and he closed his eyes and pushed up against the pressure of her fingers.

'Won't you miss him?'

The woman shook her head. 'No. We're dog people really. Anyway the kids are set on a dog now, and Tommy's a terror with dogs. They don't stand a snowball's chance.'

The curtains were vast: six of them, each eight feet long and seven feet wide. It had been a struggle to carry the material home on the bus. A William Morris print, a creeper and flowers, turquoise, blue, violet and olive, plus yards of ivory lining and a string of lead weights to put in the hems. With so little furniture she could spread the fabric on the floor to check before she made the first cut.

Tommy inspected everything, sniffing the pin box, batting the reel of tacking cotton, and unerringly choosing to curl up heavily on the piece she next wanted to sew. While she cut and pinned and tacked and sewed, she talked to him, telling him her life story and how beautiful he was. He listened attentively, one ear cocked to her voice wherever he happened to be.

Sometimes she was overcome with adoration. She took her foot off the pedal mid-seam, crossed the room, turned him on his back and blew into the fur of his stomach, draping him in her hair. He rewarded her by purring and stretching his arms above his head, letting her tickle his armpits before abruptly signalling that enough was enough and rolling away.

She worked on the curtains every evening, finishing and hanging them one by one. Tonight she'd triumphantly hung number two in the bedroom, giving her privacy at last, and was kneeling on the floor, half-listening to the radio, pinning number three, when the doorbell buzzed.

Who on earth? Mick was at home tonight, definitely, and the people in the other flats wouldn't ring, they'd tap on the door. Could it be Ann, breaking the ice at last? Zoë unhooked the entryphone nervously. A masculine voice crackled in her ear.

'Hello, Zo. It's me.'

'Pardon? Who?'

'Charlie. Charlie Evans. Can I come in?'

In Vino Veritas

'I regulated my ingestion of fluids rather injudiciously last night.'

Charlie groaned as he unwrapped his cod and chips.

Hugh tried to meet droll with droll. 'More than usual?'

They were in Hackney, slumped in disintegrating armchairs on either side of a sticky plywood coffee-table laden with bottles of Newcastle Brown. The gas-fire was on full, and the window streamed with condensation. Horatio lay sprawled on the sofa, his snores competing with mournful strains of 40s jazz. His doggy smell mingled with the aroma of salt-and-vinegar and unwashed socks. Sebastian was away, visiting relatives in France.

'Nah, I'm standardly injudicious these days,' Charlie conceded, crunching a pickled onion. 'It depends how much of the readies I've got, though. Spot of luck, you turning up. I'd run low, what with Mussolini being inconveniently absent and all my other creditors shunning me.' He began wolfing the chips down, four or five at a time. 'The pub's stopped cashing my cheques, and the fridge has become inconsiderately empty.'

Hugh was here to stop himself fretting about Lois. Hanging around her looking for ways to please wasn't aiding his cause one bit. This is the way to kill a wife with kindness. The heart-to-heart with Ann had him ruminating on how complex people were and how little he normally bothered to understand them, and he'd resolved to take the subject up as a sort of hobby.

Calling on Charlie seemed an easyish way to begin. Not that Charlie was simple. The challenge was that everyone thought he was and he played up to the image. No, the odd thing was that he liked Charlie. Though it hurt to imagine this scruffy Adonis naked with his wife, he had to admire his cheek. And Lois had mentioned that Charlie liked him.

Of course it was possible that a discarded lover's cheek wouldn't stretch to sharing a few beers with the husband, and Hugh lifted the phone with caution. But far from being nonplussed Charlie leapt at the offer, so here they were. Hugh gazed about him at the filthy, littered flat, which surpassed Lois's descriptions and grainy black-and-white photographs. She hadn't shown him any snaps of Charlie's bedroom; he struggled not to imagine it.

'Cheers,' he said.

'Cheers, mate.'

'Is this how you and Sebastian spend your evenings?'

Charlie snorted. 'Well, old Mussolini's a bit on the judicious side. He cooks a mean curry though, so I can't complain.' He tossed the empty chip paper over his shoulder, sat up straight and set about the manufacture of a roll-up.

'He seems a good chap,' Hugh offered. 'A true cosmopolitan. Plays a crafty hand of bridge too.'

'Totally fucking insufferable, as I say.'

Charlie let out a sudden groan. Hugh was baffled. 'He's not that bad, surely?'

'What?' Abstracted. 'Oh... no... Mussolini's okay. I'm just lamenting coz I do. I find it helps until the booze takes hold.' He upended the bottle.

'So what's the problem?'

'Oh, you know. Same old story. Ann.' He erupted into a Tarzan howl.

'And hasn't...' Hugh hesitated before deciding to go for it. 'Well, hasn't any other lady been able to help?'

Charlie lowered the bottle and looked at him.

Hugh allowed a short, uncomfortable pause. Then, 'It's all right. I know about you and Lois.'

Charlie's eyes widened. 'Hey... mate...'

'No, really it's all right.' He recited his formula. 'I love her, but I'm not enough for her. She's unfaithful to me, but she doesn't lie to me.'

'Hey, I like that.' Charlie shrank head into shoulders and affected an American drawl. 'Jus' like Annie and me.'

It was impossible to be cross with him. 'That's Bogart, isn't it?'

'Yeah. He's who I should have been.'

The dregs of jealousy drained away. Hugh felt a foolish joy. 'I know what you mean. With me it's Shakespeare. Well, Marlowe actually,' he confessed to deaf ears. 'People don't understand. They think I'm pretentious.'

'Yeah.' Gloom. 'Annie told me it's junk.' He had a faraway look. 'She won't have me, you know. I've tried everything, and she won't have me.'

'Mine eyes smell onions,' Hugh quoted solemnly. 'I shall weep anon.'

Charlie leant forward. 'Hugh, mate. About Lois. I didn't mean... well, I wouldn't, you know.'

Hugh cut the apology short. 'Let copulation thrive! Oh villain, thou wilt be condemned into everlasting redemption for this.' He raised his bottle. 'Well, here's my comfort.' He felt frivolously happy.

Later they ran out of beer and started on a bottle of Calvados that Charlie found under Sebastian's bed. From the record player Lester Young's tenor sax unrolled like a velvet ribbon around Billie Holiday's sad, scratched voice, and Hugh's inhibitions melted away.

'I love Annie-Pannie,' Charlie kept complaining at intervals.

'And I love Lois. Oh, how I do,' Hugh let himself sigh.

'And Annie-Pannie loves you,' Charlie moaned.

'Yes, but Lois goes to bed with you and Jack.'

'Jack?'

'Oops.' Though why not discuss Jack? 'The son and heir of a mongrel bitch, begging your pardon, Horatio.'

Charlie contributed a sizeable belch.

Dimly, Hugh recollected his new commitment to empathy. 'Jack's not all bad,' he allowed. He swallowed some Calvados. 'Not all bad,' he repeated, struggling to hold the thought in place, 'because Lois can be confusing. She can go to your head. I should know.'

He slumped, exhausted by the effort of goodwill.

Charlie's eyes focused briefly. 'D'you know what?'

'What?'

'Everybody's fucking everybody. It's getting to be like postman's knock.'

'I'm not.'

'What?'

'Fucking anybody.'

'There's Annie-Pannie. She would fuck you.'

'You're right, I think. She kind of asked.'

Charlie's eyes focused. 'She did?'

'And I kind of turned her down.'

'You what?'

'Yup.'

'You're not... you know, incapable?'

'Nope.'

'Blimey,' said Charlie.

Hugh lurched forward, clutching at Charlie's arm. 'Does it work?' he suddenly needed to know.

'Does what work?'

'Fucking everybody? Does it make you feel better?'

'Not really, no.'

Charlie looked glum. Could that be why Lois was glum?

Promiscuity wasn't helping, wasn't making her happy.

'Though don't knock it,' said Charlie. 'I had Zo the other night.'

'Zoë?' Hugh blinked and refocused. 'Just like that?'

'Just like that. Not bad. I'll probably have her again.' Charlie sloshed more Calvados into his teacup and sniffed loudly. 'But it's Annie I want.'

'Lois has everyone. And it's Lois I want.'

'It's a bugger, eh?'

'The most lamentable comedy,' Hugh managed to say. 'Very tragical mirth.' He started to hiccup, then became dimly aware that Charlie was punching his arm. 'What?'

'Wanna know something, mate? Between you and me, no offence. I always thought you were a bit of an old fart, know what I mean? Plus it was a real pisser Annie thinking the sun shone from your arse. But actually, godda hand it to you, you're an okay bloke.'

Double-think

Each morning, when Zoë got up, Tommy spoke to her, 'Ack!' and followed her like a little dog into the windowless bathroom where the extractor fan throbbed like a ship's engine, and then to the kitchenette in the living-room, where he purred fit to bust as she spooned out his food. When she left, he did too, heading off into the bushes without a backward glance. It worried her at first, but each evening there he was again, perched on the front garden wall from which he'd ousted Prunella, ready to leap down and weave around her ankles as she let herself in. His tea eaten, he'd settle on the wicker chair beside the Swiss-cheese plant in the huge bay, narrowing his eyes when she spoke to him across the room.

Tonight he slept, sphinx-like, on the end of the bed where, replete with food and sex and frothily tipsy, Zoë giggled with Mick beneath the Heal's duck-down duvet. Mick had brought champagne to celebrate the six months they'd been lovers, which he said was a personal record, and their first night together in the flat. What luxury, it was ten o'clock and her man didn't have to go home. The new curtains were drawn tight shut against the bare branches of the plane trees and the cold winter sky.

'Amanda?' smiled Zoë.

'Yes. She won't answer to Mandy.'

'And she fell for your charm, just like that?'

'Well, no, my persistence as ever. She said "No way" at first, but then she liked the ideas the creative boys came up with, and the product was bath oil, and my sales talk probably made her randy. I told her I hadn't met a sales manager as effective *and* sexy, et cetera. You know.'

'As I say, she fell for your charm.'

'Well, I've bugger all else to offer.'

'Not true. Not for me.'

Zoë rubbed her cheek on his bicep and grinned up past his chin. What better moment to tell him? 'I've been to bed with someone too.'

She waited, but he didn't say anything.

'Charlie Evans. He's at ATP.' She'd looked forward to telling this entertainingly, like Mick did with his conquests, but now she was trying to downplay it. 'He's just a clerical assistant. A layabout. Charles Evans Esquire, special subject the *Guardian* crossword.'

Still no reaction.

'Anyway, here I was, minding my own, sewing curtains, and he turned up at the door and said, "I want to go to bed with you." So, you know me, I went.'

Mick had stopped touching her. He was half sitting up. He fished a pillow from the floor and shoved it between his head and the wall. The cat woke up, rolled over and started washing its stomach.

'It's not serious,' Zoë said. She began to be cross. 'Oh come on, Mick, what's with the long face? You do it, so why shouldn't I?'

174

He had the grace to look abashed. 'You're right, but I can't help it. I can't stand to think of you with someone else.'

'I was with Tony.'

'That's different. Husbands are different.'

He was tracing the circumference of her breast with a giant forefinger, round and round and in towards the nipple, then out again, round and round. She watched, then glanced up and saw his mind wasn't with the finger. His head was turned away, his blue gaze fixed on nothing. The cat too had paused in its washing, its back leg, forgotten, stretched out in front.

All at once Mick seized her wrist. 'I knew!'

'Knew what? That I would sleep with other men? Well, yes. Why not?'

'I knew you'd done it. All evening I've sensed something. You couldn't hide it.'

'I didn't want to hide it—I wanted to tell you. That's what's good, that we don't lie to each other.'

She made him smile at her. He'd be fine now he was smiling. It was the surprise that had thrown him. She dropped down and blew a raspberry in his stomach.

He slid beneath the duvet and looked at her, nose to nose. 'You can't keep secrets from me,' he said. 'Even if you wanted to, you couldn't. I'd always know.'

She nodded. He looked happy again. It felt like a compliment, a restatement of love. But now, lying back on the pillow, watching the cat's eyes glaze and its head nod in and out of sleep, she found she was annoyed. More than annoyed. She remembered Ann's words. *He just expects a faithful little mistress waiting for him to drop by.*

Because yes, what a nerve! If it were only Elaine she shared him with, she would understand, for it was true: spouses were different. But he was seeing Tessa Golding regularly; it was as if Tessa and she were taking turns. *And* he was still having flings with these Amandas and Janets and Ruths. How dare he be jealous?

Mick's breathing had slowed into sleep. She had no one to tell this to. Not Ann any longer, or Tony, or Mick. Never her mother. Only herself; only Tommy.

Who was fast asleep too, his white stomach rising and falling, a paw draped over his eyes. What was it Hugh said at bridge the other day? She'd been waxing lyrical about Tommy, and Lois had brought her up short with a sneer about cold, selfish animals. And Hugh had produced one of his Bard quotes. 'A harmless necessary cat.'

How kind Hugh was. She could see he'd be good to confide in, wouldn't pull disdainful faces, or start telling her what to do. He'd look her straight in the eye and say something she hadn't thought of, something that would help her to see clearly and feel less isolated. And sex wouldn't get in the way.

She snuggled against Mick and smiled. She would probably never have such a conversation, but it was comforting to imagine it.

FEBRUARY

Beginners

'Every snow crystal is different, they taught me,' said Pamela.

'But how do they know?' said Ann.

'Yes, now you mention it,' Sebastian said, stroking his beard, 'how would one go about proving such a thing?'

'Who has measured the ground!' cried Hugh.

Zoë was nervous and flustered. The usual eight were playing bridge at her place, except that Tessa had opted out. Jack said she had to get her fix of *The Good Life* and *A Bouquet of Barbed Wire*. Sebastian said the Japanese had invented a machine to record TV programmes, and Zoë wanted to know more about it, but Ann interrupted and changed the subject.

A friend of Ann's called Pamela had come in Tessa's place. Zoë couldn't warm to her. She was pretty, but seemed brittle and false somehow, hardly bothering to say hello, boasting loudly about some doctor who had taken her out in a sports car and gushing sympathy at Jack about his squatters.

Zoë had been worrying for days how she would fit the Drunken Bridge Club into the flat. There was room, just, to set up the card-table—a wedding present—in the bedroom, provided one person sat on the bed, so Jack Golding only had to bring two folding chairs in his boot, which he said was no trouble at all. And in the living-room the round white table was turning out to be perfect for drunken bridge, proof against spills and burns and thumps, and with plenty of space for glasses and ashtrays. And no sneers yet from Lois.

The two rooms were wall-to-wall smoke and noise, and there was a growing line of empty bottles in the kitchenette, where Tommy crouched on the floor with an alarmed, accusing look. When she was dummy, Zoë sped round emptying ashtrays, tracking down the corkscrew, refilling the percolator—another wedding present—and looking anxiously from flushed face to flushed face. And yes, all was well. They were behaving as they did in Fulham or Highgate or Camden Town, the ash from their cigarettes dropping on the carpet, the khaki pile shrugging it off as she'd known it would. She really did seem to be accepted by these people, or at least to blend in. Like a snow crystal, she thought, unique yet integral.

She'd worried most about feeding them. Ann and Lois produced effortless masses of grub when it was their turn, and Tessa's meals were incredible: cordon bleu. She was relieved that Tessa hadn't come. She'd laboured all yesterday evening to produce a cauldron of chicken casserole, and had rushed home tonight to reheat it and whip up heaps of mashed potato and a whole jumbo packet of frozen peas.

'Boy, this is good!' Jack gobbled it down. 'Real comfort food.'

He held his plate out for seconds and Zoë sprang to refill it, delighted to be praised, and thankful she'd stretched the budget to three extra chicken legs.

'You must all come to Hackney one day,' said Sebastian. 'I'll cook a curry.'

He was encouraged by Zoë's success. He could see that she was a shy social animal like himself, who had nevertheless made it, if not to the nucleus, then at least into orbit of this gang. He might even be doing a little better than she was; he felt included in a way she didn't seem to be yet and that David Pratt, sitting on his left, never would be. Despite religiously regular attendance and graduating from collar and tie to shirt and sweater, Pratt was too mundane to appeal to the Anns, Lois's and Jacks of this world. His efforts to please were too obvious; his jokes fell flat. Whereas Sebastian, for all his diffidence, plumpness and fear of being judged boring, was finding the social game surprisingly simple; it required only a little courage. His glamorous new friends seemed taken with the fact that he was Italian and French and British all at once; and he was gradually carving a role for himself as benign boffin, bridge guru, disingenuous innocent, and understudy to

Hugh Fairchild's dependable nice guy. He was the butt of jokes perhaps, but they were kind, like those made about Horatio, who couldn't be here tonight because of Zoë's rather splendid cat. Yes, Sebastian decided, I'm another endearing mongrel dog.

He stroked his beard and watched Pratt stroke his over-sized chin three seconds later. He'd become aware of this mimicry in the office and decided to test it fifty times. Twelve out of twenty-three so far.

'Sebastian, I meant to say.' Hugh sat on his right, shuffling and dealing in that out-of-character, cardsharp way he had. 'I owe you an apology and a bottle of Calvados.'

Too right. He'd lost his temper quite badly with Charlie over that. 'Well, I wouldn't say no.' He drew a courageous breath. 'Bring it round some time and help me drink it.'

'You're a gent, I'd like that, next week any good? Great, I'll give you a ring. Did I deal these? Pass.'

'Great.' Sebastian echoed the word casually, playing down the pleasure of being promoted.

It was his bid. He cleared his throat and raised his voice slightly. 'One no trump?' He looked hopefully across the round white table at Lois, who seemed to have fallen asleep.

Ethics

'Come on, petal. It's your bid.'

Hugh touched Lois's hand, but she shrugged him off, filling him with sudden alarm.

Zoë was passing the table. She hovered, smiling anxiously at Lois. 'Can I get you a coffee? That would wake you up.'

'And if I told you to mind your own business, Zoë dear, would that shut you up?'

There was a stunned silence. 'Hey. Petal. Perhaps you're not well?'

She looked furious and miserable and impenitent.

179

'Do you want to go home?' he tried.

'Yes, I do.'

He began to rise from the table, but she shook her head impatiently. 'You stay. I'll go by myself.'

'No—'

'Yes. I want to.'

He sat down, bewildered. 'But how?'

She'd dumped her cards on the table and was fighting her way past David Pratt.

Zoë ran off into the bedroom, saying, 'I've got the number of a taxi firm.' She looked tearful, and who could blame her?

The others soon arrived in the doorway. 'What's the matter, my lover?' Ann was asking, but Hugh couldn't hear if Lois answered because Pamela was whining, 'We can carry on with a floating dummy,' and fixing Jack with those baby-blue eyes.

Zoë brought the phone on its long extension cord, and Lois was nodding, 'Go on,' and looking ready to burst with rage or misery. So he gave in, dialled for the taxi, which came in almost no time, and she was gone in a moment, barely saying goodbye.

He wanted to follow; he wanted to be with her. But he couldn't, she'd told him no and he'd let it happen, let her go, stood powerlessly by as she threw on her coat and departed. He was worried witless, but she didn't seem ill, just allergic to company, and not only his. None of this would matter if he could only understand.

'Your bid, Hugh.'

There were cards in his hand. Pamela had taken Lois's place at the table. David had doubled Sebastian's no trump. Hugh could barely think straight. He managed to pass. Then, while Sebastian pondered whether to bid again, he took deep breaths, doing his best to calm himself, to practise his new hobby, to invoke the distracting power of empathy. He looked up from the table. Jack, Zoë and Ann lingered there waiting for someone to make a fourth in the bedroom. Ann was frowning at Jack. Why? Hugh made himself concentrate on

180

working out why.

There was so much going on here. Trivial tensions like the bottle of Calvados between him and Sebastian. The new understanding that reigned between Ann and himself. The horribly malign subtext between Jack and Pamela; could that be what drove Lois away, surely nothing so simple? David Pratt sucking up to Sebastian. And for crying out loud—if he wasn't mistaken, and he wasn't, because, of course, that was why Ann was looking outraged—seductive signals aimed by Jack at Zoë. Good God, would the man never stop screwing around?

'No bid,' said Sebastian.

The bridge wrapped up around midnight, but the other antics persisted loudly for some time. Hugh felt exhausted by them. He should slip away, get to Lois as fast as he could, wake her, take her by the shoulders, insist, what the hell is the matter, and was it really necessary to be so spiteful to Zoë? But one of these characters might need a lift from him, and he must stay briefly to apologise to Zoë, must tell her the evening was great, that it was nothing she did, he was sure, that made Lois so scratchy. No one was pretending to ask after Lois, thank goodness. The sensible thing was to sit quietly until all this fuss was over.

It was finally agreed that Jack would drop Ann off, Pamela would take David, who lived somewhere west, and Sebastian would get a cab. But there was so much to-ing and fro-ing and debate about whether she should keep Jack's folding chairs for now that, as they all drove away, Zoë was quite surprised to find herself suddenly alone with Hugh Fairchild. Momentarily, she wondered if he would proposition her, but her instinct told her he wouldn't, even though Lois had lovers, Charlie for starters.

Lois was the kind of woman Mick would fancy the pants off, but Zoë suspected that Lois would belittle him. It was obvious that Lois despised her, never saying one civil word, cuddling up to Ann in front of her, ignoring and discounting

181

her, and dishing out catty snubs.

Hugh was different. He was pulling his coat on now, fishing a striped scarf from the sleeve and winding it round his neck. 'Whew!' he said. 'What a palaver, eh?'

'Yes. You lot certainly take some keeping up with.'

She could feel how excited the evening had made her: full of energy and nothing to do but wash up. Sleep was out of the question.

'Look,' he said, 'I've got to say how sorry I am about Lois. She's not herself lately, snapping at everyone. It's no excuse, I know, but I hope you weren't hurt by it.'

She shook her head noncommittally.

'Really,' Hugh insisted, 'she can seem horribly cruel, because she means what she says and shows no compunction. But it doesn't run deep—it's gone as soon as it's out of her mouth. It's mood, not malice.'

And she doesn't give a toss what people think of her, Zoë realised. Which maybe isn't such a bad thing. 'Would you like another coffee?' she dared to suggest.

'Ah... I... erm. I should be getting back. I'm really worried about—'

'Of course. As she means you to be.'

She saw surprise in his eyes, then recognition. His open mouth resolved in a smile. 'Why not? Yes. Thank you. I could do with catching my breath.'

He unwound the scarf and unbuttoned the coat, but, oh dear, did he think she was making a pass? She didn't fancy him, not in that way. But still, this was about something else besides coffee or catching a breath. She wanted something from him, and he wanted something from her. Something Lois wouldn't like.

They were standing too close together. She stepped back, gesturing vaguely. 'I must find the cat. He's hiding somewhere.' She laughed nervously. 'I've not had him long. I must explain to him this isn't typical or he may leave me.'

'Ah, good,' Hugh pulled a chair out from the table, 'you talk to animals too.'

She hesitated in her flight to the bedroom. 'Do you talk to Horatio?'

'Of course. He's my closest friend.'

'Next to Lois, you mean?'

'No.' Gratifyingly definite. 'More than Lois.' He grinned. 'At least I can understand Horatio. And he never disappoints me.'

She smiled, thinking of Mick. 'Yes, humans are harder, aren't they?'

She found Tommy under the bed and coaxed him out. She picked him up and began to stroke him and croon to him. Stealing a glance at her reflection, her flushed face, she could make no sense of it. She went back to the living-room.

'Would you do me a favour, Hugh—bring the wicker chair from the bedroom and put it over there?' She pointed to the Swiss-cheese plant.

He did as she asked. He didn't say anything, but the awkwardness was passing. She put both extractor fans on, bathroom and kitchenette, to clear the smoke, and their combined roar made conversation impossible. With Tommy settled mistrustfully on the chair, she set about making fresh coffee, smiling at Hugh each time she crossed the room collecting up cups or glasses or ashtrays. The place began to seem tidy and organised. She wiped the white table in front of him before bringing clean cups and turning the extractor fans off.

'Are you having any particular trouble with humans at the moment?' he asked.

She laughed. 'Oh, I suppose, the usual amount. You know.'

She'd imagined confiding in him, but it felt wrong to explain about Mick. And she couldn't possibly tell him about Ann.

He was fidgeting, she noticed, perched upright and looking round the room. He was probably still anxious to chase after Lois. She glanced where he glanced, seeing her taste through his eyes. Their eyes met. His were standard-issue grey-blue, the lines on his face reassuring. She managed to hold his gaze, to pretend she was calm and knew what she was about.

'I've just taken them up as a hobby,' he said. 'Humans. They're fascinating. And it's useful for my work.'

'You teach philosophy?'

'Yes. Ethics mostly.'

'Wow,' she said, and then wished that she hadn't, because she'd caught 'wow' from Jack, and she was always picking up phrases from people. At Christmas she'd found herself calling her mother 'my lover'.

Hugh raised an eyebrow. 'Wow?'

She poured coffee, supporting her wrist with her free hand to steady the shake. 'Yes, well, what I mean is, I'm impressed, I mean interested. I've always wondered about ethics. Like, what are they, where do they come from, why do they matter?' She was embarrassing herself; he was an academic professor and she was jabbering nonsense. 'What I mean is, I know this table is white. I know I'll have a headache tomorrow. But how do I know if something is good, or right, or beautiful? What does it mean?'

'Wow,' he said. 'I wish I had more students like you.'

'What about fidelity?' The word was out of her mouth. She was immediately blushing and regretting it.

He looked thrown. 'Sexual fidelity?'

'Yes.' Oh dear, he thought she meant Lois, or worse that she was making a pass. And she wasn't; she meant Tony and Charlie and Mick. She scrambled to make it more general. 'I mean, should people expect it? Is it wrong to be unfaithful, or does it depend? Isn't jealousy equally as wrong, worse? Whatever worse means.'

'Slow down.' He was smiling again. 'Do you want *my* view or the philosophers'?'

'Yours.'

'Well.' He spooned sugar into his cup and stirred thoughtfully. 'I've pondered this quite a lot, and I think it's connected with trust. The word 'infidelity' implies a broken promise, don't you think?'

She wasn't sure what he meant. 'So, if you haven't

184

promised to be faithful, it's all right not to be?'

'Not necessarily. But if you have promised, and you haven't been let off your promise, then to my mind it isn't okay. There's nothing absolute about it, I hasten to say—the web of our life is a mingled yarn, good and ill together.'

He was slipping out of it too easily. 'But shouldn't it be absolute?' she said.

'There's the mystery of ethics again. What do you mean by 'should'?'

She needed a better answer. 'I try not to make promises I can't keep, and then I mess up on a huge one like marriage. But I couldn't go on being married to Tony for the rest of my life just because I said so to a registrar. Could I?'

He leant nearer. 'Did you say so to Tony?'

'Not exactly. Well, no. He knew I still wasn't sure. He must have known it mightn't last.'

'That was the important contract then.'

'Contract?' The word sounded cold.

But Hugh seemed animated. 'Yes. Contract. Fidelity, infidelity, it's all about keeping faith with the contract. The key thing is to know what the contract is. We're bound to get in a muddle if we don't think about it until after it's broken.'

He drained his coffee and set down the cup, but he didn't get up. He lifted a finger.

'Now I'll play Socrates. Let's suppose you've made a good, clear contract of monogamy with someone, and one day you're tempted, really very tempted, by someone else. But you don't do anything about it. You resist. Would you still feel you'd been unfaithful?'

Zoë considered. 'No,' she decided. 'That's being faithful. I mean, if you aren't ever tempted, you'll never know if you're true, will you? You'll just be, well, smug probably.'

He sat back and laughed. 'I like you.'

'I like you, too.'

His eyes were soft. It wouldn't be impossible... but no, they mustn't go there. This wasn't about sex. Not at all.

He leant forward again, touching her hand. 'You seem to

185

be of the Kantian school. Now, let's take it further. Suppose you confess to this other person you're attracted to, you tell them you're tempted? Would *that* be unfaithful?'

She could feel herself blushing. She broke eye contact and looked at the cat. 'It sounds dangerous.'

He withdrew his hand; sat up straight. 'You're right. I can see that it *is* dangerous. Humans, all of us, me, we find it hard to just leave things be. We have a habit of expecting situations to develop.'

'Yes!'

'And they don't have to. We can choose. Choose to leave well alone, to do what's right instead of what we feel like doing. That's Kant again—it ain't moral unless it hurts.'

She had a sense of being about to discover something, but he looked all at once forlorn, staring into his empty cup. Had she been sharp with him? She wanted to touch, to console him, but it would be facile or worse.

He stood up and began buttoning the coat and rewinding the scarf. She didn't want him to go, not like this.

She was thirsty. She went to the sink and drew a glass of water, which she drank steadily down until it was empty. She refilled it, came out of the kitchen and leant against the screen of white-painted cupboards and shelves, meeting his eyes.

'Do you know what my problem is, Hugh? I've no contract, not with anyone. I'm not even near having one.' That didn't seem quite fair to Mick. 'Or perhaps I have, but it's kind of a contract not to have a contract.'

He looked at her, frowning slightly; then he spoke. 'Maybe you don't have to see it as a problem, not yet. Try not to worry about it. Enjoy your freedom. The readiness is all.'

'The readiness?'

'Says Hamlet. Best friend Horatio.' He held out a hand.

She took it, only half understanding. 'Of course. Thank you. The readiness is all.'

But then understanding completely. 'Because it's not about sex, is it?'

The words weren't right, but she knew what she meant.

186

'No, it isn't.' He understood. Which made it okay to be holding his hand.

'I must go now.' Lifting her hand to his lips.

'Yes. And good luck, Hugh. I mean it.'

Inadequate words.

'Thank you, Zoë. You too, though I'm sure you'll be fine.' His face was very near, and her hand still in his. 'Hereafter in a better world than this, I shall desire more love and knowledge of you.'

She was embarrassed, but then he let go and stepped backwards, waving farewell like Dr Who.

'I'll see myself out.'

Merely Players

Wow indeed, Hugh thought as he unlocked the car, what a hobby this was proving to be. He'd come through a moment in there of understanding what it was like to be a philanderer. And now, okay, though yes he was regaining himself, he was not quite so... well... smug. Hah! Resisting Ann was one thing; resisting Zoë was quite another.

Cruising south with the other small-hours travellers through St John's Wood, his destination registered, his brain emptied of fantasy, and the fear rushed in. What the hell was the matter with Lois? It was getting worse by the day. He'd lost his bearings with her. When he got in from work tonight, she'd been pacing the kitchen, banging saucepans, swearing at Horatio for getting under her feet, and announcing that she didn't want to play bridge. He'd had a trying afternoon in meetings; he was looking forward to the cards and the company, and Lois didn't seem to have cooked anything despite her rampaging in the kitchen; so he put his foot down.

'We can't cancel. Or put it this way, we won't. Not without notice, for no reason.'

Indulging her whims was a pleasure when her whims were

life-affirming. But tonight she'd been a killjoy; he was almost ashamed.

Was it Zoë who was bugging her? Was his wife resentful of a woman, younger and more classically beautiful than herself, befriending Ann, bedding Charlie, being targeted by Jack? But since when was Lois cast down by the competition? Usually it roused her to shine brighter, not to bitch and retreat. No, the only answer that made sense was that she didn't want to be where she was, indulged by him, playing at being free. She wanted out.

Approaching Hyde Park Corner, he replayed her voice: *it's you that I love,* but found no reassurance. And then, bang, he was hit by a wave of nostalgia so strong it made him groan. He never anticipated this recollection, never remembered it would come, but the sight of the park gates as he swung round The Wellington Arch into Knightsbridge invoked it like a prayer. It had been a warm evening, two or three years back. He and Lois were strolling together into Hyde Park. They'd seen a film in Curzon Street, then eaten in some dimly-remembered pasta house, achieving an edgy respite from the ongoing arguments in which they each stood their ground, daring the other to walk away from the marriage. After the meal they'd wandered through the subway and into the park, with no destination, pretending to be at ease, pretending to enjoy the violent red-and-purple sky. And there, on their right among the trees, a bandstand slipped by, haunted by ghosts of vanished trombonists and French-horn players. Without a word Lois steered him towards it, without a word he followed, and they stepped up onto the bandstand, as if it were planned or expected, and danced, silently, in the old-fashioned way, her right hand in his left, her head on his shoulder, his nose in her soft, dark curls. Not for long, for only twenty, maybe forty seconds, they danced in the silence, before heading home.

He glanced around at the scatter of her junk in the car. Tears blurred his vision as he cruised past Harrods. He could never find a way to predict which moments would stick. They were seldom the experiences that he struggled to capture and

188

hold. He could recall almost nothing of his wedding day, for example. Was it the act of trying to remember that got in the way? These moments chose themselves for reasons he never understood, and he wove the story of his life out of them. He drove on down the deserted Fulham Road towards Lois.

He no longer wanted to tell her off. He let himself in quietly and didn't switch on the light. 'Ssh,' he whispered to Horatio, who came wriggling and snorting to greet him. But there she was, her outline in the dark sitting-room doorway.

'Lois?'

'Hugh.'

He put on the light. 'No. Turn it off.' She ducked her head, but he'd seen what he feared: swollen eyes, shining cheeks. 'I've something awful to tell you.'

She turned from him, back into the room. He followed her. She'd been lying on the sofa; as his eyes readjusted, he could make out the dents in the cushions and a scatter of crumpled tissues. But now she picked her way over to the leather armchair and sat alone, out of his reach, fiddling with one of the protruding tufts of horsehair. Will I remember this? he wondered.

'Sit down.'

He sank into the warm depression she'd left. Would he feel her warmth again?

'Do you want a drink?'

'I don't know.' He swallowed. 'Lois?'

'Yes?'

'I love you.'

She made a small, choked sound. 'Don't say that.'

He could feel the pain begin to close in, pressing down on him from the shadowy corners of the room and at the same time rising up inside him, gripping his heart and his lungs so he could hardly breathe, filling his head and stomach so he felt sick, and his ears so he could hear his blood pumping.

'Tell me,' he managed to say.

'Oh God. I'm so sorry. I'm pregnant.'

For a moment the word made no sense. Then his instinct

189

was joy. He half rose. 'Why sorry? Don't you want it?'

She burst out sobbing, 'But, Hugh, it's not yours.'

His knees gave. He dropped back.

'Almost certainly not. It was November. It's Jack's, or it's Charlie's, there's no knowing. I'm so terribly sorry. Can you forgive me? Please. I'll have an abortion. Please, Hugh.'

Slowly he got to his feet again. 'Jack's baby? November?' His mouth was so dry he could barely get the words out. 'You've known this for months. What's the matter—won't the bastard have you? Won't he ditch Tessa for you?'

'Hugh. Don't. Please.' She sounded frightened. Her arms were stretched towards him. 'Jack doesn't know. I was due in December, but the coil... I thought I'd missed one, but then January... and even then, I didn't feel sick. You're supposed to feel sick. I kept thinking—it can't be true. I didn't want to believe it. I only went to the doctor today.'

He looked at her blankly. 'So now you'll tell Jack.'

'It could be Charlie's.'

Anger rushed through him. 'Jack, Charlie, Joe Bloggs, what's the difference?'

'That's unfair, Hugh,' she yelled. 'I didn't mean to get pregnant. You *said* I could sleep with them. You *told* me to do it.'

Silence. He was routed.

'What an idiot,' he said at last. 'Of course I did. That's what I did.'

He didn't want to be in his own skin. He was stuck in the middle of the room in the dark, unable to move, the pathetic fool who gave his wife away. He looked towards the door.

'I'll leave.'

He walked out and into the bedroom, switching the lights on. He found a bag and began to throw things into it.

She followed him. 'No, please, Hugh. I love you.'

He couldn't answer. He pulled open a drawer, fished out socks, pants, a sweater. Where would he go? An abortion, she said. He cleared his throat, tried to relax his shoulders. Found some words. 'Is that what you want?'

190

'Yes, please don't leave me. Please don't stop loving me, Hugh. I can't bear it.'

'That's not what I mean. Listen, Lois, an abortion. Is that what you want?'

'Yes. Yes.'

He couldn't look at her. He had to get out of here.

'Hugh, please.'

Horatio was whining. Lois was crying. 'I love you so much. No one else, Hugh.'

Easy words when she needed him. He managed to look at her. 'How can I possibly know that's the truth?'

'I love you, I love you, I love you,' she said.

He zipped up the bag. 'I'll be back for Horatio.'

'Hugh, *please*.'

He was along the hall, through the door, down the steps and into the car, where he sat a long while, rigid, unable to think straight and blinded by tears.

MARCH

Diplomacy

One bright, blustery Sunday in early spring, Sebastian and Charlie were relaxing together in their local, idly supping their second pints, savouring the fug of smouldering tobacco and vaporised alcohol, leafing through the newspaper and waiting for the Hackney Stompers to arrive. They'd bagged a good table, handy for the bar and the Gents, not too near the door or the stage, and large enough to spread the paper above and their legs below, scuffing dark stripes in the sawdust.

Sebastian allowed himself a mellow sigh. He'd just had a rise in salary, enough ahead of inflation to feel like promotion, announced by a letter signed jointly by Messrs Attwood and Thorn that thanked him for his 'invaluable contribution to our continuing success'. And, last Wednesday, he'd spent an evening with Hugh, who was an interesting chap and seemed set to become a friend. Life wasn't bad.

Charlie stopped chewing his biro. 'Diamonds for the imperial anniversary,' he challenged. 'Or altogether more basic attire, question mark. Two words, eight and four.'

'Birthday suit,' said Sebastian.

'Of course.' Charlie tutted. 'Smartarse.'

Sebastian's gaze wandered from his paper. The band members were drifting in, wild-haired and black T-shirted, collecting their free pints from the bar before unpacking their instruments. He extracted a Café Crème cigarillo from its small, flat tin, lit up and sent a lazy jet of smoke into the sun-shot haze. 'This is the life,' he said, caressing his beard.

'Too right,' said Charlie.

Charlie's back was to the window. A blaze of gold came through his curls. Sebastian narrowed his eyes so that the glare nicely blinded him. 'It's spring.' He stated the obvious with pleasure. 'And maybe we'll get one more hot summer before the ice age, who knows?'

'Talking of birthdays...' Charlie paused to release a thick, trembling smoke-ring. 'It's mine next month. The fifteenth.' He swiped the smoke from the air.

'And what does that make you?'

'Aries, the ram!'

'How old?'

'Twenty-nine.'

'Bizarre,' Sebastian mused, 'given that you're not yet out of short trousers.'

'No need to be fucking insulting,' said Charlie benignly.

Sebastian turned a page, but Charlie wasn't done with the subject.

'So. Do you fancy throwing a party?'

Meaning, please throw me a party. Still, it wasn't a bad idea. Sebastian played it cool. 'Me or us?'

'Well... you know... us. Cheap though. Buy in a few crisps and tell 'em bring your own booze.'

'We'd have to spring-clean.'

'That's easy,' Charlie said eagerly. 'Just shovel the crap into sacks. It'll be clear in no time. I'll do it—I'll put on me apron.'

Sebastian was tempted. They had friends now: the Fairchilds, the Goldings, Ann and Zoë and so on. Colourful people. It could be a good party.

'Okay, you're on.'

The band-members were playing tantalising riffs, joking and laughing with their fans near the stage. The pianist was on his second free pint and looked crazy already. The pub was filling, the buzz of chatter and laughter was growing, and the bar was fast becoming obscured behind a wall of muscular backs. 'Time to get another round in,' Charlie offered. He was on his feet pulling a crumpled pound note from his pocket.

'Good on you.'

He hovered. 'There is just one thing.'

'Oh yes?'

'Fancy dress. The party should be fancy dress.'

Sebastian shrank. 'No.' What would he wear that wouldn't

draw attention to his size?

'Aw, come on. Bit different, don't you think?'

'Optional.' Let others be ridiculous.

'Okay, optional. So we can tell who's chicken.'

'But won't fancy dress be expensive?' He tried to appeal to Charlie's insolvency.

'Na-ah. Seeing as it's my birthday and the temperature's rising, I can come as the emperor. Ba-boom!'

Charlie pulled off his sweatshirt, revealing a grubby blue vest. The band swung into ragtime, fifty feet began to tap, and Charlie swaggered his way imperially to the bar.

Joining the Dots

On Tuesday Zoë woke up shivering. Tommy padded up the duvet and stood heavily on her chest.

'Wait, can't you, for once?'

Her voice sounded odd, dead, no echo in her skull. Did she have the flu? She struggled to her feet, went in search of the thermometer under the washbasin, then hung there, waiting, trying to see in the mirror how the mercury was rising. Her reflection was blurred. The face belonged to someone else. The extractor fan seemed to be installed inside her head. The cat yowled at her.

'Do shut up.'

She felt dismal: low-spirited as well as ill. Nothing bad had happened since the gang played bridge here. Frugal weekends spent alone, one awkward one spent with her parents, routine weeks at work, some nights with Mick, another bridge evening. She didn't go to yoga anymore; neither she nor Ann had suggested signing up again after Christmas. But depression had thickened like fog, until yesterday at work she became estranged from herself, possessed by demons who whispered doubt in her ear and put wrong words in her mouth. She tried to be positive, but everything she said misfired. She willed the day to end so that she could creep home, shut the door and be quiet behind it.

Wobbly and aching, she squinted at the thermometer. A hundred and one.

She was fast asleep when the doorbell rang. She lurched up, struggling to know who, what, when?

Friday. She'd been ill for three days. Temperature still ninety-nine. Bright sunshine outside. Clock-radio showing 12.46.

Jack Golding's upbeat voice crackled through the entry phone. 'I heard you were ill. I've brought you some nice food.'

She buzzed him in and hurried to pull on her tatty quilted dressing-gown. She caught sight of herself in the mirror; her hair was chaotic, but, too late, he was knocking. He burst in smelling of fresh air and held out a large carrier bag.

'Salade Niçoise!'

He strode through the living-room. She followed. He had on a soft, brown-leather jacket over a shirt striped in clear, bright colours, turquoise, blue and white, open at the neck. His dark, wavy hair looked as though it had just been cut.

'Do you have a large bowl?'

She stared as he unwrapped ingredients. Fresh salmon— 'Look how pink'—hard-boiled eggs, anchovies, new potatoes, tomatoes, green olives—'You'll love these, they come from an amazing shop in Soho'—French beans, tiny crisp lettuce leaves, vinaigrette in a corked bottle, a French stick he was tearing into soft pieces and pale-brown, crusty crumbs.

'*Et la pièce de résistance.*' He produced wine with a flourish. 'Pouilly-Fuissé. An excellent vintage.'

She shook her head, frowning.

'And you mustn't worry about me. I never catch flu.'

'I'm not sure alcohol's good for me.'

'You can't watch me drink on my own.' He was busy pulling the cork. 'It's a restorative. One little glass will help you get better.' He poured two large glasses, 'Cheers,' and knocked back half of his. 'Wow! Superb!' He refilled it to the brim, then

195

lit one of his elegant, long brown cigarettes.

'Cheers.' She took a sip. She couldn't taste anything.

'Let the salad rest for five minutes. These smokes are fabulous.'

He nudged the open packet along the counter towards her. *More,* the cigarettes were called.

She shook her head. 'I'm not well.'

He was staring, but not in a bad way. She had no make-up on; she must look a real mess. Was he here to seduce her, or being genuinely kind?

'This is nice of you.'

He grinned and raised his glass again.

'Any luck with your squatters yet?'

His face darkened; she regretted the question. 'Not much,' he growled. 'I'm no nearer getting them out, but at least the buyers have stopped threatening and started negotiating. Offering to complete if I drop the price.'

His mouth curled; he looked sour. She scanned her brain for a pleasanter subject, but he bounded off across the room. 'Sit here. I'll wait on you.'

He was turfing Tommy off the wicker chair, turning the cushion and patting it. She followed reluctantly. Tommy looked sour now, and she wanted to protest, but Jack was back in the kitchen dishing up food. Sunlight was dappling around the bay, stirred by the rustling bare branches of the trees outside. She felt weak and sat down.

He bore the plates towards her on upturned fingers like a waiter. She couldn't help smiling.

'This is very...' She hunted for the right word in her feverish brain.

'Very what?'

He sat on the floor at her feet, topping up her glass, smiling at her. The salad was crunchy, sharp, sweet. She hadn't been eating well, just cereal, and baked beans on toast, and odds and ends from the fridge. This special food from Soho was doing her good, making her well again.

She found a word. 'Very stylish.' He looked pleased.

196

'Trendy.' He looked less so. She tried to make amends. 'I mean, you know how to do things.'

'What sort of things?'

His shoulder was touching her leg; she didn't know whether to move away. She remembered his broad shoulders were the first thing she'd noticed about him.

'Your party last summer—it was beautiful. Perfect. The grapes and the flowers and the butterflies. Everyone smiling and relaxed. Don't take it the wrong way, I don't mean it the wrong way, but I thought it was like one of those pictures in the Sunday colour-supplements.'

He put a hand on her arm. He didn't say anything, just left the hand there and held her gaze, so she knew what he wanted. Oh dear, not again.

He was raising himself from the floor now and sliding the hand behind her neck. As his face approached hers, her brain was too fuddled to think properly, and somehow she decided it was okay to sample. After all, Mick and Tessa.

It was only a little kiss. He smelled of expensive aftershave. He held her face inches from his, waiting for her eyes to give him the go-ahead. And the moment they did, before she could reconsider, he kissed her again, longer and deeper.

How glamorous and flattering and unexpected this was. But manipulative too. He wasn't giving her space to think. She disliked being ambushed. How fresh and clean he smelled and tasted—while she was disgusting. What must hc bc thinking?

She wriggled away, protesting, 'I'm horrible. I need a bath.'

'You're not in the least horrible.' He held onto her. Pulled her back. 'You're very sexy.'

Her long, auburn hair was damp and tangled. She tasted of wine and olives and toothpaste. Her hot skin smelled faintly of Vick's vapour rub. It was exciting to feel her reluctance give way to desire and confidence. Normally, yes, Jack liked his women to be clean; fresh out of a bath-towel gave such scope for oral delights. But he would lose the moment if he asked her to wash. Keep his face well away from her fanny and he'd

197

be fine. He was more than ready to slip and slide into her feverish flesh. He picked her up and carried her into the bedroom.

An hour or so later, they had a bath together, in her windowless bathroom. A nice little room this, in a tasteful conversion. Plain white suite and tiles, setting off wallpaper that Zoë announced proudly she'd hung herself.

'The room isn't square, look,' she said, waiting for the bath to fill. She'd been awkward and reluctant in bed, and she was still acting shy, starkers on the yellow bathmat. 'This corner was a nightmare, but you can hardly see the join. Tony taught me how.'

Jack sat with his back to the taps; he insisted on it. He washed her feet, picking them up and soaping each toe. At last she seemed at ease, coy and giggling like a woman in a bath should be. He liked what he'd heard, that she was happy to be the bit-on-the-side for that bloke Tess worked with. Zoë was no Pamela, nor a man-eater like Lois. She would do nicely.

'So.' He put her foot down and explored under the water with his fingers. 'We're going to do this again, yes?'

'I don't know.' She looked as if she knew very well. 'What about Tessa?'

'You can talk. What about what's-his-name?'

She squirmed away from his fingers and frowned. 'Who do you mean?'

'That bloke you see. Nick Galloway?'

'Mick Galway.'

She seemed angry; had he screwed up somehow? Mentioning the competition? Getting the bugger's name wrong? Calling her the town bike?

'Sorry. Mick Galway.'

'But how did you know?'

He dribbled water from a flannel onto her shoulder. She looked great: pink in the face with fever and outrage, and her hair dripping suds on those lovely little breasts. He was impatient to get her back in the bedroom. He shrugged.

198

'Maybe you told someone.'

'Only Ann, but she promised.'

'Once you tell, other people get to know. It's natural.'

'Ann told you?'

God, what was the fuss about? 'No, Tessa told me.'

'*Tessa?*'

'Yes, Tessa.'

She snatched the flannel from his hand. 'Let me get this straight.' She looked furious, but he sensed this was to his advantage. 'Just Tessa? No one else told you?'

'That's right. So I guess,' pushing home the advantage, 'if she didn't hear it from Ann, maybe this Nick, sorry Mick fellow told her?'

A wave hit his stomach as Zoë flung herself back in the bath. She hurled the flannel on the floor, and then the soap, which skidded behind the lavatory. He waited for her to speak.

'If you and I have an affair...'

Home and dry. 'Yes?'

She leant towards him through the steam. 'Would you tell anyone about us?'

'No.' He made the decision as he spoke. 'I've had them where people know, and it's no good, it gets so involved. You probably know about them yourself. Pamela, and Lois.'

Damn, she looked astonished. 'That Pamela who was here?'

'Yes.'

'And Lois?'

He nodded.

'Well... it figures. But no, I didn't know.'

'Still, never mind, you do now. So, all the more reason, this time it's definitely a secret, just between us. Which means you don't tell anyone either. Not even this Mick guy, okay?'

Her face broke into a grin. 'He said he'd always know if I slept with someone else. So he won't need me to enlighten him, will he?'

'So you will then?' Jack cupped her glistening breasts, one in each hand and bent to lick them.

'Yes.' She slid nearer and put her arms round him. 'Though I think,' she murmured, 'in fairness, and to make everything kind of... well, symmetrical, there's another secret that *you* ought to know.'

Contracts

'Are there any men worth fancying at Rex?'

'What?' Tessa opened a cupboard door between his face and her own. 'Where have I put the green peppercorns?'

He closed the cupboard and stepped nearer. 'At Rex. Where you work every day. Any big, sexy, juicy blokes you fancy there, darling?' He could read the alarm in her eyes. 'Well? Do you understand the question now?'

She looked away. 'Don't be daft, Jack. I've told you, they're all far too busy fancying themselves.' She began darting around the kitchen, pretending to look for the peppercorns. 'Some of them are doable, I suppose. Alan for example, he'd be a dish if he wasn't such a poisonous wanker.'

He watched her intently. 'Alan? The MD?'

'Yes.'

'I thought he was past it.' He stepped close to her again. Not touching.

She laughed unconvincingly. 'What gave you that idea?' She put a hand on his arm. 'No one who's anyone grows old in advertising, sweetheart—they all make their pile and get out. Alan's thirty-eight.'

She looked pleased with herself for changing the subject and spun off, hunting for peppercorns.

'But then there's Mick, isn't there?'

She stalled, a bird shot on the wing. 'Mick Galway?'

'Yes, that Mick. Big, ugly Mick Galway. How old is he?'

'Good heavens, Jack, how should I know? Thirty something. Heading over the hill.' She was flapping to remain airborne. 'Most of the staff think thirty's a dirty word, and, yes,

I suppose, now you mention it, lots of the men would be fanciable if they weren't so feverishly dating each other. There's Brian, the gruesome accountant, of course, single and hetero and gagging for it—but yuck, the very idea.'

He moved in for the kill. 'You wouldn't, by any chance, *sweetheart*, be extracting the Michael?'

'What?'

'Going at it with Mick-taking Galway?'

For a moment her mouth hung open. She was going to confess.

'Jack, you've got to be mad. I told you, it's Zoë who's doing that. No accounting for taste, he looks like the back of a bus.'

Her mouth was twitching with tension. Hold her eyes. Don't blink. No proof, he didn't have proof, and she would want to know how he knew. Fuck, he was going to have to think this through. He backtracked.

'So you're telling me you're not having an affair with Mick Galway?'

'Yes, that's what I'm telling you.'

Silence. Her face drained of colour.

'Fine,' he said. 'Fine. If you say so.'

'Just look. Silly me. Here they are.' A little bag of peppercorns was in Tessa's hand. Her voice softened. 'Jack.'

'What?'

'I don't know... I mean, yes I do know... I want things to be good between us. Like they used to be.'

There was pleading in her voice, but he couldn't stay, couldn't deal with this now. He was in the hall, an arm in the sleeve of his new brown-leather jacket. 'I have to go meet the buyers,' he said bitterly. 'Pray the fuckers don't bankrupt me.'

She was still clutching the peppercorns. 'Jack... darling... good luck. We'll get shot of the squatters, and things will be better then, won't they? A fresh start. Let's promise each other?'

'Yes, of course.'

What else could he say? He accepted her hands. Her kiss.

'A clean slate, Jack,' she was telling him. 'A new page. From today.'

Hugh threw a ball for Horatio in the park. He lobbed it high so the dog stalled astonished beneath it, waiting for it to fall to earth. The low spring sun dazzled his eyes. The breeze was sweet with the scent of new growth. Nearby, along the path that ran back towards the car park, came a young mum with two children, one barely toddling, the other a small girl with a red bobble-hat who pointed at the capering dog and laughed.

This is happiness, Hugh told himself. Memorise it. Bottle it. I've never been this happy before. I may never be this happy again. The delight kept on lasting and growing. He woke to renewed bliss each morning, and took it safely to bed with him each night. He sat grinning over his sandwiches in his lunch hours at the university, marvelling at his good fortune, savouring it, doubting its reality, challenging the fates to take it away.

Horatio delivered the ball to his feet. He bent to pick it up and tossed it from hand to hand, teasing.

Sometimes for a short while he would forget he was happy. He would be sucked into the routine of preparing and delivering lectures, chairing seminars, marking essays, and he would forget. But there, beneath the routine, leaping out as he turned a page, like hope from Pandora's box, ran joy, pushing its inadvertent smile onto his face, daring him to take in the immense, amazing truth of what he had.

Lois loved him, and he believed her. Lois said she would always love him, and he believed her. He would never lose her; he had her pledge.

Horatio barked politely for the ball. He hurled it a long way, flat across the grass this time, bouncing and outstripping the dog.

He knew of course that he was crazy. With his rational mind he knew he should doubt her. That he should be mortified and full of anger and tell her it was too late. And yes, he had those feelings. He could resurrect them any time he wished and imagine playing the scene out differently. Turning the ignition key, driving away. To a hotel, to Ann, back to Zoë: 'Take me in, please, I need shelter.'

But he didn't wish it. He'd stared into the abyss of life without Lois, and it wasn't for him. He loved her, still wanted her. And there in the muddle, as her despair and misery met his own, he'd seen his chance of happiness and taken it.

Pregnant by Charlie, maybe that wouldn't be so terrible. But by Jack—God help him, his blood still ran cold. She'd offered an abortion, as if it were nothing, and it had seemed to be some kind of solution, until he realised it was no good. Because she would do it and then hate him for it, and he would lose her all over again.

So somewhere around five in the morning, he had taken her hands and told her that she must do what she wanted. That she must decide and take time to be sure.

She'd tried to insist on the abortion, but he repeated, 'No. Take time. Think. Imagine. And if you decide you want the baby, I will love it, love him or her, be its father.'

She'd taken two days, before saying anxiously, 'It's a person, Hugh, isn't it? A little child with a life. It seems wrong to kill it. But are you sure you won't mind?'

And her decision didn't surprise him or anger him. It was the price of his happiness.

It frightened him, this new commitment. Not least that people would notice, might snigger and whisper: it's a wise father that knows his own child. So he minded, of course he did, horribly; but he had Lois's love, and it was the baby that had brought it about. A baby who would be half Lois.

'No,' he'd managed without a blink. 'I don't mind. I promise.'

And Lois had kissed him, and the happiness had started to grow, every day stronger. Was he insane? Would it stay?

Horatio came bustling up, wagging everything but his tail and dropped the ball. The sun had gone in. 'Enough,' Hugh told him. 'The air bites shrewdly—it is very cold.'

'Why yes, Hamlet,' he answered himself, 'it is a nipping and

203

an eager air.'

He began to stroll back towards the car park, occasionally chucking the ball ahead. The child with the red bobble-hat turned up beside him, trotting along, first at his heel and then at his elbow, like another companionable dog. 'I'm Shirley,' she imparted confidentially.

'Honoured to meet you, Shirley. I'm Hugh.'

'Is he yours?' She pointed.

'Yes. An ill-favoured thing, but mine own. Do you want to throw the ball for him?'

And so they proceeded, Shirley tossing the ball, the dog fetching it, and Hugh trying to imagine how it would be to have a child to talk nonsense to full-time.

They arrived through the trees into the car park. He glanced behind for Shirley's mother, but she was nowhere in sight. Oh heck.

'Hey, Shirl. Where do you think you're going?'

'Hold my hand.' She slipped her warm little fingers into his and tugged him towards Horatio, who stood expectantly beside the car.

'Where's your mother?' Hugh crouched down, but she dodged his eye.

'At home.'

'What about the nice lady I saw you with?' he tried. 'And the baby? Weren't you with them?'

'Mmm.' Reluctant, scarcely audible.

He began to lead her back the way they'd come. But, oh dear, too late, he heard the cry, 'Shirley! Shirley!' tremulous and frantic. And here came the mother, stumbling out between the trees, babe in arms, to find him holding her daughter's hand.

'*Shirley!*' Her eyes taking him in. 'Oh, thank you! I didn't realise she'd gone.'

'I'm so, *so* sorry.'

His relief made him otherwise speechless. Shirley, outmanoeuvred, let go of his hand and skipped over to her mother. And off they went, the mother scolding, Shirley protesting, the baby beginning to wail, the line between happy normality and unbearable tragedy no thicker than a hair, while Hugh sagged against the car, hugging his own happiness to himself.

Jack powered the Rover into the garage at Bartholomew Road and slammed on the brakes with inches to spare. Anger was consuming him, corroding him; he could barely breathe for it. And something else. Jealousy. Images of Tessa and some monkey-faced goon with a big dick and a giant ego, going at it.

And she'd stood there, white-faced, staring him down. Calling him sweetheart. Denying it.

She was supposed to confess and grovel; he hadn't thought it through any further. When she didn't, what could he say? Zoë told me? Fuck. Fuck.

He could march into Tessa's office on Monday morning and deck the bastard, but what then? The same thing: who told you? That's for me to know, he would say; but Zoë would spill. Yes, fuck it, if he landed one on her precious Mick Galway, Zoë would tell Mick how he'd found out, and then Mick would tell Tessa... fuck, he needed to think about this.

And he didn't have time now; he had this meeting in ten minutes. This bloke, Macpherson, wanting him to cash in Brecknock Road for no profit, and he was going to have to agree. He was losing hand-over-fist in interest payments on the overdraft; he should never have exchanged on Lady Margaret Road; the completion money was due in two weeks, and the boys' wages week after week, and this place wouldn't be sold until August, if then, because the buyers were in some god-awful chain, but it was too late now to tell them to stuff it. And his solicitor was fucking useless: never there, never bothered, letting the whole sorry mess drift, pontificating between games of golf, 'Well, yes, they can sue, though buyers rarely do that in practice. The best outcome's an out-of-court deal, eh? Good luck.' Christ, he was paying a useless solicitor to wish him good luck!

Five minutes. He went in through the kitchen, straight through to the front room, unlocked the drawer of his desk and pulled out the whisky. He took a slug, then another, then hovered behind the folding shutter watching the street for Macpherson. He should be calm, cool, laid back, convincing on how he wasn't desperate for cash, persuade the mean fucker to raise his offer, just a few thousand, meet him halfway for Christ's sake, split the difference like gentlemen; it was still a good deal, the squatters would be out before long, it couldn't drag on forever, and the property was worth a bomb. If only he could say forget it and hang on for another buyer, but he couldn't, he'd done the sums. He'd be losing hundreds a week very soon, and the bank had started sending him letters about loan limits. If he sank any further, he couldn't dig himself out. Time was vital in this spiralling market. Cut the loss, forget bloody Brecknock Road, a whole year's profit, a whole year's love and hard labour down the Swanee. Move on, make it up on this one and Lady Margaret. Except that it wouldn't be made up, would it? Just bankruptcy avoided. A year down the drain for fuck all if he couldn't screw a bit more out of this bastard.

A Jaguar XJ12 Coupé slid to a halt outside. You couldn't park there, but it did. The driver's door opened and a huge man got out. A great, ugly brute of a bloke coming up the front path. Like Galway. That was all that he knew about Galway: big and ugly, even Zoë confirmed it. Screwing Tessa with his big, ugly dick. Christ! But this was Macpherson, and it was he who was about to get screwed. Jack took another slug of whisky, put the bottle in the drawer, fixed a smile on his face and went into the hall.

APRIL

Child's Play

'Good grief, what a horrible mess!'

Charlie's bedroom felt colder than the rest of the flat, and there was a reek of stale smoke and unwashed feet. The mattress on the floor was uninviting, a tangle of grey sheet and orange candlewick. The woodchip paper on the chimneybreast was painted lime green.

Charlie looked wounded. 'Don't you start. Mussolini's been on at me to get it cleared up for the party.' He sighed, dropped his coat and collapsed on the mattress. 'He's getting to be like my fucking mother.'

He looked up at her, 'Come on, Zo,' and began to pull off his clothes.

Slipping in naked beside him she hugged him tightly for warmth, he hugged her back, and for a minute or two they said nothing, did nothing but hug, skin on skin.

'Mmn,' Charlie breathed in her ear, 'how comforting and rude.'

She pulled her head back and looked into his face: snub-nosed, blemish-free. Did he have hidden depths?

He was climbing on top already. Foreplay wasn't his style. She didn't mind; she wanted it too. She rolled on her back and guided him in, planning what she would say to the cat next time it sulked when she stayed out too long. 'You're very comforting, Tommy, but you're not rude.'

The sex was energetic and over in a few minutes. Charlie slumped on her chest, breathing hard, and she held him close and stroked him. 'That was nice.'

'Mmn,' he said again and then seamlessly started to snore.

His weight was hampering her breathing; she eased him off. He made complaining noises, turned his back and was asleep again. She fingered the candlewick and frowned at his grubby yellow curls. Okay, no big deal, but a quick dollop of rudeness wasn't enough. There was something else she was starved of; what was it?

The readiness is all, Hugh had said. Enjoy your freedom. Kissing her hand, absolving her. And she was trying to enjoy it, but she wasn't, not really. Freedom, free love, free sex: it was getting to seem like empty ritual, whether with Mick or Jack or Charlie.

She hutched up on an elbow to contemplate the jumbled heaps of rancid socks and old newspapers—DUTCH ELM DISEASE ADVANCES NORTH—WILSON RESIGNS— the fraying maroon curtains held together with a safety pin, the overflowing ashtrays.

The readiness is all.

Time was she'd been too ready, childishly keen. So she'd learned better; she'd settled for Tony. But that only taught her that love can't be manufactured: she couldn't decide to love someone like she could decide to be happy. So here she was, eyes open, free, wary of passion, pretending nothing she didn't feel. Bravo, she told herself, but felt no answering glow.

Mick, Jack, Charlie. Not one of them right; each so different. Might she mix and match perhaps? Assemble a man to be happy with from parts of all three. Frankenstein's lover? She smiled. But what would a-man-to-be-happy-with look like? What the hell *did* she want?

She slid out of bed, stood up shivering and began to pull on her knickers.

Charlie rolled into the space she'd vacated and yawned. 'Hey, where are you going?'

'Home to feed the cat.'

'Okay. Chuck us my fags, will you?'

She found the paraphernalia for his roll-ups on top of the cold paraffin heater and brought it to him. But his eyes were closed and he was snoring again.

Playing to Win

Jack arrived at the head of the delicatessen queue. 'A quarter each of *saucisson sec* and *jambon cru*, please. Yeah, thanks, that one. Plus some garlic black olives and a bunch of those radishes.'

He was teaching Zoë about food, and today he planned to reveal the secret of *radis au beurre*. Fresh-cut, fat radishes, laid open with a sharp blade, stuffed full of fine, pale butter and dipped in salt. The only civilised way to eat them. Tessa had shown him; it was how the French ate radishes. How did the French discover these things?

Tessa was away with the Rex management team. She'd made a big, noisy deal of it, grumbling about not wanting to go, hating to give up her Saturday but needing to score points with 'dishy wanker' Alan after missing his precious client-weekend last summer. She had shoved the agenda in front of Jack's nose and rattled on about how 'Management by Objectives' was all well and good, but Alan's craze for measuring everything that moved was verging on certifiable, everyone thought so. At which Jack had barked, 'Everyone?' with an edge to his voice that she'd pretended not to notice. She had gabbled on, 'Well, you know, everyone with half a brain,' before skipping double-quick to the times of the trains, while her face turned pink and her eyes failed to meet his. Because not everyone, just Mick, that was who. It was Mick's pillow-talk she was spouting. She had Mick on the brain, and half of Mick's brain in her knickers, while the other half was in Zoë's, and all Jack could do was follow behind, sniffing for signs of Mick's brainwork.

He elbowed his way through the Soho crowds towards the short-stay car park, his eyes flinching from the setting sun. A smell of spring permeated the evening air, and he resented it, because the property market would be rising, and he'd sold out, rock bottom, on Brecknock, and because Tessa would be enjoying this weather on her dirty weekend. He wanted to bomb down to bloody Brighton and punch tricky Micky's lights out, but all he could do was show Zoë his own tricks and pray they were the best.

Get a grip. Sex with Zoë was world-class, win prizes, no doubt about it. And there she was, snug in her NW6 love-nest high in the budding trees, waiting for him.

He swung the clutch of carrier bags onto the back seat of the Rover. Flowers, wine and food, spring in the air, and a Rapunzel with long auburn tresses. All the ingredients for the perfect assignation. His instinct had been spot on. Zoë wasn't maudlin like Pamela. Or steely like Lois. Or belligerent and false like his darling wife. She was gentle and curious and warm, open and endearingly ignorant, and sexy, like wow! Wanton, never sordid. Up for anything without being sullied by it. Into the marvel of sex: pure as *radis au beurre*, voluptuous as a scallop with white wine and mushrooms, surprising as the heart of an artichoke.

The traffic was flowing north nicely. Tottenham Court Road, Euston, Camden Town, past the turn-off to Ann's, no snarl-ups, and on through Chalk Farm. Lights all green round Swiss Cottage and straight up the Finchley Road towards a tumble with Zoë, with her glorious tumble of hair. He was late on purpose; she'd be hungry as hell, salivating as he walked in the door, wide grey eyes on his *saucisson sec*. Because who gave a toss about Tessa and Mick's little sideshow, when this was on offer? Not laughing in the wings, no. Main show, centre stage. And he'd have the last laugh. Because maybe it was Zoë, not Tessa, he was meant to be with.

Yeah. How about that, Tessa dearest?

'Oh boy! Just think of those two busily having it away, doing the dirty on us. Little do they know!'

Zoë tried not to pull a face. Jack was stretched out naked on his back with his gorgeous head in her lap. Such a pity he wasn't more likeable.

'They're not, though,' she told him. 'Mick says they've called it a day.'

'Oh, yeah, right. Pull the other one.'

She let it drop. It was no use to say Mick never lied to her. Anyway, they should be doing this for the pleasure of it, shouldn't they, not for the pain it caused others? Their sex was a pleasure, no doubt about it; the bed looked as though a hurricane had hit it.

All at once he stopped grinning and gazed. 'Oh wow, Zoë.'

Viewed upside-down, the mean twist of his mouth was transformed into a smile. She combed his dark wavy hair with her fingers; it sprang like a soft brush. She steered away from the subject she saw in his upside-down eyes.

'You and Tessa seem good together, actually.'

He snorted. 'We were. Or at least I used to think we were. But now it's one argument after another. Niggling at each other, you know?'

'Yes, I do know,' she said sadly. 'That was how it was with Tony. It got so we couldn't talk about anything. But we were very different from each other; you and Tessa seem more alike.'

'In what way?' He sat up to look at her: a pity, because his mean mouth was back.

'Oh, I don't know. You're both so... so sophisticated,' she offered. 'Dynamic.'

'Yeah.' He smiled. 'But perhaps it's too much when you're similar. I begin to see why opposites attract. Now you, for example.'

He kissed her, and she leant warmly into the kiss, rising to her knees on the bed. He was fantastic at kissing, unlike Mick or Charlie. She was thinking of her Frankenstein lover.

'Zoë?'

'Yes, Jack.' Rubbing noses.

'I think I might love you.'

She sat back on her heels.

'Seriously. And I want to ask you something.' He had hold of her hands. His face was expectant. 'Just theoretically. If I were to turn up on your doorstep one day...' She kept her face blank. 'You know, with a couple of suitcases? What would you do?'

'If you left Tessa, you mean?'

'Yes.' He smiled into her eyes.

She must speak plainly. She tried to find a friendly way to put it. 'I would put you up for a few days, Jack, until you found somewhere to live.'

His expression altered, turned sour.

'I'm sorry, but I don't think it would work out, you and me.'

'What about Mick?'

'What about him?' Jack's obsession with Mick was annoying.

'If he left his wife, would you have him?'

'He's not going to.'

'But if he did?'

She sighed. 'I don't know. Maybe. But I'd really rather he didn't. I'm not ready. I don't want anyone moving in.'

Jack was scowling; she hugged him. 'Hey, cheer up. No big deal. We're fine as we are. Situations don't have to develop. Plus I figured out something in the bath this morning. All relationships have a built-in vitamin deficiency. There aren't any perfect ones.' She was proud of this theory. 'You get starved of Vitamin A with one person, so you rush off to someone else who gives you oodles of Vitamin A. But then, after a while, you develop a whole new lot of symptoms and you realise there's no Vitamin B this time. And off you rush again.'

He looked unimpressed. 'So what's the answer?'

'I'm still trying to work it out. Just now I get different things from different people, which is okay, but it feels temporary. I suppose, eventually, you have to settle for someone. You have to decide to do without whatever vitamin that person can't provide, or get it from another source. From your work, or your friends. From yourself.'

He wasn't listening, she could tell. She and Jack were the same in some ways—emotionally promiscuous, adrift—but so different in others. Above the downturned mouth, she saw the

212

angry question still in his eyes: 'What's wrong with me?' Thank goodness he was too proud to ask.

'Hey, enough of this,' she said. 'I want some more food.'

She leant down to pull her bra from the heap of clothes on the floor. 'And then you must help me think what to wear to Charlie's fancy-dress party. It has to be dirt-cheap, and I'm stuck for ideas.'

Revelations

Sebastian's flat was unrecognisable. It delighted him with its new colours and textures, archaeological treasures that had lain hidden beneath the crust of grey-brown filth and fluff. The light flooding through the polished windowpanes hurt his eyes. 'Blimey!' said Charlie, venturing in to find yet another area gleaming. 'It's fucking amazing! Thank you, girls.'

In exchange for a party invite they'd have issued in any case, Charlie had inveigled the three students from the downstairs flat into helping them spring-clean. They'd arrived meaning business, bearing mops and dusters, and quantities of Vim, Windolene, Dettol and 1001, as well as a hoover in full working order, and set to with such enthusiasm that Charlie said he felt giddy and retreated to the pub.

Sebastian they permitted to stay. More than that, they transformed the kitchen first so he could start turning out quantities of lamb madras and pork vindaloo and chicken korma on hygienic surfaces. He'd been ashamed: 'No really. I'll do in here.' But they wouldn't hear of it. They bulldozed past him, pulling on yellow rubber gloves, and jostled him out onto the landing.

Now, as the doorbell rang for the first time, he stood on a carpet glowing with jewel-like colours, graciously sipping wine and nibbling samosas. The hi-fi played Pink Floyd's *Dark Side of the Moon*; he had reminded Charlie that Ann didn't like jazz. He was wearing a chef's hat, check trousers and wrap-around apron, and he didn't feel too fat or too foolish.

The three students were dressed, largely by colour association, as a tomato, a banana and an orange. Charlie had spent countless hours trying to become Bogart, but, lacking the gravitas, had finally settled on Charlie Chaplin, or possibly Harpo Marx impersonating Charlie Chaplin. A pair of Sebastian's trousers sagged convincingly onto ancient black plimsolls, the tailcoat and bowler were extravagant purchases from the Oxfam shop, and a shoe-polish moustache completed the effect. 'Heil Hitler,' called Sebastian as Charlie ran down to answer the door.

It was Zoë, wearing jeans and a sweater. She was kissing Charlie and telling him happy birthday, and giving him a wrapped present, which he tore open like a four-year-old.

'Oh, Zoë, that's great!' Charlie rushed off to the hi-fi, Pink Floyd bit the moon-dust, there was a scratched mumble of recorded voices, then a pause, a tinkle of piano, and the rasping, soft voice of Sam singing *As Time Goes By.*

Good present. The students were singing along.

Zoë disappeared into the bathroom to assemble her costume. 'Can I get you a drink?' Sebastian called through the door.

'Yes, please. I won't be long.'

She drank red wine at bridge. He poured one and came back with it as she emerged, dressed as a cat.

'Nice costume.'

'Thanks.'

She pointed out features. The leotard from yoga, the white patch she'd sewn on the front, the woolly white bed-socks, the felt ears kirby-gripped into her hair, which was kind of piled up, the whiskers painted on her cheeks.

'And, look.' She displayed a tail made of curtain lining. 'I stuffed it with old tights. Hey, Sebastian, the flat looks amazing!'

'Yes, doesn't it, though? All thanks to our neighbours. Charlie's bemused—he says women are peculiar. He wants to know how long before we'll achieve the comfortable, lived-in look again.'

Someone leant on the doorbell. Sebastian gave Zoë her drink and went down. There was a whole crowd on the step. Friends of his who'd driven up from Kent and Croydon. Friends of Charlie's who'd strolled round from the pub. Friends of the girls from below. Wearing all manner of disguises, each of which had to be applauded. There was a point to fancy dress, he was realising; it got people talking and gave you a glimpse of who they might be underneath.

The bell rang again, someone went down, and here were Jack and Tessa, dressed rather intimidatingly in hired outfits, Captain Hook and Elizabeth I, and bearing armfuls of claret, which was generous if a bit showy. Jack strode around shouting and slapping Charlie on the back.

The flat was thumping already. Persons unknown had turfed *Casablanca* off the turntable, thrown on *Make me smile (Come up and see me)* and turned the volume up. They'd done it: this was a real party. The doorbell rang again. No one seemed to hear. Sebastian went to answer it.

'Hi there!'

Ann bounded past him up the stairs. She was dressed as a clown, with a red nose and painted smile and huge blue pom-poms down the front of a baggy white tracksuit. At her heels bumbled Horatio, excited and barking, a white pleated ruff around his neck. When she reached the landing, she started shouting for everyone to pay attention, to come and look. The landing was filling with people and Sebastian could see Ann sweeping the ground in a theatrical bow.

'And now,' she announced, 'the moment you've all been waiting for. The spectacle to end all spectacles. Pray silence for Mr and Mrs Hugh Fairchild!'

Sebastian turned back to the street door and gasped. 'Wonderful.'

Here they came, arm in arm, greeted by screams of disbelief from the heads craning over the banister rail. Hugh and Lois, elaborately and convincingly dressed in drag.

'My compliments to the chef,' said Hugh as he passed.

215

Sebastian closed the door and followed them up, staring. Lois was severe in black tie and tails. Her dark hair was flattened with brilliantine, and she eyed the crowd haughtily through a red-ribboned monocle. But Hugh stole the show. One white-gloved hand safe on Lois's arm, the other dangling a sequined evening bag, he followed with ladylike steps. His grey Marcel wave was secured with a diamante slide; his dress was blue rayon with tiny pink flowers, and he was thin enough to look like somebody's aunt in it. Its mid-calf hemline revealed wrinkled pink seamed stockings and pale-blue buttoned shoes.

The two of them had Sebastian mesmerised. Lois was as disturbingly male as the Baron de Charlus, and Hugh... Between the pink of the pearls at his throat and the soft grey of the wig, peeped out a face Sebastian only half-recognised: charming, bright-eyed and rosy with rouge, a face with the power to tell fortunes and grant wishes.

As the explosion of applause and laughter died away and the crowd's interest exhausted itself, Ann followed Lois to the sofa to look at the leather-bound album she had tucked under her arm. It contained the best photos of their bridge evenings, and Lois had brought it to show off to whoever would look.

'I'm beginning to fancy myself as a portrait photographer.'

Ann turned pages eagerly. 'Lois, they're brilliant!' she shouted above the rising noise of the party. People were dancing now and singing along to Elton John.

'Do you think so?' Lois yelled back. 'You're not just saying that?'

'No, you've got a real knack.' Ann jiggled her bum on the sofa to the beat of *Social Disease*. 'It's like each one reveals the person, and—oh... gosh,' her excitement crashed, 'that's amazing.' Hugh, close-up, offered the lens a look of inexpressible tenderness.

Lois grinned. 'Whoops, too personal. I should have left it out.' She reached and turned the page.

Ann recovered herself. 'They're ever so good though. Have

216

you tried... well not these obviously, but have you tried selling any?'

'Yes!' Lois seized her arm, excitedly. 'I'm meeting an agency next week. I sent them some I took on the Kings Road. It's crazy down there—kids with blue hair and black lipstick, giant safety pins instead of buttons. Anyway, they actually rang me! They said, come along, bring lots more, and we'll see. Hey, how about this one of Sebastian?'

Ann was amazed again. 'It's marvellous. He looks so relaxed. So genial.'

So attractive, she was thinking.

'Oh dear, is that me?' He was leaning over them, offering weird-looking nibbles. 'Great costume, Lois,' he yelled.

'Thanks. And, well done, Sebastian. The party's really swinging.'

'Yes, I'm surprised, too. Keep the bowl. There's plenty.'

Ann grabbed his hand and squeezed it. 'The flat's unbelievably clean,' she hollered up at him. 'It must have taken you forever.'

'No. It was—'

A dancer barged into him; she lost hold of his hand. Then someone slapped his shoulder. 'Hi, there. Glad you could make it.'

He was gone. She turned back to the album and, 'Oh dear,' caught her breath in dismay to see an image of herself, in her Sassoon-haircut days, dealing cards grumpily onto the Fulham dining table.

'Don't worry about it, my love,' said Lois. 'We all have our bad moments. Talking of which...'

Queen Tessa the First was steaming towards them, her train billowing regally behind. Arriving, sinking in a nest of golden brocade, fingering her stiffened lace collar and huge drop-pearl earrings, she showed no interest in the photographs. 'We must decide about holidays.' Her red-nylon corkscrew curls quivered with indignation. 'I have to book my leave. Alan's pestering me for dates.'

Ann shook her head dubiously, remembering Italy. But

217

who else could she go on holiday with?'

Lois seemed unenthusiastic too. 'Ah... yes... well... June.'

'Okay, done!' Ann bounced her pom-poms.

'June's impossible,' said Tessa. 'I'll have the staffing projections to do. July's better for me.'

Lois shook her head. 'You can count me and Hugh out then.'

'No!' Ann protested. She certainly wasn't going without Hugh and Lois.

'God, can't anything ever be done to suit *me*?' said Tessa. 'What on earth's wrong with July?'

'Oh well, here goes,' Lois said. 'Hold on to your hats.' She leant forward, looking hard at Ann. 'Don't go blabbing, but I'll be in my eighth month by then.'

'You what?'

'You heard.'

'Gosh, how wonderful,' Ann mumbled.

'Congratulations,' whispered Tessa, the anguish plain on her face.

Ann stared at Lois's stomach. It just filled the black satin waistcoat. A baby was in there.

Lois was avoiding her eye now. 'So, it's June or nothing, and this side of the Channel. But don't let me spoil things — Hugh and I truly won't mind if you go without us. We're being all connubial—nest-building and so on.'

Ann faked some enthusiasm. 'No, June it shall be, my lover. We'll rent a cottage and wait on you. How about Wales? The Wye Valley?'

'Terrific,' said Lois. 'You're on.'

Tessa muttered something about consulting Jack and retreated, past the hi-fi where people were debating what to play next. Ann began counting months in her head; she knew all about this from her sisters. She leant forward, to ask—

'Oh lord, no, not Abba!' said Lois. 'Help, we need Charlie. What's happened to his jazz?'

Ann refused to be deflected. 'So, it's five months, am I right? Is it Hugh's?'

'Of course it is. I didn't say at the time, in case it didn't come off, but that was the main reason I went straight—to try for a baby.'

She looked flustered. And the dates didn't fit... did they? Now she was trying to divert her again. 'Tessa's never happy, is she? Look at this.' She had the album open at a photo of Tess caught scowling at Zoë, who resembled a scolded child: startled, ashamed and rebellious all at once.

Ann had to laugh. 'Oh, my lord. Though, to be fair, you can't blame Tess, what with Jack's philandering and that antediluvian boss of hers—Hey, what's up?'

Lois's eyes were closed.

'Nothing,' she said after a few seconds. 'The baby moved, that's all. The shiver went to my toes.'

Ann clenched her teeth. She felt suddenly vindictive. 'And you could call it foresight,' she said.

'What?'

'Tessa scowling at Zoë.'

Lois looked puzzled; then she got it. 'You don't mean...?'

'It's been obvious for weeks. Shagging Charlie's not enough for her apparently—she's got to add Jack to the set.'

The same way you did, she was thinking, as Lois turned to see. By the window, Tessa, taller than Jack in her mock-Tudor shoes, was busy haranguing him about holidays, while Zoë, elbowed aside, fidgeted with her cat's tail. And yes, now Jack was turning from Tessa to Zoë, with a bow and a flourish of his black pirate's hat, and a smile that was unmistakably carnal.

'Spooky little cow,' said Lois, making Ann smile.

Zoë was amazed at how surly Tessa could be. No wonder Jack wanted out. She'd barged in on their conversation, sounding half-hysterical, banging on about holiday dates, demanding that Jack come to France with her in July, just the two of them, rather than to Wales in June with Ann and the Fairchilds, and all because of some staffing report she had to write for her boss.

Jack stood his ground. 'You can tell Alan where to put his

deadline—I'm not having my holiday ruined. The Wye Valley's a great idea. Let's rent somewhere huge—we can fill it up. You'll come, won't you, Zoë?'

'Me?' He was half-pissed, she realised, leering at her in front of his wife. 'Gosh, thank you... and it sounds great, but—'

'No buts.' Jack prodded the white patch on her stomach with his hook.

Tessa looked ready to explode. 'Four women, two men and no buts?' she hissed.

'We'll ask Sebastian and Charlie,' said Jack, winking at Zoë.

'Charlie? Oh great idea! Won't Ann just love that!'

Rude beyond belief. Zoë spoke carefully. 'Or I might be able to bring someone?'

'What!' Tessa's face darkened. Zoë almost expected her to say, 'Off with her head!'

Defiance kept her going. 'Mick.' She faced out Tessa's glare. 'Mick might be able to come.'

'For fuck's sake!' muttered Jack, then, 'Oh Christ, this is all we need!'

Zoë turned to look. It was latecomers arriving: Pamela on David Pratt's arm. Pamela was straight out of a *Carry On* film, wearing a nurse uniform with micro-short skirt, black suspenders and plump white cleavage. David hadn't bothered with fancy dress at all, unless a pale-blue safari jacket could be called fancy. Pamela was aiming a simper across the room at Jack.

'You'll be asking *her* on holiday next,' Tessa growled. Then she grabbed Zoë's empty tumbler and thrust it, with her own, into Jack's hands. 'More wine, thank you!'

For a moment he defied her, but then he took the glasses and set off towards the kitchen, steering well clear of Pamela, Zoë noticed.

Tessa grabbed her arm. 'Ow! Let go.' But she pinched more tightly, digging her nails in. 'Listen. I'm only saying this once. Mick's not coming, understand? What the hell are you playing at?'

'Stop it! That hurts!' Zoë flung her arm sideways, breaking Tessa's grip. She felt her face grow hot. 'And thank you, I understand perfectly.'

Shamed by the wobble in her voice, she stumbled away through the crowd, dodging a man who was flinging his fists about to Abba, and almost collided with Ann, who was with Hugh and Sebastian by the fireplace. Ann took no notice, continued to talk. 'You have secret talents, Sebastian. These little meatballs are yummy.'

Fine, it gave her time to catch her breath.

God, what hypocrites these people were. Involving her in their poisonous games. Having affairs as if it was a bit of fun, then turning on her, telling her off for breaking some rule they'd just invented to suit themselves. Okay, so bringing Mick was a crazy idea, but that didn't justify physical assault.

'Are you all right?' Hugh, in his disconcerting old-lady disguise, peered at her with concern.

She took a sharp breath and gave her head a little shake to clear it. One of her cat's ears fell off, and Sebastian bent to pick it up. She yanked the other one from her hair, which promptly fell down round her shoulders. 'I'm coming to pieces.'

'You do look a bit flushed,' said Ann. 'How many drinks have you had?'

'I'm bloody angry, that's all.'

Damn, she shouldn't have said that; their faces were expectant.

'No. It's nothing. I'll be fine. I'll, I'll sit for a bit.'

She backed away towards the sofa. Picked up the leather album that was on it. Tried to shut out the deafening music.

Sebastian had followed her. He squatted in his long, white apron, smiling. 'Would a coffee help? I can easily make one.'

'No thanks. Really, thanks. I'll be okay.'

He went away and, to calm herself, she opened the album and turned pages, starting from the back, working forward. It was what she needed; Lois's photographs were incredibly good. Fleeting expressions exposed beyond doubt or denial.

This one of her and Tessa: didn't it say it all? Taken before she'd ever looked at Jack, and yet here was Tessa's angry contempt. And look at this marvellous one of Ann, dealing cards with a black scowl on her face, blocking all overtures of friendship. What the hell was wrong with these women?

She turned another page. Sebastian smiled out at her. He was sitting in the leather armchair next to Hugh and Lois's fireplace, leaning forward, waving an arm as though he'd just finished speaking. Open. Relaxed. Gentle. Kind. A lovely face. She hadn't seen that before.

She peered through the dancers to where Sebastian stood talking to Hugh and Ann. Holding his chin, chuckling at something Hugh said, then putting his drink on the mantelpiece and setting off for the kitchen. She dodged her head to keep him in view, feeling excited, noticing his relaxed pace, the interest he offered a friend on the way. What she'd seen wasn't fleeting, wasn't only in the photograph. It had always been there. It just needed eyes.

Waterloo—

A marvellous feeling was sweeping through her, half-lifting her from the sofa. And possibilities, banal, unoriginal and wonderful, were opening like flowers in her mind.

Sebastian? Why hadn't she thought of him?

The rest of the party played out around her like a warm day on a beach. She made no move beyond watching Sebastian and waiting for his eyes to meet hers, which they rarely did, he was so busy serving and receiving compliments on his food. She didn't mind; there was no hurry. In breaks from watching him, she drifted among the dancers and chattering groups, feeling semi-invisible and radiating affection at everyone. Their power to distress her had evaporated.

When people started to leave, Charlie found her and nuzzled her neck, 'Stay the night, Zo?' but she wriggled away. 'Sorry, the cat'll be starving. Great party. Happy birthday again.'

She returned to the kitchen and stood one last time by the

door, watching Sebastian, his blue shirtsleeves rolled up past his elbows, clearing and stacking plates and chatting to one of his university pals. 'I know what you mean about Foot,' said the pal, 'but even Callaghan looks a drip after Wilson.'

No rush. All the time in the world. For the moment it was enough to comprehend he existed. She stepped nearer and observed the soft, blond hairs on his wrist. She touched them with a fingertip, sending a bright shiver of electricity up her arm.

Surely he felt that? But no. His eyes, greenish-grey, were on hers, and all he said was, 'Hi, Zoë. You off?'

'Yes. Yes, I am. Great party, Sebastian. Thank you.'

She couldn't speak another word, to him or to anyone. She found her things and stole away quietly before anyone could offer her a lift. She went home by tube, cocooned in her thoughts. She carried her bubble of happiness from the station, down through the dark night and the scent of the budding trees in Greencroft Gardens, up the stairs and into the flat, where she scooped up the cat and fell on the bed with him laughing, daring to say, 'Tommy, I may have done it. I may have found someone to love.'

MAY

Tongue-tied

'So. Have you told him?'

Mick's eyes across the pub table were obscured by sunlight reflected from his glasses. All Zoë's instincts were to comfort him, but it was the same Catch-22 she'd had with Tony: impossible to console and to leave at the same time. And she was beginning to worry about something else, too.

'No.' She shook her head. 'It's so different—I've been savouring it. But actually, trying to explain it to you, I'm realising I don't know how I am going to tell him.'

Mick gave a sarcastic little laugh. 'Pull the other one.'

She leant forward, trying to fathom his lenses. His forehead glistened with sweat: it was airless in here. She hated this.

'What's difficult? He'll fall at your feet.'

His voice was hard to read. Kind of hopeless and caustic.

'Will he?'

'Yes.'

'You mean he'll go to bed with me?'

'Yes.'

'But Sebastian isn't...'

She stopped. It sent ripples through her, speaking his name.

'Isn't what?'

Isn't like you, she almost said. But that was unfair. Isn't like us was more like it. Because however must she seem to Sebastian? Leaving her husband. Sleeping with Charlie. And he probably knew about Mick, though not about Jack, thank goodness. How could she say, Sebastian, with you I'll be different? Why should he believe her, or care?

'Isn't what?' Mick persisted.

'It wouldn't just be about sex.'

Mick fidgeted with his empty pint glass.

'My round.' She reached for her bag.

'No thanks, I've got to go. Alan's on the warpath. One of the account managers screwed up.'

They were standing, and she could see his eyes now. He shook his head. 'Don't kid yourself. Without sex, it's nothing.'

'Yes. Of course.'

They emerged into glaring sun and loud traffic, his way left towards Rex, hers right towards ATP.

'Thursday night?' he said.

'Fine, okay.' But already this felt wrong.

He stepped nearer, his eyes full of pleading. 'What *I* feel for *you* is more than sex.'

For an instant she thought: I can't do this, I can't hurt him. But it was no use.

'Yes, Mick, I know. And I'm sorry.'

'Do you have a moment?'

Sebastian jerked awake and saw Zoë in his doorway, all smiles. He struggled to his feet, feeling fat. 'Of course.'

She advanced into the room. 'Only I'm clueless about error margins, and I wondered if you could tell me if this result is significant?'

His mind was gummy with dreams. The air was so thick with heat this afternoon that he'd nodded off. But he must do this properly. At the various team-meetings last week, when he'd announced GAS, his new 'general advice service', apart from the odd, polite chuckle, no one seemed to take much notice. Zoë was the first to turn up.

He fetched the 'guest chair' and positioned it next to him, on his side of the desk, friendly and informal. He shook his head to keep the weight of sleep at bay, and a drop of perspiration ran into his eye. He fished for his handkerchief. 'Show me,' he said.

Her question was disappointingly simple; he was surprised that she needed to ask it. And she seemed to understand his answer with no trouble at all. Was there something more complicated she was after? He drew a diagram on a piece of graph paper: the normal curve, with arrows and dotted lines; but he could see he was losing her. She was nodding, but not really listening. She was watching his mouth move, and his pencil; but did she comprehend the marks it was making? He felt peculiar, almost hypnotised, half asleep, half awake. Was he boring her? He made himself stop speaking. Lord, it was oppressive in here, and he shouldn't have pulled his chair so close; did he smell sweaty? She looked cool in that yellow dress.

She seemed about to say something, but then didn't.

'So,' he prompted. 'Does that solve the problem?'

'Yes. Thank you.'

She got up, picked up her papers, then lingered.

He smiled, feeling horribly fat. 'Any time. I'm happy to help. It's what I'm here for.'

'Thank you,' she repeated. 'You're good at explaining things.'

Still hovering. Was there something he'd missed?

'Will you be in the pub later on?' she asked.

'Not tonight. Dinner with my parents.'

She looked nonplussed.

'In Bromley,' he added.

'Right.' She kind of winced. 'See you, then.'

'Yes,' he said. 'See you. And erm, you know, any time.'

She was gone. Well, she'd woken him, but he seemed to have put her to sleep. He definitely needed to work on his advice style. Make it snazzier.

Watching Ann laugh on the phone, Zoë itched to confide in her, but it was impossible. They'd said nothing personal to each other in all the months since that night with Mick. Ann was staring out at the chimneypots as she chatted to Lois, but, shifting the receiver from one ear to the other and swinging back to her desk, her eyes closed as they passed over Zoë. She stubbed her cigarette in the red ashtray Zoë had given her for Christmas and pulled another from the gold Benson's packet. Her hair at the front looked dull, and the skin beneath her eyes was discoloured.

Zoë wished Ann would laugh with her the way she used to, the way she was laughing with Lois. Then she could wax lyrical about Sebastian and say, 'How do I do it? How do I tell him?'

Except it wouldn't be kind to wax lyrical, would it? Because Ann wouldn't welcome the news. It might even hurt her. Not that Ann fancied Sebastian; she was rather dismissive of him. But Ann wanted to be in love; she'd said so once. She would think it was her turn, not Zoë's. It was proving awkward to tell anyone.

Charlie's face came round the door, 'Wotcher,' and Zoë nodded hello. His head hovered awhile, disembodied, watching Ann on the phone. Ann didn't look at him either, but carried on talking and examining the burning end of her cigarette. Finally Charlie came in properly, ambled over and stood in front of Zoë's desk. He shifted from plimsoll to plimsoll. 'Fancy the pub this evening, Zo?' he said loudly.

And there it was in his hopeless expression, the same blessing and curse. His whole mind intent on sending signals through the back of his head, wanting Ann, angling to get her attention, to make her jealous.

Of course, Zoë thought, Charlie will understand. He'll help me find the way through. She smiled gratefully. 'It's a date.'

Chinese Whispers

The doors of the pub were propped open, and the customers sat around pavement tables, laughing and sunning themselves.

'I'm not poncing around outdoors,' Charlie growled.

Zoë didn't argue. She bought him a pint, while he commandeered the usual corner.

'Cheers, Zo. You're a mate.'

'Yes, I am.'

'You're smiling too much,' he said morosely. 'I hope you're not going to be too fucking cheerful.'

'I'll try not to be. But here's the deal, Charlie. I've a big problem, and the next round's on me too if you can help solve it.'

He brightened, 'You're on,' and downed half a pint straight.

She took a deep breath. 'The thing is, I feel foolish. Something's happened in my head, and I can't find a way—' She stopped to gather herself, then said quickly, 'You see, it's like this. It sounds daft, but I think I may be falling in love.'

'Whoa! Steady on, Zo—'

'With Sebastian.'

'Ah.' Charlie put down the pint.

'And I don't know, you know, how to make him aware.'

'Yeah, right, you have got a problem.'

Relief flooded through her. 'It's so good to tell someone. Just the fact you're not laughing makes it seem, I don't know, possible again. I was beginning to think it was hopeless, because how on earth *do* I ask him?'

Charlie said nothing, began making a roll-up.

'Here I've been, month after month, not fancying him, and now suddenly I do. How's he to know that, or believe it? I try hanging around looking likely, but he doesn't seem to notice.'

'That's it,' Charlie said.

'Or maybe he does, but doesn't want to let on?'

Charlie considered briefly. 'No, I think you had it first time. It doesn't occur to him. He's not got the radar.' He lit the roll-up and drew on it delicately. 'You know—doable totty, north-northeast.'

Zoë sighed. 'It's strange. It's one of the reasons I'm attracted. But it's almost as though he's not in the game.'

'Yeah.'

Charlie seemed to have nothing to add. He drained his pint.

'So... what do you think? Is there someone in his life I don't know about?'

'Dunno. Don't think so.'

'Think hard.'

'There's a French bird he writes to. A cousin or something.'

228

Her heart plummeted. 'There is?'

'Yeah. She sends postcards with green biro all over them.'

'Green?'

'Yeah. Lots of exclamation marks.'

'And kisses?'

'Don't think so.'

'Have you read them?'

'Of course not!'

She looked at him until he blinked. 'Well... okay... yes, if you insist. I did glance at a couple, but they're in French, which isn't my subject.'

'So, come on, Charlie, what does he say about her? Does he see her when he goes to France? What's her name?'

'Talk about the third degree.' Charlie tapped his empty tankard. 'Payment up front?'

She sprang up and fetched another pint.

'Cheers, Zo.'

She waited.

'They don't telephone,' he said finally, 'and he mentions her as if she's just anyone. My guess is she's keen and he isn't particularly.'

Of course. It had to be true. 'And she's there, and I'm here.'

She chewed her lip, wanting another half, which she couldn't afford. At the rate Charlie was drinking, she'd be on bread and scrape until the end of the month.

'Do you want a roll-up?' he offered.

'Yes, please. Thank you, Charlie.'

He flattened the Rizla and distributed tobacco even more meanly than usual.

One of her fears surfaced. 'Charlie... do you think Sebastian might not be interested in women?'

He groaned, licking the Rizla. 'Bit fucking rich—bloke doesn't fall at your feet, and that proves he's a shirt-lifter.'

'Are you sure that he isn't?'

'For definite. Now and then he kind of joins in with the lamenting about lack of leg-over.'

'He does?'

'Yes, he fucking well does.'

'And he doesn't say, "I wish I was in France?"'

'Nope.'

She bent over his match-flame, an idea forming in her mind. 'Does he ever mention who he does fancy?'

Charlie considered. 'Nah, it's not really his subject, that kind of thing.'

'Because that's what I'm asking you, Charlie. For another pint. Could you speak to him for me? Tell him I'm smitten, not just sex, that I really like him. Then he'll know—he won't need radar. It'll be for him to decide.'

'Fucking hell.'

'Please, Charlie.'

'Another pint, you say?'

'Yes.' She opened her purse, pulled out her last note.

He tugged at his hair and growled, 'Nothing doing.'

'Two more pints,' she pleaded. 'And you can keep that fiver you owe me.'

He gave in. 'Oh all right. But I'm not promising.'

Sebastian was pounding spices for a lamb dopiaza when Charlie wandered into the kitchen, stubbled and tarnished, grabbed a bowl, upended a packet of Rice Krispies over it, and reached for the sugar. The floor crunched underfoot as Sebastian moved between spice-shelf and table, and he performed his usual mental trick of not minding. Presented by Charlie with the options of being a downtrodden housemaid, an insufferable nag or a fellow slob, a fellow slob was what he'd decided to be.

'Mornin',' mumbled Charlie.

'Morning.' Sebastian looked at his watch. 'It is, too. Don't usually see you before noon on a Saturday.'

'It's fucking hot.' Charlie spat Rice Krispies. 'I had to get up for a slash and to open the window, and then I thought, oh well, here I am.'

Sebastian moved to the chopping board and began slicing

onions. He was soon rubbing his eyes. Through his tears he saw Charlie stare, spoon poised halfway to his mouth. 'Onions,' he explained.

'Yeah, onions.' But Charlie left his mouth open as though with something to add.

Sebastian opted for silence. Charlie probably needed subbing and he was low on cash himself. He turned away to the stove, lit the gas, threw a knob of ghee into the copper-bottomed pan his mother had donated and watched it melt, golden and glistening. In went the first lot of onions with a hiss and babble. He added crushed garlic, cinnamon sticks and cloves, then stirred with a wooden spoon, watching the slivers collapse and slide into yellow heaven. Better than chemistry practical, this. He set the gas low and returned to the table to consider the joint of lamb. Charlie was still looking oddly at him. It was distracting. 'Are you okay?' he risked asking.

'Yeah. Fine, mate, fine.'

Bizarre. Still, there was no point trying to fathom Charlie. He would only tease and dodge and lob insults. Sebastian slid the knife into the plumpest part of the meat.

Charlie coughed grossly and began to roll a cigarette. 'Had a drink with Zoë on Thursday.'

'Oh yes?'

Success: he'd detached a squarish slab that would divide well into cubes. It was going to be a splendid curry. 'Is she coming tonight? You're welcome to share this.'

No reply. He lifted his head to look at Charlie, who mumbled, 'She's all right, old Zo, don't you think?'

'Definitely. There's not many would put up with you.'

He'd caught Charlie's habit of offering insults in lieu of conversation. But Charlie wasn't on form. 'Yeah, a bit of all right,' he repeated lamely.

Highly bizarre. Was Charlie becoming attached to an obtainable woman for a change?

'So, shall I cook rice for three, two or one?'

'Dunno.' Charlie lurched from the table. 'I'll ask her. Pub'll be open soon. Fancy a jar?'

'Sure. I'll get this simmering.'

He threw the ground spices into the pan and inhaled. Cumin, ginger, coriander, turmeric: was there anything more wonderful than these smells?

The phone began ringing. 'I'll go,' said Charlie.

Other Engagements

'I'm getting married, Lois... To David... You know, David Pratt from ATP... Yes, isn't it? I'm surprised too, and so happy.'

Ann dug her toes into the sullied white shag-pile and inhaled the floral air-freshener. She'd been watching and listening for half an hour now, as Pamela shifted the receiver from one ear to the other, pretending to believe that people's startled congratulations and excuses about the party were genuine.

At least she wasn't plagued with envy, as she'd been over Lois's pregnancy. When Pamela first flashed her diamond, she'd had to squash an instinct to laugh. It had been easy to say, 'Pam, how wonderful! You dark horse. When did this happen?' and to ooh and ah through Pam's story of how David had booked a posh restaurant and actually gone down on one knee between the main and the pud. Here at least was someone sadder and more desperate than herself, and now, with luck, Pamela's whingeing about Jack would stop.

'Okay, Lois. Yes, I'm sorry it's short notice. Of course I understand, though it would have been lovely to see you.'

Pamela slumped despondently as she hung up. 'Thank heavens we persuaded David's sister to lend us her flat. It would've been a complete flop here in Acton.'

It was going to be dire in Swiss Cottage. Pam had invited nurses from the hospital, and David was sending a general invitation around ATP, so there should be enough people to look like a party, but too many key players were pleading other engagements, or talking of 'probably', or of 'dropping in for a while' on their way somewhere else. And there was a heavy flavour of family: Prattie's sister, his cousins from Watford, Pamela's gormless brother, who was bringing his mates from teacher training college, and two lots of parents on weekend trips to town. The parents would come early to meet one another and then, said Pam's dad, 'make ourselves scarce while the young people have fun.'

Ann patted Pamela's arm. 'Is David's sister nice?'

'Mary? Not really. There's something a bit dried up about her, and she's been horrid about lending her flat. We've told her there'll be next to no mess and we'll clear up and pay for any damage, but she's still acting like we want to ruin her life. Hang on, I need to spend a penny.'

While she was gone the phone rang. It was David.

'Tell Pam, Charlie's being stubbornly vague. Sebastian's a definite though. He'll arrive late because he's booked to meet up with a pal. Bring the pal along, I said, the more the merrier, but he reckoned it wasn't possible because they're meeting in Croydon. You're coming, aren't you, Ann? Don't you dare let us down.'

Hanging up, Ann flicked through the pile of magazines on the sofa beside her. *Getting inside your man's mind in the bedroom. How far should a Cosmo Girl go? Reform your man without losing him.* When Pamela came back, she relayed Prattie's message, but Pamela nodded absently, scarcely seeming to register it. She was flipping pages in her address book.

'There's a call I've been putting off,' she said. 'I've got to be brave. I've been sitting on the loo, thinking, now I must do it, go on, do it now.' Ann tried not to laugh. 'Because, Ann, when will I feel any braver?' She threw the address book aside. 'What am I doing? I know his number by heart.'

She got up from the settee and went to the stereo. There was a record on the turntable already.

'I promised myself I wouldn't play this when I rang him. But I can't help it. We had so much together, Ann. We could have had everything, and he threw it away.'

The music began, a regretful, downbeat intro, causing Pamela to crumple as though leaking air. Ann got up and put her arms round her.

'Are you sure it's a good idea to invite him, my lover?'

'But I have to.' She adjusted the volume. 'Not too loud,' she explained. 'Just so it's there in the background. He won't realise he's hearing it.'

She lifted her hand and looked at her diamond. Ann seized the hand. 'You don't have to do this, Pam.'

'Yes, I do, though. He misses me—I know he does. I see pain in his eyes whenever he looks at me.' She crouched on the settee and started to dial. 'He works on Saturdays now. I heard him complaining about it at Charlie's party. He has to go hell-for-leather on Lady Margaret Road to make up his losses on Brecknock—Oh, hello...' She hunched over the phone. 'Yes, hello, Gary. It's Pamela Harrison. Is Mr Golding there, please?'

For a few moments she listened, then, 'Okay, thank you, Gary.' She hung up, pulling a face. 'That man is so vile, so insinuating.'

Her voice threatened tears. She whispered, 'I'll ring Highgate. There's nothing wrong in that, is there? I'm engaged to be married. I'm inviting them to a party, that's all.'

Ann put an arm around her shoulders. 'Yes, that's all you're doing, Pam.'

Pamela was shaking. She held each number against the stop before letting the dial rattle back. She released the last one and waited, eyes shut, then jumped and made a face at Ann.

'Oh, hello. Tessa, hi. It's Pamela... yes... no, no, the thing is I'm engaged to be married.'

'*Married?*' Ann could hear the crackle of Tessa's voice in the receiver. She leant nearer.

'To David. David Pratt. You know, he's—'

'*Yes, I know. Well, I never.*'

'And we're having a party. Next Saturday. I do hope you and Jack will be able to come.'

Tessa laughed. '*I'm afraid not. Goodbye.*'

And Pamela was staring at a dead receiver.

'The bitch.' She hurled it into the shag-pile. 'The horrible, nasty bitch. You know, Ann, I knelt here pleading and crying with Jack not to leave me. But he wouldn't listen, and he's stuck now. My poor darling Jack, saddled with that horrific woman.'

'It doesn't matter anymore,' Ann tried to tell her. 'You're marrying David.'

Pamela looked up, blinking, her mascara beginning to run. 'You're right.' She found a tissue and blew her nose. She wiped her eyes, smearing the mascara, struggling to smile. 'I know, I'll invite Zoë.'

Ann watched Pamela dial again and listened in to the tinny tones of Zoë's responses. And, to give her credit, Zoë, though she barely knew Pamela, was friendly—*Congratulations. That's wonderful*—asked who would be at the party, and seemed genuinely not to mind that it would only be Ann and Sebastian and a few other bods from ATP. *I live round the corner. Of course I'll be there.*

As Zoë put the phone down on Pamela, it rang again. It was Charlie this time, crying off his promise. 'It's impossible, Zo. The subject just doesn't come up.'

'Okay,' she sighed. 'But he's definitely going to Pamela's engagement do, am I right?'

'Yeah,' Charlie conceded. 'He's not keen, but he reckons he owes it to Prattface. What bollocks. Anyway, he's cooking tonight and says we can share it. D'you want to mosey on over here?'

Yes, she did; but no, no, she couldn't.

'Come on, Zo. I fancy some nooky. You'll be at it with Mussolini soon, and I'll be without.'

'Nothing personal, Charlie, but shagging you in his flat is hardly going to help my cause.'

'So that's it then?'

'Yes. Sorry. And by the way, you still owe me that fiver.'

The Mating Game

'So then of course, I was on my own again. Which was when I decided men really aren't worth it.'

How old-fashioned this party is, thought Zoë for the umpteenth time as she shifted her weight on the sofa arm, renewed her fixed smile and tried to pay attention to Pratt's sister whose name she'd forgotten and who seemed to have so many dreary problems.

'I keep thinking the next one will be better, but you no sooner give them a cup of tea than they're off in your bathroom leaving the seat up and heaven knows what else.'

'I don't really mind that,' she put in. 'They might just as well complain that we leave it down.'

The sister stalled, frowning. 'I don't see what you mean. It's supposed to be down.'

It was like the parties Tony used to take her to before they were married. Rooms stuffed full of knick-knacks and pleasant people to whom she could think of nothing to say. Women with short, permed hair who talked earnestly about nursing or teaching and wore little gold crosses round their necks. Men standing shoulder-to-shoulder discussing football or alternative routes to Basingstoke. Anodyne, undanceable music. She missed having her own stereo. Jack said she could get a credit card and buy one, but she didn't quite like the idea: she wouldn't feel comfortable spending money she didn't yet have. It was tough being broke though; the flat needed something soft to sit on. She'd seen seating units in Habitat, cut from foam, with foam-chipping cushions and washable, stone-coloured denim covers. Two corner units and two plain would make a great L-shaped sofa, and they were really quite cheap, but she couldn't afford them as well as a stereo.

'Anyway,' grumbled the sister, 'seat up or seat down, when you haven't got a man, it's no use wasting time wishing you had.'

No one from the Drunken Bridge Club had come except

Ann, who'd borne it for barely an hour before pulling a conspiratorial face and vanishing again. Time was Ann would have stayed for her company alone. They'd have nattered nineteen to the dozen and got tipsy and not noticed how dull the party was. Zoë took another sip of white wine, though she was trying to go slowly. Tipsy was fine, but she didn't want to be pissed when Sebastian showed up.

If he ever did. She kept anxious watch on the door to the hall. Each time it moved, she willed him to appear. She raised her head, preparing to give a smile of slight surprise, one that would say lightly, well good heavens, how nice to see you, though it hardly crossed my mind you'd be here.

'So what do *you* think?' The sister coughed to reclaim her attention, then waited expectantly.

'About men?'

'Yes.'

'Well... it's not really about lavatory seats. Or sex, I've decided.'

'Yes, yes,' said the sister impatiently. 'The point I'm making is, are they worth it at all?'

'Worth it?' Zoë's irritation was rising. What was 'it', she wanted to ask. 'Probably not,' she said brusquely. 'You'd be better off going to bed with a good book. Have you read any lately?'

'No,' the sister sighed. 'I mostly watch television.'

She began to list her favourite programmes. Zoë glanced at her watch, gone eleven, and tried not to despair. He'd be here later. But this *was* later.

She had no plan beyond the smile she would give him. All day she had distracted herself with physical preparation: washing her hair, creaming her skin, ironing the long, blue cotton dress she wore to the Goldings' garden party last year, putting it on, seeing how shabby it was, dithering and taking it off again. Resisting the urge to run up to John Barnes and blow some of her savings on something new. Changing her mind to another old favourite, a dress tiered in different Madras cotton plaids, pink, green, blue, yellow, that swirled and floated as she moved. Deciding on underwear: no bra, it was far too hot, and her newest white knickers, chaste as a nun. And then she spent ages fidgeting with her hair, trying to contrive a look that was uncontrived, before losing patience and arriving here stupidly early, almost the first through the door, carrying her gift of a white china plant-pot.

Pamela was so effusively grateful that Zoë knew from the off it would be one of those parties. And now she'd been here an eternity, her bottom numb on this sofa arm, smiling false smiles, eager, then anxious, then bored, and now hopeless, and still with no plan.

The sister was talking about *Coronation Street*.

He wasn't coming.

It was just as well; she had no business being here. Sebastian would see through her selfishness and despise her. He would decode her smile, know it was meant to entrap him, and escape back to Hackney thinking less of her, not more. She was trivial, she was shallow, she had nothing he needed. She should read more, join the Swiss Cottage Library, because good men and good books were not either-or. If he wasn't here by eleven-thirty, she would go home. She glanced at her watch again: nearly ten-past already.

'So I have to admit it, I'm hooked. Do you watch it? I'm sorry, your name's gone from my head. It's always the way with me. I try to remember, but I'm useless at names. Now faces, that's a different thing. I never forget a face. If I see you next week, I'll remember you straightaway. But where I saw you, or your name, no, don't ask me.'

Behind the sister's mournfully rabbiting head, Zoë saw the door move again, its handle depressed by someone who lingered talking in the hall. She watched it listlessly, expecting nothing. And then the door swung open, and there he was. Sebastian. Looking straight at her. With a smile that said lightly, well good heavens, how nice to see you, though it hardly crossed my mind you'd be here. And there was no guile in his smile. And across her face there spread a smile of welcome that said simply, hello.

238

Sebastian could have done without this party. He'd had an excellent evening and an over-large meal with his affable, laid-back buddy Pete, and now he was yawning and ready for bed. Still a promise was a promise, and David had few enough mates. Steering his heavy feet between train and tube at Victoria Station, he'd consoled himself with the thought of a long lie-in tomorrow.

'Sebastian! How wonderful to see you,' Pamela gushed at the door, embracing him as though they were old friends. Her cheek, as he kissed it, felt fleshy and soft, and her cleavage jiggled just out of focus beyond her urgent smile. Three young women in the hall paused in their conversation. 'Moira. Jill. Emily.' Pamela pointed and flourished. 'This is Sebastian, David's wonderful boss.'

He grinned, embarrassed by the introduction, not wanting to be a boss, unwilling to play the part. To his relief, their interest was transitory and he was allowed, first into the kitchen to be given a drink by David, and then into the lounge, where the clamour of conversation competed with the subdued sound of an old Beatles LP.

He was relieved to see Zoë; he was too tired to make much sense of strangers. She made her excuses to the woman she was talking to and came over.

'Good to see you,' she said.

'Yes, indeed.'

It was odd her being here; though maybe not, she lived close by. Anyway, it was his good fortune: he wouldn't have to pretend to be awake. He liked Zoë: she had a calm, quiet way about her and humorous eyes.

'Have you had a good evening?' she asked. 'Pamela said you were seeing a friend.'

'Yes.' He patted his stomach, trying to pull it in at the same time. 'We had a blowout, Chinese for a change. To be honest, I'm whacked. I'd give anything to sit down.'

They found a space between the sofa and the television where they could squeeze in with their backs to the wall. He slumped down, sighed, 'Ah, that's better,' and closed his eyes. When he next opened them, he saw Zoë was smiling at him. She didn't say anything.

'I'm sorry,' he said. 'I'm not scintillating company.'

She arranged herself alongside him, shoulders touching, looking out into the room. 'Scintillation isn't required. Seriously, you don't have to say a thing.'

It seemed easy to take her at her word. He let his head fall back, sighed, sipped his beer, allowed the music to wash over him. *Martha, my dear.* Zoë joined in, singing along softly, knowing the pauses and inflections. She had a good voice.

The track ended. He knew what came next; he'd heard it so many times. The music dragging with fatigue. *I'm so tired.*

'How will you get home?' said Zoë after a while.

He yawned, longing for bed. 'A cab, I guess.' The evening was starting to blur.

'Or you can stay at my place.'

He opened his eyes. 'Okay. That would be good.'

He closed them again. He didn't understand. Did she mean—? Maybe not, but what else could she mean? Better let her take care of it. Her soft voice sang along with John Lennon's.

Still she had no plan. She was mad. Crazy. There was only one bed. He knew that, didn't he? Perhaps he didn't. Perhaps he thought she must have another, a put-you-up she would pull from a cupboard with a flourish. She didn't even have a spare blanket.

They were walking back now, through the warm May night, under the plane trees whispering with their new summer leaves, strolling slowly side-by-side. Relaxed and calm. It was easy to be calm with Sebastian. She felt she could let him take care of things, take care of her forever.

And yet he wasn't holding her hand. He gave no sign that he expected to sleep with her. Why should he? How could he know? You can stay at my place, she'd said. Not, oh by the way, I think you're amazing and it seems daft you going all the way back to Hackney when you can spend the rest of your life round the corner with me, what do you say? No, idiotic, tongue-tied woman. She'd said nothing like that. Just, you can stay at my place. What was any sane, sleepy man to make of that when he hadn't even winked at her? And what would he think when he realised? Oh help. She was a lunatic in serious danger of being taken for a tart.

They climbed the stairs together and stood in her living-room. As he bent to stroke the cat, she scanned the room desperately, trying to conjure up a softish surface six feet long, but none appeared.

'Would you like a coffee?'

Perplexing. When it was past two o'clock and she offered yet more coffee, Sebastian got up the nerve to kiss her. He found sex daunting, he didn't know how one was supposed to initiate it, and he feared being rebuffed. The three women he'd been to bed with had each led him there or climbed in with him, and that was what he'd been hoping Zoë would do. But now he saw she was embarrassed. He would have to have some kind of a go.

He stumbled across the gap and landed in her arms.

And that was it, it was easy. All of a sudden, she was kissing him and laughing and blurting out how embarrassed she'd been and what must he think of her and how she'd been trying for weeks to tell him.

And then they made it through into the bedroom, and it was happening, and he was struggling to do it right and to hold his stomach in and to last for more than two minutes, but it didn't seem to matter that he didn't. She really seemed keen.

Afterwards she lay quietly, smiling and touching his face.

'I can't quite believe this,' he said.

'Nor can I.'

Her eyes were very close. In the darkness, he couldn't see their colour, only their shape, and the softness of the look she was giving him. Her arms were round his neck and her lovely hair was all over the pillow, smelling of apples and vanilla, and

241

her cool skin was under his hand, which was free to go anywhere.

'I'm sorry,' she said. 'I've kept you up all night, when really you're dying to sleep.'

He shook his head. 'This is worth staying awake for.'

'That's 'it'!' she exclaimed. 'That's what 'it' is. Worth staying awake for.'

He laughed. He didn't understand, but it didn't matter. And she was right, he had been sleepy; but now he wasn't at all. All he wanted to do was to look and touch and hear her voice and do it again soon, less urgently, taking more notice, and hopefully more time. He'd be okay, he'd not had any practice; he just needed more practice. She was speaking.

'So tomorrow, Sebastian, what happens tomorrow?'

There was going to be more. Though, oh dear, what about Charlie?

'Tomorrow? Well, I think tomorrow we should have a lie-in and lots more of this.' He dared to explore with a finger. 'And possibly some croissants and coffee. How does that sound?'

She hadn't said anything about Charlie. Maybe Charlie wouldn't mind. He'd never called her his girlfriend, and he was still whingeing on about Ann.

'Sounds great,' Zoë murmured.

He wished Charlie hadn't been here, in this bed, touching what he was touching.

'Shall we have a bit more right now?'

She was climbing on top of him, taking hold of him, making him catch his breath and say, 'Yes'.

He reached up, brought her face down to his for a kiss. Her hair fell in a soft curtain around him. He would probably stop minding about Charlie quite soon. He just needed practice.

A Bad Call

On Monday morning, Ann raced back from her meeting with the partners, eager to spill her good news. She found a scribbled note from Zoë on her desk. *Lunch with M, then taking pm off. Hope OK. Tons of leave left. See you tomorrow.*

And yes, it was fine. The new project was launched; nothing much to do until the questionnaires came back. Ann lit a cigarette and gazed happily through the open window at pigeons huddled in the shade of a chimneypot. What a sweltering spring, and still the whole summer stretched ahead. She felt a touch woozy: Ron and Doug had cracked open the champagne. It was happening. She was going to be a partner!

She rang home first, to hear her mother squeal with delight. She made her promise to swank unbearably to all her brothers and sisters. Hanging up, she did a little dance around the office, before picking up again and dialling Lois.

'Ann, that's just brilliant. You really deserve it.'

Lois's pleasure was genuine. She too was happy, selling her photos and growing her baby. 'Heavens above,' she said, 'we've started doing all the middle-aged crap.'

And then she was asking about the holiday in three weeks time. 'Have you booked it?' she wanted to know.

'Yes. That converted barn we all liked, with the river at the bottom of the garden.'

'Sleeps how many?'

'Eight.' Ann clicked her lighter. 'I know it's a lot between five, Lois, but we're all working. Well you aren't, but Hugh earns enough.'

'Don't be daft, Ann, since when was I penny-pinching? It's the company I'm worried about.'

Ann focused. 'Do you mean Jack? I've noticed he's off with you.'

'Both of them. I don't think I can bear a whole, undiluted fortnight of the Goldings. It wears me out, listening to them fight. Hugh says, in that case let's cancel.'

'Hey, no,' Ann protested, 'you can't leave me with no holiday. I'm not going on my own with those two. And the deposit's non-refundable.'

'Exactly. That's what I told Hugh. So what I thought was, ask a couple more people, yes?'

'Okay. Brilliant. Though it rather depends who.' Ann blew smoke towards Zoë's empty desk. 'How about Pam and David? I was at their engagement do on Saturday. They'd kill for the chance.'

'Oh, yawn, do me a favour. We'd die of boredom watching David lick our boots. And Pamela would mope about gazing at Jack. No, I've a much better plan. How about dear, sexy little Charlie and nice, cuddly Sebastian Santini?'

Ann giggled. 'Lois, you're incorrigible. Middle-aged and pregnant and still after the men!'

She quite liked the idea though.

Lois was laughing. 'But, of course, did you imagine I was permanently retired? This is definitely just a fat and farting phase I'm going through. So... Sebastian and Charlie. Go get 'em, right now!'

Ann set off in search. The more she thought about it, the better the idea seemed. She'd be the unattached woman in a party of seven with two unattached men. Sebastian and Charlie were good company and, what the hell, in the boozy idleness of Wales, she might well overcome her objections to one or other of them. Didn't Tessa keep nagging 'Just choose someone and see how it goes'? Suddenly the champagne and the good news had her wanting to do just that.

They were with one of the computer guys, poring over some printout, and there was no sign of David Pratt, thank goodness. It felt easy and friendly to invite the two of them together, so it didn't look like a come-on, which she wasn't at all sure that it was, or for which of them.

'I'll come if you pay my share of the rent,' dear, sexy little Charlie said brightly, 'and if you'll be my woman while we're there.'

Ann laughed, 'Steady on, Charlie,' as the computer guy's eyebrows shot up.

Charlie scowled. 'Count me out then. Even if I could afford it, there's no way I'm going to pretend to be fucking bourgeois and watch you lot play bridge.'

His funeral. She wasn't going to plead. And there was still nice, cuddly Sebastian. She touched his wrist. 'So how about you?'

'It's very kind of you, Ann, but, er...'

He looked attractive today, smiling and relaxed, and that blue-denim, button-down shirt suited him. 'Er what, Sir Sebastian? Spit it out.'

'Well, I'm not sure if—'

'Come on. Don't be shy. It's a brilliant converted barn, really gorgeous, four bedrooms and a garden with apple trees right by the Wye. Live dangerously. Say yes. It'll be great to have you along. Everyone says so.'

'It sounds wonderful,' he said. 'The thing is, I'll have to check... What I mean is, there's someone...'

What on earth was his problem?

'There's a person that I'm probably, you know, erm, with.'

She understood him at last and found herself stuttering, trying to cover her tracks. 'Of course... yes... how rude of me, I should have asked.' God, did he realise she'd been flirting? 'You must bring her. She'd be very welcome. I'm sorry, I had no idea.'

Charlie snorted, which didn't help. The computer guy grinned.

'It's okay.' Sebastian's face had turned pink. 'There's no reason why you should. It's only just happened. This weekend. I thought she would have told you. It's Zoë.'

'Zoë?'

'Yes.'

Ann salvaged her smile.

'But thank you, Ann, it's really nice of you to ask us, and I'd love to come. And Zoë, too, I'm sure. I was being inane. Of course, we'd both love to come. It sounds really excellent.'

Endgame

Walking up from Highgate tube, Zoë's alternating feelings of elation and sadness gave way to dread. Her feet dragged as she rounded the last corner and saw Jack's sleek, green car on the gravel behind the beech hedge, in front of the posh door with its long, black-painted hinges. This was Tessa's house; she had no business here. She hung back in the lane.

On the phone, Jack had insisted she come. She said no, but he wouldn't accept it. 'Take the afternoon off. We have to talk about this.'

It was only fair, she supposed. She'd met Mick for lunch and told him. She wouldn't have dreamed of ending it with Mick on the phone, though it was hell face to face.

'I should have left Elaine,' he kept saying, repeating it no matter how many times she protested that she hadn't wanted him to.

'It's Elaine you love really.'

'No, it's you, Zoë.'

And she loved him too, and it was horribly hard to part from him. His eyes were bloodshot, he was blinking, and she couldn't bear it, that Mick was near tears because he believed she was wonderful when she wasn't at all. She found herself confessing about Jack to him, wanting him to be angry or his relaxed, philandering self, because his grief was too awful.

It was a mistake telling him about Jack; it hurt him more. Which had her blathering how she'd been annoyed at his jealousy, the way he'd told Tessa about her, which was why she betrayed him. And meanwhile she was thinking, what the hell am I playing at, because now he was blaming himself, calling himself a fool. And she was protesting, no, no, you're not, blurting how she didn't even like Jack. Which was when Mick sat back and looked at her and said, 'But the sex was good, wasn't it?' Not bitterly, just sadly, and why did men always want to know that? And then he was asking was the sex good with Sebastian, which she wasn't going to discuss. The whole conversation was horrible. Couldn't she have found a better way to do this to someone she cared for?

Which was why she didn't want to see Jack now. It was easy to concede on the phone, okay, I'll come. But pussyfooting here in his driveway, she saw it was wrong, because she didn't care for Jack, and it devalued Mick to act as though she did. And she was exhausted after two nights and a day spent mostly awake with Sebastian. And this relentless heat was making her jaded and sweaty. All she wanted was to go quietly home, push up the tall sash windows, take the cat in her arms, and fall asleep listening to the cries of the swifts wheeling and diving above the plane trees. She turned to go. She would ring Jack and tell him she got held up at work.

'Zoë.'

He was standing in the open doorway. And she was suddenly terribly thirsty.

'Jack.'

He ushered her in and gave her water that she gulped down. He was wearing denim flares and a white linen shirt, and he smelled of alcohol. He'd set out radishes, butter and salt on the kitchen table. He'd made soup and warmed bread. The back door was open onto the terrace, where the vine was coming into leaf. She took a step into the garden, seeking the magic of the party last year, but recalling only Tony that day. Tony... then Mick... it was frightening, all the pain she kept causing, the good men she kept throwing away.

'Bordeaux.' Jack put a cold glass in her hand. 'A nice Merlot.'

'Lovely,' she said lamely. 'A farewell feast.'

'Not at all, that's what I'm saying. No one knows about us. There's no reason to stop.'

She had broken her promise to Jack, telling Mick, and she was going to break it again. The minute she was clear of Mick and Jack, she would tell Sebastian everything. About Jack, about Mick, about Lois, Tessa, Ann, Pamela, everything, because she owed him no less and she needed to clear the poison out of her system.

Jack clinked her glass. 'Cheers.'

'I'm sorry, Jack, but I mean it. I'm going to be true to Sebastian.'

True just for once in her life.

Jack looked as if he'd bitten on a bad radish. 'You'll get bored. He's a nice enough guy, but you're not telling me he's sexy?'

Like Mick, wanting to know. She didn't answer.

'You'll soon miss me.'

No she wouldn't.

'I'll treasure the memories,' she lied. 'I'll think of you whenever I eat *radis au beurre*.'

She tried to stop drinking, but he kept topping up her glass, and she felt nervous, almost afraid; he was saying so little through his compressed, cruel mouth. Very soon she would leave. She would take the tube to Belsize Park and walk home along the sunbaked avenues. And then she would ring Sebastian and say there've been others besides Charlie, but there are no others now.

'Time for bed,' Jack said.

'No, Jack. I'm going to be faithful.'

'This one doesn't count. You can't ditch me without a proper goodbye.'

His eyes went to the ceiling. 'Not here, Jack. Not in Tessa's bed. Hey, what are you...? Stop it.'

He'd grabbed her bag and was tugging her out of the kitchen, through the hall, to the front door, thank goodness, and across the gravel to the car. Opening the passenger door, trying to shove her inside.

'Hang on. I didn't mean somewhere else.'

He ignored her. He was locking the front door. 'Shut up and get in.'

How dare he? She set off across the gravel, half-running. And immediately he was there, at her elbow, grabbing it and forcing her to stop.

'Let me go.'

248

'A lift home, what's the big deal?' He wouldn't let go of her arm.

She wanted to shout, 'Fuck you, don't push me around,' loud so the neighbours would hear. But there was pain in his eyes, and the words died in her throat. She didn't like Jack, and now she almost hated him, but that wasn't fair. She should have said no in the first place. Did he love her? Was he hurting like Mick?

He was pulling her back to the car, and she was too exhausted to argue. Her knees were bending, she was inside, and he clunked the door shut. The interior smelled of hot leather and his cigarettes. He crashed in beside her, not saying a word, slammed the driver's door, revved the engine and fast-accelerated into the lane.

She fastened the safety belt and watched him change up through the gears, glaring at the road ahead. She willed him to look at her. 'Please don't be so angry. I do care how you feel.'

He threw her a glance. 'Okay. So give me one to remember.'

She turned away. Saw the hot, bright streets hurtle by. Fought against nausea as he swerved and braked. Remembered her aversion to smart, fast cars.

The readiness is all. It wasn't about sex. Mick and Jack insisted it was, and she couldn't prove otherwise. So, what the hell? Let Jack have his way, one last time that would belong to the past? She didn't want to, but it wouldn't mean anything or cost anything.

It was a horrible mistake. There was no comfort to be had this way. She kept her eyes open. Met Jack's angry stare or, when his face was in the pillow, watched the clock radio on the bedside table. 4.32.

She wanted to think of Sebastian, but she mustn't while she was doing this. Why was she doing this? She shut her eyes, focused her ears, and eventually heard the soft click of the little digital flap falling and revealing the next minute. 4.33.

Jack pulled out, knelt astride her and looked down with

249

furious eyes. He presented his cock to her mouth. She took it and started counting seconds in her head. One... two... three...

He tugged her hair, rocked her head back and forward. Fourteen... fifteen... sixteen...

Come, she thought, come. But he didn't. Twenty-seven... twenty-eight... twenty-nine...

He withdrew, dropped down and burrowed his head between her thighs. She tensed, but he persisted, his tongue, then his finger, finding the spot and working it.

Fifty-eight... fifty-nine... sixty. She stopped counting. This was no good. She would have to come, so his honour was satisfied. Lots of women faked it, she'd heard. She wished that she could fake it, right now, get it over with, but she didn't dare. What would he do if he realised? Yell at her? Hit her? She shut her eyes and concentrated, trying to go with the tickle, shifting so his finger stopped bruising. It didn't take long. It felt as meaningless as sneezing. She faked some sound effects to go with it, then pulled him into her and applied herself vigorously to making him come.

'I hope that isn't the one you'll remember.'

It seemed odd to be speaking.

He got up. Started to pull on his clothes. 'Could be worse, I suppose.'

'Meaning what?'

'It's not that troglodyte, Galway.'

Now she did hate him. He sat on the edge of the bed, yanking on his shoes. 'You don't know the first thing about Mick.'

She ducked as he swung round. 'I know all I want to know, thank you.'

She felt bleak, almost desolate. 'Jack, don't be like this. Can't you be happy for me?'

'No, I can't.'

He stood for a moment, glaring. There was nothing to say.

'Goodbye, Zoë.' He turned and strode from the room. The door slammed. She heard his footsteps descending the stairs.

The clock radio showed 4.51.

It was suddenly very quiet. She got up, put on her dressing gown and stepped into the living-room. Tommy, on the wicker chair in the bay window, lifted his head and blinked at her. She went across and slid up each of the four giant sashes, then picked Tommy up and sat with him on her knee. The world outside blazed with light, and from the sky came the sound she wanted to hear: the shrill, airy sound of the swifts calling to one another, wheeling and diving high above the plane trees.

JUNE

Gloves Off

Sebastian scanned the front page of *The Times*. The riots had spread from Soweto to other townships. Vorster insisted 'maintain law and order at all costs', and the police kept on firing their bullets into black children. Yesterday the tally was eight dead; now it looked to be hundreds, though they weren't allowing the journalists in. Yesterday's image was enough. A lifeless boy, barelegged in shorts, limp in the arms of a student in dungarees. A young girl, her palm raised in horror or denial. Running together, their two faces contorted with grief.

Sebastian lifted his head from the newspaper and contemplated the six people and one dog who lounged about him on a patchwork of towels and blankets in the dappled light of the apple trees. For once no one was speaking. Most of them looked asleep. Only Zoë was busy, cross-legged on the grass, braiding daisies. His gaze followed the slope of the garden down to the picket fence and beyond to the gleam of the river, the fields and the heat-hazed horizon.

Yesterday, they'd talked about South Africa a bit over lunch, competitively expressing their outrage. And then the conversation had drifted; and now massacred children had passed out of their thoughts. They would be out of his in a minute or two. He turned pages. The Ecology Party trying to drum up support. Viking One in orbit round Mars. What should he do? Think of that boy each time he didn't buy a South African orange? Was that it?

He drew in a deep breath and exhaled slowly. Because he couldn't help it, he was happy, and he was no better than the people he was with, and he was glad he'd let Zoë persuade him not to pull out of this holiday. When she told him the details of who'd slept with whom, he was shocked. More than that, repelled. He couldn't understand how such things could go on, how this incestuous circle could smile and play bridge and drink wine as if none of it had happened. His first instinct was to break off with her, but he didn't say so and the moment passed. She seemed angry with them all, and hurt for reasons he didn't fully understand. She wanted reassurance that she wasn't a bad person. He said, let's not go to Wales, but she seemed set on it. 'We shouldn't have to punish ourselves,' she insisted. 'Why should we let them exclude us?'

As far as he could see, no one was trying to exclude them; but what did he know? And actually the holiday had been fine. The place was idyllic, everyone was basking in it or pretending to, and though he could guess at some of what lay beneath the surface, mostly he didn't bother. The respect verging on awe with which he'd regarded these people had evaporated now. And things felt good with Zoë, better each day. Especially kissing felt good. He looked at her mouth now, smiling to itself as she added another daisy. He thought sometimes he could go on kissing her forever.

He yawned, pulled a handkerchief from his pocket, polished his lenses and then wiped his forehead and neck. This heat was incredible: they were all of them sweating and pink. His back was sticking to the deckchair, and his head ached a little. Perhaps he should eat something salty? Or shave off his beard?

The tensions had threatened to break the surface last night when Ann had them playing that truth game. The idea was to say which plant, animal, bird, and so on each person resembled. Someone suggested landscape as a category, which was a toughie, and he was struggling to decide whether Hugh was more like a lake or a meadow and how he would explain either, when Ann said that Zoë was like foothills, which seemed unkind although apt. And then Ann looked wounded when Zoë retaliated in the next round by likening her to holly, which Sebastian couldn't quite see. Shiny and colourful, Zoë maintained, but what about the prickles? Tessa or Lois seemed a lot more like holly to him. Zoë confessed later she felt rotten about it. She'd meant Ann was closed off, not as friendly as she used to be, but holly wasn't right, not at all; it just came into her mind, and popped out of her mouth, and sounded horrid, and then it was too late.

Anyway, the bad feelings weren't evident today. Everyone was being pleasant, or subdued at least, enervated by the never-ending blaze from the sky. Lunch had been excellent as usual: gourmet and alcoholic. Tessa and Jack certainly knew how to cook, even if they were a bit fractious and wearing on the nerves. They'd insisted they didn't mind doing it for the whole fortnight, leaving the skivvying to everyone else. Well to Zoë and Ann actually, since Hugh and Lois were happy to be waited on, and Zoë said she enjoyed cleaning.

He glanced back at the paper. 'Office workers stripped off and plunged into Trafalgar Square fountains yesterday,' he relayed to no one in particular.

Ann rolled onto her side and opened her eyes. 'Boy, am I glad I'm not in London.'

He read on. 'People got stuck in a tube train north of St John's Wood. From 10.30 till noon. It was so hot that they broke windows to get air. Some stripped to the waist.'

Lois had picked up her camera and was doing a bit of view-finding. 'Some *what* stripped to the waist?' she asked and clicked the shutter at him.

He grinned. 'Men, I suppose. *The Times* doesn't specify.'

Hugh gestured lazily at the sky. 'Maybe there were topless women. *The Times* chooses not to specify.'

'It's the drought that worries me,' said Tessa, fanning herself with her book. 'Some of the reservoirs are completely empty. It hardly rained last winter either.'

'Still, look on the bright side,' said Ann. 'It must be the best year ever for a holiday in Wales. Such a shame we have to go back tomorrow. What shall we do with our last afternoon?'

'Climb the Brecon Beacons,' said Jack.

'Walk along the Wye,' said Lois.

'How about you, Sebastian?'

'Really, I don't mind.'

It was bound to be wonderful, whatever they did.

Wandering in the meadows beside the river, hand in hand with Zoë, he'd seen a kingfisher zip low across the water like an iridescent arrow. 'Look,' he'd said, and she'd seen it too, where he pointed, perched briefly on a root that twisted out from the bank, a silver fish in its beak. Or scaling the easy peaks of the Black Mountains, standing there on one of those craggy fingers, looking out across the multicoloured patchwork of summer fields below, he'd felt marvellous.

Mostly it was the nights that filled his head. Naked under the thin sheet in the sultry air, watching Zoë's hair spread in ruby waves and ripples, like a calm sea at sunset. Private time while the others slept, when they could make love and talk softly about anything and nothing.

Ann was laughing. 'Oh Sebastian, you're incorrigible. You let other people make all the decisions.'

'Why not?' He stretched up to pick an apple. 'Provided they're small ones. I truly don't mind.' He polished the apple with his handkerchief.

'I don't notice you making any big decisions either.'

Was she trying to goad him? Zoë reckoned she was jealous. 'Yes, I do,' he said amiably. 'No one takes those for me.'

Zoë gave him a slow smile over her daisy chain. He had an urge to take her to bed.

'Like what?' said Ann.

'Oh... you know,' he teased, still looking at Zoë. 'When to change my underwear. How many pints to have. Whether to shave off my beard.' He crunched into the apple.

'Don't shave it off,' Zoë said.

Jack snorted irritably and got up from the grass. 'I'll fetch another bottle.'

'You've had quite enough,' Tessa snapped.

'What am I, a kid?' he snapped back.

'I'll have some more, Jack,' said Lois.

Ann frowned. 'Should you be drinking so much, Lois, my lover?'

'Nonsense. Hugh tried that on, didn't you, prawn?' Lois gave Hugh a kick.

'Yes, petal.'

'And I said, sod off, the little bastard's going to wreck my life soon enough.' She reached for one of Ann's Benson and Hedges.

Ann pretended to tut. 'I wonder if the little bastard feels tipsy.' She put her cheek on Lois's tummy. 'Hey, I can hear hiccups!'

'Seriously,' Tessa said. 'It can't possibly be good for the baby.'

'Baby. Baby. Baby,' Lois groaned. 'The minute you're pregnant, everyone's at it, determined to turn you mumsy. It works too. The silly bats at my antenatal class are going soft in the head, all done up in Laura Ashley and smiling serenely. Parroting rubbish about fulfilment. Lord, it's bad enough waddling around looking like an ad for contraception without having a personality transplant into the bargain.'

She inhaled furiously and blew smoke. Sebastian smiled. Lois was intimidating, but he admired her spirit. She hardly looked pregnant, wearing that shirt and shorts, and with her hair cropped like a man's.

'Oh curse of marriage,' intoned Hugh, 'that we can call these delicate creatures ours, and not their appetites.'

'Shut up, prawn.'

'Yes, petal.'

Jack growled, 'I'll get the wine then.'

'And have another look for the kitty,' said Tessa. 'I'm sure I gave it to you to look after. It has to be somewhere.'

Zoë was worried about the missing kitty, which they only topped up this morning with yet another three pounds each. They were so carelessly extravagant; she'd already spent far more than she could afford.

'I need the loo,' she said and followed Jack in.

He was across the kitchen, facing away from her, his head bent, twisting the corkscrew as though he were wringing the neck of a chicken. He seemed so embattled. 'Do you need help looking for the kitty?' She touched his bare shoulder.

'Might it be on the floor of the car?'

He spun round, snarling, 'Hands off. What are you playing at, little girl? Want to keep me on a string, do you?'

She stepped backwards, shocked. 'No, of course not.'

'Well, it fucking well looks that way.'

'I don't know what you mean. I just meant, hello, can I help.'

'Oh yeah? Flaunting yourself? Dangling your daisy chains?'

She could find no reply. She blundered upstairs to the bathroom, her face hot with shame, thinking, oh my God, is he right? Was that why she'd insisted on coming to Wales? She thought it was sticking up for herself. She could have been on holiday somewhere else, alone with Sebastian.

She searched her face in the mirror, struggling to be honest. Okay yes, she'd been showing off a bit, but not to torment anyone. It was such a relief to be done with skulking in bedrooms and concocting alibis; she'd wanted her friends to be glad for her.

She went downstairs nervously, but Jack was back in the garden, persuading people to drink more. She crept towards them and sank onto the rug next to Sebastian's deckchair. Sebastian gave her his beautiful smile, mending her in a moment, making her happy again.

When she woke the next day, he had already gone down. She must have been fast asleep not to hear him. She threw on shorts and a T-shirt, visited the bathroom, slipped her feet into the new clogs she was trying to break in and clumped downstairs to the kitchen.

Breakfast was in progress. Jack was busy at the stove wearing only shorts and an apron. Ann, Lois and Tessa shared the bench behind the long table and were munching away.

'Morning,' she said.

They said nothing, barely even looked up. She took a chair opposite them, and Jack dumped a plate of bacon, scrambled eggs and grilled tomato in front of her.

'Thanks. This looks delicious.'

He returned to the stove, refusing to speak to her. The others' silence felt pointed too. She realised the problem. 'Where are Hugh and Sebastian?' They made things seem friendly just by being around.

Nobody answered. Then Ann said quietly, 'In the garden with Horatio. They've eaten.'

Jack plonked his plate at the head of the table, pulled up a chair and started shovelling food into his mouth.

Zoë tried smiling at Tessa. 'I shall miss being cooked for. You've spoiled us.'

Tessa wiped grease from her mouth with a napkin. 'Have you found the kitty yet, Jack?'

He lifted his head from his plate and growled, 'I'm positive you had it. You said I couldn't be trusted.'

'Have you tried the floor of the car?' Zoë asked again.

'It doesn't matter,' said Ann. 'We can always start a new kitty.'

'We should have let Zoë look after it,' said Lois. 'Always clutching her purse and doing little sums.'

They all smiled, even Ann. Zoë bent over her food, feeling her face grow hot. The bacon in her mouth lost its taste. She envied the disorganised, spontaneous people who sailed through life not minding about money. She'd never thought how she must seem to them. But there was no cause to be rude. And having money didn't give them the right to throw hers away. There was the best part of twenty pounds in that kitty; why shouldn't she be worried?

She raised her head, but no one met her eyes. Tessa had risen and was moving around the table, filling bowls from a pan full of milky coffee. It was how the French did it, apparently. 'Ooh, Tessa,' said Ann, lighting a cigarette. 'Wonderful stuff.'

They were all worried really, just hiding it to make her look mean.

The back door opened, Horatio padded in panting, and a blast of sweltering air delivered Sebastian and Hugh, framed in a dazzling rectangle of light. Thank goodness. 'Hi, you two.'

And the words tumbled out of her. 'The kitty's still missing. It could be in one of the cars, or maybe we left it in that café.'

'Just bloody drop it, Zoë!' Jack was in her face, shouting so loudly that her hands flew to her ears. 'It doesn't fucking matter. All right?' Jabbing his finger.

She was too stunned to think straight. No one was moving or speaking. Hugh and Sebastian were stalled in the doorway. Jack was glaring, his finger still prodding her shoulder, but beginning to smile too, vicious and triumphant, while, across the table, Ann, Lois and Tessa all had smirks on their faces.

Her chair scraped the flagstones. She was taller than Jack in her clogs. She stood, trembling, gripping the edge of the table, staring down into her *café au lait*, struggling to find words.

None came. She thought her head might burst. She took a step backwards. She would run from the room. But that was what they wanted.

Her head cleared. She knew what to do. For a fraction of a second she hesitated. Would it be better, more dignified, to walk away?

No. No, it wouldn't. She sank her thumb into the tepid coffee and spread her fingers wide around the bowl. She lifted it, swivelled back on her heel, then swung her arm in an arc like a discus thrower, launching a parabola of pale-brown liquid through the poisonous air to land precisely on Jack's cruel mouth.

For a moment it was wonderful; she was powerful and free. Then Jack was coming at her, his fist drawn back for a punch, bellowing, 'You bitch.' But Sebastian was there, grabbing his wrist, and Hugh, too, his arms locked around Jack from behind, shouting, 'Don't you dare.'

Jack was still glaring and struggling, but suddenly Tessa was screaming that he was a shit, and the dog started barking, and Jack's energy died.

He went out into the garden, slamming the door. Zoë smiled at Hugh and Sebastian. 'Thank you.' The others could go hang. Ann could go hang. She didn't look at Ann. She reached for the pan and poured herself more coffee. She sat at the table and took a mouthful of food. The bacon tasted good again, salty and sweet.

Showdown

'You unspeakable arsehole,' Tessa exploded. 'I thought I would die of humiliation.'

Jack braced himself for the onslaught. With Ann as passenger, Tessa had been sitting on her fury for a hundred and fifty miles. Nothing would stop her now.

Nearly home. He wouldn't rise to it. Let her blow herself out. He put his foot down, took a corner too fast, then hurtled up the Kentish Town Road. No traffic: it was two in the morning.

'Answer me, Jack.'

'Fuck.' He screeched to a halt at some lights. 'I can't think what you're talking about.'

The decibels rose. 'You're not shrugging it off. You know very well what I mean. That scene with Zoë, it was obvious what it was about. How could you do that to me?'

Quick, counterattack. 'To *you*?' The lights changed; he was away like a test driver, bellowing above the noise of the engine, 'What the fuck is it to you? God, that's your trouble, you think everything's about you.'

'My trouble?' she yelled. '*My* trouble?'

He refused to answer. He had her gripping the dashboard as he jumped the next set of lights. 'Jack, stop it!' He took the corner onto Highgate Hill in a squeal of protesting rubber.

Before the tyres had stopped churning the gravel, she was out and through the front door. He followed her into the kitchen. She flung open a cupboard, grabbed a glass, filled it with water, and downed it in one. She didn't look at him. Had she said her piece?

He crunched back to the car for the luggage. And then he was inside again, closing and locking the front door, before braving the kitchen with the bag of washing. Tessa hadn't moved. Empty tumbler in hand, she was staring at a vase of dead roses on the table, whose rotten stink filled the air.

He lobbed the bag in the direction of the washing machine and turned to leave, but she lunged across the room and grabbed him by his shirtsleeve. 'Oh no, you don't. You're not running away this time. You're going to bloody well answer me.'

She was dragging him to the table. She pulled out a chair and tried to push him onto it.

He resisted. 'I need a drink.'

Her face puckered with contempt. 'Of course you do. You've got a drink problem.'

'What crap! Don't talk fucking daft.'

'I know what I'm saying. I've read books.'

'Oh, for fuck's sake.' He fetched whisky and two glasses, poured generous slugs and downed his in one. 'Okay. Okay. I'll be a dipso if it makes you happy. You've always got to be fucking right, haven't you?'

At least they weren't talking about Zoë.

'Sit down, Jack.'

'There.' He plonked himself on the chair. 'Satisfied?'

She sat too, took a sip of the whisky and pulled a face. Then she leant closer, made him look at her. 'I've had all I can take, Jack. We're going to have this out.'

He pushed his chair back, away from her. 'What? That I'm a disgusting alcoholic who doesn't deserve such a sweet, kind wife? My arse.'

'No, Jack. Your womanising.'

He poured more whisky before meeting her eyes. 'I don't know what you're talking about.'

'Zoë.' She pulled her chair nearer, watching his face. 'And there was Pamela of course. I'm not stupid.'

He held her gaze. He could feel his lips twitching. There was a tremor in one of his eyelids. He swallowed more whisky.

'I can't stop you screwing everything that moves. But then one of the little slappers drops you, and you have to air your

261

grievance in public.'

'She drenched me in coffee, the cow.'

'Yes, Jack. But why was that, do you think?'

'I've no fucking idea.'

'Everyone in that room could see you were the jilted lover.'

'Bollocks.'

'Bollocks, nothing. I've had to put up with Ann's condescension all the way home. D'you think you can fool me? Go on, tell me you haven't fucked her.'

He pushed up his eyebrows. 'Who? Ann?'

'Don't play games. You know very well who.'

She glared, wanting an answer. He looked away; busied himself lighting a cigarette.

She swallowed more whisky, 'Ugh,' and banged the glass down. 'Don't you see why I'm mortified?' There were tears in her voice now. 'When Ann and Hugh and Lois all know I'm a mug?'

'Fuck Lois.' He spat the words. 'All the world can see Hugh's a prize mug.'

'What?'

Shit, why did he say that? He could almost see her mind working.

'Lois...? You've had Lois?'

Say nothing.

'You've had Lois!' she screamed.

Shit. Say nothing at all.

She lurched to her feet. 'Christ Jesus, whose baby is that?'

It was his. He hadn't believed it until this moment, but the baby was his.

Tessa was shrieking. 'No. God. You bastard.'

He flinched, drawing himself into the chair, refusing to speak. She leant over him, screeching, 'You pig.'

He put a hand on her chest, pushed her backwards and stood up unsteadily. 'Whatever you say, Tess. I've had it away with Horatio, and Zoë's fucking cat. Will that do you?'

There was a long, deadly silence. Her eyes held his. A mongoose eyeing the snake. Then, 'Get out,' she said quietly.

'What?'

'Pack a bag. Go. Now.' She pointed at the door.

'Come off it, Tess. You're being stupid.'

He tried to touch her. She stepped clear of his hand. 'Stupid or sensible, get the fuck out.'

'What about you and that pile of shit, Galway?'

'Are you deaf? I said leave.'

She was shoving him towards the door. His feet and his body were allowing it, as panic took hold. 'But the house, Tess? This is my house.'

She almost spat in his face. 'I think you'll find that I've helped with the mortgage. We'll have to sell it, that's all.'

JULY

Telling the Truth

Hotter and hotter. Drier and drier. Ann arrived home unsettled by another day of Zoë's brisk office politeness to find two half-naked navvies in the process of tearing up the tarmac outside her flat. One juddered with his drill. The other, his eyes gleaming in a mahogany face, winked at her half-heartedly as he shovelled the debris away. What time was this? Shouldn't they have packed up by now? She scowled, slammed the door on the racket and dumped her bags in the hall.

It was stifling inside and the mildew smelt horrible. She charged through to the living-room and began to unlatch the French window. Shit, the doorbell. It was Pamela of all unnecessary people, in a frilly pink frock. She had a bright smile pasted over her perennial neediness and was shouting above the din. 'I was passing and I thought, heavens, it's been ages since we had a good natter.'

'Pam, I only just got *in*.'

'Well, if I'm not welcome—'

'No, look, don't take it personally. I'm frazzled, that's all. I'll be fine when I've changed out of these things.' She gestured vaguely. 'Grab a seat. No, open the window—I was going to. We'll sit out. I won't be a mo.'

She ducked into the bedroom and tore off her sweaty clothes. Fuck, she could do without Pamela. She found a wraparound cotton skirt in the washing pile. Not too creased. Put it on. And a bikini top, why not?

Alcohol. She could hardly wait. She burst into the living-room. 'G and T? I've got ice.'

Pamela trailed after her into the kitchen. She hadn't opened the window. Dear God, couldn't she follow a simple instruction?

'I'm sorry to be a trouble, but could I have tea-tea?'

Ann felt like slapping her.

'Of course. Just give me a minute.' She poured gin, found the ice and some tonic, threw it together and grabbed a swallow. 'Christ, I was ready for that. Okay. Tea. Look, Pam, I need you to help me. Open the French window, there's a love. Get some air circulating.' She filled the kettle, took another gulp of gin and started laying a tray. 'And Pam?'

'Yes?'

'Can you fetch me my bag from the hall? I need a cigarette, right now!'

'Good God. Look at all these ladybirds.' She held the card-table out through the window. 'Here, put this up.'

Pamela took hold of the table reluctantly, as though it might infect her. When Ann came back with the deckchairs, she was running her hands over the stained green felt, flicking off the ladybirds that kept landing, and smiling dreamily at her diamond ring, ablaze in the sun.

Ann went back again for the tray. 'Here we are.' She dropped into a deckchair and sighed heavily. 'Boy, what a day!'

Pamela showed no interest, just simpered, 'Shall I be mother?'

'Oh, please.'

Ann lit a new cigarette and waved the smoke from her face. The drill was still pounding the road out front. She groaned, 'This won't do,' and sat forward. 'So tell me, how are you? You're right, my lover, I haven't seen you for ages, not since your engagement do. Have you and David fixed a date?'

'Yes.' Pamela poured tea demurely. 'The thirty-first of this month. You're invited, of course.'

'Goodness, that's soon. You must be excited.' Try as she might, her voice emerged flat and dull. 'And will it be London or Exeter?'

'Exeter.'

'Oh Pamela, *must* you?'

Pamela said nothing. Looked wounded. Sipped her tea.

Ann exhaled sharply through her nose. 'Never mind. I

suppose I can combine it with a visit to the parents. I haven't been down since Christmas.'

She flicked ash, leant back, closed her eyes.

'You haven't asked why.'

'Why Exeter?'

'No. Why so soon.'

She paid attention. 'Good lord, Pam, are you really?'

Pamela nodded and laughed, shoved out her stomach as far as she could from a deckchair and patted it.

Bloody hell, the whole world was podding. 'How wonderful. Congratulations. Do you want a boy or a girl? What are you going to call it? All those things.'

'All those things?'

'Well, you know what I mean.'

'You sound as if you couldn't care less.'

'Of course I care, Pam. So tell me, what names have you thought of?'

Pamela pouted. 'You don't want to know.'

'Yes I do.'

No, she didn't.

'Emily for a girl.'

'That's lovely.'

'And Jake, we thought, for a boy.'

'Mmn. Jake Pratt.'

'There's no need to call attention.' Pamela looked woebegone. 'Actually, it's a pity—why am I saying this?—but I'd prefer Jack to Jake. But it would hardly do, would it?'

'No,' Ann shook her head firmly, 'it wouldn't. Ouch, these ladybirds are biting!' She swatted her arm. 'I heard about it on the news. There's not enough for them to eat.'

'Is that it?' Pamela said.

'Is what it?'

'Is that all you can say about my baby?'

'I'm tired, Pam. I'm sorry if I seem less than ecstatic.'

She blew smoke and flicked an inch-long cylinder of ash onto the concrete.

'How was Wales?' Pamela said abruptly.

'Oh, a real drag.' She squashed the dog-end underfoot. 'It made me glad to be single.'

She stared at the tea Pamela had poured for her. The sound of the road-drill bored into her head. Did she have the energy to fetch herself another gin? She sure as hell needed one.

'Why?'

'Why what?'

'Why glad to be single?'

'Oh, you know. Zoë and Sebastian so full of each other.'

Pamela smiled. 'Oh, I see, you mean jealous.'

She took a breath. 'No, actually, I mean glad to be single. Too slushy for words. Plus Jack and Tessa bickering. And Hugh and Lois tediously pregnant—oh God, sorry—'

The drill stopped. 'Jack and Tessa bickering?'

Fuck, here we go. 'Yes, never do things by halves. Two rats in a sack.'

Pamela's face brightened on cue. 'Oh dear. Poor Jack. My poor, lovely Jack.'

'For Christ's *sake*, Pamela!'

'What?'

No. Don't say it. Say nothing. Grin and bear it. Go and get the gin. She struggled out of the deckchair.

'How dare you smile like that!'

'Like what? Can't I smile in my own garden?'

'Like you know so much better than I do. You don't. You only know what suits you. You never believed he loved me, did you? You never wanted to believe it, but he did. No, Ann, he did. He still does.'

Say nothing. There was no point in arguing with her. The drill started up again.

'You can see how unhappy he is, but you won't admit why. He hasn't the courage to leave her, that's why. He tells himself he has to stay, has to try and make it work. He's so confused, Ann, under such stress, you wouldn't believe.'

'No, I wouldn't.' She couldn't take any more of this rubbish. 'Jack's a philanderer. He led you a dance.'

'No!'

Damn it, here came those tired old tears again. 'I'm telling it how it is, Pam, not trying to upset you.'

She reached out a hand, but Pamela refused it.

'I'm not upset. It's my hormones. I'm really very happy. I...'

She pulled out a tissue and bent over it, blinking and swallowing.

Fuck all these secrets. Ann crouched down next to Pamela, took hold of her wrist. Pamela twisted her head away, the noise of the road-works doubled in volume, but Ann was determined. 'You have to understand the truth about Jack. He's had affairs since you. And he'll go on having them. They mean nothing to him.'

'Affairs?' Pamela repeated the word, as if trying to comprehend it.

'Yes. He'll never be true to anyone or make anyone happy.'

'Who with?' Pamela asked. 'With *you?*'

Ann rocked back on her heels. 'No, Pamela, fuck you, not with me.' She felt vicious. 'With Zoë, and Lois, and don't you dare say I said so, but I'm pretty sure Lois's baby is Jack's.'

'No.' Pamela's eyes widened with panic. 'You're wrong. You're lying.'

'Why should I? I'm giving you the facts. Unvarnished. Forget bloody Jack Golding. He's worth nothing, don't you see? Nothing at all. Pam, love, you're getting married to David. You're having David Pratt's baby.'

Pamela's face went through several contortions. She half rose from the deckchair, then fell back and curled up around her stomach, her knees to her chin.

'I'm sorry, my lover.' Ann stooped over her, stroking her hair. 'Would you like that G and T after all?'

Musical Chairs

Jack sat in Gary's kitchen in Islington, knocking back stale Bordeaux and fingering a large, white, rectangular envelope.

He stared through the smeared window into the backyard, on whose arid surfaces the sun hammered relentlessly. Could it be any hotter on Mars? The Sunday paper was full of hype about the Viking One landing.

Gary was at his girlfriend's place; he was hardly ever here. Jack had been lucky to find him in on the night Tessa went ape, sounding groggy when he answered the phone.

'Sorry to wake you, mate. Thing is, any chance I can doss at yours?' Hotels were expensive and Jack had mislaid all his friends.

Gary could hardly say no, because Jack knew he had a room going spare. He'd crashed here a few weeks earlier after a boys' night in Soho. He'd been drunker than he'd wanted Tessa to witness and had passed out on a neat single bed with his head full of strippers and whores.

'How do you mean, guv?'

Gary had sounded unwilling, so Jack had staged a chuckle. 'I need a bolt-hole till the crockery stops flying.'

'A spat with the missus, eh?' He'd still seemed reluctant. Then, 'Give me an hour, all right, guv?'

'Thanks. I'll be there.'

He'd spent the hour drinking bad coffee in an all-night café near Kings Cross and planning his next move with Tessa. A 'spat' sounded right, reassuring and temporary. Tessa would relent. She would calm down and see how hasty she'd been.

The next day he'd sent flowers, expensive white roses, with a card. 'My darling wife, I love you. Please forgive me.' And then, in the evening, he rang.

'Hello?'

'It's me.'

'Yes.' Her voice small. Not angry. Not scoring points.

'Did you get the flowers?'

'Yes.'

He waited. He could hear her breathing.

'Tess. Darling. Forgive me. Please.'

'No, Jack. I've seen a lawyer. You'll be hearing from her.'

Bluffing. Upping the ante. Suppress the annoyance, speak

gently. 'Hey, Tess love, you don't mean that.'

'Yes, I do.'

'Come on now. You know you're the only woman I care about. I've learned my lesson. It won't happen again.'

Silence. Time to grovel big time.

'I've treated you badly, and I'm so, so sorry. You can't know how sorry I am. I'll make it up to you, I promise. It'll be just you and me, that's all I need.'

Silence. What else?

'And a baby, if you really want one.'

He heard the catch in her breath.

'Say yes, Tess. Tessa, my darling. A baby. Two babies. Please say you'll forgive me.'

Silence. Then, 'No, Jack.'

'There's no hurry. Give it time. Say at least that you'll try.'

Another long pause. He waited it out.

'I have given it time. I've been thinking about it for the best part of a year. Watching you, Jack. Listening to you. And it's no good—'

'Tess.'

'Not anymore, Jack. Not ever again. It's over. In my head it's over. It won't come back. I could never trust you.'

'Yes, you can. I promise.'

'It's too late. I tried to trust you. I wanted to trust you. But now I don't want to anymore. I've stopped wanting to. I've stopped even wanting to want to.'

'It'll pass, Tess. You'll feel better.'

She gave a strange laugh. 'I don't want it to pass. And yes, I think I will feel better. It's good to be free of you, Jack. To be free of the lot of you.'

'Tess.'

'I have to go now. Goodbye.'

And she hung up.

That was three weeks ago. Damn it, hadn't she told lies too? At first he kept ringing, wrote letters, went round to see her, pleaded, sent more flowers; but nothing shifted her. Sometimes he thought he could see struggle in her eyes, or hear it in her voice; it seemed she was a tremor away from relenting. But last weekend she rang and asked him to come for his clothes. She'd filled four bin-bags with them, tied tightly with string, and lined them up on the front step. And when he tore one open, he found the right sleeve missing from his new leather jacket. And below, from each shirt and each jacket.

'You bitch,' he screamed through the letterbox. 'Why the fuck have you done this?'

'I felt like it,' she said.

And yesterday this heavy envelope had fallen on Gary's doormat. A letter from the lawyer, offering a fifty-fifty deal on the house, politely asking him to confess to adultery, politely asking him to sign away his marriage. Jack drained his glass, slid the declaration out of the envelope, and stared at it, still not believing Tessa wanted him to sign.

He glanced up at the kitchen wall-clock: gone noon already and here he was still slumped in his one-armed bathrobe. He could think of nothing to do with this day. Nothing at all. He was tired of watching the West Indies thrash England. He wanted company, but all at once his world seemed to have shrunk, as though Tessa had been his ticket to life. And this bottle was empty, just when he needed more booze to dull the panic.

He did a quick search of the mainly empty cupboards. Solid beech, not only the doors; it made him wonder how Gary could afford it. The whole flat was surprisingly classy, and impersonally done up like a show house. Gary was selling apparently, though he'd only recently moved in. He was on the way to being a small-time developer himself. Jack wandered through to the living-room and opened the stylish teak sideboard. Fuck it, no alcohol. Where had Gary hidden it? How fucking petty, he was paying his way, wasn't he?

He slammed around the flat for a bit, pulling open cupboards and drawers. Try the mean fucker's bedroom. He yanked open the door of the built-in wardrobe, but still no luck. Gary must have taken it all with him, the bastard. He was going to have to get dressed in one of the few things he still had with two sleeves and go to the off-licence. Oh shit, it was Sunday. Fuck, fuck, fuck.

The wardrobe wouldn't shut. A heap of stuff inside had collapsed and was blocking the door. A framed photo of Gary with some mates was on top of the landslide, his arm around a bird with a baby. Something oddly familiar—

What? *Fucking hell!* The big man standing behind Gary, hand on shoulder, was Macpherson! And the woman, down-market blonde, and the baby, he'd seen them before too. At Brecknock Road! Sweet Jesus *fuck!*

His solicitor's new-fangled answering machine rambled on about opening times. He dialled him at home, but his wife said he was out playing golf.

'Should be back by six. Shall I ask him to ring you?'

'Yes—though *no!* Not on this number.'

What in hell other number to give? Bartholomew Road? The phone was still on there—

Holy Christ! Contracts exchanged on Bartholomew and Gary with a key. Fuck, fuck.

'Look, tell him I'll ring back this evening, okay?'

He slammed down the phone. Found a sleeveless T-shirt; put it on. Was half out the door when another idea struck. He dived for his business diary. Turned pages. Found the number for Macpherson, grabbed the phone, dialled.

The receiver blared out the unobtainable signal.

'Screw. Fuck. Bollocks.' He snatched up the car keys and was out of the door.

Then back. Riffling through his diary again, in search of the locksmith.

'Be in, damn you.'

The locksmith agreed to be at Bartholomew in half an hour. 'Double rate on a Sunday, okay?'

And Jack was out and into the Rover, and haring across town, three-quarters-pissed and half-crazy, towards Bartholomew Road, expecting to find its locks changed already and its windows filled with jeering faces.

He screeched to a halt in front of the garage door. 'KBW' was daubed drippily in silver on the new red gloss. Bloody National Front. He leapt out, key in hand. Christ, the relief as it fitted and turned. He stowed the car in the garage, went in through the kitchen and dashed around looking for squatters. Not a sign, thank fuck. And the locksmith would be here in ten minutes. Plus it made sense. Calm down. Have a shot of the emergency scotch. They wouldn't do him over twice. The whole point was that the sting was invisible; even Paul Newman knew that. Macpherson, Gary, that woman, all in it together. And that bloody baby was Gary's. What a fucking betrayal! He'd get them though. He'd be on to his solicitor tonight and—

Sweet Jesus, could he even trust *him?*

Tessa. He needed to tell Tessa. She was good in a crisis, and she loved him, goddamn it. She would be as angry as he was, she would drop this divorce shit, she would help him.

'Hello?'

'Hello, Tess.'

And he told her, falling over his words, getting in tangles. He blurted it all out: the photo, the baby, the solicitor, every damn thing. 'So what should I do, do you think?'

'You're drunk, Jack.'

'So would you be—'

'No, I wouldn't. And if it's sympathy you're after, no dice. It's time someone ratted on you, don't you think?'

He was going to start shouting about his leather jacket and Mick fucking Galway, but she hung up. And the locksmith was coming up the path.

By the time the locksmith was done, Jack felt calmer. He'd made some decisions. He would change his solicitor on Monday. Meanwhile, he wouldn't face Gary with what he knew, but would move out pronto. He toyed with the idea of a counter-squat to stop Gary's sale, but it would only put him in the wrong, especially as he couldn't trust himself not to break

273

the bastard's nose.

Grabbing the scotch, he bombed straight back over there and packed up his stuff, throwing all the incriminating evidence he could find in on top. No papers, nothing about Brecknock, just a couple more photos from the floor of the wardrobe, enough to demonstrate that Macpherson was some kind of buddy or uncle and that was definitely Gary's brat.

And now, bloody hell, he was a vagrant again. He could doss down at Bartholomew, but there was no bed there; he might be better off sleeping in the car. He lugged his possessions towards it. His Rover, green and gleaming amidst the peeling stucco and rusty railings of Islington, obediently accepted the key and admitted him and his bottle and his bin-bags to its elegant interior, closing its door on him with a soft clunk. But the hot, leathery smell failed to console, for he had nowhere to go.

He turned the key in the ignition, eased into gear and started to drive. 'Come on, girl. Take me somewhere.'

There wasn't much traffic, just Sunday drivers. He cruised down to the Angel and then along Pentonville Road to Kings Cross. He turned on the radio. A jazz band was playing *Sweet Georgia Brown*. It caused him a gripe of sadness that he couldn't explain. Then his mind filled with the memory of the long, white-clothed table under the vine and, beyond it, his Highgate garden full of roses and honeysuckle, and the passionflower with its unnatural blue blossoms and heavy yellow fruit, swarming over the wall. He stifled a groan and turned off the radio.

At Euston, for no reason, he turned north towards Camden Town.

And then it came to him. Ann.

Ann sat in a deckchair on her patio, smoking and sipping gin and tonic, and trying to read. Eventually she flicked her cigarette away and flung the book down. It wasn't David Storey's fault, she could see why it had won the Booker prize; she just wasn't in the mood for a gritty northern tale.

She stared at her garden. Only a few geraniums survived; everything else was dead, or if not dead, hunkered down, leafless. The worst drought for two hundred and fifty years, they kept saying on the news. Great areas of the country with taps empty most of the day. Forest fires out of control.

She didn't want to think about it. There was no point in sitting here; she should do something else; but there was nothing to do but the ironing.

She could ring Lois, she supposed. And Lois would say, 'Come on over. Come and watch my bump grow.' But she didn't want to. 'I want my own life,' she whispered to the clinking ice-cubes.

It's not Hugh, she told herself. She'd been kidding herself about Hugh. She loved him, of course she did, but she'd never been turned on much by ginger-haired men. She couldn't really imagine having sex with him.

She squirmed in the deckchair. The thought of sex had her feeling randy, and she was thinking how easy it would be to ring Charlie. Nothing simpler. For the millionth time she considered it, but it was still hopeless. He would drive her round the twist in no time, and she'd have the trouble of explaining why not all over again.

And now she was biting her lip, remembering how Sebastian was with Zoë. He'd blossomed and revealed himself as quite possibly sexy. It was far too late to be seeing it, and maybe he still wasn't her type. She could smell judgement in his silences.

Mick Galway? More than once these past weeks, she'd been tempted to ring the big Irishman. 'Would you fancy a drink?' Sex on tap without the least whiff of judgement, and a potential good friend, a man who, like Hugh, appreciated women. Like Hugh with knobs on! But, hold on, he knew where she was. He knew she was available. If she rang him, he might say no, which would be humiliating. Or yes from politeness. She shrank with remembered shame. Really, it was out of the question.

She lit up again and let herself think about Jack. Jack

Rabbit—she'd fancied him from the start. Watching him work his way through her friends, she'd pretended to disapprove, envious that he didn't choose her, insulted at being the one woman he overlooked.

She should steer clear for a while; she owed that much to Tessa. But eventually it would be all right, wouldn't it? 'Eventually' could be a heck of a long time, though. It could be years, literally, before it would seem all right to say to Tessa, 'Oh, by the way, I'm seeing Jack. I hope you don't mind.' That was if Tessa ever spoke to her again. But if Tessa threw Jack away, she couldn't expect him not to land.

Ann's bladder was nagging. She got up from the deckchair, swallowed down the ice melt, and mooched in through the living-room towards the bathroom. In the hall she jumped and drew back, seeing the shape of a man behind the glass of the front door.

He had probably been ringing and knocking for ages. The bell didn't work properly because the battery was flat. It gave out a sort of helpless death-rattle. But, before she could decide to step forward, the man was fumbling with keys, and finding one and trying it in her door. And her door was swinging inwards, and her stomach was doing a somersault, and she was opening her mouth to cry out—

And then laugh. Because of course, the key was the one she had given Pamela, way back. And here he was again, Jack, bang on cue, showing off his muscles in a sexy, sleeveless T-shirt, holding out a bottle towards her and smiling his winning smile.

AUGUST

Prizes

Sebastian wedged the sash as high as it would go in hope of getting a breeze into the room. He paused to stare for a moment at the dusty, broken slates and blackened bricks before turning back to the double mattress on the floor. Zoë was awake now, looking at him with big, soft eyes.

The phone began ringing in the living-room, and he could hear Charlie going to answer it. He slipped back under the sheet, discarding his dressing-gown at the last moment and holding in his stomach.

Zoë put her arms around him. 'Why did you put that on?'

'I don't know,' he lied. 'Habit. The neighbours might see me. Charlie might barge in. Tommy might be shocked.'

The cat sat on the chest of drawers, glaring down at them. It hadn't stopped sulking since it stepped from its cardboard carrying-box last night. It had turned up its nose at the tinned pilchards and evaporated milk that Zoë had brought along to placate it. She'd nipped out for some bog-standard cat-food, but it rejected that too.

'Bollocks, Sebastian.'

She burrowed into his arms and squeezed him tight round his middle, making him grin. He liked the way she seemed so innocent in company and then wasn't at all.

'Complete bollocks. Come on now, be honest, admit it.'

He liked her exacting truthfulness.

'Okay. You win. It's because I'm too fat.'

'So I haven't noticed? So I'm going to shriek and run from the room and say I've made a terrible mistake, forget I ever said I loved you madly?'

Loved you madly? That was alarming. But it was great to be allowed to be fat.

She was pulling the sheet back and looking him up and

down, which had him feeling shy, but he rode out the feeling and didn't try to cover himself.

'Come on, big boy. Don't you know I've always had a passion for chunky men?'

And yes, he was ready and willing, and it was natural to begin, so they did. But there it was again, the thing that he didn't like, that reference to 'men'. She had told him the history of her love life. Or rather she had started to, but when she got to number six or seven, he'd interrupted, 'Why? Why are you telling me?'

'I don't know.' She had stalled, looking embarrassed. 'To confess, I suppose. To come clean. To get it out of my system. I'm sorry, I'll stop.'

She had barely referred to her past lovers since, or only obliquely, saying that he was special, like caviar after baked beans. But he sensed they were still in her thoughts, a story she couldn't stop telling herself.

Confession was part of her truthfulness, he supposed, but some things were difficult to hear. That last time with Jack after the first time with him. Why did she do that? Why didn't she say no?

She was smiling down at him now, rocking gently, and it was very easy indeed to smile back. All this sex was wonderful, and he didn't want to find fault. He couldn't possibly dislike her or judge her. She was so anxious that he shouldn't think ill of her. So beautiful and somehow, in spite of everything, innocent. And often quite funny.

He would come too soon if he wasn't careful. He rolled her onto her back, so he could slow down the pace, and tried to distract himself. Did she mean it about loving him madly? Sometimes she spoke as if she expected them to be together forever, and he wasn't ready for that, or at least not with her, which was just as well because she was married, and his mother still went to mass every Sunday and didn't believe in divorce. No, she wasn't the one. But this was fine for now.

Zoë held Sebastian close, felt him move in and out of her,

heard him sigh. She was so happy. She couldn't remember being happier.

This wasn't good sex exactly, but that didn't matter. It was sex with Sebastian, whom she loved, and she wanted to make love to him again and again. She wasn't missing Mick or Jack, not at all, and maybe, if this ever got boring, she would show Sebastian how; but just now it wasn't boring, not in the slightest. Just the feel of him was good, and the easiness of it, and the fact that he was in her arms and she wanted him and he wanted her.

And now he was coming and saying, 'Sorry,' which she must ask him not to say.

It wasn't bad sex; he looked after her. Last night, they'd both been touching each other, and she had slowed down her hand to let her body catch up with his finger, and then it was happening, and they were both going for it, and they'd come, big-time, together, which was fantastic, amazing, so easy; she'd not done that with anyone before.

And it wasn't like Mick, and it wasn't like Jack, because it was real and mutual and not about making someone else do something or feel something.

And right now it felt good to have the weight of Sebastian on her, to feel her breathing constricted by the pressure of him on her ribs. After all the travelling, at last she'd arrived. It was easy to be natural with him, to confess and be absolved. She'd told him her faults, and he'd said, 'Yes. I know. I've seen. It's all right.' He wasn't interested in her history; he didn't mind who'd gone before. He hadn't spoken of love yet, but she wasn't impatient. He was a reserved, private person, unused to voicing his feelings. Not impulsive like Mick or manipulative like Jack. When Sebastian one day told her he loved her, he would mean it; it would be true.

I'm lucky beyond all measure, she thought, gazing up at the cat. I was out of time, almost lost. I could have ended up like Ann. She couldn't imagine a worse fate than living with Jack.

'Decent within?'

Charlie was knocking. Tommy leapt down and ran to the

door. Sebastian rolled sideways, spilling stickiness, yelling, 'Hang on a mo!'

Zoë grabbed his pyjama jacket from the floor and struggled into it. Which was silly in a way, because there was nothing Charlie hadn't seen.

Charlie stuck his head round the door and smirked. 'Blimey, what a sight.'

'Good morning,' they said.

'Thing is, we're out of cornflakes and bread. Give us a couple of quid and I'll go down the corner-shop.'

'Wallet's in my jacket.' Sebastian pointed to where it hung over the chair-back. 'Can you get *The Times* too? And a couple of grapefruit.'

'*Si*, Mussolini.'

She watched Charlie cross the room and fish in the pockets of Sebastian's pale-blue cotton jacket. On the chair-seat, her pink shorts and striped T-shirt were folded, with her bright white knickers on top. Did Charlie miss her, she wondered? He seemed cheerful today, after last night's renewed lamentations about Ann's taste in men.

He turned around, waving a fiver. 'The Stompers should be on. Do you fancy a few jars later on, when you've dug yourselves out of your pit?'

'Sure thing,' said Sebastian.

'Great,' echoed Zoë. 'You seem happy, Charlie.'

He Bogart-posed in the doorway, tugging his curls. 'Well, yes I am,' he rasped, 'Just a little.' Then he broke into a grin and back into himself. 'Because, whad'ya you know? That phone call just now. I'm an uncle.'

The Waiting Game

'This was supposed to be about fun and love, not violence,' said a black organiser in Notting Hill. The television news cut from rampaging crowds to smashed windows to bloodied policemen to a burned out van. Hugh couldn't watch any longer. He left Lois in the sitting-room and put the front door on the latch while he carried a pile of newspapers down the front steps to the bin. He dumped them in, replaced the lid and stood a moment, one hand on the railings, staring along the street. It was still boiling hot. A savage wind was pushing thin grey clouds across a tight grey sky and ripping small branches from the trees, whose leaves drooped and rustled. The strip of bleached grass between pavement and tarmac was defeated. The earth was tired. It wanted autumn and rain.

And Lois's bump wanted to turn into a baby.

He was frightened, and he knew Lois was too, though she pretended not to be, and he didn't tell her he knew. Sometimes, wakeful in the night, he was actually terrified. Hardly able to stop himself from clinging to her, whimpering like a spooked child. Even if nothing terrible happened, even if she sailed through this, he was afraid of her pain, which he was powerless to prevent or alleviate. It wasn't right for her to suffer; she wasn't used to it; how would she manage? It made him miserable and helpless.

But also, he had to face it, he was terrified for himself. Part of him didn't want to climb back up these steps. Because how would he feel when he saw this baby who kicked and shoved at him from inside the bump? The books told him that parental bonding was an instinct beyond the control of the rational mind, something that just happened. By the same token, might it be something that just didn't happen?

The uncertainty tormented him. He'd promised to accept this baby as his own, but when he saw the shadow of Charlie, or please God no, Jack, in the child's face, and heard the echo of one of them speaking through its mouth, wouldn't he recoil?

He hoped not. He fervently hoped not. He willed it not to be so. But was he was capable of loving this child? We know what we are, but know not what we may be.

Good old Marlowe, always nailing the question. So what was the answer this time? Hugh hesitated in the doorway, thinking of Marlowe's punishment for mocking God. Headlong flight into exile, then dead to the world while his genius flowered in another man's name. Forever and ever, it never would change. There was no proof, and Hugh had learned to hold his tongue on the subject, tired of people tutting and edging away from his modern blasphemy, his doubt of their inscrutable actor from Avon. His two English faculty colleagues were particularly scathing. The bolshy one began ranting against 'toffee-nosed conspiracy-theorists who think you need a degree to be a genius', while the conservative one queried with a small smile why anyone lacking a degree in English literature should feel himself qualified to hold an opinion. Hugh backed off, shut up, took himself back to the sonnets and plays, to Hamlet, and still heard what he heard and believed what he believed, and said nothing to anyone ever again. His faith in Marlowe was no more mad or presumptuous than the next man's faith in a personal god, and no more worth arguing about.

He shut the front door on the wind and leant against it for a while, rubbing his eyes and shaking his head. He had his answer. Whatever happened, whoever's baby this was, however he felt, he would show nothing, not ever. If Marlowe could suffer in silence for four hundred years, so could he. He pulled himself together and went back to the sitting-room.

Lois had turned off the television. She lay in a hot heap on the sofa; the air was like glue in the darkness. She lifted her head to smile wanly. 'You've been gone a long time.'

'Hello, petal.'

He bent to kiss her. She wound her arms around his neck, pulling him down, but then let go and half-pushed him away again, sighing, 'I wish the little bastard would get a move on. This bit is so boring.'

He sank into the leather armchair. Horatio, on the knotted rug, thumped his tail wearily.

'I thought of ringing Ann,' she said, 'asking her over, but she'd want to bring Jack, and I can't be doing with him.'

'No,' Hugh agreed.

'It's lovely being drunk, though,' she murmured. 'Very, very nice. Sherry's wonderful. Hits the bloodstream fastest, apparently. Something about the percentage of alcohol.'

'So where did you read that? Doctor Spock?'

'Ha ha,' she said.

For a while they said nothing. Then her voice came again.

'I love you, prawn.'

'I love you too, petal,' he told her. 'And the little bastard.'

'I don't deserve you,' she said.

That night he half-surfaced from a dream to hear the thunder break at last and the heavy, wet insistence of the rain. The curtain blew out from the window, and a cool, damp breeze caressed his face like the answer to a prayer.

The quality of mercy is not strained.

He rolled towards Lois, giving the dream leave to re-start. He was floating adrift on an open raft on a wide sea, searching the horizon for a landfall. Horatio stood alert on the prow, wearing a hat like Nelson's, growling and saying, 'Look, my lord, it comes.'

All of a sudden he was wide-awake. Lois wasn't here. And the mattress beside him was wet.

'Lois!' He scrambled from the bed, then stumbled from room to room, calling her. She wasn't in the bathroom. Or the sitting-room. Why didn't she answer?

She was kneeling on the kitchen floor beside the empty sherry bottle, gripping a leg of the table, her teeth clenched, her face white and eyes tight shut. Letting go of the table, she waved a hand blindly towards him.

He took the hand. Knelt beside her. Rocked her, kissed her, willed the pain to pass.

Finally she slumped and gasped, 'I didn't want to wake you. But they're coming so fast. Ever so fast.'

He couldn't leave her. But he must. 'Stay there,' he said stupidly. 'I won't be long.'

He ran back to the bedroom, threw on the first clothes that came to hand, and grabbed her dressing-gown, the car-keys, the small case that was already packed. In the kitchen, he found her whimpering and the dog padding anxiously back and forth.

'Angels and ministers of grace defend us,' he muttered and tried to lift her to her feet.

'Oh shit, Hugh.' She broke into a wail. 'It hurts like bloody hell.'

By the time they arrived at the hospital, she was screaming. She couldn't walk. He helped two porters extract her from the car and get her onto a trolley in the pelting rain. 'Fuck! Fuck! Fuck!' she shrieked at the sky.

Inside were harsh lights, the echo of footsteps, the stench of disinfectant. There were nurses, but no one did anything to help or seemed to be in charge. Soaked to the bone, dripping rain onto her face, Hugh clung to Lois's hand as she raised her knees and screamed again, a dreadful, wordless screech that he didn't think he could bear.

At last a young woman was racing towards them across the polished green lino, frighteningly young in her crumpled white coat and with huge, dark smudges below bloodshot eyes. She pushed Hugh aside, lifted Lois's nightdress and started work.

He staggered backwards, collided with a wall and paused there, leaning against it and panting, with the rain running into his eyes.

And grinning inanely.

Full of joy and love.

Oh wonderful, wonderful, and most wonderful! And yet again wonderful, and after that, out of all whooping!

For he had seen. Seen the top of the baby's head.

And was that only blood he had seen, or did the baby have red hair?